ACCLAIM FOR
SAINTS AND MONSTERS

"With enchanting prose, a captivating world to explore, and characters you can't help but root for, this heartfelt romantasy will delight fans of Elizabeth Lim and Asian dramas, reminding you of what it means to truly be whole."

— **ERIN PHILLIPS**, AWARD-WINNING
AUTHOR OF *A CROWN OF CHAINS* AND *A BOND OF BRIARS*

"*Saints and Monsters* is a thrill of a read that will grab your heart from the first page and never give it back!"

— **RENEE DUGAN**, AWARD-WINNING
AUTHOR OF *THE STARCHASER SAGA*

"A rich world full of enchantment and political intrigue, perfect for fans of Studio Ghibli and The Lunar Chronicles. The romantic entanglements and character arcs had me on the edge of my seat! Positive messages of self-worth and the value of humanity on top of magic and high-stakes adventure make Saints and Monsters a perfect fantasy read."

— **ASHLEY BUSTAMANTE**, AUTHOR OF THE
COLOR THEORY TRILOGY

"Entirely captivating plot paired with beautiful writing, McGinty establishes herself as a must read author! One of the best releases this year."

"In the fantastical novel *Saints and Monsters*, a girl fights for her family and kingdom, bearing the burden of two hearts within her."

"Clever. Original. Mesmerizing. Captivating from page one, McGinty's Saints and Monsters draws you into an imaginative and complex world filled with high stakes, stirring romance, and unforgettable characters that just may steal your heart."

"Simply stunning! Dazzling worlds, deadly curses, and treasonous alliances set the stage for this beautiful masterpiece. A must read for fans of fantasy!"

SAINTS & MONSTERS

ELLEN McGINTY

To Patrick,
If I had two hearts they'd both be yours.

ALSO BY ELLEN MCGINTY

THE WATER CHILD - YA Historical Fiction

SAINTS & MONSTERS - YA Romantic Fantasy

THE LAST WAYFINDER (coming 2025)

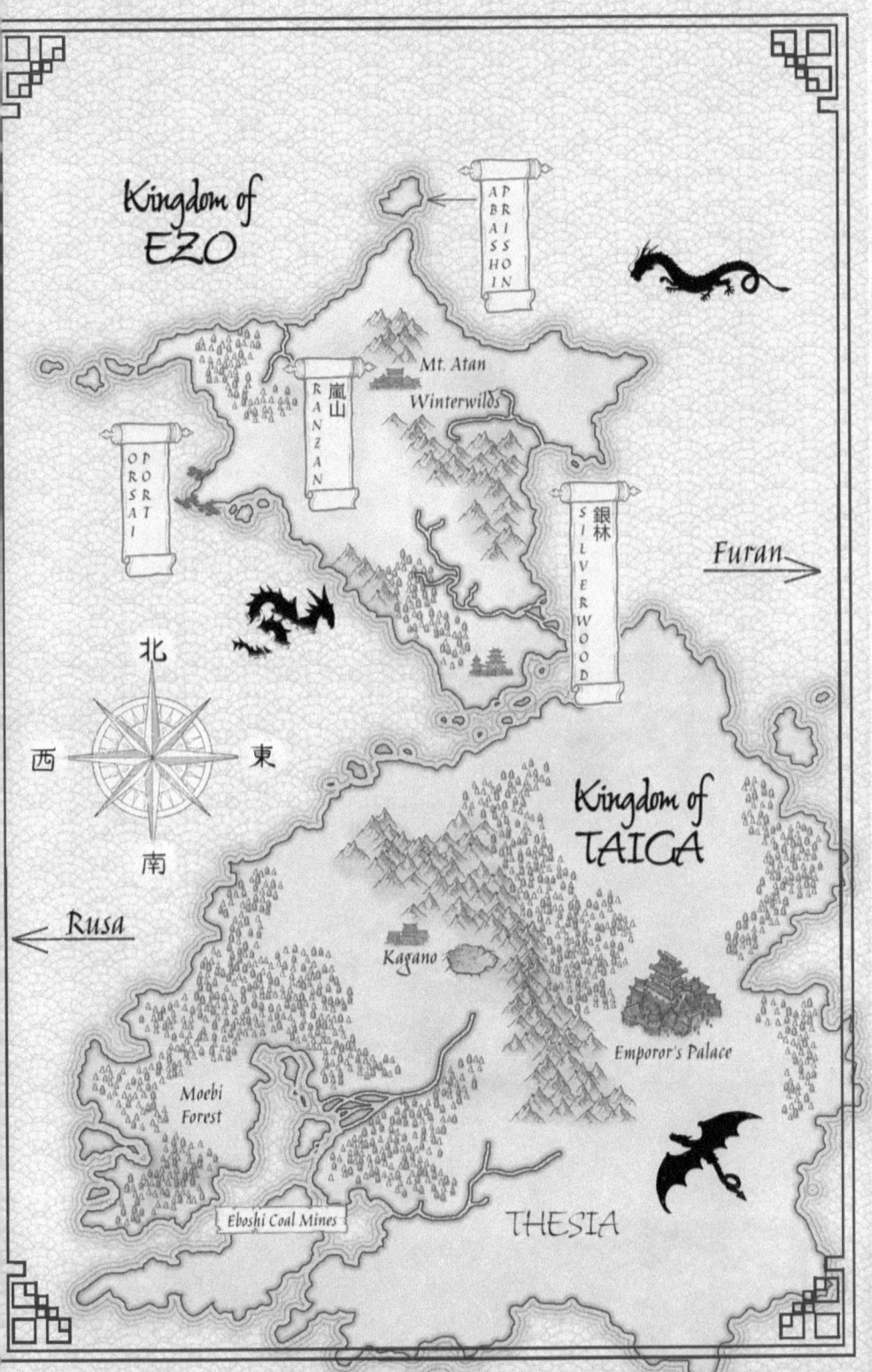

Kingdom of
EZO

APBRAISSHOIN

Mt. Atan

Winterwilds

RANZAN 嵐山

OPROSARTI

銀林 SILVERWOOD

Furan →

北

西   東

南

Kingdom of
TAIGA

Kagano

Emporor's Palace

← Rusa

Moebi
Forest

Eboshi Coal Mines

THESIA

CHAPTER
ONE

MORNING BEGINS with the cry of dragons. I sit up in bed, heart pounding as the first shriek pierces the air. Hunger laces the low, haunting melodies, rivaling only the wolves prowling the Winterwilds. The sea serpents' wails return every year when the snow melts, dappling the mountains with green and a blush of fresh blossoms, when steam curls from the hot spring canyon, and when sticky-sweet chestnuts fill our kitchen . . . but this time is different.

I'm not ready to lose my sister.

"Runa," I hiss.

My sister lies in the bed next to mine, her curved form longer, fuller than my own. Her forehead wrinkles and her lips pucker as if she'd just kissed a newt. Dreaming, again.

"Runa?"

My eyes flick to the ceiling before I swing my legs out of bed with a wince. Dull pain laces my spine, spreading to my hips. Seventeen, and I feel like an old maid with rheumatism. But pain won't stop me.

Not today.

Runa has trained every day for the coronation on her twentieth birthday, because in Ezo, the firstborn daughter doesn't simply inherit the crown, she earns it by facing a dragon. And I'm to be at her side, to be her courage when her heart fails. Papa always said I have enough courage for two hearts . . . though, he also said it was a shame for all that courage to be wasted on someone fragile.

A muscle twitches in my jaw as I attempt to bury those words, shoving them into a dark corner of my mind. My back brace lies open like a cracked oyster on the bedside table. I sling the form-fitting leather shell around my torso and strap it across the back. The wood-framed interior bites into my ribs, but I try not to notice it.

My fingers glide across the smooth deerskin, a brilliant white with lacquered cherry blossoms. Papa had it designed by the famed artisans in Thesia and engraved with protection charms. Not that it'd stopped me from falling down the stairs or crashing through a paper screen when my legs gave out at random.

I hobble to Runa's bed, grateful we now share a room on the castle's ground floor, and give her shoulder a sharp nudge. She rolls to the side, pulling the blanket to her pointed chin, and mumbles under her breath.

"It's time," I say with a huff. "The dragons are here. Do you want to see them before the ceremony?"

Tawny eyes fly open and a hand darts out to grab mine. Runa gulps, throwing off the covers. The boys say she's pretty no matter what, and they're right. Chestnut hair falls over my sister's face in tussled heaps, sleep lines crease her cheeks, and shadows cup her eyes like tea saucers, but she's still the most beautiful girl in Ezo.

"Here?" Wide brown eyes search mine, her hand bearing down on me like a vise grip.

"Yes, if we sneak out now, we can get to the beach before Papa wakes."

A rueful smile cuts across Runa's pink lips. "You just want fish cakes."

I flash a grin and adjust the leather brace where it rubs beneath my left arm. "Someone has to have their priorities in the right place."

Runa's eyes sparkle with mischief as she sweeps herself off the bed and throws a robe in my face. Slubbed silk pools over my bare arms as I wiggle into the soft fabric cut from a single roll of beetle-brown silk, the same worn by our kitchen staff, which we had pilfered for disguises the previous day. Runa bites down on a clothespin as she rearranges the layers of her stolen dress and the white apron with the royal crest, a plum blossom encircled by a vicious sea serpent.

"I've avoided looking at them every year, knowing this day would come," she says, tracing the embroidered serpent. "I'd rather secure the kingdom with marriage instead of magic."

"Trade you," I say, whisking a thick scarf from the wardrobe to cover my bright blue hair, the bane of my existence. My hereditary 'disorder' as the physicians called it came with not only a bent spine, but painful weak joints and telltale blue hair. "At least you can choose your king after the coronation. I'm doomed to marry the Duke of Taiga."

"Meera, you're complaining about this?" Runa plucks a sketch from beneath my mattress, admiring it with a dreamy sigh. "He's coming tonight, isn't he?"

I make a show of rolling my eyes and stuff the sketch into my apron pocket, away from her prying fingers. There's no denying the duke is handsome, and he'd been kind when we met as children, but the fact is—I wasn't given a choice. I don't want a loveless agreement, to be shipped off to a fierce kingdom on the other side of the sea so Papa can get a better bargain on rice.

Rice!

Anger heats my cheeks, but I lift my chin, endeavoring not to let it show. "He is. But that's hardly a concern. Princes and dukes are predictable and boring. You, my dear sister, will face a dragon and become queen by tomorrow morning."

I pry the window open, thanked by a fistful of damp, salt-licked wind and the sweet aroma of chestnuts roasting over a stove. A dragon cry splits the air, rattling the thin glass panes. I wince, one hand frozen on the cold glass while the other flies to block my ear.

"Saints, they've never been *this* close to shore. Not in our lifetime." Runa rushes toward me and peers out the window. Silver-gray cherry trees dot the castle's pristine garden, each bud restraining a shock of pink. The lawn slopes into a steep embankment that leads to a rocky harbor and the ever-changing sea beyond.

I pull my hand away from the glass, cold radiating down my palm and setting my nerves on end. "Papa will have heard it too. Let's go."

We climb out the window, Runa letting me use her arm as a support. Together we crouch beneath the kitchen windows, all open and breathing fresh steam like sumptuous clouds in the morning air. My side pinches from the bending motion and a sharp ache fists around my spine. A constant reminder that I'm not what the kingdom of Ezo needs, not pure and worthy like my sister—not a proper living sacrifice to the dragons.

Near the kitchen window, a stern voice barks out commands followed by a chorus of mumbling maids and the clanking of iron pots. Woven baskets hang from the windowsill to collect discarded chestnut hulls and eggshells. Carefully, Runa plucks a basket from its hook and empties it. As soon as we pass the kitchen, I take the weightless basket and strap it to my back. A dull pain throbs against my backbone, causing me to wince.

Runa's worried eyes scan my face.

I force a half smile, leaning against the wall with one hand cupping my wooden brace, and focus on my other senses, the ones not registering pain: the scents of fresh rice, honey citrus, and roasted chestnut puffing from the windows.

"Good?" Runa mouths.

I nod.

Together we scurry out the castle compound, a strong gust pushing at our backs as if the wind is on our side. I grip the straps of the empty kitchen basket, hoping the disguise will be enough to grant us one last day of freedom.

With a single glance at our brown kitchen robes, the guards wave us through the imposing gates. Dozens of kitchen staff will be crossing into town to fetch supplies for the coronation banquet tonight, no questions asked. Sharing grins, we break clear of the castle walls, crossing the deep canal that serves as a moat, and turn down an alley of zelkova trees shimmering green in the early morning light.

I whistle for the nearest rickshaw and lean against Runa's shoulder. "Anything you want to do on your last day as a free woman?"

Runa takes my hand as we climb into the two-wheeled cart. "You'll see." She grins and calls to the runner. "To the port, Yamashi Park."

A crowd bustles against the steep port wall of Silverwood Bay, children atop their parents' shoulders, old men leaning on crooked canes, a twitter of young ladies fighting the playful breeze that tugs on their broad hats and billowing skirts. All of them stare down at the sea or walk the long cobbled path lined with colorful vendor carts—all come for the queen's coronation and the dragons.

I check my scarf before exiting the rickshaw, careful lest anyone see through our disguise. My fingers curl around the port fence, a wooden rail separating the smiling onlookers from the scaled beasts below, as I pull myself higher for a better view.

What does everyone see in the wingless death?

Up and down the sea serpents writhe in the jade sea, a coil of metallic scales and fins. Rows of razor-sharp teeth tear into a giant elk sacrificed on their behalf before plunging it beneath the dark, churning waves.

I blanch, a chill snaking down my back, curving with my too-bent spine. It's one thing to read about the sacred dragons in the holy testaments of the saints, quite another to see them this close in the wild.

A bone-white dragon turns. Its black eyes flecked in gold snap to mine. I match them with a steady gaze, a hard lump in my throat, and reach out for Runa. My sister's knuckles turn deathly pale on the rails. "They're so cold."

"Aren't all serpents?"

"Do you think they're lonely?" Runa turns to me, the question in her eyes sincere. "We humans have only one heart and suffer a great many things. How much pain must they feel with two?"

"None," I say, pulling my sister to the park fountain. In the center, a gray-green stone in the shape of a wingless dragon towers over us with antler-like horns and the claws of a lion, its color faded by time. "The dual hearts pump more blood into their elongated bodies," I explain. "Simple physiology. They may be immortal beasts, but they only deal with us to stave off war and bloodshed."

"And to honor their promise to the first queen. She was only a little girl when the dragons fell from the sky during the Ashfall." Runa reaches out to touch the pedestal, her fingers lingering on the engraved poem beneath the dragon's claws. An ancient script carves deep into the stone:

By scale and blade, the dragons' oath is bound
A gift of the gods for a human queen
If worthy she is found
A heart for a heart to keep the peace
A life given in servitude for bloodshed to cease

Nothing but empty words etched in stone. Mother had survived the ritual, offering her life in service to the dragons, to be a good queen to both man and beast, but it hadn't been worth the cost. Sure, her borrowed dragon magic had enriched the land, enlarged crops, and even sweetened water like golden honey. But like the queens of decades past, death came too young, too sudden. It was as if the dragon had stolen a piece of her. And magic has faded from the earth with every year since her passing until poverty now sinks its teeth into our kingdom.

The white dragon plunges its head into the waves, circling another beast to create a whirlpool of scales in shimmering gray, tide pool green, and palest bone. The festive crowd presses in, hugging the fence along the deadly precipice, eyes alight with wonder at the majestic, twisting serpents.

I trace the colorful ribbons of death weaving into the sea and my mouth goes dry like cotton and sticky spiderwebs. I could go everywhere with my sister, but not after today. The dragons that would grant her a piece of their heart magic would never find me worthy, not even to stand in their presence. Everyone knows what happened to the last cerulean princess with a crooked back . . .

Suddenly, two hands grip my sides and hoist me into the air. I'm tilted toward the sea, feet kicking and side smarting beneath the brace.

"Put me down!"

The hands relent immediately, and a dark-haired boy slips his elbow over the rail, a smile dashing across his lips. "Not feeling reckless today, Princess?"

"Bastian!" My lips pinch into a firm line, though I'm sure my eyes betray me with a smile. My older brother leans against the rail with a carefree air, his long white shirt unbuttoned at the top and a rough seafaring coat loose over his shoulders.

He tosses a leather bag and catches it in his palm, zeni jingling inside. "Did you miss me?"

"Glad you could join us." Runa's eyes glimmer with pride at the well-kept secret. "I see you got my message?"

Bastian smiles, wide and ridiculously dimpled, wind-tousled hair sweeping across his eyes. "Couldn't miss my little sister's big day. Are you nervous?"

"Please, I've still an afternoon to think about my blessing or my execution, Bastian." Runa smiles as if it were a joke, crossing her arms over the cliffside rail to hide the tremor in her hands. "I didn't invite my siblings here to talk about *that*."

"Saints, Runa, this tradition has been going on smoothly for decades. The dragons will accept you. Nothing is going to go wrong." Bastian jostles her elbow.

Runa sighs, tearing her gaze away from the dragons as they thread silver into the ocean waves. "Tomorrow morning I'll be facing a dragon, claiming a life-bond with it to prove that I'm the rightful ruler of Ezo. If I succeed—"

"You will," I say, squeezing my sister's hand. "I have no doubt."

Runa forces a smile. "I wish I had your confidence."

"If I could take your place, I would," Bastian says, his voice earnest.

My heart lurches, wishing I could say the same.

"Sometimes I wish you could." Runa shakes her head, face tilted toward the sea. "The dragons would love you."

"I do look worthy, don't I?" Bastian grins and runs a hand through his dark brown hair. He winks at a quartet of ladies down the railing, all of whom promptly blush.

"Has anyone told you that you would've made an extraordinary pirate, Bas?"

"How do you know that's not what I've been doing this past year?" He waggles a brow. "We all have secrets, little sister."

"Not me." Runa squares her shoulders and pushes off the railing. "I'm where I want to be, whether the dragons accept me or not. Ruling the queendom, guiding it. It's an honor to lead the maternal line in Ezo. The other nations depended on us once, and they will again. We will keep the balance with our abundant resources and peaceful example."

"If you've a secret, Miss Perfect, the dragons will find it," Bastian warns, tossing his coin bag. "What about you, Meera?"

My siblings turn to me with anticipation, the sea wind ruffling their brown hair and tawny eyes that match, like siblings often do. Unlike me.

"I shouldn't say. You'll laugh at me."

"I always laugh *with* you." Runa elbows me. "Not that I can say the same for Bastian."

I raise my chin. "Fine. I want to join the saints in the monastery. I envy their freedom."

"A nun life?" Runa's mouth parts in surprise.

I nod. "What else does this world have for someone like me? Most second daughters serve in the queensguard or on the council, but Father won't even let me try."

"You're the first I've met who dreams of that life," Bastian says. "I'd promise not to tell any of the visiting princes, but it's *nun* of my business."

I nearly choke on a laugh. "Tell them, please. I'd just as soon marry a dragon than the Duke of Taiga."

A few pedestrians further down the seawall whisper behind their scarves, eyes lingering on our little trio. Bastian tosses his leather coin bag again, but I snatch it from the air and stash it in my apron. Sailors and kitchen maids don't display their zeni.

I nod toward the vending booths and lead the way. A sharp jolt of familiar pain rips fire down my leg, forcing me to hobble.

Runa's at my side, the weak side, before I can protest, and Bastian takes up the rear. Once she becomes queen, we won't have these seaside strolls or mornings sneaking food from the kitchens. We won't even share a room anymore. No one will be there when I fall. I bite my lip, turning my attention to the bright vendor stalls and the salt-damp air that cools my cheeks.

"So, when did you arrive?" I ask Bastian, trying to distract them from my limp.

"Ship came in last night," he explains. "Two days' journey from Taiga. I actually rode with your duke. He's not as bad as you think, despite the rumors." He pauses for effect. "But the dragons almost didn't allow our ship in the harbor. Captain had to wave them off with harpoons and throw out a sacrifice to distract them."

"Why? They've never blocked the harbor before." Runa's voice turns sharp with alarm.

"We've never had this many visiting diplomats, not in our lifetime," Bastian continues. "Everyone wants to see if the magic is real. If the dragons are as merciful—or vicious—as they say. I'm sure it's like this every coronation season. Of course, they don't have the beasts in Taiga."

"That's because the duke had them hunted to extinction," I snap, suppressing a shudder at the thought of the sacred beasts' blood leaking into the ocean, their hides sold for zeni and teeth for elixirs. "And it *is* unlike them to intercept the ships. The ancient texts say they never meddle in human affairs within the Enkai Sea, as long as the oath remains intact."

"We aren't living in your books," Bastian says, his voice unusually hard. "The eight kingdoms are fraying."

The phrase hangs between the three of us almost like a warning. I notice he doesn't correct me about the duke.

"The books are always right." I lean toward the nearest stall where steam rises from a steel vat. Subtle spicy notes of clove, salt, and honey warm my face in a gentle cloud. I pull the basket from my back, setting it before the vendor.

"I'll take two pounds." I point to the round chestnuts turning in the drum. We can't return to the castle empty-handed.

"Where did you find these books?" Bastian says, plucking a chestnut from the pan while the merchant's back is turned. He skips it once in his fingers, hissing from the bite of heat. "I've a hard time imagining Papa letting you into his library."

I raise a brow. "The monastery has a library. I wasn't joking about becoming a saint. They explore the eight kingdoms, find ancient treasures, even cultivate herbs and secret tonics. It sounds exciting."

Runa snorts and reaches for the bag as I pay the elderly woman, giving her an extra zeni for the nut Bastian had stolen. As if in repentance, he shoulders the heavy basket.

I lean into my sister, dropping my voice. "I'm glad you brought us together again."

"Someone has to look after you when I'm queen. I almost invited the duke. I mean, you keep his picture—"

"I don't need anyone to take care of me."

"Not even me?" Runa's lips pout before splitting into a wide smile.

"Not even you," I say, smothering the lines of my apron to avoid her gaze. "I have to be self-sufficient; you taught me that. We've both worked hard to be worthy for this day. I . . . I just remembered. I need to get the last of the supplies. The saints make the most delicious butter."

I turn to leave, but Runa catches my hand. Her tawny eyes bore into mine. "Worthy doesn't mean perfect."

Easy for her to say with a body that listens and a heart the dragons would kill for.

"I'll be back in a blink," I say, my voice softening. "Why don't you and Bastian fetch the vanilla for the custard?"

"We shouldn't part ways unprotected," Bastian says, falling in step with us. "Take my personal guard." He cups his hands to his mouth and imitates the cry of a white-eyed warbler.

A shadow moves beneath the awning of a bakery, blending into the dark wooden walls and thatched roof. The figure's clothes shift color, mottled by sun and shade, until he stands an arm's length away. He'd been so still, I hadn't even noticed him.

The man nods toward Bastian, his dark brown eyes darting up from the cobblestones beneath us. A callousness in his gaze, coupled with black hair cropped like a foreign soldier, throws his youthful face into confusing lines.

"Jey, keep watch over Princess Meera," Bastian instructs in a whisper.

"Her safety is my life." The man slams a fist over his heart.

"It most certainly is not," I correct him, pulling a golden chain from inside my tunic and stringing it around my neck. "Mother Ema will protect me."

"A charm?" Bastian arches a brow.

I point down the street that wends around the bottom of the cliffside and loops a trail up the small forested mountain creeping with homes and shops. An old woman in white knotted silk with a thick periwinkle-blue robe bends over a stand, weaving amulets and selling carefully wrapped butter. "A saint. You find them at the monastery. Perhaps I *shall* become one when Runa becomes queen. I prefer their protection."

The shadowed guard nods, a spark of admiration in his eye. But Runa and Bastian give me no such look. "You're serious?" Bastian says with an exasperated huff. "I think Father and the duke would have something to say about that."

I raise a brow, daring him to remind me of my arranged marriage again. "Come on, the entire market is enthralled with the dragons right now. No one will pay attention to a hobbling maid."

Runa sighs. "You won't be long? Just to get butter from the nuns, right?"

I nod and flash a smile before cutting to the nearest side alley. *Blessed Saints.* I need to be alone. Before the dragons consume part of my sister's soul. Before I'm to marry a handsome duke and move across the sea to a rival kingdom—to Taiga. Before my world dissolves at the whims of people stronger and more whole than me.

I eye the bright blue awning of the nuns' stall ahead. Maybe they can protect Runa's heart from the beasts and grant her success. I'd searched their library for clues, a secret wisdom, the history of the dragons' oath—and nothing.

But I could ask.

One. Last. Time.

CHAPTER
TWO

MY LEGS BURN LIKE FIRE as I crest the top of the hill, heart hammering. Banners pop in the breeze, each one displaying the name of a traditional shop from the eight kingdoms, come to display their best wares for the coronation festivities. Wood sculptures beneath a vibrant green tarp for Thesia, honey jars in exotic flavors under Taiga's crimson tarp, even a sword stand from Ezo's own Sorachi mines.

The saints greet me with wind-chaffed faces and a low bow that suggests they know who I am beneath the disguise.

"Sisters," I breathe through a smile, my lungs aching. "I'll take two butter sticks."

The older nun wraps two bars of brilliant golden butter and places them in a bag, tying it closed with a ribbon. "There you go, dear. Did you only come for butter?" Her knowing eyes shine.

I open my mouth and close it before daring my question. "My sister, Runa. Is there a way you can help her?"

"Does she need help?" The question is calm, thoughtful.

I falter. "I-I think so. She's afraid about tomorrow."

A clatter of metal sounds behind us, drawing the nuns' attention. Shouting erupts, followed by a slew of curses as a smack echoes across the market—the sound of leather on flesh.

"It's urgent," I press, leaning across the saints' table and dropping my voice. "Is there a way to guarantee the dragons will accept her?"

The eldest nun eyes the commotion behind me, and I glance back at the ruckus. Fists swing beneath the sloping banners, one smashing a tureen of candied yams, which now roll about the cobblestone. The nuns light a prayer censer and a wisp of milky smoke laces the breeze, then they bow their heads and begin to chant.

Great, they're praying. They won't talk to me again until the fighting stops.

I push out from the butter stand and step toward the fray. Today is about changing destinies. Mine—and Runa's.

The first man is a blacksmith with broad sweeping shoulders and long, shaggy hair. Blood streams from a cut on his brow, but he wipes it with the back of a coal-stained hand and holds his arms up to block his opponent.

The other man is a lanky blond lieutenant bearing the Taigan crest, dual dragons fighting in a blaze of fire. The black suit, black hat, and sharp gold buttons of the Imperial soldiers are hard to miss. He lights a cigarette with one of the new flame canisters as if bored. "Where's my dagger?" he growls.

"I already told you," the blacksmith says with a ragged breath. "I don't have it."

"Wrong answer." He swings at the blacksmith with a feinting punch and then hammers him in the side on the next blow. A bloodied cough spurts the ground.

The nuns pray louder.

"Enough," I shout, snatching a frying pan from the nearest vendor, still hot and dripping with batter. No one's going to stand between me and getting answers from those nuns. "Clear out, now."

The blacksmith leans, doubled over, one arm gripping the bar of his shop to keep himself upright.

The lieutenant sneers. "I don't take orders from kitchen maids."

I glance down at my apron, forgetting my disguise. *Saints, I should've thought this through.*

My foot taps in rapid-fire rhythm with my thoughts. I can't outrun this man, and if I reveal myself as the princess . . . I gulp. I'd rather face this man's fists than the whispers of the crowd and Papa's wrath on the eve of the coronation.

"I'm not ordering you as a maid. I'm calling you out as a girl who has more guts than you." I throw the pan in his direction, and it clatters against his arm, blocked by a swift move.

A dark scowl clouds the lieutenant's face as he brushes off the newly charred spot on his uniform. He drops his cigarette and steps toward me, an angry tic in his jaw.

I swallow hard and dart behind the nearest shop counter, praying the queensguard intervenes soon.

"In here," a small girl whispers. The urchin points to a trap door inside the pop-up vendor cart, inching the wooden hatch open for me to crawl inside.

"Thank you." I nod, wedging myself into the makeshift hiding place, a small storage hold between piles of raw yams and charcoal. "Go to the baker at Yamashi Park and ask for Prince Bastian. He'll help."

The shop girl's eyes widen. She gives a sharp nod before shutting the door behind me. Footsteps pound outside, followed by an angry roar.

"I know you're here." The lieutenant's greasy voice spills through the wooden cracks. "Come out or we'll have another sacrifice for the serpents, and it won't be a deer this time."

A terrified squeal sounds outside, and I push my face toward a crack in the makeshift cart. The lieutenant holds a hot tong to the shop girl's quivering throat. She claws at him with charcoal-stained hands, her feet barely touching the ground.

Boiling saints.

"Stop!" I crawl out of the booth on hands and knees, standing slowly, my eyes never leaving the dark, murderous leer of the lieutenant.

"It's always easy to find the trash," he purrs, sniffing the little girl's hair. "It all smells the same." He hurls the child aside with a flick of his wrist and then brandishes the hot metal.

The shop girl scurries down the hillside alley, and I fix the man with a glare fit for a beast, even though my legs quake. I only hope the girl remembers to fetch Bastian. I raise my hands tentatively as the man steps closer with the iron. My back brace hits the booth, and my throat goes tight.

A sizable crowd circles us, murmuring, and a few collect the fallen goods from the merchant's cart. I sorely wish I hadn't dismissed Bastian's guard. *Where is the queensguard? Shouldn't they be patrolling this side of the harbor?*

"I should end your miserable life right now."

I gulp. "But should you? The penalty for manslaughter is quite high in Ezo."

"Yes, but you're just a kitchen maid." He leans forward, hot tong still in hand and a short sword belted at his waist. "A pretty one at that with those blue eyes and smooth skin."

Heart racing, my eyes dart to the beaten blacksmith and his tools littered on the cobblestones. An anvil, hammer, chisel, anything to help me defend myself. No one in the crowd meets my gaze, offers to kick a weapon toward me, or tries to distract this insane lieutenant. *Cowards.*

Fine. I'll take him on alone, then.

I pull the gold chain from my neck and thrust it out for all to see. "In the name of Mother Ema, I demand that you stop. Violence is a curse on the souls of men."

The lieutenant pauses, his sneering face within arm's reach, and the gold pendant dangling between us. "A sister of the light?" His eyes skim my face and linger somewhere below my shoulders. "I highly doubt that."

"Ask the nuns," I shout, my voice catching. I scan the crowd, their attention riveted on the simple charm. "Only a sister of the light carries a pendant. Call them over. I am one of them."

The lie trembles in my throat, but I hold it there. Silence catches on the breeze, broken only by the piercing cry of a sea serpent and the flap of tarps in the wind.

The lieutenant works his jaw, eyes darting to the shifting crowd. Only one thing causes greater fear than the militants of the other provinces all thirsting for Ezo's natural resources—and that's the Order of the Light. They stand outside the rule of the eight kingdoms and are the only ones besides the queen to understand the dragons' unruly magic. The western kingdom of Furan's weight behind them doesn't hurt either.

The lieutenant's blue eyes bore into me, weighing my threat. He doesn't fear the saints; his eyes are too cold, too jaded.

I straighten, trying not to gulp as fear knots my stomach. "The queensguard will be here soon. I-I . . . suggest we both go on our way."

A wicked smile brushes the lieutenant's lips as he leans forward. "You shouldn't pick battles you can't win, *sister*. The blacksmith refused to sell me a certain tool to control your vicious beasts. Dragons crossed into Taigan waters, and I'd like to do a little hunting on the way back, you see."

My breath becomes shallow.

"Harming the dragons here would break the oath. The dragons would destroy us."

"There's an 'us' now," he jeers, one hand trailing the scarf holding back my hair.

I reel to the side, shoving his hand away. "Leave or I'll report you to the sisters."

"You're not one of them." He lunges for my neck but seizes my scarf instead. Tight silk whips past my throat, burning like a rope. Blue hair falls down my back and strings into my face as I trip forward, clawing for the scarf.

The crowd's murmurs turn to gasps.

"The cerulean princess! I thought she was bedridden."

"That's no saint. A curse, that one."

"She can't walk without sorcery."

I grab at my hair, desperately trying to hide it behind my back or balled into my fist, but it's no use. The blue strands rival the sky and sea, blinding in their strangeness.

The lieutenant pauses, momentarily stunned as the scarf hangs limp in his hands.

"Princess Meera?"

I spin around at the sound of my name. A man identical to the picture kept beneath my mattress storms down the narrow cobblestone along the cliffside, stopping with a winded breath and my name on his lips. Dark eyes shaded with concern—and anger—snap to mine. *My eyes*, not my blue hair or crooked spine.

My gaze wanders over the short, whiskey-colored hair, the slanted brow, and the unmistakable scar trailing his cheek, as if someone had aimed for his eye and just missed.

"Casmir . . . ?" I scan the Duke of Taiga, searching for hints of the boy I'd last seen five years ago when our parents signed the papers for our engagement. He's taller, darker too, as if he's been working in the sun and not counting scales in the emperor's golden palace.

"Are you all right?" His voice is calm, trained.

Hot tears rush to my eyes, all the stress spent and pouring out. I hate crying, especially in front of a boy—this boy in particular. I swat the tears away with the back of my hand. "I'm fine."

Casmir closes the gap between us, loosening the collar of his shirt and tearing the silk cravat from his neck. Using it as a ribbon, he ties my hair into a simple knot. I reach back to touch the camellia-red silk that now tames my blue tresses, and my eyes drift to Casmir's open collar and the stubble shading his jaw, as though he'd just arrived from sea and had not the time to appear presentable.

How had he found me so soon?

With a flick of his fingers, Casmir summons two Taigan guards to right the disarrayed alley, breaking my trance.

The soldiers snap to attention, herding the startled crowd and picking up the fallen potatoes as if one missed vegetable would be their head.

"My lord." The lieutenant claps a fist to his heart with a sharp bow. "My apologies. I did not know it was the princess. She intervened when I was dealing with a thief and—"

"And you dare assault a citizen of Ezo? My betrothed no less." Casmir's jaw clenches.

"My lord, but the dagger of the saint, it's—"

"Silence." Casmir backhands the lieutenant with his ringed hand, knocking the man to the ground. "You'll meet your punishment on the ship."

I stifle a sharp breath at the cruelty—and the power behind that hit—but the man had deserved it.

The lieutenant pushes up from his humbled position, body trembling and eyes wide with terror. Casmir nods, and his officers haul the man away by the arms. The lieutenant yells in protest, writhing and kicking to escape, but a harsh jab to the head with a wooden baton silences him.

I don't realize I'm stepping backward until Casmir lays a gentle hand on my shoulder. "Are you hurt?"

Casmir's eyes remind me of the forest we played in together so many years ago as children, a dark green maze with flecks of sunlight. *Before he became a dragon slayer and agreed to a betrothal without even asking me.* He searches my face, no doubt smeared in charcoal from the yam hut. "Are you hurt?" he asks again.

"I'm fine." I brush his hand aside, warmth swooping below my brace. "Thank you for helping, but I had it under control."

He raises a brow and nods to the crowd. "It's not me you need to convince. It's them."

I grit my teeth, anger blossoming in my chest because he's right. It doesn't bother me so much when it's Runa or Bastian who helps me. It's not out of pity or distress. It's a bond. Siblings. But Casmir? I don't even know why he agreed to marry someone like me.

I scour the cobblestone street, my heart humming like a hawk moth paused in midflight. "Where's my sister?"

"Is she here as well?" His eyes drop to my kitchen robes, a smile sliding across his sun-kissed face. "Running away on the big day?"

"Runa would never run," I say. "The unity of the kingdoms depends on her leadership."

Casmir turns, a laugh escaping his lips. "Spoken like a true ruler. But it's that very conceit that makes them wrong."

"Runa's not conceited, she's—"

Casmir holds a finger to his lips, his ruby signet ring glinting in the sun as he scans the crowd and the soldiers righting the fallen carts and produce. His voice drops to a whisper as he leans closer. "It's simple physics, Meera. Kingdoms are made to fall."

I steel my shoulders. *Is that a warning?* "If you know something about a threat to our queendom, speak freely."

"It's my job to find threats," he says. "That's why I'm here. To make sure the coronation goes smoothly for both our kingdoms. And to honor your sister, of course."

I can't help but wonder if there's another "and" with the way he looks at me. "Well, I suggest we find her before we're both in trouble."

I throw one last glance at the saints' booth, now empty, and sigh, cursing my luck.

A dragon cry breaks the silence and Casmir stiffens. I forgot Taigans aren't familiar with the serpents. My fists tighten at my sides. Runa will face them tomorrow morning. And whether or not the dragons find her worthy, I will lose her. To the fangs of a beast or the power of a crown.

THREE

I CLIMB THE PALACE STEPS, thick silk knotted in my fists, careful not to trip over the long hem of my dress. It shimmers around my ankles like blackest night—the color for mourning. Sixteen hours before my sister loses either her life or part of her soul.

"Your Highness!" A timid voice calls after me. "My lady, please. I have a dress for you to wear to your sister's ceremony."

My jaw clenches as I step onto the sixth-floor landing, a wide hallway trimmed in cypress wood with an open view of the cliffside town. Pain pulls at my back, a persistent ache, but it's nothing compared to the worry squeezing my chest. I catch my reflection in the full mirror that stretches the length of the opposite wall, angled to catch the warm orange glow of the setting sun. Is there no way I can help my sister?

"The dress . . . please." Footsteps slap louder, faster up the stairs.

"I already have a dress." I stare at the mirror with the sea reflected behind me. Long blue hair piles on the top of my head, braided and woven into clever arches and curling fronds that tuck neatly at the nape of my neck. Black nestles against my skin, tight silk folds held together by my bone-white brace. It hugs my spine, looping under my arms and holding my twisted back upright. My fingers trail the thin wood covered with lacquered leather that stops abruptly above my hips.

"Your father insists," the maid continues, stepping beside me.

I meet her gaze in the mirror and take a deep breath. Seira, the weaver's daughter. Her talent belongs in a school for seamstresses, not here in the castle mending laundry and running errands for the head maid. The girl could fashion dresses from any substance, even tree bark if asked to, trained by the skilled hands of her ancestors, the Ainur who dwell in the northern mountains.

Soft brown eyes dart away the moment she notices I've caught her staring. I turn, shifting my gaze to the dress held in her arms. My stomach twists. It's blue, the same color as my hair. Silk layers touch the gown in various shades and textures, the outer a light, summer silk with open weave to let in the light.

"It looks like the ocean in the morning sun. Your father had it custom made for the celebration." The maid shifts the dress in her hands, presenting the changing colors and soft weave.

My eyes cut to the flowing waistline. "He wants me to hide my brace."

Seira squirms, fingering the fabric. "He said—" She swallows like his words are hard to pry from her throat. "He noted how ambassadors from every country will be here and it's important to look . . ."

"Don't search for a nicer word." I raise a brow, my jaw set. "I want to know what he said."

"Whole."

The word is a knife to my spine, almost snapping me in two.

Seira's eyes jump to mine. "I don't think he meant it like that."

"Of course he did." I turn away from the dress. "I'm not wearing that. My strength comes from not hiding my weakness like a coward."

I will show them all that I'm not broken. Not worthless or a pawn to be bartered, no matter how I feel on the inside.

I glide down the hall, dizzied by the high ocean view and the mirrored waves. My throat tightens, and I struggle to fill my mind with more important things than dresses: reviewing schedules for the ceremony, memorizing the names of dignitaries, ensuring the cook bakes my sister's favorite pudding.

"The king told me you'd say that." Seira's voice is a timid whisper. "I-I'm to inform you that if you don't wear this, I'll lose . . . my job."

I freeze, my eyes snapping to the wooden ceiling as I take a fortifying breath. Papa always knows where to strike. "He wouldn't do that."

The maid hurries to my side, bowing low and holding out the dress like a ritual sacrifice as if to remind me what kind of man my father is. One hardened by the throne.

Seira braves a pleading glance at me. "Are you willing to test that?"

My father sits on his silver throne in the Grand Hall, robed in midnight blue silk trimmed in white fur. The head of a wolf stares down at me with glassy eyes from behind the throne. I don't like the way its teeth glimmer in the candlelight, frozen in a perpetual snarl. A message to all who approach the throne —the prince consort is no longer a figurehead, not since Mother's death, but a regent vested with power. One who dares to call himself king when only a queen can sit on the Ezo throne.

I bow before Papa, my brace chafing the underside of my arm from within rolls of blue silk. He meets my gaze with a hard glint of triumph.

"Is everything a game to His Majesty?" I rise and note the

guards on my left and right. "Even the coronation ceremony for his most prized child?"

His jaw hardens. "Only pick the games you can win, daughter. Enjoy the festivities. You'll have your own ceremony before too long. No need to stain your sister's."

Heat burns my throat, but I swallow it down. I lost Mama when I was only eight, and my papa soon after that to the grief that turned him hard and bitter. I don't have memories of my parents' love, at least none strong enough to block out the cold training, endless lessons, and selling of my future to save the queendom from certain financial ruin. Runa has memories. A lullaby Mama used to sing over her, morning strolls with Papa to fetch the freshest puddings at the market.

But I've none of that—only Runa. It's like losing a mother, a sister, and a friend in one night, and I can't even make a statement with the clothes on my back.

I bow and welcome the brace's bite against my ribs.

"Don't forget your schedule," the king says, his voice softening a shade. A servant scurries to me, bowing as he holds out a silver platter with a small, square envelope.

I pluck it off the tray, bow, and turn my back on the man who didn't raise me.

6pm Mingle with the lords
7pm Dance with alliances
8pm Celebration dinner
9pm Runa's Farewell

The last line jumps off the page. *Farewell to life as she knows it.* I crumple the paper in my fist, squeezing until my nails dig into the fat of my palm. Then I drop it on the floor and make my way to the ballroom on the darkest and lowest floor of the castle. Tonight won't be Runa's farewell, not if I can help it.

Doors clank behind me with a thunderous rumble as I step

into the chamber dominated by an enormous window holding the sea behind it, underwater. In daylight, the sun dips golden fingers into the blue, and the light through the water paints rainbows on the floor. But tonight, I see only the guttering glow of torches and my own reflection in the wall of water. Sweat beads at the back of my neck from the heat of firelight and the eerie rush of water behind the glass. *Are the dragons watching?*

I'm announced before I can catch my bearings. "Her Royal Highness, Princess Meera of Silverwood."

Dignitaries blur into view like spots of too-bright color, disorienting. I catch whispers of Thesian accent and the crimson of Seshu brocade as I scan the room, hunting for the one person I need to see.

Warm candlelight pours over a lacquered table from a chandelier on the high ceiling, the newest invention from Taiga, created by Furan engineers. Crystal prisms attached to the fixture magnify the light by reflecting its brilliance. It glows with the warmth of a hundred lanterns. But the chill air, and even colder stares from the dozens of nobles, extinguishes it from thought.

Runa stands at the far end of the table, extending a subtle nod as I make my way toward her. The nobles hold their silence until I take my seat at her right-hand side, then a wave of general murmur fills the cavernous room. Runa grips my hand beneath the table with a reassuring squeeze.

"Did father make you wear that dress?" she asks, turning to nod at a passing noble from Thesia decked in green robes woven with horsehair.

"I chose to wear it," I say, Seira's concerned face flashing in my mind. "Papa may twist my arm, but he can't take away my choices."

A smile breaks Runa's perfectly red lips, wrinkling the fine lines of her makeup. "The indominable Meera. Casmir has no idea what he's getting into with your engagement."

"I still might choose the nuns," I whisper.

Runa laughs into her wine goblet.

My heart gives a painful lurch. Would that be her last laugh? Her last taste of the spiced tones of Katsuma wine? I scan her painted face, purest white with rose-red lips, black lashes like the wings of a raven, and eyes so warm and clear that you'll want to spill your deepest darkest secrets because you know they'll be safe—you'll be safe.

The dragons will accept her as their queen. They'll change her slowly, or shorten her life like the queens of old, like Mama. That's the best-case scenario. And I'm . . . scared.

"Have you talked to any of the nobles?" Runa asks, recovering from nearly spilling her goblet on her scarlet dress. She rises to her feet and takes me by the elbow, leading me to the dance floor.

"Is there one who doesn't want to slit my throat?" I ask sulkily. "They're only here to see if you become queen and Ezo regains its power. If not for that, they'd tear us apart. Look at them, they're practically salivating for an opportunity to steal the queendom."

"Yes." Runa casts a shrewd gaze about the milling crowd, some sampling wine, dancing, or secreting into the shadowed corners for scandals of one kind or another. Whispers of the kingdoms' discord float over my ears: the bakuto gangs in the capital of Taiga, droughts and the rise of tariffs, the resurgence of the Black Dragon Society, and Rusan ships interfering with our cargo. "But there is one noble who'd like to see you."

Heat rises to my face at the thought of meeting Casmir again, as a duke and not just a childhood acquaintance from a warring province. He's never seen me in a formal dress. My hands fly unbidden to the loose fabric at my waist, the gauzy blue threads that make my hair seem even brighter in the warm light. I sorely wish for a simple tunic to hide in.

"You look beautiful," Runa whispers.

"Oh look, it's Lord Alexandu of Rusa talking with Bastian." I nod toward an older gentleman sporting a chartreuse cravat with an inky black suit. "Maybe I should invite him to our table."

"Because he represents the largest rival to the Taigan Empire? Casmir will only find it a welcome challenge."

Nervous tension pools in my stomach. "If you had to marry one of these, which would you pick?"

"Had to?" Runa chews on the words as if testing a new culinary morsel. "As queen I'm free to choose my match. My only requirement is that it's for love. But that's the least of my worries right now. It won't matter if . . ."

I wait for her to clarify, to add "if the dragon eats me" to the end of that sentence, but she doesn't. It hangs thick in the air between us.

Runa takes a long gulp of wine and swallows hard.

My chest gives a painful squeeze. How can someone so kind and beautiful not know her own worth? The dragons would be blind to reject her. I want to ease her fears, to see her easy smile return.

"What matters is that you enjoy right now," I say. "Besides, all the princes in the eight kingdoms are here."

"Not all of them." Runa scans the room as if hoping for a spark of love to light her way.

"Well, most of them. Why don't you go dance and see if someone interests you?" I nudge her in the ribs.

"Love only happens that fast in fairytales."

"So I'll be your fairy godmother." I loop my arm in hers and wrap a finger round one of my blue curls. "They all think I'm a sorceress anyway, as if only old witches have curved backs."

I lead Runa across the dance floor. Nobles congratulate her on the upcoming ceremony, wish her favor, and more than a few scan the warm glow of her skin and the tight curves of her scarlet dress that flares behind her with a rounded hem studded in rainbow garnets and golden threads.

Runa dances with the Prince of Seshu, a handsome blond-haired youth, and Sir Richter, the silver-haired ambassador of Taiga, before returning to the table for appetizers with the brooding young Lord of Kagano who controls the region's best hot springs.

Father toasts as the servants arrive, effectively distracting the dignitaries as the food is arranged on the table and the wine glasses refilled. I slink into a corner, making note of the Seshu prince should Runa ever ask my opinion on her future partner.

"Sorry I'm late."

I jump at the sound of Casmir's voice behind me, my wine goblet sloshing against his chest.

"Good thing it was white," he says, plucking at the silk suit tailored across his broad chest and lean, muscular arms. "Still, the silk is done for."

Father clears his throat, and heat brushes my jawline. "They're all staring at us, aren't they?" I whisper.

Casmir leans down, a conspiratorial smile on his face. "Yes."

"Boiling saints. They'll never see me as a normal princess."

"Why would you want to be normal when you're exceptional?" Dark eyes skim over my blue hair and the billowing gown before flickering to my lips. "And you'll never be a nun with that cursing. Bastian told me all about your preferred profession."

Heat engulfs my face, threatening to drown me. *He's doing this on purpose to unnerve me.* I shove my now-empty wine glass into the duke's hands. "I shall endeavor to become more worthy—of the nuns, that is."

He grins, but I turn to face the crowd and find the toast is over and my sister is tossing back the dregs of her second goblet of wine. Her face flushes a tad pink as she sets the chalice down and lifts a silver spoon for the royal pudding. Per tradition, she takes the first bite.

I stare across the room at my own plate, the creamy orange pudding topped with red berries and a dark caramel syrup dripping onto the white porcelain. It's tradition for the royal court to eat foods that smell pleasing to the dragons on the coronation eve. And for the princess to choose one food of her choice as a kind of last supper before taking the crown. Of course, Runa chose pudding.

A fist slams against the table, rattling the plates and drinks. A smack of flesh against the hard wood. Coughing.

My eyes jump to the source of the commotion. Runa stands, bent over the table, one hand to her throat and another bracing herself against the table. Eyes red, watering, bulging. Her skin goes ghastly white, then blue. Her mouth opens, but no words come out. Veins pop against her forehead as she coughs, coughs, coughs.

Blood splatters across the serviette in her hand, and then my sister collapses into her chair, face hitting the table with an unholy smack.

"Runa!" I scream and run toward her.

"Quick! Send for a physician!" The Seshu prince drops to his knees and presses his fingers against her neck.

My sister lies across the table, her body twisted at an odd angle, one hand reaching out, fingers curled, and the other hand at her throat. Chestnut hair spills across the splattered plates.

"No! No, no . . ." A tangled cry rips from my throat as I run to her.

"Meera, don't!" Casmir grabs my arms and pulls me away. "It could be foul play; you could be next."

I fall against him, slamming my elbow into his ribs. He grunts, but his hold only tightens. *How dare he hold me back!*

Servants rush by, righting my sister and wiping the blood from her mouth.

"Runa!" I writhe to be free while tears overwhelm my eyes.

"Call for a physician," Casmir orders. Then to me, "Meera, look—she's breathing."

I pause the struggle, letting his arms anchor me for this one brief moment. Runa's chest rises and falls with a gentle cadence, almost like she's listening to a lullaby, breathing to its calming rhythm.

I reach out to her again, but my fingers pause before touching her. My eyes round in horror at the faint greenish tint beneath her skin. "It's magic."

Casmir releases me and steps toward Runa, bending down to analyze her face, frozen in fear and as if choking.

"Don't touch her," I order. "The first rule of magic is never touch."

"Where did you learn that?"

"In *The Saint's Book of Serpents*," I say, and a look ghosts across his face. "Ezo may be the most wild and rural of the kingdoms, but we have a power no one else does."

"And a great many nations would kill to have it." He straightens, scanning the room.

"To stop the coronation and keep us from that great power, all the nations are here on our doorstep." My eyes linger over his, suspicion brewing as I trace the lines of his face. He helped me at the market. Why am I questioning?

"We'll find whoever did it," he says with cold certainty.

"*I'll* find them," I say. "And make them pay."

"She's . . . she's dead?" someone gasps.

"No," Casmir speaks loudly. "Asleep. Princess Runa has been cursed."

I search the crowd for a sign of guilt or recognition as Casmir states the facts. That's when I notice a guard and the Prince of Seshu collapsed on the floor, asleep. A loud thud follows as a servant collapses on his way out to send for a healer, then another into a tureen of radish soup.

"What do we do?" The question comes from every corner of the room, as surely as it comes from every corner of my mind. The dignitaries closest to Runa step back, others peer against the glass ocean wall for a glimpse of the dragons, saying what everyone is thinking: "The dragons are waiting for their queen."

"She will wake." Papa's voice booms with a certainty I don't feel. "The dragon will have its queen. Send for Mother Ema and the best healers in the land." His voice shakes as if he's single-handedly trying to hold the kingdom together, and it's cracking beneath his words.

"If she doesn't?" the young Lord of Kagano demands with a calloused air.

I wait for Papa to give us some hope that he can save her. That anyone can save her. Instead, after giving Runa a hard look, his eyes slide to me. "We have another princess."

I go numb at his words—it's a death sentence for me—but he turns to speak to the nobles crowded around him as if I'm already forgotten. My knees shake, threatening to collapse. My sister's body isn't even cold, and my father's going to throw me to the monsters without a second thought.

I brace myself against the banquet table, palms pressing into the wood. *Don't collapse. Don't be weak.* An ear-shattering cry shakes the windowed wall that looks into the sea, and my legs buckle.

The dragons know.

CHAPTER
FOUR

"POISON." The word spreads like the plague hours after the healer arrives. Whisper upon whisper, faces turn to horrified expressions as they stare at Runa's limp body. A cursed poison.

She's okay. There has to be a way to fix this. My teeth grit against the image of my sister collapsed over the table, her chestnut hair spilled across the plates and dishes, blood running a slow, thick river down her face. I shake my head, stepping back, back, back.

There's nothing okay about this.

My spine slams into a wall of solid flesh.

"Princess Meera?" The worn voice of my father's personal guard. A gloved hand takes me strongly by the arm and propels me to the back door. "Your father requests that you wait in your quarters until the coronation."

"Wait, he . . ." *Wants to keep me prisoner.* My head goes dizzy, all warmth draining from my body. The coronation, the dragon . . .

I spin round to catch my father's eye, but his attention is elsewhere. A few nobles spare me a cursory gaze before dismissing me as just another pawn in their plans. Conniving, the lot of them. All here to watch if our kingdom falls so they can scavenge the pieces. Well, I won't be locked away, not when my sister needs help and a poisoner is on the loose.

"I need some privacy," I whisper to the guard. "In the washroom," I add, so he catches my meaning.

"I'll stand by the door."

"That won't be necessary." I lift my chin. "My sister's just been poisoned. I think the queensguard has better things to do than wait outside the ladies room."

He reddens, lifting his hand from mine in a subtle acquiesce. "Protecting you is my highest priority. I will wait outside the door."

I take one last glance at Runa, only her sprawling hair and pale fingers visible with the crowd surrounding her. A few limp bodies decorate the cold floor: the cook, a physician, three servants, and the Prince of Seshu. A cry curdles in the back of my throat. I dash out of the room.

I run like I was made of sea and sky, like nothing can stop me. Rushing the stairs—up, up, up—my heart slams against the brace, lungs burning. I fly out the castle's staircase, away from the guard, feet crashing against the slick wood that pools into the main hall. Runa's plucky smile flashes in my mind, her sharp nose and the way she stood tall to face any problem, no matter how she felt inside. No matter how scared.

Runa would tell me not to worry. Pull myself together. The kingdom needs a queen.

I am not my sister.

"Meera!" Bastian calls to me over the top of the stairs, his voice etched in worry.

"Leave me a—" My hip catches and I fall, palms slapping the hard wood, followed by a smack to my head.

Mumbled curses sound over me as a hand turns my waist and sits me up. I rub my forehead, vision blurring back into focus.

"Hey," Bastian's voice is a warm invite, accepting me.

I grab onto his strong arms, and he pulls me to my feet. "Father was going to lock me in my room." My lips tremble against my will. "Runa won't be there. I can't. Not with her empty bed and . . . and her asleep in that chair. She has to wake, Bastian. She has to." I don't have words for the pain that flashes hot in my chest, the swirl of thoughts and numb disbelief twisting inside me. Tears pool in my eyes, but I strike them away with the back of my hand. "I'm not a queen."

"I know." His warm arms tuck me into a hug. "I know."

Bastian's wool jacket smells of spiced vanilla and old cedar like the room where Runa was poisoned. I blink and pull back. "What am I to do?"

"My little sister is asking me?" He runs a hand through his dark hair, mouth pinched in worry. "I'd say think it over, get some sleep. But there's no time." He straightens, glancing about the room to make sure we're not overheard. Footsteps sound in the outer hall. My brother nods to the door of Father's library, and we slip inside. As soon as the door closes, Bastian lets out a deep exhale and leans over the large table-map in the room's center.

"We should be safe here," he says. "Look, Meera, I've been living in Taiga for the last year as Father's ambassador." He points at the largest kingdom on the map, south of our island. "They have Ezo's best interests in mind. But Rusa, Thesia, even Seshu wouldn't hesitate to cut our throats if it meant winning the kingdom. They all want our resources, the coal and silver in the mountains, the earth enriched by centuries of dragon magic. The only thing stopping them right now are the dragons protecting us because of the oath. But if there's no queen tomorrow, the oath is broken and we lose everything."

My breath snags against my brace. I need to sit, to think. "You know what happened to the last cerulean princess," I say, curling a lock of blue hair around my finger until a few brittle strands pull free.

"Yes, grandaunt was burned alive by the dragons and then torn to pieces in front of the crowd." Bastian says it unflinchingly, his tawny eyes so like Runa's. "Meera, you can't go through with the coronation. Father's not thinking straight."

"I have to," the words rub raw against my throat. "You said it yourself, the kingdom will fall if I don't. I have to try. Maybe the dragons will be merciful—"

"No," Bastian says with sharp finality. "It's too risky. If you die, Ezo will fall all the same. But we found another way."

"We?" My eyes narrow, blurring over the portraits in the library, including the vacant one where our grandaunt used to stare down at us with blue eyes and hair, like me. She, too, had the same creaking bones, blue hair, and crooked spine—an inborn disorder, a fault—the reason the dragons would kill me if I stepped up to that throne. The reason my portrait will never grace the castle walls. Because I'm not *whole*.

Not perfect like my sister.

Bastian nods, his mouth set in a tight line.

"How?" My mouth goes dry at the morsel of hope Bastian is offering. But what plan could possibly work? Runa needs me to do what she can't—to reseal the dragons' oath and secure their magic for the kingdom. Because it's more than a throne, it's the lives of thousands of men, women, and children needing protection. It's Mother's home, our pride and heritage.

"I'll show you." Bastian turns and opens a door opposite the one we'd entered.

A shadowed figure stands in the doorway, arms crossed as if he'd been waiting. But the fierce scar against his jaw softens as he offers a sad smile and steps into the lantern light. A shock of whiskey-colored hair and eyes like a summer forest sweep to mine.

"Casmir?" I clasp a hand to my startled heart, looking from my brother to the duke. My brother nods, acknowledging the duke, and then slips out the library door, shutting it behind him.

Panic flutters to my chest. What does the Duke of Taiga want? Had he found a cure or leads to the culprit so soon?

"Princess Meera," Casmir begins, stepping up to the wide table, littered with dozens of books and partially translated scrolls. "My sincerest apologies about your sister."

His formality hits like a splash of cold water, setting my nerves on edge. I swallow hard and steel my face though my heart is breaking. "I don't have time for pleasantries, Duke. No matter how kind. What have you come to say?"

A nervous smile tugs at his lips. He flips a page in *Myths of Saints and Monsters* before turning to me. He moves closer, until our fingertips touch on the edge of the table, over the engraved map of the eight kingdoms. My spine tingles, remembering the startling thrill when his eyes had found my lips at the ball. This is no time for that.

"Do you have news of my sister?" I press, withdrawing my hand. "Have they found a cure? Surely the healer—"

"It's a curse," he says, studying his rejected hand on the table. "The Ladies of the Light came and stopped the poison's progression with their incantations and herbs, but your sister will be asleep until she dies."

"No. No, she can't—it's not possible."

"I'm afraid it is. But the saints saved her life. Your father ordered that floor of the castle be emptied and boarded up. Too many servants and dignitaries have contracted the curse and sleep within the castle walls. It'll spread if we're not careful."

My eyes snap shut. This can't be happening. Truth begins to settle in my bones. "So I am to attempt to be the next queen."

Casmir nods. "Unless there's another way to save the kingdom without the beasts."

My eyes narrow. "Says the dragon murderer."

"There's reason," he says, lips pursed as if trying to conceal what we both know to be true: The sacred dragons are by no means safe or friendly. "Meera, what if I told you that there's another way? I spoke with your brother—"

"What do you propose?"

"Marry me," he says, his voice going deep, breathless. He bows on one knee and pulls a gold ring from his finger, brilliant diamonds encircling a fiery ruby. The jewel is so bright that it almost sings. "Taiga is the sun and Ezo the moon, our two great kingdoms were meant to stand together. It's the only way to save Ezo."

"Marry you?"

"We *are* betrothed." A soft laugh plays in his green eyes.

Heat flames to my cheeks and it takes me a moment to remember to breathe. I turn, my aching back resting against the thick wall of books like a second backbone. The gauzy layers of the blue dress twine with my fingers. I want to run my hands across the patterns of my brace to comfort myself, but it's buried in silk. *Breathe.*

"Marriage won't give the kingdom magic," I say, trying to find words. "Or save my sister. Or protect our shores from Rusa . . . or even from Taiga."

"Astute." A glint of admiration enters his eye. "But I've a bit more sway as duke than you give me credit for. The emperor may not always listen to me, but his advisers and soldiers do. Taiga will protect Ezo from the other kingdoms. You have my word."

"I don't know how much weight that carries," I press, my confidence wavering. "Taiga could easily turn on us. The emperor is always expanding his borders. Not exactly a trusting relationship."

"We don't have to trust each other right away," he says slowly, taking my hand and rising to his feet. "Or make anything final . . . except on paper. To keep the other kingdoms at bay, to keep Ezo safe while we work out a plan."

"And the dragons? To ignore them would be to break the oath. To release hellfire."

"Not if you're married before the coronation."

His words fill the library like an ultimatum, because they are. He's right. The dragons only take an unmarried princess, one whose heart doesn't belong to another. One worthy, whole, pure. I wasn't the intended, Runa was. If I married before the selected time, I wouldn't be eligible, the oath would pass over me. The kingdom would still be without magic and the dragons' protection, but at least they wouldn't attack us—*in theory*.

"But that means . . . we'd have to marry before the coronation tomorrow morning."

Cass runs a hand through his hair with a nervous chuckle. "I admit, it's not a perfect plan. If it makes you feel better, the arrangement would only be a formality, for now."

"Not perfect!" I gasp. "Formality or not, we'd have to—"

"Be in the same room?"

I cross my arms, insufferable heat rising to my cheeks. It's all too fast, too soon. Marriage isn't something to rush into lightly. "I'd rather offer myself to the dragons," I say, hating how ridiculous I sound. "N-no offense."

Casmir smiles, biting back a laugh, and then fixes me with a smoldering stare. "Are you sure?"

My heart slams against my brace. *Saints help me, I'll never be a nun at this rate.*

"My sister might still wake," I say, searching for an excuse, for time to think.

"I'll take that as a 'no,' " Casmir says, putting a respectful distance between us. "But your sister will not wake, Meera. And neither your brother, nor I, want to see you die."

Frustration churns in my gut. "So you would marry me to save a kingdom? To save my life?"

"Yes." He almost laughs, a pleading look in his eye. "Is that so hard to accept? What is love if not to save a life?"

Love. I gulp at the word. *He shouldn't say that so lightly.*

"There are many reasons to save a life," I say, schooling my features to hide the turmoil within. "I-I need more time. I'm sorry, Casmir. If you want to help me, find out who did this to my sister."

I turn, whisking the library door open, and nearly barrel into Bastian at the bottom of the stairs.

"Meera, wait!" Bastian calls, snagging my arm. "Did you turn him down?" he asks with disbelief.

I round on him, hair lashing my face. "I won't marry to save the kingdom, not when it means leaving Runa to die. I'd rather face the dragon. They have magic. They could—"

"What? What could they do?" Bastian takes me by the shoulders, grief showing in the dark hollows beneath his eyes.

"The dragons will kill you because of your disability. This is the only way. If you don't marry Casmir, our kingdom will drown in dragonfire or bleed with Rusan bullets." Bastian swears, drawing a hand over his face, pale with worry. He's never looked at me like that before. Like I'm . . . in his way.

"Marrying Casmir won't save Runa," I say shakily. "We can't give up on her so easily. The dragon's magic might save her. I-I have to try."

Bastian takes a deep breath, his back sagging against the wall. "Meera, we both have to face that Runa might not—"

"Don't say it," I whisper, squeezing my brace as if to hold me together.

Bastian takes a measured breath. "She's my sister too," he says. "But the kingdom is breaking. Don't do this for yourself. Do it *for* Runa. She would want you to put the kingdom first."

It's an effort to breathe. To take in his words and accept them. A chill wraps around my shoulders as I think of Runa alone in that room, and the dragons writhing in the ocean with their sharp fangs and twin hearts. Why can't there be a way to save both Ezo and my sister?

Casmir's warm eyes and the ruby ring flash in my mind. The ring . . .

My mouth goes dry. Casmir had worn it at the market. The lieutenant's words crawl from my memory. He'd said he was trying to find something to control the dragons. A dagger belonging to a saint. Casmir had silenced him. Could it be *the* dagger of the saint? If it's true, then maybe there is a third way.

I clear my throat and place a hand on Bastian's arm, an idea glistening in the back of my mind. "I won't let Runa down."

"And Casmir?" Wariness creeps into Bastian's eyes.

"I just need time. I'll give him my answer first thing tomorrow morning."

"Father's already arranged for the coronation at daybreak," Bastian says. "Tomorrow will be too late. If you're going to marry Casmir, Father needs to know—now. Otherwise he'll throw you to the dragons."

"It's my decision," I say. "And I'll make it soon. Please, Bastian, trust me."

He sighs, pushing off the wall. "I hope so. But please consider, I can't lose another sister."

CHAPTER
FIVE

DUE TO MY OUTBURST, Father stationed guards inside my room as well as out. So much for privacy to mourn my sister's eternal slumber. I grit my teeth, pacing my room—ahem, *prison*—and ignoring Runa's empty bed and the flowers one of the maids had laid there. I'd come up with a plan, but it involved a bit more risk than I was comfortable with. Even Runa wouldn't have approved.

Slipping behind an ornate folding screen, I pull open Runa's wardrobe and change into one of her favorite outfits, a white silk shirt and honey-brown skirt with taffeta. Anything to feel like my sister is still here with me. Strapping the brace over the top, I rifle through my sister's desk.

The queensguard had already taken most everything, searching for any clues to the poisoner's identity: Runa's dairy, letters from Auntie Margo in Furan, even her lipstick. But my sister didn't keep secrets, not from me. If someone had a grudge against her or if clues were hidden within her room, I would know.

I knock over a bottle of ink to gauge the guards' attention level. A thick-set guard shakes his head at me while the other one stands perfectly immune. Getting out of here will be harder than I thought. I clear my throat, giving myself a brief once-over in the mirror and tucking my blue hair into a long braid that falls down my crooked spine before approaching the guards.

"I need to see the Duke of Taiga," I demand, standing before the door.

The guards widen their stance, blocking the passage. "No one is allowed in or out until the coronation," the thick-set guard says.

"Am I to starve?" I feign offense. "Tell my father I wish to see Casmir. Or take me to him, now."

"We have orders," comes a quiet but familiar voice.

My gaze softens on the youngest guard, the twin brother of my maid, Seira. "Did you see my sister in that chair?"

He drops his gaze to the floor.

"I know you would do anything for yours. Let me help mine. I need to speak to the duke. Take me to him, please. It might be the last favor I can ever ask." I groan inwardly at pulling the pity card. But if I'm about to become dragon chow, I might as well use it to my advantage.

"Thirty minutes," the guard says, eyeing the other sentry for approval. He nods, faintly, and Seira's brother opens the door.

"Thank you," I mouth, whisking out the door before he can change his mind.

He leads me up three flights of stairs, waiting as I climb slowly after him. My legs feel like pudding and I've half a mind to return to my room. We enter the guest quarters for the visiting nobles, a long dark hallway painted with silver dragons and emerald waves glistening in the moonlight.

"Last door on the left," he says, stopping a few paces from it and offering me the candle that had lighted our way. "I'll wait outside. Remember, only thirty minutes."

I gulp, my heart pounding. "Right. Thank you."

"Seira told me what you did for her," he adds, his voice a grateful whisper.

I smile, finding strength in those words. "Sisters are worth fighting for," I say. "Take good care of her."

I turn and rap on the door. Silence. And then the scruff of sleepy footsteps against wood. I turn, half-thinking to abandon my desperate plan, when the door cracks open. Casmir blinks at me, eyes half-open. He runs a hand over his face before smoothing his unkempt hair. "Meera? What are y—"

I push the door further open and slip inside, closing it behind me.

"I need to speak with you." My voice catches as I bump into his bare chest, the candle nearly falling from my grasp. My hand brushes against his warm skin for a second too long as I steady myself. A spark radiates down my arm and into my stomach as he catches my hand and guides me into the room. This close, he smells of the hot spring baths, hinoki cypress, and soap.

I clear my throat and he steps back, reaching for a robe on his bedside table. My gaze lingers on his back and the countless scars threaded across his skin. *How many secrets lie stitched beneath those wounds? Are those scars from fighting dragons?*

"My apologies," he says, voice still groggy. "Thought I was dreaming for a second." Wide muscular shoulders slide into the silk robe, tapering down his impossibly fit waist. Even Bastian doesn't have tone like that, and he trained directly with the queensguard.

My nerves flutter. Perhaps this was a very bad idea.

"Maybe I should go," I say, wanting to avert my eyes. "I didn't mean to wake you."

"Stay." Casmir eyes me questioningly from where he ties his robe, and I turn away quickly, heat crawling up my neck. "I want to hear what you have to say."

"I wish all this were a nightmare," I mumble, taking a turn

about his room, one hand on my brace as if it would hold me together. "The poison, the coronation, all of it."

"If you're worried about nightmares, you should've called a physician," Casmir says, his voice guarded as he lights a second candle and gestures to a chair by the window. "But as it is, you've woken me without coffee. A crime no good soul has ever committed. So, whatever it is must be extremely important."

"It is." I nod and take a seat, thoroughly unnerved by Casmir's green eyes in the candlelight, beautiful and yet calculating. *Focus. Ask about the dagger the lieutenant was after and how to control the dragons . . .*

Casmir sinks onto a chair beside me. Our fingers brush as he hands me a small lap blanket. I hadn't realized that I was trembling, but one glance at my hands tells me otherwise.

"What can I do for you, Princess?" The question is kind, if not a tad amused.

"I have two problems, Cass," I begin. His eyes light at the sound of his nickname, the one I'd used when we were children. *Good, gaining his trust back is step number one.* "First, there's an assassin on the loose. The person who cursed my sister is most likely still in the castle, and it could be anyone—even you. I need to find who did it and what poison they used."

"Is this how you usually ask your friends for help?" Casmir's eyes shine with humor.

"I wasn't aware that we were friends," I say.

"Let's amend that." Cass retrieves a thin notebook from his bedside table and hands it to me. "I've done some research in the last few hours, like you asked of me in the library. I was planning on telling you tomorrow after the coronation. But I have a lead."

He opens it and points to the first page.

"The poison?" I squint at the hurriedly scrawled words for the names of various plants, calculations, and . . . a name. "Jey. Is that the lead?"

"My informant," he corrects, snatching the notebook and

settling back in his chair. "Now, can we start over as friends? Or have you reconsidered my proposal?"

"About that . . ." My stomach flips, but I force myself to carry on. *It's near-certain death or this man. And I can't save my sister by dying.* "That's the second reason I came. In the library, I spoke too harshly."

Casmir tilts his head, and dark eyes like a shaded forest meet mine. "So you wouldn't rather throw yourself into the dragon's mouth?"

"No." My lips pinch in embarrassment. "I wouldn't. Not like that. I've an unfortunate habit of saying what's on my mind. I'm sorry if it hurt you."

"Apology accepted," he says. "But you didn't sneak past the guards to my bedroom to apologize, did you?"

"It's not like I wanted to come to your bedroom. I . . . have questions and not much time." I pause, studying his face. He watches me intently, politely ignoring my embarrassment. Taking a deep breath, I go on. "My brother said that you hunted down the last of the dragons in Taiga. But you said there was reason. I need to know the truth. Why do you hunt that which we consider sacred?"

He leans forward, raising a brow as if to challenge me. "I carry out the tasks the emperor would rather not. Like eliminating the dragons within Taigan borders. They're vicious beasts with no regard for human life. In Ezo, they say the dragons helped restore the world after the Ashfall. But Taiga has a different story, one where the dragons started the flames. You view them as fallen gods tasked with protecting the earth. We see them as demons trying to destroy it."

Casmir twists the ruby ring on his hand and takes a deep breath. "Naturally, I wanted to avoid a discussion on dragon hunting in the library. Just like you didn't want to talk about marriage after your sister was poisoned. Secrets are nothing but a door to hidden pain. Why don't we leave that door closed this early in the morning?"

I nod, glancing at a narrow gap of moonlight coming from the window. "You're right. Perhaps that wasn't a good way to start."

"What's really on your mind?" he says, his voice softening.

"I've been thinking about your proposal. Is it still on the table?"

He sits up straighter, eyes searching mine. "Only if it's what you want," he says cautiously. "You've been through a lot in the last few hours. I hadn't planned on asking you like that. Not the kind of proposal a lady wants to remember."

"You planned to ask me?" My eyes dart to his.

"Yes. Just because our parents signed an engagement contract for us doesn't mean that it's set in stone. The future is yours, Meera. Not for anyone else to decide."

My lips part and my heart pounds against my ribs hard enough to feel a bruise. How could he make me feel this way? We hadn't seen each other in five years. He'd sent letters and his picture once, but I'd thrown most of it away. Studying with the saints was the life for me, not marrying on my father's order as a bargaining chip. I close my eyes, mentally pulling away. But his words stick in my mind like honey. *The future is yours to decide.*

Runa would want me to save the kingdom, but she'd also want me to marry for love. The one thing she'd wished for herself, I could make a reality. But it would take time and I'd have to face the dragon—and not die. That's where Casmir comes in.

"I would like to consider your proposal on one condition," I say.

"It's already on shaky ground," he teases. "Adding a condition will only make it worse. If this is to last, we need to at least try to trust each other."

"It's not a condition, exactly. But, if there was another way to save Ezo, outside of marrying me, would you help? I need to know if your commitment is real. That you're not interested in marrying me just for political gain."

"You mean, is there a way for you to save Ezo without me? I've no interest in forcing your hand. Of course, I'd help if there was a way."

I swallow, relief washing through me. "Good. At the market, the lieutenant said he'd come for a dagger to control the serpents. But there's only one that could do that. If you killed the dragons, you would know."

"There are many ways to kill a dragon, Meera."

I shake my head, leaning closer. "Not with a dagger. And he wasn't talking about killing them but controlling."

"The fable of the Bleeding Saint?" His brow raises even higher.

"Yes. What do you know about it?"

Casmir drags a hand over his face and neck. "I really need coffee for this." He casts me a bemused half smile and sighs. "It's a fairytale. The Saint created all the dragons from his tears and placed them on the earth to govern man and beast. But one dragon craved things against his nature—the flesh of men, the blood of his fellow beast, and the power of the Saint. He slayed whole villages and nearly destroyed Taiga with fire, luring the Saint to intervene, to stop the madness.

"But the Saint conquered the dragon and sealed him within the deep dark of Mortua beneath the sea. As the dragon fell, with one last flick of his tail, he stabbed the Saint through the heart. A servant boy witnessing the event ran forward and cut the spiked tip off the dragon's tail." Casmir shrugs. "That relic is the dagger of the Bleeding Saint. A fairytale."

I take his hand, willing him to listen. "But what if it's true?"

He leans forward, matching my posture. "The story says that if you pierce a dragon's heart with the dagger, then the beast will grant you any wish. But it isn't real. I would've used it if it was."

"The lieutenant was looking for it," I press. "It's here, in Ezo, isn't it?"

My eyes cut to his. I see the calculations spinning in his mind. "He was just looking for an Ezo-made dagger. You have the best silver and iron mines in the eight kingdoms."

"Please, Cass. He called it the saint's dagger."

He sighs. "*If* it's real, it'd be somewhere safe."

"And where would you hide it? You're a strategist."

His eyes take on a clever sheen. "In the cathedral, beside the home of the Ladies of the Light. They guard the kingdom's largest library and house an armory of relics. And they know more about magic and curses than anyone else."

"That's where the queen goes after the coronation to be tested by the saints," I say, my thoughts clicking together. "But I won't be there for the journey, not if I meet the dragon."

"Unless?" He cups my hand with both of his. Hope lights in his eye.

If there's any way to cure my sister, to survive the dragon coronation and take their magic, the saints would know. But I've only eight hours to find out. Eight impossible hours.

Unless everyone is distracted by something else.

"What are you planning?" Cass leans back, a knowing smile sparking in his eyes.

"My future," I say. "Do you still want to get married tonight?"

CHAPTER
SIX

A LICENSE HAS ONLY two uses in Ezo, obtaining a gun or marriage. I'm here for the latter. The cathedral's ancient brick walls, strangled with vines and moss, rise before me like a fortress a short distance ahead. Our horses slow, their heads tossing in excitement at the brisk midnight run through the woods.

Father will be livid when he finds out what I've done, and he *will* find out. The stable hands will notice the horses' hooves clogged with dirt and snow, the sweat stains from the saddles' girths—all clues we won't have time to hide to make this work. But I don't care.

In seven hours, I'll either be married or eaten by a dragon. Father can yell at me all he wants and I won't bat an eye. The next seven hours are *mine*.

Our horses lurch to a stop outside the cathedral walls. The wind bites through my thick wool robe and hat as I stare up at the enormous stone arches stretching into the dark sky. Silver grass ripples in the wind beneath it, surrounded by a rose garden, all thorns in the early spring, and tucked into the mountainside on the edge of the city. Only yesterday, I'd have given anything to belong here with the saints. How things have changed in the last few hours.

Cass reins in his horse as I dismount mine.

"You ride like a wraith." Cass flashes a smile as he ties his black horse to the nearest tree.

"I'll pay for it later," I say, my back already aching.

My palms sweat as I fumble with Mikan's reins before tying the chestnut mare. She paws the ground, nudging me with her head for a treat. I relent, pulling a sugar cube from my pocket and letting her warm lips nibble it from my palm.

"So, what's the plan?" Cass says.

Right, the plan. Getting a marriage license, piece of cake. Breaking into the saints' vault for a fabled dagger . . . about as risky as my sister's pudding.

"We go in and ask for the license and a saint to return to the castle with us for the marriage ceremony. Then, while they're distracted, I'll go to the relics vault and look for the dagger. You have the schematics?"

"No." Cass makes a low whistle. "But he does."

A shadow emerges from the forest and lingers on the edge of the clearing. A gray hood obscures his face, but wide shoulders and otherwise lean build suggest a soldier, albeit a short one. He's dressed in common wool and cotton; even the soles of his shoes are cloth, soundless.

"Meet Jey." Cass nods toward the shadow.

The man pulls off his hood, revealing cropped black hair, and bows.

I stiffen as recognition hits. My eyes shift to Cass and then back to the shadow again. "Bastian's guard. What's the meaning of this? Are you spying on my brother?"

Cass shrugs. "Never forget that I'm first the Duke of Taiga; keeping close tabs on the neighboring kingdoms is my job. But I'm showing you my hand as an offering of trust. If you want a real shot at trying to find the dagger, you'll need a shadow's help. Jey is the best there is. Of course, I'll have to pull him from shadowing Bastian, now that you know."

"Do you have a spy on me too?" My voice goes tight.

"No."

I narrow my eyes, studying him. *Can I trust anything he says?* He's helping me look for the dagger, my last hope against the dragon. But he's also trying to gain my trust so I'll go through with the wedding. Runa was better at politics . . . and boys.

"So this is the informant you told me about," I say, schooling my features. "Jey, what do you know about the poison used against my sister? Casmir showed me your notes."

"It was handmade and steeped in magic," he says. "None of the nobles could have made it without the help of an apothecary or a saint."

"A saint?" I ask in surprise.

"They are well versed in magic and medicinal properties. The poison used on your sister was a rare medicinal remedy for sleep and when used in excess, it's lethal. But whoever concocted it also applied magic to lengthen its effects and render it contagious. I found traces of it in the kitchen and also at the market, in the bakery your sister visited."

I breathe hard. Cass really had done his research. Someone had gone to great lengths to plant that poison for Runa. But why? To ruin the coronation and take over Ezo once the dragons turn on us and cease to protect our borders? That could be any of the delegates, including Cass. But he already has a small claim to Ezo with our betrothal. Why poison my sister? Why make it a contagion? There are easier ways to secure a kingdom. It's not adding up.

I pace the outside wall of the cathedral. It has to be someone with an intimate knowledge of Runa's taste. No one knew we were going to the market that morning, much less the bakery. Except Bastian and Cass. My eyes slide to Jey questioningly.

"Who do you think did it?" I ask point blank. Before we get the dagger, I need to trust this man, and right now that would be a very big leap.

Jey points to the wall behind me.

"The saints?" I ask, incredulous.

He nods. "I can show you why my suspicions lie there."

"What do you say, Princess?" Cass shivers in his wool coat as he holds out an arm for me. "We don't have much time."

I steel the nerves in my gut and take Casmir's arm. "Let's get that marriage license, shall we?"

Jey slips into the shadows once again, blending into the cathedral's wall as Casmir and I take the wide stone staircase to the entrance. Saints greet us in periwinkle-blue habits and practiced silence, palm-sized prayer censers hanging from their waists. They wave us through the door as though they'd expected a midnight visit.

Inside, torches flame in metal sconces, casting a warm glow on the towering stained glass in the central chamber. Wooden benches lined in soft crimson form two aisles leading to a long altar at the front. Behind that, a copper statue of the Bleeding Saint stands tall with a hole in his side and arms extended to the audience. More statues line the rooms to the side of the center aisle for the other lesser saints, all honored for risking their lives for the good of man and beast.

The abbess, the saint Mother Ema, greets us with a short nod, gray eyes scanning my face in the flickering torchlight. Her gaze hesitates a moment too long, and I tuck a wayward strand of blue hair into my shawl. "Welcome, Princess Meera and Duke Casmir. How may the Light guide you today?"

She doesn't mention the time of night or the fact that we are here, alone.

"We'd like to get married," Casmir says. "The princess would like a saint to wed us in keeping with her faith."

Mother Ema's knowing eyes meet mine before dropping to

my neckline where the pendant rests hidden beneath my robes. "We recognize Princess Meera as an adherent of the faith, like her mother," she says with emphasis on the latter. "I'll send for one of the saints to ready themselves for the journey. You may rest in the sanctuary until then."

"Thank you." I breathe a sigh of relief as she turns, her robes wafting the scent of rosemary and benediction oils. Once her footsteps recede, I scour the room for Jey. He appears in one of the alcoves, leaning against a statue of a saint as though bored. He pockets a few zeni from the offering box as he sweeps toward us.

I scowl at Jey before looking to Casmir. His warmth bleeds into me this close, and my stomach flips with a different set of nerves. "Stay here," I whisper, aware of the nuns watching us from the side of the sanctuary. "Tell them I went to visit my mother's ashes if they ask questions. To seek her blessing. I've come here often enough, it shouldn't raise suspicion."

"Be quick," he whispers.

I slip away from his arm, but our fingertips catch at the last second.

"And Meera . . . good luck."

I cast him a faint smile and then turn to follow Jey. How he keeps himself concealed from most eyes, I'll never know. Bastian had trained under a shadow as part of his tutelage as the prince. He credited their camouflage to the secrets of Moebi warriors, the study of dragons, and relentless hard work. We trail a few narrow corridors, slinking past nuns in silent prayer or painting books or tending plants, and go down another passage, and then up, up, up.

"I hate spiral staircases." I groan at the next turn.

Jey motions to a landing at the top and then flies up the steps without a sound. I eye the metal stairs, framed on all sides by stained glass cut into the shapes of dragons, saints, and roses. But what I notice most are the thorns, sharp and pointed like the dagger of the Bleeding Saint. In the daylight, the stained-glass column would probably be like walking through a rainbow, but at night it's an eerie flash of indigo moonlight.

"Where's the map of this place?" I pant, clutching my side.

Jey leans over the top railing, holding a recently found torch, and taps the side of his head. Of course, he has the layout memorized. I hurry up the last several turns, a fierce ache throbbing down my lower back by the time I reach the top.

My eyes go wide. "We're in the tower."

Jey leans against a brick pillar near the staircase. "It's all right here."

"Right where?" I scan the circular room full of solid bricks and bookshelves thick with dust and ancient tomes.

"Your necklace," Jey says, holding out his hand.

"Excuse me?"

"Trust me." He motions for me to hand it over.

"I just saw you steal from the offering box." But when he only raises his hand higher, I tug the gold chain over my head and pass it to him. "It belonged to my mother. You have five seconds to return it."

He tilts his head, staring at the round pendant smaller than a Taigan copper. "That should work," he says and presses the pendant against the worn spine of a book. "You know, it's extremely hard to get one of these. They're not given, but earned."

"You don't think I earned it?"

His muffled laugh sounds against the stones. "No, I don't. You have to be truly worthy to earn one of these."

My stomach drops at the ease of those words. The certainty. Still, I raise my chin. "Three seconds."

He tries the necklace against a few more books.

I peer over his shoulder as he dusts the tomes on the lowest shelf. "What are you looking for? A secret door?" I hold out my hand. "Five seconds."

When he doesn't return the pendant, I snatch it from his untrustworthy fingers. He scowls as I take a turn about the room. "These are forbidden books," I whisper. "Look, this one is on alpine poisons from Moeb."

Jey takes the tome, grimacing at the patina of dust. "It's sealed like the rest."

I hold out the pendant to the next book. The round shape almost matches the lock embossed on the spine like a key. My eyes widen. "The dagger's hidden in the tomes."

"And if we're lucky, more than a dagger," Jey says, a greedy glint to his eyes. "Look for a book that doesn't belong."

We rifle through the tomes until I've seen one book louse too many and a sizable cloud of dust grates our lungs. On the last shelf, I notice a thin illustrated book of children's fairytales. The cover shows a white dragon and a lamb in a field of narcissus with gilded edges.

"Found it." I give a triumphant smile as the pendant glides smoothly into the lock.

I stare as the book opens, revealing a velvet box where pages should be. A map nestles inside, which Jey promptly steals and then begins feeling the wall beside the bookshelf. There's a loud crack and the wall slides open. I cringe, hoping the sound doesn't give us away.

Stacks upon stacks of ancient relics, gold, and unusual objects line the narrow hallway that runs a full circle around the tower—a room within a room. "I thought this place would be more guarded," I say.

"The saints don't believe in violence," Jey whispers, ducking inside the hall with the torch and snatching a golden object the size of a crow's egg off the nearest shelf. He weighs it in his hand before tossing it to me. "The *Faberche*, a birthday gift for the little tsarina of Rusa crafted by a metallurgist. Wonder what it's doing here?"

The tiny golden egg weighs a fortune. Hastily, I replace it on the shelf. Then I scan for any glimpse of the dagger. The shelves lining the wall are caked with treasures, all rammed together like a golden rat's nest: jewels, glass vials of mysterious liquid, swords and silks.

"How did you know where to find this?" My fingers scan a suit of armor trimmed in lacquered leather similar to my brace. "The saints are supposed to keep it a secret, safeguarding treasures the kingdoms would otherwise fight over in order to keep the peace."

"The pendant." He nods toward the necklace still in my palm. "I've seen it in too many accounts of the treasure for it to be a coincidence. The building schematics told me the rest."

My eyes narrow. Surely he hadn't been researching the treasure on Casmir's orders. This kind of knowledge took months to acquire, if not years. Either Jey is a well-informed single agent, or Casmir's been looking for the dagger too. His sleepy face comes to mind talking of the Bleeding Saint, the way he ruffled his hair and shook his head at the story. Cass is not one to believe in fairytales.

"But if the pendant is the key, that means anyone working here could have access to this chamber." I study the colorful vials of potions and dried herbs against the wall. Could the poison have originated here?

"Not just any pendant," Jey whispers, coming alongside me. He twirls one of the colorful vials before tucking it into his pocket. "The only pendant capable of opening this room is one of Mother Ema, the abbess." His eyes flash to mine. "That means you, Princess, are the most likely culprit in your sister's murder."

"There's more than one pendant with her image," I say, anger heating my cheeks. "Have you told Casmir your theory?"

He laughs. "Casmir's heartless. He wouldn't care if you poisoned the entire royal court."

"You're lying." I bump into the shelf behind me, wishing his words didn't give me pause.

"Trust me or not, it doesn't matter." Jey sinks into a plush chair with a satisfied sigh and places a gold crown on his head. "I don't want you to marry the duke. Let's just say it's not politically advantageous. If you marry, he settles down and there's less strife between Ezo and Taiga, and less in my coffers. I make money by bleeding kingdoms, not fattening them. But that also means I'm inclined to give you the dagger. If you'll gift me one tiny little token."

I cross my arms, favoring my bent side. "And what's that?"

"A title—before you stab the beast, of course." He smirks. "There's no telling if you'll actually survive using the dagger."

Blood drains from my face and pools somewhere in my stomach, making me nauseous. *Am I willing to stab a sacred dragon? For Runa.* My hands tremble.

Jey laughs quietly. "It *is* a dagger. What did you think you'd do with it? Tickle the beast?" He straightens, a look of mock sympathy on his face. "Don't be so appalled. You won't kill it. With that dagger, the dragon will grant you any wish. Even bring your sister back. One wish. So make it count."

"Then why haven't you used it?"

"Because I don't want to die, Princess," he says with a smile. "But you seem desperate enough to risk it. All I ask is that you make me the lord to some forgotten province, and the dagger is yours."

"But I'm not in a position to give you a title," I say, indignation pounding in my veins. "Enough games. Casmir asked you here to help me. Now where's the dagger?"

"Casmir doesn't think the dagger exists," Jey says, tossing the crown to his feet with a clatter. "And when you're queen, you can grant more than a title. In fact, I'd prefer if you wrote it down before facing the dragon. Just to be safe. Time is ticking, Princess."

Saints, the man would double-cross his own mother. First Bastian, then Casmir, and now me. Does he really know Casmir that well, or is he toying with me to get what he wants? I weigh my words carefully. While promises can be broken, there's always a cost. And something tells me that this man won't stop until the oath is fulfilled . . . like the dragons.

"Deal," I say. "The title of Mayor of Ranzan, a city in the central plains."

"Sign it." He scrawls across a roll of parchment and holds it out to me, the deal inked onto the page.

"The dagger first."

He slaps his hands together and bounds from the chair, grabbing an ancient leather box from one of the stacks. Inside is a familiar case of King's Crag.

"A board game? Is this a joke?"

He stands, dangling a silk bag for the game's wooden pieces. Only when he opens it, a bone-white knife falls into his palm.

"Use it wisely," he says, extending the blade's handle. "I would've used it myself, but I value my skin. The coronation is a rare opportunity to get so close to the dragons and live. All you need to do is stab the serpent with that dagger and the wish is yours."

My fingers curl around knife, and I shudder. The dagger's blade is a raw, razor-sharp bone with a serrated edge, exactly like a dragon's tail. The handle presses cool and smooth against my palm, crafted from steel and inlaid with silver serpents. "Is it . . . real?"

The question hardly seems necessary, but I ask it anyway. Even as I hold the knife, dread sinks into my bones, a sickening feeling that my world is shifting again.

"Yes," Jey says, seizing my hand and pressing the blade against my finger. It nicks the skin, and blood beads to the surface. I gasp and wrench back my hand, the blade still clenched in my palm. He wipes the dagger clean with a damp handkerchief as I stare at my bleeding finger.

"What was that for?"

"Sign." He holds out the parchment again.

My stomach tightens, but I lift my chin. *For Runa.* Reluctantly, I drag my finger across the page.

A grin twists his lips as he pockets the deal. "One more thing," he says. "Tell no one about this. Keep it a secret, even from Casmir. If anyone finds out, your brother might accidentally try to see Runa and join the slumbering in the dining hall. Do we have an understanding?"

The threat isn't lost on me.

I scan the shadow, almost invisible as he clings to the dark patterns against the wall. I've an inkling to fight him, to stop his blackmailing heart right now. But it's a battle I'd surely lose and even with the dagger in my hand, it feels wrong. I made a promise, and Jey's not harmed me or anyone else . . . yet. Then there's Cass—how in the Saint's good earth am I to keep from telling him?

Jey raises a brow, waiting for my decision.

I nod. Placing the dagger back into its scabbard, I tuck it into my brace. My ribs ache in protest as we head back downstairs to the sanctuary.

I hear Casmir's laugh before I see him, a warm rumble of nerves and cheer. Three nuns wait with him, one covering her mouth as she laughs at some story he'd been telling. His eyes find mine as I stumble into the hall, and everyone turns.

"Sorry, I-I got a little lost," I say, attempting a weak smile. I glance around for Jey, but he's already vanished into the mottled shadows.

"She's terrible with directions," Cass whispers to one of the nuns. Then louder to me, "Come, dear. We have the license and a sister to come with us. You need rest before tomorrow."

"It already *is* tomorrow," the youngest nun adds, merry laughter tugging at her eyes.

"A royal wedding," another says, rushing forward to take my

hand. "Come, come. We'll take you back in the carriage and lead your horses. It will be a beautiful day!"

Beautiful.

With a white dress, a hideous dragon, and Cass' forest-green eyes looking at me like they do now—almost a caress, concern pinched at the corners—what could go wrong?

Instinctively, my hand travels to my side where the dagger hides, smoothing the brace beneath my wool traveling coat. We sit side by side in the carriage as the nun drives us back to the castle.

"Did you find it?" Cass asks, shrugging out of his cloak and placing it over me.

I lean into his shoulder, taking in the warm scent of cypress and fresh soap. He shivers, probably from the cold so foreign to a Taigan spring, and my heart melts a little.

"No. You were right, it's just a fable." My voice is low and disappointed, because I almost wish it were true, that I hadn't found the dagger. That I didn't have to do the unthinkable to save my sister and second-guess everyone—especially Cass.

His hand brushes my brow, tucking a stray piece of hair behind my ear. "I'm sorry."

"Me too," I say, nestling my head against his shoulder and wishing the morning would never come. Wishing my sister wasn't all alone, asleep at a banquet with rotting food. Wishing couriers weren't, at this very moment, heading toward the castle and knocking on every door announcing a wedding in four hours without my father's consent. That the dragons weren't waiting for a perfect queen to reseal their oath and grant our kingdom magic once more.

Wishing that I didn't have to choose.

CHAPTER
SEVEN

THE CASTLE IS a hornet's nest of delegates, couriers, and queensguard by the time we arrive. This time, I'm locked in my room with seven guards on the outside. Seira's twin brother is noticeably missing. His sister waits in my room, pale-faced and bent over a long white gown with delicate embroidery—my wedding dress.

Thankfully, Casmir insisted no one speak with me, including my father—*not sure how that went over*—so I could rest. Saints bless him. His cloak still wraps warmly around my shoulders, carrying with it the smell of cypress and soap—of him.

Developing feelings for someone tonight was supposed to be Runa's miracle, not mine. I don't have that luxury anymore, not when it's clouded with saving a kingdom and my sister.

I shrug the cloak off and make for the bed. Sleep tugs at my eyes even as my mind runs laps. It must be near three in the morning. Only four hours left. I collapse on the feather mattress.

"My lady," Seira squeaks from the corner of the room. "Is it true that you ran away with the Duke of Taiga to get married?"

I groan, shifting to get more comfortable. It's a struggle to speak. "We didn't get married . . . just the license. Haven't . . . signed . . . yet."

"Oh," Seira says. I can't tell if it's disappointment or relief that rushes through her voice, but I'm too tired to care. "Would you like a song to help you sleep? You've been through a lot today."

I nod into my pillow.

A voice like the spring breeze spills soft into the room as Seira sings.

I sleep, and in my dream, I'm with Runa. She's a glowing light in an otherwise dark world filled with twisted roots and sharp thorns growing up the castle wall from the inside. It takes me a moment to realize that we're in the banquet hall. But it's an overgrown forest, the walls crumbling and scorched as if it'd been burned to the ground and abandoned for years.

Runa squeezes my hand, imparting courage to my trembling heart. But I'm not quaking in fear, it's her realness that shakes me to the core. She looks exactly as she did on the day of the ball —after the poison—her crimson dress splotched with spilled wine, her hair an unruly mess, and her face tinged green. Tawny-brown eyes watch me, sparkling with affection.

"You came for me," she says, her voice tight as if someone were choking it.

"I could never give up on you." I squeeze her hand, amazed by how real it feels. "I won't stop until I wake you. I'll find who did this. I promise."

"Wake me?" Runa turns, eyes widening with fear. "My dream . . . you're in my dream."

She whips her head side to side, a frenzied look in her eyes as if a monster were chasing her. But all around are only towering thorns and the distant crash of waves. "Hide, Meera. Get out of here, now! Don't come back."

Runa shoves me, and I fall into a pile of rotting food on the banquet table. Wet pudding squelches between my fingers and a ham filled with maggots wiggles beneath me.

Runa's hands fly to her throat. It's like watching her poisoned all over again.

"Runa!" My eyes fly open, heart pounding so hard my chest aches. "Runa!"

"Shh, you had a nightmare." Seira's calloused hands prop up a pillow behind me. She sweeps my long hair to the side and helps me to a sitting position. Sweat drips down my neck from the terrifying dream. "Would you like some tea?"

Sunlight peeks through my curtains and the birds sing outside.

"What time is it?"

She sucks at her lower lip before forcing a fake smile. "Time for tea."

I stare at her and then yank the curtains wide open. The sun sits bright and yellow on the horizon, the shadows of the trees screaming the time: seven o' clock. Only one hour before the wedding ceremony and coronation.

One hour before the dragons will be closest to the shore.

My ribs throb from where I'd slept in my brace and where the dagger had dug into my side. I check that the blade is still there and not another dream.

"I need to see my sister," I say.

"That's not possible." Seira eyes me pityingly. "The king has barred the doors. Her name is not even to be spoken. He forbids it. They say it's grief or denial. He sent a letter this morning, calling your decision to marry the duke reckless."

And sending his last daughter to face the dragons isn't?

Anger flashes through me. And something else. I can't place the firm resolve that washes over me. The readiness to do what I must to save this kingdom and bring Runa back. "Do you have anything stronger than tea?"

Seira lifts a brow. "As a matter of fact, a certain duke may have sent for coffee."

I smile, but it fades the minute I glance at the long white dress draped across Runa's empty bed. Seira turns to leave, but I snatch her hand, turning it palm upward.

"You're bleeding," I say, staring at the reddened cracks and pinpricks on her palm. "How many hours were you bent over that dress with a needle? Did you sleep at all last night?"

Seira jerks her hand back, cradling it against her chest. Her jaw tightens, even as her eyes are soft. "We're all doing what we can to help," she says. "Some marry dukes and others sew dresses."

I sigh, the dagger digging into my ribs from under the brace. Seira has no idea what I'm about to do, to risk—but she stands by me regardless. I don't miss the puffiness rimming her eyes. It's possible that my father punished her brother for helping me last night, but it's not my place to ask.

"Use the silk bandages," I order, taking her hand. "And Seira, ask Casmir for two cups of coffee. You're right, we're both doing what we can to save Ezo."

CHAPTER
EIGHT

THE DAGGER FITS within my wedding dress perfectly, tucked beneath my brace. I wear the brace my way, not hidden on the inside like my father insisted. My hands slide down the smooth leather surface, admiring how strong it makes me feel. A reminder that confidence is a choice, one I must wear boldly if I'm to survive.

Pure white with a luminous sheen covers my waist and climbs up my ribs like a corset before wrapping around my back in an elegant form-fitting design. White silk drapes across my shoulders and down my arms in long, crimson-lined sleeves that trail the ground and reflect the sunlight. The dress itself hugs my curves and sweeps to the floor in a beautiful train of shimmering cherry blossoms to match the brace.

My eyes flick to the mirror Seira holds.

"You're beautiful." Her words are a hushed awe.

A cold breeze snakes around my bare neck, carrying with it a strange and distant song, the dragons' cries. I stiffen, shoulders hunching as I meet my reflection full on. I am . . . beautiful. And I'm going to break Casmir's heart, Bastian's, and maybe even my own. But I have to do this, for Runa.

If there's a chance the dragon's magic can save her—can save us all—it's worth the risk, isn't it?

Escorted by a troupe of personal maids and queensguard, I'm led to the rocky beach where the coronation is to take place. A wooden gazebo painted in red with brilliant copper tiles waits on a short cliff near the water. Ascending the hill in tiny silk slippers is torture.

Casmir waits with morning hair sticking up in spite of his best efforts, a sharp wool suit of midnight and shocking white underneath. But it's his face that I can't stop looking at. He's fully awake, and like me, there's an alertness to him, a stiffness that has nothing to do with the cool morning breeze and dozens of eyes watching us.

Does he know what I've planned?

I stand opposite him and he takes my hand. My breath hitches at the warmth of his touch. These hands that could make my breath snag, that could make me forget the horrors of the last twenty-four hours, if only for a moment. Forest-green eyes meet mine, searching for answers.

"On this fortunate day . . ." The saint begins, a nun blessed by Mother Ema to lead the ceremony. I'm grateful it's not the mother herself or I might not have the nerve to go through with it. The nun's gaze slides over us like a mirror, and I'm afraid of what I'll see. "We gather to join this man and woman in holy matrimony with the saints and ashfallen and all of Ezo as witness."

Casmir holds both my hands now, his eyes on me as if the saint were of no importance—as if the world were of no importance. "Meera," he whispers.

I look to him and then to the crowd. A dragon shriek pierces the air from the waves below.

"Do you, Casmir, Duke of Taiga, offer a lifelong vow to Princess Meera, to live in peace and prosperity with your descendants, to respect and protect her as your wife?"

His eyes lock with mine, a plea in the warm green gaze. "Yes, I do."

Heat races between my ribs. I can't do this. I want to say yes to the possibility of a future with him, to lean into him, to feel the press of his lips against mine, but I . . .

"Do you, Meera, princess of Ezo and the Northern Sea, take this man to be your husband, to share your joys and sorrows with him as long as you live?"

I lean into him, my forehead brushing his jaw. "Thank you for helping me," I whisper. I've already calculated this moment, that pulling back would enable him to hold onto me—to stop me. So I do the one thing I can to distract him. I kiss him goodbye.

My lips slide over his, hesitant at first, but I melt at the warmth I find. My hand trails to his face, pulling him closer as he kisses me back, hungry yet gentle. He's holding back, aware of the crowd watching us, but his hand travels to my waist. A question hums between us as I pull away, my head buzzing as if I'd drunk too much wine. The dagger seems to burn against my ribs. Saints, I wish there was another way. But Cass can't save my sister.

Before he can react, I slip from his hands and dart past him.

"Meera, don't!" Casmir's voice breaks like a wave upon the rocks.

I don't dare look back. Before anyone can stop me, I run and jump off the short cliff to where the dragons wait in the sea below. A million choices whirl past as I fall, possibilities I'd thrown to the wind. There's no turning back now.

The water's surface is harder than I'd expected. Icy waves slam against my body, filling my ears. A shiver forces my muscles to cramp as I fight for the surface. I gasp for air, blinking back the water as I tread.

Shouts call from up above, but I can't make out the words. Even if I could, I wouldn't care. My dress weighs mountains. The long flowing sleeves drag me down, and it takes all my energy to swim out to the nearest sea stack. I climb up the sharp black rocks, hands slipping against the barnacles and my silk slippers tearing. Grabbing the knife from my brace, I dash it against my palm and let the blood drip into the sea.

There's only one way to get the dragons close enough for this to work . . .

"I'm here to take my sister's place," I yell at the waves and sky and dragons.

I hear them before I see the silver, black, and pale green scales break the water's surface. Three dragons surround me, only their coiled bodies visible as they weave in and out of the sea like living threads.

Their cries reverberate from the water, booming, shrilling, and piercing my skull. I cover my ears, still clinging to the saint's dagger, and shift my stance to keep track of the sacred monsters moving in the deep, each one longer than our fastest ships.

The pattern becomes clear. They're threading a death trap, surrounding me on every side so that there is no escape, no coming out of this alive. Unless I use the dagger.

Bastian was right—there really is no hope for a cerulean princess. The dragons had counted me unworthy the moment I set foot in the sea.

Cold wind bites into my wedding gown and shifts direction, gusting blue hair into my eyes and salt-dampened lips.

"I offer myself as queen," I shout at the dragons.

A scaled beast rises from the water, terrifying in its size and power. Sharp white scales, each as thick as my arm, drip water as the dragon rises, high as a cedar in the Atani mountains. Its face bends down to mine, narrow and foxlike, an intelligent expression in its dark eyes glittering with gold. Curved horns jut from the impenetrable scales at the back of its head and rows of razor-sharp teeth glisten beneath black gums peeled back in anger . . . or hunger, I can't tell which.

I reel from the stench of its breath, rotting crabs and bones. I trip and fall, clawing my way backward against the rocks. My dress snags and holds me in place. The dragon looms over me, teeth bared.

Jey didn't mention how to stab the dragon. Just get close enough and stay alive. *Right, easy.*

A memory of Runa flashes in my mind, her rosy pink lips pinched in thought as she leaned against the railing at the market. "Do you think they're lonely?" she'd asked.

She'd cared about the dragons, not just for the sake of our kingdom gaining protection or out of religious reverence, but for the beasts' sake, as living things.

I stare into the dragon's black eyes flecked in gold, trying to see it in a similar way. But I can't. These serpents had once laid waste to the kingdoms, nearly burning Taiga to the ground. They'd protected our shores and given us magic, yes, but for a price. My grandaunt, my mother, Runa . . . and now me.

I fist the dagger in my hand, behind my back where the dragon cannot see. Then I hold out my bleeding palm, asking it to accept me as its queen, to place its snout against my exposed vein and breathe its heart magic into me.

Magic that could save us all.

If I'm worthy.

At any moment it's going to bite my hand, rip it from my arm. My breaths come in and out too quickly, my vision going spotty, but I force myself to look the beast in the eye. Runa would want me to do this in her stead.

"I've come to . . ."

The white dragon narrows its impossibly dark eyes at me, black as obsidian but flecked with gold that whirls as if a galaxy dwelt beneath its stare. As if the world were at its command, its secrets held in its talons. The beast's chest glows, warming to a golden amber.

Fire. It's going to breathe fire.

The slap of oars on water. Voices shout from the boats: "Meera! Turn back! Jump!"

I recognize Bastian's voice among them and fight back tears. "I can't lose another sister," he'd said. The dragon's head snaps toward the sound, and I'm momentarily forgotten. Pushing off the rock, I lunge at the warm glow around its heart.

The dagger finds its mark, sinking into the thick skin between its scales. A horrid shriek rends the air, the dragon's body twisting back in agony. The dagger glistens from where it sticks into the serpent's hide.

My grip slips and I fall. But I don't plunge into the sea. Smooth scales wrap around my body, tighter and tighter until I can't breathe. My brace cracks under the weight, ribs curving inward. Talons scrape against the rocks as the dragon tries to right itself. I wince, imagining the sharp claws tearing into my body.

Images flood my mind: Bastian and Casmir watching in horror, my body being severed and then burned before the attending delegates.

I won't die like the last cerulean princess—like Grandaunt.

I scratch at the scales until my fingertips bleed. The dragon snorts, anger darkening its eyes. With a whip of its tail, the beast pins my arms, crushing them against the sides of my body. A bullet pings against the dragon's scales, ricocheting into the water.

My head jerks round to the boat where Casmir stands at the front, a pistol in hand. Bastian shoves his arm down, yelling something about the monster, but it's too late. The other two dragons I'd seen earlier cut the water's surface with their spines as they plow toward the boat.

"No! No, no . . ." I struggle to free myself. This is not supposed to happen.

The dagger.

Freeing one arm, I reach upward and grab the dagger still

wedged into the dragon's hide. With a sawing motion, I pull it out, loosening a scale. Watery blood pours from the wound and over my arms, followed by an unearthly shriek.

"Your oath, dragon!" I yell over the waves, holding up the dagger. "Grant me a wish. Your magic to save my kingdom and my sister."

The dragon's head swerves, mouth gaping open. Is that blood on its tongue? It was only one scale. How could there be so much blood?

The coils around me tighten and tip. The dagger breaks from my hold as the pressure numbs my arms.

Then I fall.

Squeezed.

Pulled.

Cold.

Water scalds my lungs as the dragon takes me into the sea.

CHAPTER
NINE

OATHBREAKER. Heartless. Mortal fool.

The words flood my mind, bubbling up from somewhere inside of me, but they're not mine. The dragon hurtles beneath the waves, a winding ribbon of blood in its wake. Breath burns within my lungs and my head throbs from the pressure. I beat my fists against the muscular coils that hold me tight, but it's no use.

Down we spin, deeper and deeper.

Fear threatens to swallow me before the ocean does. Pain doubles with each second. A violent urge pounds at the back of my throat, scratching, pleading for me to just open my mouth and let the agony out.

Shuddering, I resist the impulse to breathe in water. I crane my head, desperate for a glimpse of air. A sparkle of sunlight and palest blue winks at me as if saying goodbye.

Two dragons weave across the water's surface like twins of thunder and lightning. I catch the glint of their bellies, coated in pale scales to mimic the surface above. Three row boats spin frantically, caught in a whirlpool of the dragons' making. My heart lurches.

Bastian, turn back! Casmir . . . What have I done?

I shove against the dragon, careless when its scales scratch my arms. I must warn them. How many souls fight for their lives because I threw away my future for a fairytale? Freeing myself to my waist, I slam my elbows against the beast. Once. Twice.

The dragon unfurls its body, releasing me. I swim toward the surface and calculate the distance. Impossible. I'm going to die, just like the last cerulean princess, like Grandaunt.

The dragon pauses, its dark eyes watching with mild interest as I struggle with the heavy wedding dress pulling me down. I blink against the burn of saltwater, refusing to accept my fate. But the weight of it presses against me like the mountain-high distance to the surface.

I'm sorry, Runa.

A snarl crackles through the sea like a flame. It fills my ears with a threatening roar and fills my mind with . . . words.

What have you done to me, human?

The dragon bares its sharp teeth as if cornering me while the other two beasts circle down to join it. Years ago, a pack of wolves in the Atani mountains cornered Mother this way. Our carriage had broken down, and they'd followed us to a hot spring, trailing the blood left when I'd skinned my knee climbing out of the broken carriage.

Runa covered my eyes, her body trembling next to mine as she witnessed everything. Bastian chased them off in the end, but it was too late for Mother. I should've helped instead of sitting frozen, the howls and snarls swelling in my ears long after the wolves had vanished. I swore I'd never sit idle again—not when action was needed.

I guess I went too far this time.

The memory chokes off with a suffocating gag. I can't hold my breath any longer. My body gives a violent spasm. The dragon's going to watch me die and then probably drag me to the surface for a bonfire in front of my fiancé. Blackness creeps into my vision.

I forget you can't breathe.

The dragon blows a ring of bubbles at my face. They stick to me with a silky sheen like jellyfish puddled on the shore. Thousands of bubbles crawl up my neck and explode across my skin, drenching me in a strange warmth.

Breathe, the voice commands. *It's not poison.*

I gasp, sucking in the slippery liquid until the bubbles are gone. Relief fills my aching lungs. And along with it something like sleep. The blackness that had encroached on me earlier now covers me like a woolen blanket. I claw weakly at the air . . . no, the sea, trying to escape. Above, a boat bursts into flame and men jump into the ocean. Fire ripples across the water in a blaze of molten orange and sunlit amber.

In my daze, the fire seems beautiful. I stare, mesmerized by the brilliant colors, while a dull pressure builds on my chest. I want to scream, to beg for Bastian's life. To claw out the dragon's eyes and save the men fighting for life at the surface.

But my limbs fill with lead.

Talons press against my brace.

And sleep takes me.

The air tastes of seaweed and rotting crabs. Saints, let it be a dream. I'd marry Casmir and take the throne while my sister slept. I'd socialize with a dozen nobles to root out spies against our kingdom. I'd pray every day at the foot of the Bleeding Saint for my sister to wake and our kingdom to survive.

Just please, let it be a dream.

I crack one eye open and the effort is gargantuan. Are my eyelids sunburnt? Blinding light forces me to shield my eyes as I take in my surroundings. I'm lying on my back, rocks pressing against my spine and numbing my legs; a gentle slap and swoosh tells me that I'm on a beach. Birds caw in the sky above, circling me. They must think I'm dead.

But death wouldn't hurt this much.

Bastian. My eyes snap shut as images assail my mind. My brother's boat overturned, flames engulfing it as he tried to rescue me. Casmir . . . his lips on mine, the trust in his hands, the pain in his eyes when I chose magic instead of him. I squeeze my palms against my temples and order the thoughts away. They'll both be okay. I just need to find a way home to set everything right.

Wait, the dragon.

I urge my muscles to sit upright, but pain erupts along my spine, and I'm forced to roll onto my stomach first. A dull pressure builds on my left side, my heart aching as if swollen and forced against my ribs. Even my throat burns like I'd swallowed a bit of smoldering coal. I push up and the movement causes my stomach to empty on the beach.

After a few ragged breaths, I stand and find the source of my pain—at least some of it. My brace's wood lining is cracked and split into slivers. One of them wedges into my side where dried blood cakes against my once white wedding dress.

How long have I been here? Did the dragon drag me to shore and leave? Is he coming back to finish me off?

Maybe I wasn't worth the trouble.

I unfasten the brace, gauging the wooden fragment piercing my side. It's about the length of my palm, narrow as a chopstick, and wouldn't be too hard to remove.

Bastian always said the anticipation of pain is worse than the pain itself. I hope he's right.

Taking three quick breaths, I tear off a sleeve of my wedding dress to use as a bandage and then jerk the splinter free. I double over.

Bastian lied about the pain.

I tie the torn sleeve around my side as a bandage. Blood

soaks into the white silk, fanning crimson feathers into the fabric's elaborate threads. Gritting my teeth, I throw the remainder of the shattered brace onto the beach and make for higher ground.

If I'm to survive, I need to find a town and get word to Bastian quickly. He must send for help and hold off the dignitaries. The foreign leaders currently housed in Ezo must not spread word of today's events to the outside kingdoms. Fears and rumors will grow like weeds with every passing minute I'm gone. The only thing holding Ezo together now is my father and keeping the dignitaries unwittingly hostage so they can't rally forces against us without the dragon's protection. I only hope Bastian can stall them until I return.

A grove of trees lines the shore, flanked by a short sandy spread and tall black rocks on either side. The coast is similar to Ezo, but I've never set foot on this particular beach. I can't be too far away from home, across the Southern Strait perhaps or on another part of Ezo facing east by the position of the sun.

Faint footprints dart across the sand to one of the larger rock formations. It opens toward the beach, a trickle of water from the mouth of a cave forming a miniature tributary to the sea. I follow the footsteps with caution. Pirates did dwell in the northern seas; Bastian had seen plenty in his travels. Had they chased the dragon off? But then, why leave me to die?

The footprints are set close together, unbalanced, with an occasional drag against the damp sand as if the person sustained an injury. At the mouth of the cave, I hide behind the rock wall and listen.

"I hoped you would die out there," a voice growls.

I jump at the sound but not soon enough. A hand closes around my wrist and jerks me into the cave. I gasp at the pain in my side as I'm shoved against a damp rock wall, a hand squeezing at my throat. My eyes trail the pale muscled arm, the broad shoulders and bare chest heaving with anger, unkempt black hair, youthful face, and midnight eyes flecked in gold like stars.

"What have you done to me?" he asks, but it's more of a snarl.

That voice. I still, my hands frozen on his wrist ready to claw him to shreds. My eyes drop to a wound below his collarbone where the skin is charred black with patches of silver beneath. Exactly where the dagger would have sunk into the dragon's flesh above its heart.

"You're . . . no." I swallow, unsure if it's his hand that chokes my words or the sinking fear of what stands before me. The same gold-flecked eyes I'd seen below the waves now stare at me from a handsome face. The warm hand at my throat is undeniably human, but those eyes aren't. "It can't be. It's not . . . possible."

"It shouldn't be," he says, his cold gaze scrutinizing. "What did you do to me?"

I pull at his hand, and it loosens at my throat.

"You tried to drown me." That's as close as I dare to the words *you're a dragon* without sounding like a lunatic. I shove against his chest in an attempt to free myself, but he's immovable and altogether too . . . *perfect.* The muscular slope of his shoulders, the soft angles of his face, as if the Bleeding Saint had sculpted him from something other than dirt like the rest of us.

A muscle twitches in his jaw, and he drops his hand before turning and pacing like a wild animal within the cavern. My hand flies to my freed throat, thankful for the breath in my lungs. I slip against the cave wall, pulse slamming beneath my blistered, sandy fingers.

"To set the record straight, you're the one who stabbed me," he snaps, pointing to the scar on his chest. "And I saved your life. Not that I expect a 'thank you' from a mortal slug."

"I think I preferred dragons when they didn't speak," I say, breathless, my pulse thrumming in my ears. "And you can't call it saving a life when you tried to roast me in the first place."

I cross my arms against the damp cold, slouching my hips to compensate for the loss of my brace. It's unfathomable that the young man pacing before me is an immortal monster of chaos and magic. Dragons only shapeshift in the old legends. Not today. Not for real.

But this *is* real.

He looks away, taking a deep breath that could drain an ocean. Then he turns to me with hardened eyes. "What was on the dagger? What poison?"

"Poison? It was the dagger of the Bleeding Saint. You were supposed to grant me a wish, to give me magic to save my kingdom as the dragons have done for centuries past and—"

"It's not *your* kingdom," he interrupts. "It was your sister's coronation today. You are not worthy of magic."

I gape, heat prickling my skin. "Then why didn't you kill me? I know I'm not perfect like Runa. I've never been. I was born this way." I gesture to my long blue hair now clumped in wet knots down my back and to the awkward curvature of my spine so prominent without the brace. "I came for your magic. My sister is dying and only your magic can save her!"

I sink onto the cold sand and lean against the nearest rock for support. "The kingdom of Ezo will be picked apart by wolves without your magic. I thought if I used the dagger, you'd have no choice but to help us . . . I was wrong. It's nothing but a fable."

A wave of frustration slams against my aching heart. Anger and shame writhe in my chest, whispering that I share responsibility for the pain. I grit my teeth. "Why didn't you finish me in the sea? *Why bring me here?*"

Dragon, for lack of a better name, watches me closely, his eyes softening like the warm glow of an evening fire. "I'm sorry to hear about your sister."

"Your apologies won't save her, but your magic could."

"It's not so easy." He slumps onto the nearest rock facing the ocean and stares at his hands with disgust. "Not like this. And you're still not worthy."

"I don't need a reminder," I say, crossing my arms over my knees and sorely wishing for a shawl to cover my wet wedding dress.

Failure settles over me like a familiar coat. I'd made mistake after mistake that could cost the entire kingdom. I'd trusted the wrong person. I broke the law by entering the saints' vault and would never be allowed to enter a cathedral again. I'd broken most irreparably the heart of the one man who had a glimmer of hope to save Ezo. My father would never forgive me, and Runa . . . my eyes squeeze shut.

Am I such a worthless fool?

I cut a glance to the dragon sitting on his rock and shrug off the twinge of guilt for wounding him—he'd mostly deserved it.

What is failure if not an opportunity to succeed? The old proverb hums in my mind and sparks a thought. Why hadn't the dragon killed me? He still hadn't answered my question.

I study the creature perched on a rock, his spine perfectly curved, the sharp angular features of his face young and flawless. Jet black hair dips to his brows, his skin smooth as snow kissed with the sun's golden light. My eyes drop to his chiseled waist and a pair of pink wide-leg pants. I cough, clearing my throat. "Why are you in women's trousers?"

He glowers and heaves a sigh that would surely have been flames were he still a beast. "I've never shifted before. It's . . . not something dragons do, not since the Ashfall"—he swallows —"I've never worn clothes."

My eyebrows skyrocket. "Oh, I . . . where did you get them?"

He shifts sideways, lips pinched into a tight line. "From a clothesline on the other side of the woods. I liked the color."

An uncomfortable silence falls between us, broken only by the swoosh of tide and scattering of seashells dragged with it.

"My sister likes it too," I say. "Pink. And orange. Red. Anything that looks like a sunset."

He nods faintly. "She has good taste."

I scoot closer, testing my resolve. "We can fix this," I say, looking up at the dragon. "If we work together. I need your magic to save my home, and I'm guessing you need me to get back to yours or you wouldn't have spared me. Dragon, are you listening?"

He stands and moves to the mouth of the cave, staring out at the sea. "It's not so simple," he says. "I need to know, what poison did you use?"

"I don't understand. It was only a dagger."

"You're right that the dagger of the Bleeding Saint is a fable," he says, looking over his shoulder, gaze searing into me. "The story is real enough, but the relic itself has no power. True power comes from the heart, from the substance of things unseen. That dagger was the real artifact, but it was dipped in poison. It's become corrupted—cursed." He steps forward and seizes my hand.

I step back but freeze when he moves my hand to his chest. His skin is warm to the touch, like the air simmering over a well-kept hearth. A steady heart beats beneath my palm.

Dokun . . . dokun . . .

I shake my head, brow pinched in confusion.

"How many hearts do dragons have?" He stares down at me, the gold flecks in his eyes like fire.

"Two, but . . ." I swallow, my throat suddenly a wasteland of dead dreams and scorched sand. "You only have one."

He drops my hand and reaches out to feel for my own heart. I jolt back and shove his hand away. Raising a brow, I place my hand on my chest and feel for that familiar beat.

An unsteady thrum meets my palm followed by a second

fluttering beat. My eyes dart to his and I jump back. The ache I'd felt in my chest on the beach, the heaviness in my ribs.

"Saints! What have you done to me?"

He smiles, a sad lilting smile that tugs on my two hearts.

"The curse," he says, eyes boring into me. "You've taken part of me with that dagger—my heart. My life force is tied to yours until I grant your wish. But to do so, I would need to return to my original form, which I cannot do without my dual hearts. I cannot give away my magic, the thing you wish for, or I will die. I am anathema to my own kind. There's only one such curse in the ancient tomes. I'll ask once more, where did you get the poison?"

I pale, dual hearts slamming against my chest. The thought of it dizzies me, but the pressure pounding beneath my ribs is unmistakable now. "I-I . . . didn't know. None of this was supposed to happen. No one was supposed to get hurt."

"Does a dagger not hurt?" He arches a brow.

I cover my face with my hands and groan at my own stupidity. Had Jey laced the dagger with poison? Or had it been stored like that in the saint's vault? My thoughts flash to Jey wiping the dagger clean after pricking my finger, the vial he had pocketed before that . . .

"Listen, I know little of poison and curses," I amend. "Whoever did this is probably the same one who poisoned my sister. I have to get back. I have to fix this. I don't know what was on the dagger, but we can ask the man who gave it to me."

"He won't talk," Dragon says. "Whoever gave you that dagger wanted you dead. I saved you, against my better judgment. Unlike humans, dragons think about others before they act."

"I am thinking about others! My sister, my brother, the kingdom, the duke—"

"The dragon slayer?" Dragon laughs. The sound is beautiful, unlike any laugh I've ever heard, it reminds me of being a child again, of summer wind chimes and the little crepe dolls Seira used to make. I could listen to that rich timbre like the lull of the sea. I shake my head, clearing the sound, and frown.

"No one's ever talked to a dragon. I didn't know you had . . . feelings."

"We are sentient beings. We have hearts, a soul. This all men know but have chosen to ignore, except the queens. They hear us and we them. Why should I help you return to your people when I can't return to mine?"

My mouth opens but I shut it.

"How do I help you return to your people?" I ask, realizing that dealing with this monster is no different from striking a political bargain back home.

"You don't," he says. "They are coming for you."

"What do you mean?"

He points back to the ocean. "I'm no longer immortal. As far as they're concerned, you've killed me."

"That's ridiculous. You're not dead."

"That's a matter of perspective."

I take a deep breath and move to the mouth of the cave where the sunlight drags its golden fingers across the sand. "We can still fix this. Are you saying that you brought me here to wait for some kind of tribunal?"

"Yes." Dragon eyes me sidewise, no pity in his gold-dust eyes. "You're to stand trial for murder."

CHAPTER

TEN

WAITING AROUND for a horde of dragons to find me—and likely sentence me to death—isn't my idea of a good plan. I don't need to tell the half-naked man with a flawless spine and dreadful taste in clothes this. Dragon seems equally appalled by his fate to live as a perfectly normal human without magic and claws.

He stares at the ocean, his mouth set in a firm line, as if waiting for something morbid that he can't escape. Why haul us both to this cave if he's so desperate to go to the tribunal? Couldn't he just whisk us away with whatever magic he'd used to bring us here?

I cannot give away my magic, or I will die. His words beat a drum in my mind. I fist my palms. He's not the only one who needs that magic.

Dual hearts war within my chest. Now that I'm aware of them, the pressure against my ribcage makes sense, and so does the warmth coursing beneath my skin. Under normal circumstances, I'd be a shivering mess.

I resist the urge to feel the heartbeats again, to verify once more that it's real—the twin hearts tethered to my chest. Questions about the curse and the dragon heart flood my mind,

but I don't have time to seek answers. Not when Ezo's very existence is at stake.

I need to get word to Bastian that I'm alive.

I need to know what has happened in the last eight hours.

Stepping past Dragon, I march outside the seaside cave and
welcome the warm kiss of wind that clears my head. Diamonds
of light skitter across the waves in the late afternoon sun. To the
west, a forested hill leads away from the beach and inland, where
the dragon had said a small town nestled in the mountains. I start
toward it, cutting a trail through the warming sand.

"Where are you going?" Dragon's voice snaps after me.

"To find civilization," I say, not looking back. I imagine
Dragon sulking on his rock, those black eyes narrowing on my
departure with warnings of doom. But within seconds, he's at my
side, his footsteps silent on the sand.

"You can't leave."

"Do you see what I'm doing?" I snap, entering the wide
swath of bamboo trees. "Leaving." I lift my right arm to cue to
my exit, but it's draped in spoiled silk that hangs to my knees.
The motion renders me off balance and I stagger.

It's a cruel reminder that I'm still in my wedding dress, the
one day in my life I actually felt beautiful, wanted, whole . . .
now reduced to a simmering nightmare. Undoubtedly, the worst
wedding in the history of the eight kingdoms. What will the jour-
nalists scribble for tomorrow's announcers?

Medical Examiners Question Princess' Sanity.

Another Cerulean Princess Devoured!

Most Eligible Duke Rejected.

My lips pinch into a tight line. No, I'd rather not think about
the rumors spreading throughout Ezo. It would only spiral me
downward into a sea of thoughts I can't control. I must keep my
wits to get back home.

"Stay at the beach." Dragon steps in front of me, blocking
the overgrown forest path with a scowl and too-perfect chest. His

words seem to take effort, as if he's still finding his human voice.

"You should come too"—I arch a brow and match his scowl with my own—"and get a shirt."

I duck around him until I'm well into the forested grove. "I'm going to find a town, get medical supplies, and send word to my brother that I'm all right. The kingdom can't wait for whatever the dragons have planned. You know what'll happen to Ezo without their protection."

"The dragons will hunt you," he presses, walking in sync with me on the narrow path.

I want to cover my ears and ignore the earthy sound of his voice. Every syllable taps against my skull: inhuman . . . dragon . . . beast . . . monster.

"They will raze the city in their search if you hide."

I pause, my lips pressed into a firm line. "I'm *not* hiding."

"I see that." Dragon's dark eyes study my face with a puzzled expression. "You don't fear the Celestial Courts or even death. Maybe you fear being alone. That's why you invited me to join your irresponsible venture into town."

I roll my eyes. "I assure you the invitation was just to clothe you. I don't want to look at . . . that"—I gesture to the whole of him—"Now, if you don't mind, I have business to attend to. Unless you want to help and fetch a horse."

Dragon glowers. "I'm an immortal being who can bend fire and poison at will, not a servant."

"You *were*," I press. "Keep your tenses right." I turn away from him as soon as the words are spent, my conscience prickling. Dragons may be sacred, but now that one's turned against me, it changes things. I've no time for his dragon courts and politics. The queendom is slipping through the cracks while we're tromping through this sandy grove.

A pleasant jumble of sounds catches on the breeze, the gentle peal of wind chimes, a chorus of children's laughter, and the low hum of distant voices. My lips break into a smile even before I smell the warm hints of burning coal and savory roasts over a fire. A town. I'm saved.

"It's not wise to involve this village." Dragon lays a firm hand on my arm as I step out of the wood. "Return to the beach and surrender."

I let out an exasperated sigh. "It won't take long. The kingdom needs to know I'm alive. And I need something else to wear besides this."

Dragon eyes my torn wedding dress, one sleeve completely ripped off and tied around my waist as a bandage, blood glinting off it like damp paint. The once white silk is now a dull gray, sporting odd patches of white and silver as it dries. It clings to my body like a leech.

"Your appearance will hardly matter at the trial," Dragon says. "But I understand the desire to warn your countrymen. Even if it is futile."

I raise a brow and scour the town as my mind settles on a plan. "Well, you don't have to follow me. Wait at the beach and tell the dragons that I have political immunity."

"No one has immunity from the Celestial Courts."

"I prefer to stand trial in Ezo."

"You don't understand what you have done," he growls, arresting my attention. "You have my heart. I will not leave your side until it is mine again. It's probably being corrupted by your tainted soul as we speak."

My feet grind to a stop. I listen to the beat of my hearts, one slamming against my chest like a wave. I'm not the only one who lost something today.

"I promise to take good care of it," I say, covering my hearts with a hand. "But that requires food, clean bandages, and proper clothing. If you insist on staying with me, then please, help."

"Fine," he snaps. "Wait here."

The words are so cold that I'm rooted to the spot. Dragon

walks briskly toward town, padding barefoot between the thatched houses until he slinks out of sight.

I wait for what seems like half an hour, mulling over his words, listening to the dual beating of my hearts, and thinking of home: Runa sleeping in the ballroom, my father walled off in grief and anger, Bastian suddenly vice-regent with no queen to take the throne. Casmir . . . would he stay to sort things out or return to Taiga? Does he think I'm dead?

A pile of clothes plops in front of me. I stare at the bare feet beside them, kneading at the earth, before glancing up at Dragon. A silk black robe that must have cost a fortune covers his shoulders, his bare chest still exposed by a gap in the front. He stands in raw perfection, like a diamond dredged up from the earth.

"An improvement," I say, appraising him. "Though you could've stolen something less expensive—whoever you took that from is going to be very angry. That's Amami silk."

"Here." He shrugs off a bamboo canteen roped over his shoulder and hands it to me.

I snag the bamboo, careful not to touch his fingers, and down the water in long, hurried gulps. The water tastes almost sweet.

"Get dressed and be quick," he says, nodding at the pile of clothes before turning his back to me, as if that would be enough privacy.

When I don't reach for the clothes, his broad shoulders heave a sigh. "I'll turn back around on the count of twenty."

I huff and snatch the clothes. "I guess I shouldn't expect a dragon to be a gentleman."

"The sooner you're done in town, the better," he says, facing the bamboo forest ahead. "I've secured horses as well. If you really want news of Ezo, then we should head to Kagano."

"That's in Taiga! We're across the strait of Ezo, aren't we? On the mainland?" I pry myself out of the ruined wedding dress and slide into freshly dried folds of rough-hewn silk—made from the throw away scraps of silk husks—he definitely didn't try to steal something nice for me. The charcoal dress rubs against my bruised skin and the hem is too short, cresting far above the tops of my ankles, but it's dry.

Dragon nods, his back still toward me. "Kagano is your best option to find a post registrar. This town is too small, and they won't like that we've freed their horses—"

"Really, Dragon. You *stole* the horses." I slip on a pair of socks and boots, grateful the dragon thought to provide them. Then I tie the last piece of the ensemble, a black scarf with embroidered butterflies, tightly around my tangled blue hair.

"Your concept of ownership is barbaric," he says, offering the gray horse a handful of sweet clover. "Kagano is a day's ride. Either we take the horses and tell your countrymen that you're alive, or we wait at the beach and forget this foolishness."

I place a hand on one of the horses he'd *freed* from the village, rubbing the dense hair along its neck. "I'll take the horses. But tell me, why are you willing to follow me on this errand suddenly? Is it just to safeguard your heart?"

His jaw clenches. "I would spare this village the dragons' wrath. And yes, I will see that you do no harm to *my* heart."

"What if the dragons come looking for me in Kagano? Do you not worry for the fate of that city?"

"It's sacred, the dragons will not harm it—only you for disregarding their orders. You're at their mercy, Princess. And we have precious little time."

Time I need to save my kingdom. I swallow hard, blinking back images of dragon flame and watery graves, before summoning my resolve.

"Why so impatient if you dragons are immortal?" I ask, assessing the horse's saddle and how best to mount without a stool. I groan inwardly. I don't want to ask him for help, but I can't mount alone with my spine as it is.

"Immortality makes time more precious, not less so," he says, watching me thoughtfully. "You must live with the consequences of your choices for eternity, so every second matters. I won't suffer my heart to endure more of your corrupt soul than necessary."

"Can the council of dragons put your heart back?" I ask.

"It's never been done before." He steps toward me, black eyes as indifferent as the stars, and lifts me onto the horse as if I were nothing but a crippled sparrow being placed back into its tree. No act of kindness could save such a bird's life. "But I'm going to ask them to try. Removing a heart shouldn't be too hard."

His warm hands slip away from my waist as he turns toward his horse, and I'm left with a sickening feeling in my gut. He's going to ask them to try—to attempt to remove the still beating heart from my chest.

I gulp, kneeing my horse toward the open road.

No way I'm giving him the chance.

By the time we reach Kagano, torchlight gutters into the damp streets slicked with rain. Hot pain laces my back with the horse's every step. I've long since abandoned my head scarf, using it as a brace for my waist after a back spasm nearly threw me from the horse.

Dragon offered to make camp then—a small kindness—but I tied myself to the saddle and pressed on. Time is a luxury neither of us can afford.

A banner flaps in the mountain wind, the air wild with hints of sulfur and pine. Even though it's dark, I still make out the canal running through the city center, its water a turbulent, boiling stream. The immense fortress of Kagano is a hilled maze of cobblestone streets tucked into the volcanic mountainside of mainland Taiga. A day's ride from the beach and three from the capital city that dominates this part of the empire. Casmir's world.

The thought cuts me like a knife. The Duke of Taiga would one day help rule this city. And I'd turned him down. The memory of our kiss, warm and questioning, slips into my mind.

I give a forceful shake of my head, strands of wet hair sticking to my aching spine. What would Casmir think if he saw me now?

I pull my horse to a stop before the large orange banner for Fever House, the central bathhouse and lodgings for the city. Royals from across the four winds come here for its healing waters and renowned hospitality. Being from Ezo, an island nation in the frigid north, I'd never made it this far in my travels.

After Mother died, Papa had forbidden most outings. Traveling was for my brother, the dignitary and military commander, not for his daughters, the only heirs to the queen-dom. The farthest I'd been was the royal garden of Taiga, where my father had arranged my marriage to the duke.

Not that it mattered anymore.

A servant rushes from the large wooden house carrying an umbrella and a lantern. She bows before me and takes the horse's reins. Another does the same for Dragon and his pale horse.

"We need lodgings, and I need to send a letter immediately," I say as the servant leads my horse to a thatched shelter.

The servant nods, her long bangs covering her eyes, and places a stool beneath the horse for me to dismount. I wonder if my blue hair is too dark from the intermittent rain showers for her to recognize me. I clear my throat. My back is too stiff to move, much less dismount a horse. But the request sticks to the roof of my mouth.

"The lady is defective," Dragon says, a rich smoothness to his voice that makes me hate the words all the more. He steps to the horse's side and places his hands at my waist again.

I stifle a groan as he pulls me inelegantly from the horse and sets my feet on the cobblestone. My body sways rebelliously, and I slam a hand on his arm for support, surprised by the hard muscles I find there. "I'm not defective," I whisper harshly. "I've a condition."

He ignores the comment and steps aside to put space between us. "I'll take your best bath," he says to the serving girl. "And a cave."

The girl's eyes widen as she takes in Dragon's bare feet and my paltry boots, no doubt wondering where we came from and how we'll pay for the inn.

"A room," I correct, clearing my throat.

"Right," she says, recovering with a polite bow. "Will that be one room or two?"

"Two," Dragon says.

"One," I say at the same time.

The servant's head swivels. "Which will it be?"

Dragon glares at me. I can't decide if he has a sense of propriety or just can't stand my presence.

"These rooms aren't free," I hiss, pulling him aside to whisper. "And you don't have any coin. Or do you keep some in your dragon pockets?"

"I can get money," he whispers.

"Like you got the horses?" I throw a brief glance to the servant girl pretending not to eavesdrop as she orders another attendant to settle the horses.

"I'm a dragon," he says, his voice a whisper of hard edges. "I was here when gold was buried in the earth. Believe me, I know where to find it."

I study him as he breaks away and speaks privately with the attendant, his manner much more polite than with me. I almost wonder if he would be kind were it not for the heart I accidentally stole from him.

We're led inside the elaborate wooden archway and into a cavernous hall. The air is thick with mountain lemon, salt, and sharp notes of pine. I breathe deep and my legs want to collapse onto the nearest sofa. It's been too long since I've seen a sofa.

"Your letter." The girl passes me a piece of parchment and an ink pen.

I take it gratefully and sink onto the nearest cushion, hoping I'll be able to rise without the dragon's help.

I write in careful strokes:

Bastian, Prince of the Silver Isle,

My hand trembles over the next words. Should I apologize for what I did? Explain why I didn't marry Casmir? I grip the pen tight and continue:

> *I'm alive. I'll not mince words or explain my actions at this moment. But know that I place the kingdom and our family above all else.*
>
> *The dragons cannot help Ezo, and I don't know if they will attack our ships. I washed ashore on the Taigan mainland and will attempt to return posthaste. Keep the dignitaries in Ezo. Do not, under any circumstances, allow them to return to their homeland or write to their respective countries. As soon as the kingdoms realize that our defenses are down, we will suffer attack.*
>
> *I believe that the same individual is responsible for my current predicament and Runa's. Please tell no one about this letter or that I'm alive. We need to draw out the culprit.*
>
> *If I've not returned within a fortnight, then something has happened to me, and you can show*

Casmir this letter. He'll know what to do. Keep your guard up, Bas. I'll see you soon.

Your sister, Meera

I seal the letter with wax from the nearest candle and hand it to the attendant. My hand clamps around hers as I force her to meet my gaze.

"This letter is for the Prince of Ezo alone. The castle will pay you handsomely to deliver it to him. When you reach the castle gates, give the guards the code word 'peach dumplings' and they'll let you in."

"Peach . . . dumplings?" the girl whispers.

Clearly, she thinks I'm crazy. What had Dragon told her at the entrance? My eyes sideline to Dragon who paces the hall, scowling at a pair of crimson slippers provided for him.

"Yes, peach dumplings," I say with a nod, wishing Ezo had a more dignified sounding password. But my lips curl into a rueful smile remembering how Runa and I made the weekly code words to give the guards a laugh. What if it takes longer than a week to arrive and the password changes? I push the thought aside. "Make it quick."

The girl nods and rushes from the room with my only hope to save the kingdom. Hearts pound in my chest until the letter is out of sight. Dull pain laces my ribs and aches throb in every joint as I sink further into the cushions. Perhaps this sofa will be the end of me.

Dragon stares at me from the curtains partitioning the hall into the men's and women's sections of the bath house. "Don't worry about the payment for the establishment," he says. "I've taken care of it. You should get cleaned up." His eyes trace my damp dress and tangled hair. "You need it."

I would say likewise, but the dragon looks like he was born for the mountains and wild rains. He kicks off the slippers, a satisfied smile dashing across his face as his bare feet meet the floor.

"And Meera—don't try to run from the dragons."

I laugh, hobbling to my feet. "Like I could outrun you."

I stumble, the last of my energy spent. He catches me by the elbow and helps me to stand. My breath snags at the strength he makes look so easy, but I don't miss the hard glint of his eyes. "Take care of my heart. It won't be yours for long."

Dokun dokun. My hearts thunder, one of them humming like summer rain on a glass window, unmistakably warm. It draws me toward Dragon, forcing a burning heat to my cheeks.

Saints. Maybe I do need to get rid of this heart somehow . . . and fast. But first, I've a kingdom to save.

CHAPTER II

CASMIR

SAINTS AND MONSTERS BE CURSED. Casmir stares down the long, lacquered table to the girl with chestnut hair and blood caked onto her scarlet dress. Citrus and salt lace the thick, cramped air from the purifying crystals Bastian ordered, but nothing combats the rotting stench from the days-old coronation feast. No one besides the healers and apothecaries have entered the room since that night.

Casmir covers his mouth with an embroidered handkerchief, watching the sleeping princess. Runa still breathes. Her low-cut gown reveals a bare back that rises and falls with each inhale and exhale. Casmir would never be caught dead sleeping while others watched. What an unfortunate curse—*the killing sleep.*

The name is already infiltrating every corner of the kingdom from the fish-laden wharf to the spotless throne of King Talos, who'd even used the name in the royal pronouncement of Princess Runa's condition.

Casmir didn't need to move farther than the door to know that whoever orchestrated this was brilliant—and powerful. His jaw tightens, an age-old wound souring in his gut. There is always someone more powerful. Stronger. More creative. But not more determined.

He hadn't become Duke of Taiga by winning a game of rock, paper, scissors. He'd earned it in the most ruthless tournament in the eight kingdoms, The Dual Dragon Invitational, as the youngest champion in history.

Casmir calculates the possibilities of who the culprit could be, and who they'd wanted to eliminate. True, the poisoned pudding could have only been intended for the princess, but why make it contagious unless they wanted to catch someone else . . . and evade detection. Someone close to the princess. Like Bastian. The king. Or the next heir.

Fierce blue eyes and hair flash to his mind, but he shuts it out —shuts her out. A kiss shouldn't remind him of betrayal.

"Did you find any clues?" Casmir turns to the two apothecaries accompanying him, pinning them with a calculating stare. The men visibly shudder as they tiptoe around the broken plates and sleeping persons: a half dozen servants, two healers, and the fair prince of Seshu.

"No, my lord," the apothecary from Blackspire, one of the more famous medicinal guilds in Taiga, grunts into his handkerchief as he waves a lantern about the room. "There are no traces of the poison originating from any other source."

"And the other victims?" Casmir asks.

"The kitchen maid won't make it through the week," the second apothecary adds, a tremor to his voice. "Whatever Mother Ema did is holding the curse at bay, but it hasn't stopped the poison completely."

"What of Princess Runa and the Seshu boy?" Casmir lowers his own handkerchief and takes a few bold steps into the room. Fear would have men hide from the invisible and unproven, but Casmir would only bend his knee to logic. So far, the curse had only proved contagious through personal contact, not airborne. "I was under the impression that they would remain asleep until death. Not that the sleep would actually kill them. How long do they have?"

A long silence follows. "We'd be fools to say."

"You'll be dead if you don't," Casmir counters, his voice alarmingly calm.

"I can't be exact," the first apothecary whimpers. "Two weeks maybe. Unless the Bleeding Saint intervenes. It's possible Mother Ema could do more—"

"The saint's power is but a vapor." Casmir steps farther into the room for a better look at the princess. "I don't pay you to spout fairytales. Out!"

The apothecaries bow profusely and back out of the room as hurriedly as mice before a feral cat.

Casmir waits until the scurry of footsteps fades before approaching Runa, close enough to touch her pallid skin. That's what she would become in a few weeks—a corpse—if he didn't find the poisoner and force him to spill the antidote.

Jey had scoured Ezo for signs of the elusive assassin. He'd even threatened the baker and his wife, interrogated the lieutenant who'd picked a fight with Meera in the market, and eavesdropped on the nobles still housed in the west wing of the castle. Under Casmir's advisement, Bastian ordered that the nobles be placed in quarantine since they couldn't ascertain where the curse had originated.

He would find it and soon.

Casmir's hands twitch at his sides as he stares at the sleeping princess . . . the next ruler of Ezo. He twists the ruby signet ring around his finger. The one he'd offered to Meera along with his heart. He'd never offered it to anyone else. The rejection still stings like a fresh wound.

Would she have married him if he had the power to heal her sister? *Dragon magic.*

That was the only way, and she'd known it. But not just any dragon. Each one had a different ancient art, an innate power connected to the earth to heal, create, or destroy. Casmir had killed enough of the vicious beasts to feel their power, to taste it.

He hadn't told Meera the whole of it—how to kill the beast. How to master its heart.

Casmir reaches out with his left hand, unthinking. His fingers hesitate above the chestnut tresses that spill across the table. *How much power did this poisoner have?*

Double doors barge open, clanking against the walls. Bastian flinches as he steps inside the room, no doubt repelled by the smell. His usual sun-warmed hue is now an ashy shade of brown, his eyes red-rimmed as if he hadn't slept in days, and he's traded in his seafaring coat for a wool doublet and askew cravat in an attempt to wear the vice-regent's crown. Sorrow doesn't look good on him.

"What are you doing in here?" Bastian says gruffly, motioning to a set of guards on either side of him to escort the intruder out. "You shouldn't be here, Casmir. You're supposed to be in quarantine with the other dignitaries. The council is getting suspicious, and you're number one on their list. You already let your ambassador return to Taiga without clearing it!"

Casmir offers a compassionate smile and meets him at the door. "I'm well aware of the fact. Which is why I'm trying to find the poisoner first—and prove them wrong."

"The poisoner's long gone by now. Shouldn't you be searching for my sister?" Bastian's sharp eyes follow Casmir out the doors as the guards secure the room and lock it with extra chains.

Is Bastian suspicious? He wasn't earlier, not when he asked if Casmir would be willing to marry his sister at a moment's notice.

"She made it clear that she doesn't want me," Casmir says, his voice harder than he'd anticipated.

Bastian clamps a hand on his shoulder as if to apologize for his sister's reckless spirit, then waves for Casmir to follow him.

They climb the steep stairs to the upper floor where the morning sun peeks through the castle windows overlooking the bay. "She cares for you," Bastian says, weariness lacing each word. "I know my sister. She may be stubborn and wild, but she's fiercely loyal."

"To you."

Casmir shrugs him off and shifts his gaze to the sea outside. The dragons had been conspicuously absent since the attack yesterday. The primary threat to Ezo had been retaliation from the sea serpents, for which they'd made preparations. But they'd heard nothing from the beasts. Only silence.

"Do you believe she's alive?" Bastian's voice trembles.

No. The word lodges in Casmir's throat. His palms go sweaty as he stares at the sea, wild and blue like Meera, and just as fierce.

It's impossible she made it out alive.

He'd gone face-to-face with dragons and lived, but Casmir also knew their weaknesses, practiced for years, and his katana was forged in the Kagano Mountains, the birthplace of the dragon's first flame. Few blades could pierce dragonhide, and he'd seen all but one of them.

The dagger Meera had found in the cathedral and lied about. Had she been afraid to tell him? Afraid he would stop her?

He would have.

Casmir's hand drifts to rest against the sword hilt belted to his waist. The steel never leaves his side, polished as bright as a mirror and sharper than glass.

He wished it could sever the memories of the last twenty-four hours, the feel of Meera's lips against his, the way she'd leaned into him in the carriage, trusted him. He should have never told her about the fabled dagger, never led her on to try the impossible. He'd underestimated her bravery, and the love for her sister.

"Your face says it all," Bastian says. "You don't believe she's alive, do you?"

Casmir turns away, schooling his emotions into a mask. He doesn't have to answer that question or put his doubt into words. He wouldn't. If that was the only way he could rebel against the dreadful calculations that Meera had died—and still hope—then he would avoid the question forever.

"I need coffee, badly," Casmir mutters, signaling goodbye with a backward wave and striding down the hall. Plans begin to tick in the back of his mind, as they often do whenever pain hits.

"Oi!" Bastian shouts. "You haven't given an answer. My father will make an announcement tomorrow. I need to know your thoughts, not as the Duke of Taiga but as a friend."

"My thoughts?" Casmir pauses, keeping his back to him.

"Yes," Bastian says, covering the ground between them and blocking the hallway with an arm. "I can't carry this kingdom if I've lost them both. My father's role as regent was supposed to end yesterday. He's pushing me to pick up the reins, to take my sister's place. But I can't. Ezo has been a queendom for centuries. It would change everything."

"It won't change the tides, my friend." Casmir lays a hand on Bastian's arm before pushing it aside. "*Everything* is a word best used with caution."

"Like the words *poison* and *curse*," Bastian says, eyes hardening. "The nobles are getting restless. We can't keep them locked up forever. Once they leave and tell their kingdoms, there will be war." He swallows hard, a muscle twitching in his jaw. "I have to know, without a doubt, what happened to both of my sisters before then."

Casmir sighs. "Bastian, your sisters are gone. The fate of Ezo is on your shoulders, whether you wish to bear it or not."

"I've never run a kingdom before," he says, fisting his hands.

"Neither have I. But it wouldn't stop me from doing the right thing. Your sister believed in you. Don't squander her trust with doubt."

Bastian's shoulders tense. "I won't. Which is why I want to ask you to lead Ezo for the interim. No one was close enough to know what Meera said to you at the wedding before she . . ." He gulps, looking away from the ocean window. "Rumor has it that the marriage was official. You haven't denied it. That makes you the next—"

"Be careful what you suggest." Casmir tilts his head in warning.

"Hear me out," Bastian continues. "I think she's still out there. Call me crazy, but it's a hunch. I need to find her. While I'm gone, you can manage Ezo as regent. I'm losing my mind on land. I need to be out there looking for answers." He gestures to the open sea with a calloused hand, his eyes wild with raw hope and grief.

"She didn't say yes," Casmir says, making the truth clear. Though the alternative is sorely tempting. "She said goodbye. I'll respect her wishes."

"Meera would want someone to protect Ezo. You're the best soldier in all of Taiga and her *husband*. Who better to safeguard her homeland? It'd only be for a week, until I return."

"I'll consider it," Casmir says. "We may have been friends for a long time, Bastian, but I am foremost Duke of Taiga. And I doubt your father would like me commandeering Ezo."

"It's just temporary," Bastian insists. "And the other kingdoms respect you."

Power is never a temporary gain. Casmir wouldn't go easy on Bastian because he's desperate and grieving. Power is a cruel game without regard for its players. The stakes are always high. Casmir takes a deep breath, his thoughts spiraling into forbidden territory: Meera, the girl who would be his wife right now if not for an unforgiving sea and a stupid beast.

Maybe if he'd asked her sooner.

Maybe if he hadn't been afraid to tell her how beautiful she was, how her courage lit a flame in his heart that only beat faster when she walked into a room.

Casmir closes his eyes, forcing away the useless thoughts. Meera is gone. Their future torn away with talons and fire. He'd make those beasts pay. Every last one of them.

His only flame had been extinguished and all that was left was cold, calculating power and a chance to prove himself. No matter how many chances he had, it never seemed enough. He would find the poisoner. And he would take the throne. But on his own terms . . . which don't include the word *temporary*.

"Go, find your sister," Casmir says with a nod. "If she's alive then maybe the Bleeding Saint still lives. I'll guard Ezo with my life."

"Thank you. You won't regret it."

"I know." Casmir's lips quirk into a rueful grin, one Bastian was sure to mistake for pity. "I never regret my choices."

CHAPTER 12
MEERA

FIRE BREATHES down my neck as a dragon unhinges its jaws, sweeping down on the inn. My fingers press against Mama's pendant of the Bleeding Saint, prayers rolling off my tongue until I'm hoarse. Glittering black scales slash through the inn's tiled room. I scream.

Smoke burns my throat, choking me.

I can't breathe.

I jerk awake, the nightmares following me as I scour the room for any sign of Dragon. *They're coming for you*, he'd said at the beach. I believe him. It's only a matter of when.

Sunrise crawls over the mountains, dispelling a bruised purple sky with hints of persimmon. I slip into the inn's public hot spring bath, eager to shake off the bad dream. The water is like medicine for my aching bones. I don't care that Runa would call me a granny for taking a morning bath. The waters of Fever House are as close to heaven as I'm going to get—now that I've poisoned an immortal being.

Smooth water dances around my skin, warming me from the inside out as steam caresses my face. I wonder if Dragon is still sleeping, or if he sleeps at all. It must be strange for him in a different body—an entirely perfect one. Heat flushes my face and it's not from the hot bath. I don't want to think about Dragon. I *shouldn't* think about him.

His curse is unfortunate, but my kingdom matters more. And I won't let it be burned to the ground by him or the other kingdoms.

One of my hearts beats faster than the other. I'm beginning to sense that it has a mind of its own. It's loyal to him. I'm sure of it. It's probably black and scaly too.

Soft morning light filters through the thatched roof that covers the outdoor pools carved from basalt and fragrant cypress. I'm shielded from view but fully exposed to the natural elements: the blush pink sky, the rustling breeze in the garden, and the fearless song of birds. I inhale the steam, letting it cleanse me from the inside out.

It's too early for most guests to enjoy the baths. I relish the solitude. It's almost as glorious as a hot meal—almost. My stomach growls, reminding me that it's not forgotten that my last meal was yesterday, and that I'd most certainly hurled it onto the beach. I'd been too tired to eat last night, falling into bed with wet hair and a pounding headache.

Hot water soothes my stiff back and the pain shooting down my legs. I trace the faint pink circle where the brace had splintered into my rib. Yesterday the wound had bled and crusted over. But the power in this hot spring is real, stitching me back together with threads of magic. I dip my fingers into the silky water, the minerals so rich I can almost taste the alkaline tang.

What does Dragon think of this place? Are the healing waters truly the gift of a dragon like in the stories? They say the waters of Fever House run with the blood of an ancient art passed down from a dragon to a girl with a pure heart who lay her life down for the city and thereby imparted the gift to the springs eternally. But no ancient art lasts that long.

They only exist as long as the beneficiary still lives. Like the queens.

I flick the water, stirring it with an irritated stroke. I bet Dragon would know more about the secrets clinging to this place. *Enough.* No more thinking about him. I'll deal with the dragon later—after I've returned home.

Bastian should get my note within a few days, and I have a long three-day trek to the capital of Taiga to charter a ferry to Ezo.

I climb out of the bath and dress quickly, putting on a set of fresh clothes provided by the inn: traditional wide-leg pants and a tie-waist robe dyed with rich color. Every time my hands brush new fabric, I think of Runa. She'd taught me which colors go best together, which artisans made the best silks or had the most creative dyes. This was Kagano made, vibrant purple and crimson hues with a faint stencil design of a whirlpool to symbolize the healing water that keeps this city afloat.

With a grateful sigh, I lather my skin with the horse oil provided. The scratches along my hands and legs are now pale lines as if a week had passed and not just a day.

Ezo needs magic like this. It'd had it with Mama, a gentle magic that healed the land and enriched the harvest with warmth and life. The dragon who'd given her its ancient art must've had a kind heart, unlike the one I was dealing with.

I finish dressing by tying my hair into a black scarf to hide the blue tresses and slip into the hallway.

I'm not alone.

Dragon waits with his back to the ornate wall, one foot anchored against it, his arms crossed against his chest, and still donning the same pink pants and black robe without slippers. I take in the soft sheen of his dark hair, damp on the ends, the way his cheeks flush with color, and the stubble shadowing his jaw. I wasn't the only one who'd enjoyed a morning bath.

"Why are you following me?" I quip and turn toward the breakfast hall.

"I'm not following you," he says, pushing off the wall—and following me. "I'm keeping tabs on my heart. Wouldn't you do the same?"

"Perhaps."

An attendant bows as we enter the dining room and motions for us to take the window seat. I square my shoulders, trying to ignore the soft padding of Dragon's bare feet across the rug. What does he have against slippers?

The dining hall is a tasteful room heated by a standing hearth and embellished with the latest fashions from Furan and Taiga. A delightful fusion of wooden transoms carved into flying carp and dragons, lacquered tables, and soft cushions in wisteria purple and cypress green. My eyes turn upward at the unusual coffered ceiling painted with alpine plants from the mountainous region. Runa would love it here.

Dragon pulls out a chair for me by the nearest window over-looking a garden. I raise a brow at his sudden interest in manners and take the seat, my eyes narrowing as he sits across from me.

"What are you doing?" I ask, settling my napkin.

"I'm listening to my heart," he says with a scowl, leaning closer from across the table.

"And what does it say?" I raise a brow, wondering if he can really hear it from the constricting space between us.

"It wants you to eat," he says. "It's famished."

I smile, holding back a laugh. "A hungry heart, perfect. That's so . . . dragon of it."

His lips tug at the corners, the most unyielding of smiles. But it softens his jaw, the black in his eye sparkling for the briefest moment. If I hadn't been watching closely, I would have missed it. "What do you recommend eating?" He fingers the parchment menu spread between us, his brow furrowed in concentration, too much so for a simple menu.

It dawns on me—he can't read. My chest squeezes in pity as his eyes pretend to decipher the inky characters mapped on parchment.

"They have almost everything on this menu," I say, pretending I can't decide what to eat so I can read the menu to him. "From sweetfish to eel, pork and lotus soup, and even oranges. Maybe I should order it all. What do you feel like eating?"

"Fish." His stomach rumbles. "And oranges."

I pinch back a smile. "What a relief. Here I thought you would say young maidens."

"Only when they stab me," he deadpans.

I meet his eyes, the gold flecks at once angry and amused. It's a threat and a jest in one breath, and I can't keep from smiling. He leans back, crossing his arms as if I wasn't supposed to find him entertaining.

The serving staff steps up to our table with a notebook in hand and takes our order. I ask for the seabream sashimi with steamed rice, simmered bamboo shoots, and caramelized sand eels.

A few other guests enter the dining room as our drinks are served. I peer at Dragon over the rim of my coffee cup. The drink is smooth, if not a tad bitter. Not as good as when Casmir brewed it.

"You're thinking of him," Dragon says.

I nearly spew a mouthful of coffee but gulp down the too-hot liquid instead. "Excuse me?"

"The dragon slayer."

"I was thinking about the coffee for your information," I say, setting down the cup with an audible clink. "You're a terrible mind reader."

His lips quirk into a challenging grin, a slash of warmth against his cold face. "I wasn't reading your mind, only your face. You're blushing. That's what humans do when infatuated, or embarrassed."

I squeeze my napkin beneath the table, resisting the urge to kick him in the shin. "You know, people are usually more tactful at conversation. It's considered rude to ask personal questions. Or worse, make assumptions."

"People never like talking about what's real," he says. "They twist the truth, ignore it, use it to their advantage. But they rarely accept it as it is."

"It's called being polite."

He doesn't reply but watches me with the same judging scowl I'd seen too often on his face. Those black eyes with golden sparks that hate me for simply being human—or maybe it's just for stabbing him.

Our food arrives and I dig into it as if I haven't eaten for a week. The seabream melts in my mouth and the warm miso soothes my stomach. Dragon scarcely touches his plate. He holds the orange and smells it before turning to the window and watching the koi slowly churn in the garden pond.

"What will you do?" I ask between mouthfuls. "If you stay this way."

His jaw hardens and something cold enters his eyes. "I'll die."

I set down my chopsticks. "You mean . . . you'll be like me, and still have a long life ahead of you. Mortal isn't the same thing as death."

"That's one opinion."

"No need to be dramatic. You could have a long life, do something you've never done before, even make friends if you drop the scowl."

"I have friends," he says, not meeting my eyes. "And a life in service to the Saint. Before this, I was the guardian of a village in the northern mountains. Before the fall of the Bleeding Saint, before Ezo tricked us into a bargain for our powers after the Ashfall. If I must stay in this form, then I would return to that village to care for it. But that won't happen because I *will* get my heart back."

I choke down the last of my coffee, hands trembling around the warm cup. "I don't want your heart. You can have it. I just want to care for my people and for my sister to wake up. But once I've accomplished that, your heart is yours."

"And if you die in the process?"

My eyes snap to his, wishing the second heart in my chest didn't beat harder in response.

"I'd prefer to avoid that, naturally."

"That's understandable," he says, rising from his chair. "Are you ready?"

He offers me a hand.

"I don't need help," I say, finishing off my plate and rising to my feet. The hot springs did wonders on my back, and now I can stand for a good hour without the pain returning. I must if I'm going to ride into Taiga to charter the ferry—alone. "Wait . . . am I ready for what?"

He takes my hand, this time without the kind offer, and pulls me to the back door leading into the garden. I follow mutely, aware of eyes trailing us from the serving girls and the other guests in the room. Dragon doesn't answer my question as we stroll into the damp morning air, thick from yesterday's rain.

"It's not proper to run off dragging someone," I protest, jerking my hand free as soon as we're alone. "Society has rules, you know."

He shakes his head softly, as if I'm the one without decorum, and then turns down the forested garden path without asking me to follow. I grit my teeth. The nerve of that dragon to drag me out here and then leave. I shouldn't follow him, but I do. Curiosity pulls at my hearts with questions that demand answers.

The pleasing roar of a waterfall reaches me before I take the next turn among the rocks and twisted pine trees. Dragon stands before a small waterfall, the pool beneath it a brilliant azure without end.

"Why bring me out here?" I demand, crossing my arms against the chill. My eyes skim the pond, noting a red three-legged gate and dragon statue in a coppice to the left, a shrine dedicated to the sacred monsters. "They're here, aren't they . . . the dragons?"

He nods. "This is the sacred birthplace of dragons."

"This?" I stare at the small waterfall, wide and brimming over a wall of moss, not more than four meters high. "I thought dragons came from the tears of the Bleeding Saint."

"Yes," he says, a smile touching his lips as he dips a hand in the water. Our eyes meet, and my hearts beat a wild dash against my ribs. "This is where He cried and spoke life into us. A soul —like He did for man when he fashioned them from the earth. Only we were born of water." His jaw clenches and he extends his hand to me. "We can meet the tribunal together, if you wish."

I wasn't planning on going to the tribunal. My queendom comes first. But, strangely, his words comfort me. Not that I'd tell him that. If I must face the tribunal, I'll meet it head on like I face all my trials. Like I should've the day my mother died.

He's right that I don't fear the Celestial Court or whatever fate the dragons mete out for me. I fear . . . I stare at my reflection in the water, my crooked spine, and the look in my eyes that whispers the words, *alone, not enough, broken.* Like when the wolves took Mama and when I watched my siblings trying to be strong.

Deep down, I'm afraid it's not even my physical limitations holding me back, but me—who I am. Like I was born broken on the inside.

Even so, I don't take his hand.

He steps barefoot into the pool and gestures for me to follow. I raise a brow and consider. Gentle steam rises from the water;

it's warm to the touch, part of the hot spring flowing into the bathhouse.

I could run. Not that I would make it far if the dragons came after me. But I slip off my shoes and step into the pool. Silky water laps against my ankles and warmth needles my feet. One of my hearts tugs against the pull of the tingling water. I could wait for the dragons to force me, to haul me to saints knows where. But I'm not guilty of murder. I did what I had to for Runa and my kingdom.

Squaring my shoulders, I step over the ledge of the pool.

Dragon helps me down, and I fall into his chest. My hand rests against the thick silk threads of his black robe, the other against the hard muscles of his arm as I brace myself. He dips his chin toward me, inky black hair falling across his brow as he studies me like someone trying to piece together a treasure map. Heat blooms up my neck and I push myself away with a stagger. My dual hearts beat frantically, one in alarm and the other—

"Did you know that your eyes have sixteen colors?" he says.

I gape, a hand trailing to my face as if I could feel the color myself. *Why would he say such a thing?* "They're blue," I say, pulling off my head scarf in frustration. "Like my hair and the curse I was born with."

"I see more as a dragon," he says, turning to stare at the waterfall. "Your eyes are not just blue. They are the color of the summer sky, the strength of iron, the heat of a flame, the blush of silk crepe, wisteria before it blooms, lapis lazuli . . ."

His eyes meet mine again. "Your sickness isn't a curse," he says. "But how you view it is. That's why I didn't count you worthy that day. It's not a judgment on who you are, Meera. But on who you think you are."

"I don't *think* I'm cursed. I know it." I sink onto the stone wall surrounding the waterfall and pond. Heat skims over my skin, and I'm angry at myself for listening—for wanting to believe what he says. Dragon knows nothing of brokenness. "I feel pain in my body every day. The limitations. The weakness. But you didn't come out here to tell me what I already know."

"No," Dragon says, watching me closely. "But I think everyone should have the chance to see themselves clearly before meeting their fate." Then he turns and his shoulders duck beneath the waterfall and disappear. He's letting me choose.

Fight or flight.

I'm done fleeing, even if my chest pulls tight and my human heart taps a frantic staccato against my ribs like a bird throwing itself against glass. I close my eyes and fist Mama's pendant between my fingers. *Keep me safe.*

My fingers graze the waterfall, warm and dazzling. A rainbow of colors shimmer over the cascade as the morning sun catches it. *For Runa. For Ezo.*

I step beneath the water. For a moment, I'm blind from the rushing torrent and the pounding loud against my skull. My hair hangs wet and heavy from the relentless thunder and then the water at my feet stills on the other side. A slow ripple laps against my ankles, drawing my eyes to the opposite end of the cave.

Two eyes glow at the far end of the dark cavern. A scream gathers at the back of my throat as my eyes adjust and sickly green scales come into view. An emerald dragon fills the cave, its serpentine body as thick as a horse, and its wolf-like head touching the ceiling, craned at a predatory angle as it watches me. A snarl sparks against the side of the cave as it lowers its head, narrowing on me with a mouth full of razor-sharp teeth, each one the length of my hand.

"Don't move."

I startle at Dragon's voice from beside me, and a scream escapes from my throat. Dragon covers my mouth with a gentle hand. My knees buckle.

Had he tricked me here to feed a monster?

"I told them you'd come quietly," he whispers. "If you resist, they will kill you. Promise not to scream again?"

I nod feebly, and he releases me. My whole body shudders, and I hate myself for the show of weakness. "If I come where?"

"To the tribunal," he whispers. "In the Deep Dark."

A cry curdles in the back of my throat like a whimper. I don't care what he says, I'm going to scream. The Deep Dark is a world of monsters, so far beneath the sea that no mortal has seen it. A place of fire and glass and bone where the dragons first fell when they lost their wings and were banished into the sea after the Ashfall. I might be too old for fairytales, but I've seen enough in the last two days to know he isn't joking.

I spin around, launching myself toward the exit. An angry roar sounds behind me, followed by a blast of heat.

"No!" Dragon yells.

He slams into me, knocking me into the waterfall and down into the outside pond. Scalding hot spring water swirls around me as I plunge downward. His arms anchor me to his chest. I hold the air in my lungs, eyes wide, our faces a breath apart. Fire erupts above the surface, scorching the water in angry crimson ripples.

He's watching me drown—again.

But this time, his hands are warm, his face human, and his heart burns within me.

Dokun dokun.

I feel the water's heat drift away, but my lungs beg for air.

Sharp talons dip into the water. The green dragon from the cave slips into the pond, hatred vibrating from every emerald scale. The monster tears us apart; clenching Dragon in one talon and me in the other. Water scalds my lungs as I scream in protest.

The green dragon blows the same strange bubbles in my face. Only this time the drugging effects of sleep don't subdue me. I see it all.

We plunge into the pool, hurtling toward the dark.

CHAPTER 13
MEERA

TWIN HEARTS BEAT in my chest as water streams past me, stinging my face. The hot spring turns cold the deeper we go. The emerald dragon threads through a narrow tunnel of water, its belly a stroke of pale light and its claws sharper than a dagger constantly threatening to slice me open. It holds Dragon in its other talon.

He hangs limp in the serpent's claws, his short hair wild and darker in the cold sea. His black robe waves like an inky ribbon behind him, dragging behind a seemingly lifeless body. I watch his chest, his eyes, his lips for a sign of life.

He isn't breathing.

Panic squirms in my chest. *Had the other dragon not given him those strange bubbles?*

I tire of holding my breath and let the water flow in and out, searing but somehow keeping me alive. Dragon must be okay too. Why bring him to the tribunal otherwise?

After what seems like an hour, an enormous iridescent dome appears at the bottom of the pond, like a pearl. Water stretches all around it as if we have entered the sea and not the bottom of an abyss. Dragons of every color and size swim into the large pearl, knifing through it with ease like a kitchen chef carving a gelatinous chestnut pie. I brace myself, casting a worried glance at Dragon's limp form.

The green beast tucks its chin and cuts through the pearl with its horns. A filmy substance that reminds me of jellyfish slides over me. Gravity suddenly drags my ribs against the hard talons. The water is thinner here and more like air. Time, too, as if hours and minutes are indistinguishable without the sun. I breathe, finding my head less cloudy and my thoughts returning without the bubbles' drowsy influence.

The green serpent soars over unusual sandy tunnels that appear to be roads and tall seaweed gardens terraced over oyster fields. Houses made from living coral and volcanic rock frame the outer layer of the pearl. We dive down, bending into a maze of sand-blasted glass and carefully worn paths. A civilization. A home.

Nothing like the images I'd seen in books.

These aren't merely beasts. Not like the wolves and bears that dominate the untamed northern lands of Ezo. I crane my head, catching a glimpse of other dragons flying across the underwater kingdom within the pearl. A few smaller dragons chase each other through the sandy tunnels with shrill barks and colorful scales. Upon seeing me, they give a startled yap and disappear behind corners or into elaborate seaweed gardens, some large enough to rival the royal maze in Taiga.

The emerald dragon arches its back, preparing for a descent. Its talons tighten around my waist, but it flicks open the other claw, dropping Dragon's body.

"No!" My voice cracks as Dragon plummets and then hits the sand with an audible thud. His neck crooks at a painful angle, the black Amami robe twisted around him like broken wings.

I push against the talons holding me, but suddenly I'm plunged down. The green dragon lands in the middle of a wide arena flanked with rows of dark stone benches. My body slams against black sand.

Peering up from my prone position on the floor, I push my fingers into the damp sand. *Is Dragon alive? Why have they brought us here?*

A crescent throne towers over the colosseum's arena and tiers of seats. Three dragons perch atop it, staring down at me with dark, gold-speckled eyes and fire glowing in their veins.

I tear my gaze away and search for Dragon—*my dragon.* The thought startles me, but not as much as what I see. He lies face down on the ground, covered in sticky sand, an uneven breath the only sign that he's still alive. My second heart gives a painful squeeze.

"Let me go," I cry, squirming beneath the talons. "Someone needs to help him!"

The emerald beast shoves me harder against the dirt and pressure explodes along my spine. I seethe but lie still and watch helplessly.

After a full minute, Dragon pushes up on his palms, coughing. The coughs rack his body with violent lurches. None of the dragons react, seemingly indifferent. Finally, he rocks back onto his knees, wiping a hand across his mouth.

They could've killed him.

He stiffens as if sensing my stare and scowls in my general direction.

I raise a brow. It's not my fault his own kind disrespect him. *Well, maybe it is.*

Dragon pushes to his feet and strides over to me, his face too high to see from my embarrassing angle. I can only make out his bare feet, those ridiculous pink pants, and the talons of the green dragon hemming me in like a cage.

"What are we doing here?" I ask, elbowing the rough talon that pins my stomach to the ground.

Dragon doesn't bother bending down for me to see him. Instead, he moves to my side. "I'm to translate for you."

"I see. Well, can you ask your *friend* to let me up?"

"*Friends* don't usually try to kill each other," he quips, anger bristling off him. "But I've broken their code, so it's understandable. She won't listen to me."

"She?" I shrill the word, attempting to glance at the dragon holding me. "Please tell me it's not your sweetheart?"

"I don't have a mate if that's what you mean," he says. A long silence follows; I'd give anything to see his face. "And we don't feel the same shyness about such matters as humans do."

I laugh dryly, rewarded by a mouthful of sand. "Please, tell her to let me up."

"I don't *tell* her to do anything," he says. "I ask."

Dragon's feet turn as he approaches the green monstrosity, and then the talons lift.

My ribs expand in a thankful gasp as I scurry out from under the sharp claws. The beautiful robe and hakama from the inn are ruined, and my spine aches as I struggle to right myself. I breathe deep of the strange air—or water—whatever it is.

The three dragons on the rim study me with ears rotated back and unblinking eyes. I incline my head to better hear if the dragons are speaking, but I'm met with silence and the rush of water from outside the pearl. It's like listening to a seashell, the roaring hum and song of the ocean playing in the background while I'm dry and safe on shore. Only this isn't the shore, it's an underwater pocket of air keeping the world of dragons a secret from the rest of humanity.

My breath catches at the thrill of seeing it, wondering who else has, but my excitement is quickly snuffed out by a shuddering roar from one of the sacred beasts.

"You have broken the understanding between dragons and men," Dragon says, apparently translating. He stands beside me, close enough I could take his hand if I wanted to. Which I don't.

I just want to hurry back to Ezo, where Runa sleeps waiting for me. Unless . . . I can get the magic I need from one of these monsters. The dragons once saved our world from ruin; could they not save my kingdom?

I glance up at the three dragons staring at me from their perch. All scales, horns, and sharp teeth. None of their mouths move, but all of them stare at me with the same deathly certainty.

"Who is speaking?" I ask Dragon.

"We do not share our names with humans. You stand here today because you have killed one of our own," Dragon continues to translate, his voice monotonous, if not a tad murderous.

This time no roar preceded his words. *Do they communicate telepathically?*

"You can seriously talk about yourself like that when you're standing right here . . . alive?" I turn to him, but he refuses to look at me. Coldness radiates off his hard shoulders. "Tell them you're alive! You can't have a murder trial when the victim is still standing. We can fix this. It was all a misunderstanding. Someone else poisoned that dagger. Let's find the real enemy. Don't let them throw away peace so quickly."

Dragon's shoulders tighten as if my words are pebbles pelting his back. "The peace you speak of is only an illusion," he says. "True peace is not so easily broken."

I cross my arms, angling my hip to soothe my aching spine, and eye the silent tribunal. Do they feel the same way about Ezo? About the pact between my kingdom and the dragons' magic that has fed it for generations? That has brought life and help to those who need it?

The green serpent shifts behind me, and I turn. Her eyes fix on me like burning coals. The other dragons sit in stormy silence, an armory of impenetrable scales and teeth.

"What are they saying?" I whisper, edging closer to Dragon until our arms brush together.

He scowls as if my presence is offensive. "Death. Murderer. Burn her. Feed her to the sharks. Let her drown in a pool of jellyfish—"

"Point taken."

One of the dragons growls from its perch, the entire beast an iridescent black from snout to tail. It could fill a room with the length of its ribbon-like body completely ribbed in muscles and obsidian scales.

"The Grand Elder asks your name."

"What if I don't share my name with dragons?" The snark comes out faster than I anticipated. I throw a hand over my mouth, wishing I could hide the reckless words. Runa really is better at the social aspects of court.

Dragon raises a brow.

"Will he understand if I speak or do you have to translate?"

Dragon inclines his head as if listening to the other serpents. "We know a thousand languages; we have no need of translation," he says. "It is my punishment to provide this . . . service to you. And to spare your mortal mind the pain of hearing a divine voice screeching within your skull."

"How thoughtful." I force a pained smile and clear my throat before stepping toward the raised perch where the other dragons stand. "I'm Princess Meera of Silverwood," I say, meeting the black dragon's gaze with a bow, remembering that these are not only creatures of judgment and magic, but former guardians of the earth. "Daughter of King Talos and Queen Meranya."

A brief silence follows, but none of the dragons take their eyes off me.

"They accuse you of being a sorceress," Dragon translates. "And you are further accused of poisoning an immortal being, reducing his life to ash and corruption. Your motivations matter not, only your actions. The penalty for murder is death. A life for a life."

"No!" I clench my fists, stepping forward again. I'm going

about this all wrong by trying to defend myself. What had I learned from watching Runa deal with court politics? These dragons have a civilization, honor, life. They won't listen to me unless I show them respect. Quickly, I lower myself to my knees and bow with my forehead to the ground.

"Please," I begin. "The future queen of Ezo has been poisoned and lies asleep in the castle. I was told that in order to protect the kingdom, I must either take her place or marry the Duke of Taiga, the one you call Dragon Slayer. But my heart belongs to the Saint." I fish the gold pendant from my dress and hold it for them to see. "I found the dagger in their trove of relics and sought to take the magic by force—to guarantee an ancient art for my people to save them—"

"Taking magic by force is the definition of sorcery," Dragon mutters.

"It was to save my sister and the kingdom," I continue, rising to my knees. "I swear, I didn't know the blade was cursed. Please, have mercy."

The dragons shift on their perch, some tossing long necks or gnashing teeth. A slow ringing grows in the back of my skull. Pressure pounds beneath my temples with the sound. If I hadn't already been on my knees, it would've doubled me over.

Dragon steps in front of me and holds up a palm, asking them for silence. The kindness of the motion takes me off guard. The serpents seemingly obey, their eyes pinning him to the arena floor like a beetle on a corkboard. A long moment passes between them, Dragon growing paler as the time lengthens.

"What are they saying?"

He turns to look down at me, eyes scouring my face as if searching for a trace of his heart. "You poisoned me without a thought of right or wrong," he says. This time, he isn't translating. The words are his own, full of sadness and pain. "You will never get the heart magic you seek. You will never be worthy of it, not after what you've done."

"What have I done, Dragon?" I say, heat rising to my cheeks. "I fought for my kingdom, for my sister."

"You stole an immortal heart and corrupted it," he says, the cold anger of his words like a dagger. "Reasons don't matter." His head jerks up as if the dragons had spoken to him, and he pauses to listen. "They are taking a vote to determine if you deserve death."

"What about your heart?" I whisper, rising to my feet now that the headache has ceased. I reach out and grab Dragon's arm, partially for support, and mostly because I need him to listen. "What happens to you if they kill me?"

"I stay this way until I die." His hands clench. There's something he's not telling me.

"You asked them for your heart back, didn't you?"

He nods faintly, gold flashing in his dark eyes. "It's ruined," he barely whispers. "They've refused. The elders say that the heart—*my heart*—will be a plague upon both our kind until it's destroyed. The only remedy is to extinguish it."

"I'm sorry." I drop my hand from his arm. Cold reality settles into my bones. "I didn't mean for this to happen. You're right, it doesn't matter what my intentions were. It's not only the outcome that counts, it's the choices that got me here. I was wrong. But that doesn't mean we need to go down without a fight."

"We?" The word seems to jar him. "You don't fight a dragon, or have you not learned that yet?" His eyes narrow in thought, but suddenly his head snaps up as if on instinct. I follow his gaze but feel the heat before I see it.

Dragon grabs my hand and pulls me to his chest as fire scorches into the arena from a dragon on the high perch and the green beast at our backs. A blaze of amber, tourmaline, and liquid ruby flames around us with shocking speed. Heat blazes against my face, singeing my hair and dress. Instinctively, my hands jerk up, shielding my eyes. The ground shakes and I risk a glance.

The enormous black serpent curls around me and Dragon, its body taking in the flames like sunlight, warm and fierce, absorbing what was intended as my punishment. When the drag-onfire ceases, the black beast turns and locks eyes with me. It's so close now that I can see the soft ebony fur between its eyes transition to scales along the top of its head, the sharp wolf-like face and ears, long flowing whiskers and a mane of feathery scales known to harden into blades when it cuts the water's surface.

Dragon releases me, the safety of his arms melting away with a cold distance. He stares at his bare feet, face flushed from the fire and fingers curling and uncurling to release the tension. He's only protecting his heart, but the way he rushed to my defense like that . . .

The black dragon doesn't look at him. In fact, none of the dragons do. As if they refuse to acknowledge his existence.

He's done nothing wrong except to spare my life when I broke the oath. How can they punish him this way? It's not his fault that he's mortal now.

Dragon clears his throat and translates once more, "The Grand Elder says, 'We are just but also merciful. None who ask for mercy will be turned away if their heart is sincere. We will give you one chance to prove your worth. One chance to live.'"

My body nearly crumples with relief. "Thank you."

"Do not thank him," Dragon says, his voice gritted like sand. His eyes remain fixed on the now scorched floor.

"Why not?"

"He says that you must complete three tasks of the dragons' choosing. Complete them all and you will live."

"I need more than that," I whisper, my voice dry and cracked from the smoke. I square my shoulders. "I can't go back home without the magic to save my kingdom. There will be no Ezo without it . . . *please*."

Dragon glances at me this time, his head cocked to the side with a look of disbelieving awe. In the silence that follows, I take it that he's explaining my rude demands telepathically to the others. Dragon pales.

"Well?" I say. "Will they grant my wish?"

"The Grand Elder says your case for an ancient art rests with the dragon you murdered and wishes you luck." His eyes slide to mine with a look that says *impossible*. "He also said that I now have to accompany you on all your tasks to make sure you do not cheat."

"I don't need a chaperone—"

"And," he continues, stepping closer. "If you fail, he will raze all of Ezo until it's nothing but ash and bone. Too long dragons have been tied to the dark sea because of our oath. You lose, you set us all free to roam the land once more."

"Dragon," I say, wondering at the intensity in his eyes. "What does it mean for you? If I win . . . or lose?"

He shivers as if the sea is now cold to him. "I don't translate everything they say." His eyes cut to mine. "If you win, I remain like this"—he gestures to his body with disdain—"and I am no more one of them. I am human in every way."

"And if I lose?"

"You sacrifice your life to give me back my heart." A rueful smile cuts across his handsome face and he reaches out hesitantly. His thumb strokes my collarbone above my heart, barely touching, but the warmth of his skin radiates up my neck.

Dokun dokun.

"It misses me," he says before snapping his hand away. "And I aim to get it back. This is my second chance too. Now, are you ready for the first task?"

I stagger, eyeing the dragons with their powerful jaws that could swallow me whole or burn me until nothing remains. But something tells me that dying while parting with my second heart will be even more painful. I gulp and try to hold onto my courage. I may not be adept at politics, boys, or fancy ballrooms, but I do have enough courage for two hearts.

Three tasks.

One dragon completely invested in my failure.

And a chance to save Ezo and my skin.

"I'm ready," I say, squaring Dragon with a look meant to match his own. A fiery scowl to take down monsters. "What's the first task?"

CHAPTER 14
DRAGON

THE MOON GLITTERS like a lantern in the emerald river, though it is still daylight. The princess sleeps on the boat deck, her mortal mind numbed into slumber by the spume—an oxygen saliva that coats the lungs made by a chemical reaction of algae and dragon spit. Dragon's breath comes easy, filling the aching void left by his once steadfast heart.

He studies the slow rise and fall of the girl's shoulders, the expanding and contracting of her lungs. The mortal's heartbeat is faster, an ever-panicked thrum that knows its time is limited. He should wake her. The trial will commence within the hour. One hour before he would watch the princess die—and his heart along with her.

The dragons never planned to return it.

He hadn't translated *all* the Grand Elder said during the tribunal. Only the third trial would preserve his heart in a state that would enable him to take it back—if the girl survived that long. It was a cruel tease of hope.

The elders had forbidden his interference in the trials, forbade him from protecting his own heart.

Is it really a second chance if he's set up to fail?

Dragon's fingers dig into the side of the boat, hating the way feelings surge in his chest instead of logical thoughts. He *shouldn't* be angry with the elders. That's not the dragons' way. But this body refuses to listen to reason. He grits his teeth, wishing he could be like the water again—immortal, long-suffering, pure without these . . . feelings.

Meera had been a fool speaking so boldly before the Grand Elder. *Asking for an ancient art.* Dragon flicks a fallen cherry petal at the water's surface, marring the splendid reflection of the moon. Like he would ever give her the ancient art after what she did.

Imparting magic to a mortal required he have two hearts and give her a small piece of one of them. But for her to return his heart in any way . . . that would kill her. The elders hadn't shared that information. Even if he *could* give her the gift she so desperately wanted, she wouldn't be around to receive it.

Had Meera known the truth, she would've begged the dragons to burn her on the spot and save her the pain of hoping. But he couldn't think about that. He wouldn't. She brought this on herself and he wouldn't be sad for her. Dragon had to find a way for the girl to survive until the last trial. Only then did his heart stand a chance. His brows knit, staring at the impossibly beautiful emerald waters and the cherry petals floating across it white as snow.

How does his heart stand a chance within such a tiny and broken girl? It's like those cherry petals trying to control where they fall only to be swallowed by a ravenous carp.

Meera squirms from her spot on the tatami floor, pushing up onto her elbow. She blinks bleary-eyed at Dragon before the blue irises round in horror and she flings herself back.

"Where am I? How did we get here?"

Dragon watches her calmly from the boat's rail, one foot propped against the slick wood and the other planted barefoot on the reed mat. An imprint of the mat marks her cheek with a reddened thatch pattern. As if noting his stare, Meera's fingers brush the indent along her cheek from where she had slept. She rises to her feet with a slow wobble and approaches the railing.

Red lanterns bob in the late afternoon breeze, a welcome warmth after the coldness of the sea and mountains. Other boats dot the calm river, ducking beneath stone-arched bridges and carrying extravagant parties down the canal accompanied by the soft tinkling of stringed instruments and laughter.

Meera's jaw goes slack as she takes in the expanse of buildings and docks on either side of the river. The capital city of Taiga pulses with energy and motion. "How did we get here?"

"The sacred pools are connected," Dragon says, reclining against the rail. "There's one in Taiga where the first trial is to start in an hour. I rented this boat to give us privacy until then. It's safer on the water."

She turns on him with fiery blue eyes and balled up fists. "Why didn't you wake me? What is the trial? Never mind"—she holds up a hand and shakes her head—"I'm tired of asking you questions. Dock this ship. Now."

"Please?" Dragon says, raising a brow. He dips a hand into the water that flows alongside the boat. It's beautifully crafted, a rare piece of art fashioned to distinguish it from the other houseboats.

Her lips purse and she crosses her arms. "Please."

"I'd prefer not to," Dragon says, sweeping to his feet. "I'm famished. Would you like something to eat before the trial? You'll need strength." He pulls aside the hanging curtain into the boat's main cabin. A low-lying table arranged with various dishes, elaborate paintings on the sliding doors, and soft cushions beckons. Meera enters, a slight hobble in her step as she takes a seat on the floor pillow.

He doesn't miss how she arches her back, shifting away from the pain. This trial will destroy her. Dragon takes the opposite seat and offers her a bowl filled with fresh simmered eel with sesame tofu and steaming rice.

She turns up her nose, tossing her matted blue hair, but the rumble of her stomach is unmistakable. Dragon pulls the bowl toward him and empties it before reaching for the next. Meera goes straight for the sweet rice wine. He blocks her hand, offering her water instead.

"Wine isn't good for my heart."

The look she gives is murderous.

"What's the trial?" she asks, lifting her chopsticks to take a battered lotus root from the tray. "And why do you look so worried? Think I'm going to win?"

Dragon smiles with a mouthful of sashimi and swallows hard. "On the contrary, I'm concerned that you'll lose. You can barely walk."

"But . . . you want me to lose." Her brows furrow.

By the stars, it makes her look like a painting, all color and blurred edges with a dash of soul. Dragon's stomach squeezes. He closes his eyes to shut out the meddlesome feelings that dare spring on him. He never had this problem as a dragon.

"You said the dragons promised you could have your heart back if I failed the tasks," she says. "Was there something you *forgot* to translate? Back home if a translator fails their duties, Papa sends them to the arctic prison colonies."

"Sounds like a man not to cross," Dragon says. "I see translating as a fluid art, like music. It conveys differently to each person depending on their relationship with the artist."

She shakes her head and takes another swipe at the wine, which he promptly snatches away. "That won't help you on the trial," he says. "But you're right, I didn't tell you everything. There wasn't much time for details. The trials are such that, should you fail, nothing will be left of my heart to save. Except for the third trial. That one I have every interest in your failure."

"Reassuring, I'm sure. So what are they? The trials." She

swallows hard, chin tilted up, trying to be brave. Few mortals would give Dragon such an indomitable stare if they knew what he was. Meera might not be strong enough for the trials—but she's brave enough.

"They're setting three assassins loose on Taiga tonight."

She pales. "Who are they hunting?"

His lips twist, hating the elders' sense of mercy. Which of them had devised this particular trial? It was unlike the Grand Elder to suggest a task so gruesome. "You. Be the last one standing, and you win."

Her eyes fall to the shutters blocking the windows and then to the banquet table. "I suppose that explains the boat. Harder to track us on the water. We couldn't just sail out of here to Ezo, could we?"

"You and I both know the waters between here and Ezo are too rough for a small vessel like this. And the dragons block the path in the strait. To make it home, you have to win the first trial."

"How? I'm not a fighter. And my back is killing me. I doubt my legs will hold up another day without my brace. Do you know anything about the assassins?"

Dragon sets aside the last of his meal and stands. "Come with me."

He leads her into the cabin's only room, a small square with a thatched roof and painted doors featuring two traditional entertainers in long silk robes with gold hairpins and red lips. But it's the subtle details that arrest his attention: the crest emblazoned on the painted kimonos, entwined hawk feathers within a circle —the motif of his mountain village up north. The reason he charted this boat instead of another—out of an abysmal desire for nostalgia. Never in a thousand years did he think of himself as nostalgic. This body will be the end of him.

Meera tucks into the room beside him, her cheeks flushing at the cramped space. His eyes catch on the sweep of her lashes across an imperfect cheek still marred by slumber. The black lashes guard her eyes like the wings of a raven. Why are his eyes constantly drawn to her?

He wouldn't call her beautiful. What is human beauty anyway? But the imperfections—like the million variations of a sunrise, the ragged path the clouds plow across the sky, the hazy dip of distant mountains—make him want to look a second time.

She clears her throat, a warm flush coloring her cheeks. "I hope you brought me in here to outfit me with weapons and not to stare at me."

Dragon blinks and schools his features. He hadn't realized he was staring. "Yes," he says and reaches into a narrow closet.

The brace he pulls out is nothing like the one she'd worn at his murder. His fingers fumble with the bare chestnut wood and the white straps made from tough muslin. "It's all I could find on such short notice," he says, holding it out to her.

Meera's eyes shine with emotion. "Dragon, you . . ." her voice is soft, disbelieving.

"Will it work? The merchant told me that the weight and balance vary based on the condition. Dragons have excellent photographic memory so I tried to draw him a picture of your last one and—"

"It's perfect." She takes the brace from his hands and slings it gracefully under her arms. It looks like a clunky walnut shell compared to her previous form-fitting brace. She smiles, radiant, as if he'd gifted her the Jewel of the Tides. "Thank you."

"It's to protect my heart," Dragon says, a breath knotting beneath his ribs. "I'm not helping you."

"I don't expect your help," she says. "But I'll need more than this to fight assassins."

She nudges him aside and begins ransacking the closet. She swipes a long scarf and hurls it to the floor, followed by a handful of gold hairpins and a silk robe. Then she brandishes a knife with a grin. "A dagger? Never thought you'd trust me with one of these again. Really, Dragon?"

"It's not trust," he says, jaw clenching. "It's survival. And Dragon is not my name."

She raises a brow as he pushes her hand down and turns the dagger away. "I thought you didn't give your name to mortal slugs?"

"You're more like a snail," he says, indicating the brace with a sweep of his eyes.

She laughs. It fills the narrow chamber like rain on a thatched roof.

"I shouldn't tell you. But I'm also tired of you calling me 'dragon' all the time. Just please don't yell my name when the assassins come to kill you. I'm forbidden from interfering."

"I won't be calling your name. I'd rather swear it."

"You can swear it if you like. I'd say it's a compliment as much as you swear about the saints."

"I—" She flushes red. "I shouldn't do that. And I never say it about the Bleeding Saint. He's different."

He nods. "My name is Soran."

"Soran, like the fishing song?" Meera's lips purse as she begins to hum and then sing. "Seagulls jabber on high . . . we won't give up fishing our whole lives! Soooran, soran."

Heat bristles up his neck. "They named it after me. I, uh, helped a fisherman once." She keeps humming, and Soran snatches the silk garment off the floor. "Put this on and strap the dagger to your brace. The assassins will be here in a few minutes."

Her smile fades at the reminder. "How will a silk dress help me defeat assassins?"

"It's a disguise," he says. "And it'll be harder for them to kill a noble lady than someone who looks like a drowned street waif. Now get dressed."

Soran turns and storms out the doors, shutting them with a

loud rattle. He presses a hand to his chest, a hollow ache squeezing his ribs at the missing heartbeat.

The girl doesn't stand a chance, and the dragons will be watching with their spies should either of them bend the rules. The Grand Elder made it clear that Soran couldn't touch the assassins, couldn't intervene in the trial physically. But if there's one thing a dragon is good at, it's being loyal. And Soran wouldn't stop until he found a way to rescue his heart.

"Hey, Soran."

He jumps at the sound of his name and the rattle of the sliding door. Meera peeks out from the painted screen with a scarf fastened around her blue hair, the noblewoman's robes absent and only her now-tattered hakama in place. He raises a brow. "I thought I told you to get ready?"

"I am," she says, grabbing his arm. "But you aren't. I've an idea to save both our hearts. You can't stop the assassins if they come after me, but no one said anything about if they come after *you.*"

Before he can protest, she drags him back into the little room. He nearly bolts for the door at the realization of what she's intending to do. But he doesn't.

She's right—why is that so hard to admit?—this ridiculous plan might save both their hearts.

CHAPTER 15
MEERA

SORAN DOES HIS JOB BEAUTIFULLY. Even I couldn't tell him apart from a courtesan. As long as he's quiet and keeps his head down, no one will know it's him and not me dressed like a riverside entertainer.

My lips twitch toward a smile as I trail several meters behind him. He wears the noblewoman's rich silk robes tied at the waist with an elaborate obi that took me nearly a full thirty minutes to tie into a butterfly like I'd seen Seira do for my sister. My arms ached by the time I'd finished.

"Humans are too enslaved to what others think of them," he'd complained, glowering at the long-sleeved silk. "No wonder you're not free to care about other people with so much focus on yourself."

I may have tied the obi too tight in response, but he'd be fine. Anyone with a back that straight and the strength of five men should be fine fighting in a dress.

Soran walks ahead of me and summons a rickshaw, head tucked down beneath a western-styled hat and feigning a limp, as planned. I can only imagine his scowl. Few men would endure dressing in formal robes and face paint to save someone they hate, but he's not doing it for me.

My second heart beats treacherously fast in agreement.

I scour the darkening cobbled street for any sign of the assassins. On rooftops, beneath bridges, tucked into the thousands of alleys stitching the capital city in a chaotic weave. Whoever they are, the assassins were probably informed that their target is a crippled princess with blue hair who can't walk long distances. They won't be expecting an old lady with a basket of rice balls or a dragon in disguise.

A shadow moves outside the nearest store awning, and it takes all my focus not to jump in alarm. I'd love nothing more than to put my back against a wall and hole up somewhere, but Bastian's lessons tell me otherwise. *The safest place to hide is in the open.*

I walk along the side of the street lined with brick-and-mortar stores and pop-up venders hawking cabbages or the latest trinkets from the west: pocket watches, flames in metal canisters, and bowler hats. Dealers slink along the narrow side alleys, displaying crooked wares, boar teeth hawked as dragon fangs and vials claiming to be magical elixirs.

I turn my attention to the lanterns flickering to life along the street. Each one a gas flame trapped inside a glass cylinder, their copper pedestals imprinted with the seal of this city—Casmir's seal.

Does he know that I'm alive? What is happening in Ezo?

I shake away the thought and lean against my wooden cane, a basket of seaweed-speckled rice balls nestled in the crook of my arm. A shawl spreads across my back to imitate an old lady and hide my wooden brace. It feels like so long ago that I wore it proudly, boldly, but hiding it is a matter of survival today.

"Evening News!" a boy shouts, practically skipping through the crowds and brandishing a roll of paper like a sword.

A few purveyors shoo him away, others plunk thick zeni into

his palm and snatch their papers with gloved hands. They hold the fresh inked parchment to the glowing lantern light. A few of the poorer shop owners peer over their customers' shoulders for a scrap of news.

My eyes dart to Soran who slips from view in a plush rickshaw pulled by a man with a wide-brimmed hat and forked running shoes. He hunkers down as if to evade notice, acting the part as planned. I only hope the assassins go for the bait. If they target Soran by accident, he won't be breaking the dragons' rules to take them out.

I need to keep up—somehow—but my spine refuses to move faster than a snail.

"A bit of news?" I rap the street waif gently on the ankle with my cane.

He startles, and I slip a rice ball into his pocket. His eyes swivel to make sure no one notices the deal, and then he leans in to whisper. If only his voice were as loud as his smell—he reeks of northern garlic and acrid ink.

"The Princess of Ezo tried to stab the Duke of Taiga and they fed her to the dragons," he says, his voice sticky-sweet from the salacious gossip. "They say she was overcome by sorcery or a plague and lost her mind. But the Duke still loves her and is protecting Ezo, blah blah"—he shrugs and steps back—"I think they're keeping him prisoner. Why else hasn't he returned home? He's the Master of the Tournament and Ezo's nothin' but a block of ice."

Not waiting for an answer, the boy slides through the crowd again. "Get the news! Breaking news!"

They think I tried to stab Casmir?

The news keels me over faster than the pain in my legs. I stagger into a flower shop, squashed between fronds of cherry blossoms and yellow rapeseed, catching my breath.

Who could have reported such a thing? I didn't pull the

dagger out until after I met the dragon. And Casmir's still in Ezo? Why hasn't he stopped the rumors?

It's hard to breathe. I remember the assassins and try to examine the square, but too many eyes skim over me with a flicker of curiosity. I'm drawing too much attention.

"Do you need help, miss?" asks an aproned girl at the flower stand.

"I'm fine, thank you," I say, tilting my head to examine her. Isn't she too young for a trained flower artisan? An apprentice perhaps.

She smiles, her eyes shaded like pink half-moons. "In that case, you're crushing my daisies."

"Oh, I didn't mean—"

A pair of pruning shears cuts across the petals and continues forward directly at my chest with an audible *whoosh*. I spin to the side. This time, the young woman kicks at my shins, buckling me. The shears plunge down and smack against my breastbone. My breath catches at the impact. Sharp metal wedges into my wooden brace, right over my hearts.

I thank the saints for Soran's lifesaving gift and jerk the shears from the splintered wood. The puncture nearly ripped a hole through the brace to my sternum.

The girl's hand shoots to my throat, but I smash a vase of flowers against her ear. She reels back, giving me enough space to dart aside.

"Thief!" the florist assassin shouts, grabbing a second pair of shears.

I bolt down the pedestrian-filled walkway. *How had the assassin found me so quickly?*

I look back and chide myself. Bastian would say never look back, always be one step ahead. The girl is nowhere in sight as a crowd sweeps her from view. Rickshaws and horse-drawn carriages crisscross an open square ahead where the street parts into four different roads for merchant travel. Soran and I had planned to meet back at the river if we got separated. But now that doesn't seem like a good idea.

Had the assassins found him too?

I stop at the crossing, breathing hard. A chill of sweat beads down my back. The female assassin could be anywhere. A thousand scents and sounds infiltrate my senses, my mind buzzing with ideas. The dagger tucked inside my brace is now slick with sweat. I'd used one on a dragon, but could I wield it against a human?

If only Bastian were here . . . or Casmir.

A dog barks at my feet and I'm jostled in the shoulder as the crowd pushes forward. My hearts skip a few beats. I hobble across the square, shoulders pressed against men in velvet hats and stiff suits, women in buttoned dresses with wooden umbrellas. Rickshaws wait on the road for their turn to cross, runners dripping with sweat. I peer into the soft velvet seats and beneath the black awnings for a glimpse of Soran.

Suddenly, pain scorches my left foot and I fall. The crowd parts around me as the ground rises to meet my face. I block just in time, my forearms slamming into the hard earth, sparing my head. No one stops as I curl into a ball and reach for my ankle, which is suddenly burning with pain. Sandaled feet shuffle away from me like mice on the sidewalk.

The metal tines of a rake grate the ground beside my ankle, stained with blood. A farmer's tool made from bamboo and iron, not the weapon of an assassin.

"What year were you born?" the voice is indifferent and cruel.

I sit up, one hand clamped over my bleeding ankle spiked by the rake. The wound is deep. Blood oozes between my fingers as I bite back a cry.

The man swings the pronged rake over his shoulder, the crowd parting for him with a few disgruntled cries. He's taller than Dragon and as muscled as Cass, but the dark indigo jerkin and pants don't hide the tattoos inked across his skin—a clear sign of the notorious gangs, the bakuto, that roam Taiga.

Motifs from almost every noble family mark his tanned arms and neck. The five teardrops of the Katsuma clan, the royal oak tree of the Ainur, even the interlocking hawk feathers I'd seen on the houseboat. But one motif stands out from the rest. An ink-black dragon claws at his left eye and another at his right—the dual dragon crest of Taiga.

A whimper forms in the back of my throat as my thoughts spiral. The man tilts his head, his pointed straw farmer's hat casting a shadow over me.

"What year were you born?" he asks again, this time his massive sandaled foot stomps on my punctured ankle.

I shriek and attempt to kick with my other leg, but it's no use. Fire shoots up my leg. "The year of the rabbit," I gasp, my voice twisted in pain. "Why do you care?"

Dual hearts thunder in my chest, the blood pumping too fast. My vision blurs. *The dagger.* I could reach for it, but he'd easily knock it from my grasp with the length of the rake at this distance.

"Hmm," he ponders, twisting his foot on my ankle. "I usually say it's not your lucky year before collecting a kill, but this *is* your year. I've not skinned a rabbit yet. Or added the bunny in the moon to my collection of family crests."

My breath shudders. He knows who I am. My mother's motif, the rabbit in the talons of the moon, the one stitched on my bedside blanket and hung in the tapestries of our home. This assassin hunts royal families for fun.

Oh saints, I'm going to die.

I grit my teeth. No. I won't curse the saints. It's not they who stand aside and do nothing while people suffer. It's the crowd, the masses, the people afraid of standing out who refuse to do what's right. "It's not a bunny," I spew through gritted teeth.

"And you won't taint my mother's crest by adding it to your filthy skin."

He laughs and swings the rake in my face threateningly. "You don't get a choice."

"I always have a choice." I grab the spiked end of the rake and shove the handle into his gut. He staggers back surprised, freeing my ankle.

I stand with effort and attempt to run, but my legs only hobble. Tears threaten my eyes. Of all the times for my joints to give out. Maybe I can make it to the patrol office, surely they will help me.

The assassin laughs behind me, and a hard bamboo pole smacks against my leg. I hiss between clenched teeth and stumble.

A cry for help lodges in my throat. I said I wouldn't shout his name. But there is no one else. "Soran!" My knee hits the ground as my leg buckles. "Soran, help!"

The assassin rears his head back, scanning the crowd. Several bystanders stop and stare at the two of us before eyeing my attacker's tattoos and hurrying on their way. The thug pops his neck and grins. "Looks like no one is coming."

"He'll come," I say, and my second heart beats fiercely as if it would fly from my chest and fight the assassin on its own.

The tattooed man hits me again with the blunt end of the bamboo rake. Pain explodes along my side. Then he grabs me by the waist as if I were a five-kilogram sack of rice and hauls me off the street. He throws me against a wall in the nearest alley, a slash of moonlight filtering through a gap in the buildings.

My hand flies to my stomach as if to calm a panicked breath, but I'm ready to pull the dagger from my brace at his next move. I have only one shot. He needs to be close for it to work. I don't have the mobility to attack if he retreats or deflects. One chance.

"I had her first," a familiar, silky voice purrs.

A feverish chill runs down my spine. The girl from the flower shop.

"Stay out of this, Kobaya." He sneers, scanning the darkening alley roofs. "How much did they offer you?"

The girl whistles from a slanting rooftop, and then she's squatting next to me in her pasty green apron dotted with daisies. A pair of shears presses against my throat. "Revenge," she purrs. "And gold. Enough to buy my freedom."

"I can pay you more," I say, blinking back the heat that beads sweat on my brow.

The girl's shears press tighter against my throat. She might slash the blade any second. There's no time to counter it with my dagger.

"How kind," she says. "But I don't trust death bargains." She leans over me and tears my shawl away, exposing cerulean hair piled on my head in a long braid with gold pins. She grins, knowing she's found her mark.

Heat burns through my blood, clouding my mind with fever. I'm not sure if it's that wretched dragon heart or the pain swelling in my ankle, but I've little time to think about it. The tattooed assassin lashes at the girl with his rake. She ducks, keeping the shears at my throat with a steady hand, and the rake slaps against the wall with an empty clatter.

I seize the opportunity to snatch the dagger and wedge the thin handle between the shears and my neck. Kobaya jerks her weapon to finish me off and then frowns. The eerie clash of metal grates as my dagger deflects her shears. She growls, her attention torn between me and the other assassin who takes another swing at her.

With my free hand, I snatch a hairpin and swipe at her eyes.

The girl screams, reeling back and clutching her face. A jagged line oozes over her right eye where the hairpin had sliced. Blood beads from her thick lashes and down her youthful cheek. "You terror!" she shrills, lunging at me.

My heart hammers, but the other one gives an uneven flutter. Fever slicks my skin and I shake my head to keep alert. Kobaya looks younger in her shock and anger, like a child who didn't choose this path but was forced into it. It causes me to hesitate.

The tattooed assassin's rake barrels toward her. Kobaya leaps over it and somersaults to block my exit from the alley. I fist the golden hairpin tight in one hand and the dagger in the other, forcing myself to stand with the help of the wall. My legs quake, fever sapping the remaining dregs of my energy. Pain throbs from my ankle.

Was the rake poisoned?

A flash of copper glints in Kobaya's palm.

"Is that a trivet?" I ask, gaping at the round teapot holder.

She rips a soft cover from the edge, revealing a nine-pointed throwing star. She bares her teeth as the tattooed assassin lunges again. But the giant is no match for her speed. Kobaya leaps, easily evading him, and charges toward me.

Dokun dokun. My second heart counts the seconds, the beauty of the metal star, the arch of the pearlescent moonlight.

A third shadow enters the alley, changing my calculations—a girl with an elmwood cloak and eyes blue as fire. An Ainur wayfinder.

No one's ever survived a battle with the benders of fate before. I've never even seen one, only heard about them from Seira when she told tales of her people in the Northern Winterwilds, hidden deep in the Ezo mountains, the special few born with magic and ice in their veins.

Blood cakes the wayfinder's woven coat threaded from elmwood as she enters the shaft of early moonlight. The third assassin. But whose blood is on her coat? My eyes widen in horror. I scream Soran's name.

It can't be.

Don't let it be.

Not his blood.

CHAPTER 16

CASMIR

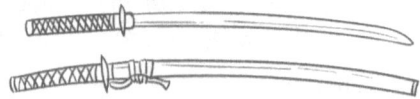

CASMIR LOWERS the binoculars with a gloved hand, a cold wind barreling from the west and unsettling his horse. He opens an insulated canister and takes a warm drag of coffee. The heat burns his throat and settles in his stomach like fuel. It would be unholy to patrol the Northern Winterwilds without coffee.

Unthinkable, really.

The Rusan commander had seen him, their eyes connecting over the narrow strait that remained frozen for most of the year. It was too early for boats in this region of Ezo, but the Rusan general had equipped an icebreaker to pave the way for the fleet. General Alexi Reznik stood atop the commanding vessel in a bundle of black bear fur, a spark of victory in his eyes pinning the top of the cliff where Casmir and his scouts waited.

Even from there, the loud crunch of the icebreaker grates over their ears and causes the lingering snow to tremble. The vessel's iron plow cuts large sheets of ice as its deep metal hull crashes over the surface, just like the Rusan forces would trample over Silverwood if they made it inland with their superior armory and slash and burn tactics.

The dragons hadn't intercepted the encroaching ships. In

fact, they'd been sighted and were reportedly ignoring the activity in their waters. This was all the proof the eight kingdoms needed to confirm that Ezo's borders were exposed for the first time in a century. Open. Vulnerable.

Casmir eyes the smattering of ships, twenty-five at his last count, now coasting toward the westernmost harbor of Orsai.

"What do you command, my lord?" a soldier boy asks, shivering beneath his oversized wool uniform. His horse shudders, too, thick brown withers flinching at the dusting of snow turning the supposedly spring air frigid. Casmir had requested this soldier specifically, the brother of Meera's personal maid since she seemed to care for her servants. He couldn't fathom why. Still, he would see to it that the things she loved stood protected.

Casmir waits until the coffee has fully settled in his stomach before turning the horse with a nudge of the reins. "We invite General Reznik for brunch," he says. "And then we take him back to the castle, by force if necessary."

The young soldier pales, though it's hard to tell in the cold how much is from the weather or nerves. "Won't that be considered an . . . act of war?"

Casmir smiles and leans over his saddle. "Not when he sees that the ambassador of Rusa has already contracted the killing sleep—"

"But he hasn't yet. He's quarantined in the east wing . . ."

Casmir's eyes cut sideways to silence him. "General Reznik won't want him returned. Or perhaps we *should* return the ambassador." A twisted smile dimples his cheek. "It would stall the invasion. Provide us three days to prepare a more . . . permanent solution."

"You mean, release the killing sleep on Rusa. But won't that risk spreading the contagion outside the palace? Even in the city itself?" The boy eyes the ships with a furrowed brow, his voice raw from the cold.

"No choice comes without risk." Casmir straightens and

snaps the horse's reins. "It's the ones willing to pay the price who rule the world, remember that, Kazuya."

"I've no wish to rule the world," he mutters, turning his horse. "Just for me and my sister to belong in it."

"Then stay with me," Casmir says, signaling for the scouts to make their way to the beach to intercept the general. "And you won't lose."

Barging into Silverwood castle with an angry Rusan general on his heels caused more than a stir. But Casmir liked the attention. It fed smoothly into his plans no matter what words the King of Ezo would dish out later. Winter boots clomping across the marbled floor, Casmir led the general to the banquet hall where his ambassador waited.

Of course, General Reznik could smell a trap hundreds of yards away and promptly attempted to escape. With a flick of his wrist, Casmir ordered the scouts to drag the protesting general the rest of the way—not a pleasant journey down three flights of stairs.

"It's not a trick," Casmir says, opening the enormous banquet doors with gloved hands. "I take my word seriously, General. You asked for the release of your ambassador. He's right here. And you're going to take him back, as you demanded."

General Reznik narrows his gaze on Casmir, hatred written across his stony face. "Why are you helping Ezo?" he snarls. "You're just trying to claim this island for Taiga. You've been expanding from the start."

"I could say the same for you, General." Casmir raises a brow, his jaw tight. "All the eight kingdoms want a piece of Ezo. But I'm not one of them." He offers a sad smile. "It's for love, if you must know. I take my vow with the princess to the grave. And anyone who crosses me likewise."

Casmir nods to the scouts and they haul the general toward the putrid banquet hall, shouldering him through the doors. Casmir was used to the smell by now. He'd visited more often than he'd like. When he couldn't sleep at night, which was becoming far more frequent. Or when the dragons cried too close to the shore, reminding him of Meera in her white wedding dress facing the monster.

He was going to fix it—all of it. The kingdom, the curse, and his broken heart.

Casmir twists the ruby ring around his finger as General Reznik shouts in the background. He'd found the ambassador's body and was no doubt shriveling away from it in fear of the curse.

The bluish tint on Runa's skin is now purple, creeping up to her hairline. She doesn't have much time. Jey had found some promising elements for an antidote, a toxin similar to the poison she'd ingested, but they'd been unable to synthesize it for a cure yet.

"Take them back to the ships," Casmir orders from outside the room.

The scouts wrap the ambassador in sheets and carry his body out the doors, wrestling a snarling Reznik behind them with his mouth gagged. Casmir felt sure that Bastian would approve of his handling of the situation. There was something pirate-like about sending a plague onto a host of ships.

He casts one last look at Runa before the doors shut. Her time wanes like the moon. And it's not just for Meera's sake that he needs to save her. Come tomorrow morning there will be a whole world trying to contain the killing sleep. And if he intends to rule it, he'll have to cure it first.

"CASMIR!" Never had his name been yelled so crudely since the day he got the scar beneath his eye. Still, Casmir does not flinch. It belittles the King of Ezo to yell. It shows the fear behind the rage.

"What have you done?" the king demands from his throne. "The queensguard tells me you've let a victim of the plague out into the streets. Are you mad?"

Casmir rolls his neck before meeting the king's gaze. "Only mad that anyone dare assault Ezo on its own ground. Rusa is amassed to the west, reports tell of Seshu coming from the south to avenge their prince. I'm sending a message."

"I should send a message by demanding your head." The king leans forward on thick arms with an impenetrable scowl, but his lips pinch together, restrained from saying what they both know is true. The emperor would never allow it.

"It's difficult to rescind a message," Casmir says. "Especially if it involves someone's head. But you needn't worry about Ezo. I took precautions not to unleash the sickness in this kingdom, only in Rusa."

The king snorts and leans back in his throne. "What of my son? Have you found him?"

Casmir bows, whiskey-colored hair falling into his green eyes. "Your best Shadow scouts are on the matter," he says. "It won't be long now until they find him."

The king nods, his square jaw tight with displeasure. Long cut eyes, darker brown than the deepest wood in the Winterwilds, stare down at Casmir from the silver throne. "What of Taiga? I would speak to the emperor about a partnership. He can't be pleased that you're extending your stay in Ezo."

"My uncle isn't interested in treaties. He prefers taking," he says. "But I can sway him."

"You speak confidently for the son of a disgraced warrior. But you have more than made up for your father's lack of judgment, not to mention your brothers. You've gained the emperor's favor. I only wish my daughter hadn't been such a fool. No matter—I will speak with the emperor myself. I don't trust mediators, no matter how influential."

Casmir stiffens, taking a deep breath. "It's not advisable to speak of the princess in that manner."

"I'll not be advised on my speech."

Then you're not a true ruler. Or father.

Casmir's thoughts swirl into a maelstrom. Meera reminded him of everything he wanted to protect, everything that was right and good in the world. She made him want to be good. This man didn't deserve to have her as a daughter.

"The emperor will not leave Taiga to meet you," Casmir says, hands fisted at his sides. The king is sharper than he'd expected, gripping every piece on the proverbial chess board with an iron grasp. But the control is because he's afraid of losing. Casmir releases his fists and turns to walk away. That's the difference between them.

Casmir had long since decided to make fear a friend instead of an enemy.

He grimaces and the scar across his face tugs at the movement, burning with memory. His father, a prominent warrior, had married into a noble class and attempted to carry both swords. But warriors seldom make good politicians or have much patience for the nobility. He had dueled illegally in the streets of Taiga, and won, but the police detained him and publicly humiliated him. After that, he pressured his five sons to show the nobility that the warrior class would never die. Never give up. Never be shamed again.

His brothers excelled in weaponry and strength. They strove to put Casmir down at every turn. He wasn't the youngest, but he'd been the smallest, the one with the biggest smile, the most zest for life, and with Mother's heart in the palm of his hand.

It was spring when his father and brothers came home drunk, celebrating an invitation from the emperor. One of them would join the Dual Dragon Invitational to become an apprentice in the castle, in the emperor's own court.

Father leaned drunkenly over the table, upsetting a tureen of radish stew and a rare bowl of simmered beef. "It's the perfect opportunity," he'd slurred. "One of you will stab that blind dragon in the back. The Endo clan will have its revenge."

Mother's eyes snapped up. "You'll do no such thing to the emperor. Have you no honor?"

"I've only shame, woman," he said, hurling a glass bottle across the table at her.

Casmir jumped to his feet, but Mother laid a hand on his arm. The bottle had missed, but barely.

"The emperor doesn't deserve that throne," Father continued, each word more slurred than the last. "Married a pauper too. His judgment is worse than his blindness. Imagine one of my sons sitting on the throne instead."

"I would see them serving at his side," Momma said. "There is honor in service. Only shame in taking. Speak no more of this. You're drunk. Tomorrow all will be forgotten."

But Father didn't want to forget. His shame grew every day like a disease and Casmir's brothers lived by it, fed from the same spoon. Father grabbed the tea pot and dashed its contents at Momma's face.

"Service is for the ugly and poor," he spewed, rage contorting his face. "You can join them, but not me."

He stormed from the room, Casmir's brothers trailing after him like fearful pups though they were all bigger than him. Only Mitsuo stayed behind with a worried crease on his brow.

"Get out," Casmir screamed at him until his youngest brother fled. Then he rushed to Momma and held her face in his hands. Red, splotched, burned.

She bit back tears and held his hands as if holding the world, her strength so small but fierce. Those hands that had fed them all. Given them all life.

"Momma, I'll fix this. You'll be all right. What do I do?" Casmir said, swallowing the panic and forcing himself to be strong for her.

"You forgive," she said. "But we need to go someplace safe. Will you take me to Auntie's?"

He nodded, dabbing her face with a cloth, unsure what to do. "I will. I'll go get her."

But Casmir didn't fetch his Auntie first. He ran after his father with the family sword, trying hard not to drag it as the weight pulled down on him. The same sword his father had used in that duel against the nobleman years ago. The one his grandfather had made in the Kagano mountains. He ran after his father with a fury no wind could tame.

His father blocked his blows with a sloppy defense. Drunkenness showed red on his face and in the slip of his foot. Casmir held the sword angled to his throat. Mother's words rang in his ears and her burned face twisted his mind into a raging knot that nearly stopped his heart.

Forgive.

He lowered the sword. *Forgive, how?*

Father seized the moment and motioned for his brothers to restrain him. The two eldest held him stiffly as Father beat him until he crumpled. Then Father pulled out a dagger and slit his face.

"I never want to see you again," his father said as the brothers threw him to the ground. "I hope you go blind after protecting the emperor like that. He's responsible for this!"

"It wasn't for the emperor." Casmir coughed, attempting to push up onto his hands and knees. "It's for Mother. If you can't see that, you're the blind one."

That was the last time Casmir had spoken to his father. After that, he had done everything in his power to take a spot beside the emperor and shame the man who no longer deserved the role of father.

He protected his mother, bringing her into the castle and giving her a comfortable life. But she didn't care for comfort. Momma only wanted peace and for Casmir to let go of his hate. But he could not do the one thing she asked of him. He couldn't forgive. Not again.

But Momma had.

And like Meera, she wasn't afraid of her scars.

CHAPTER 17

MEERA

THE WAYFINDER DOESN'T MINCE WORDS. She doesn't have to. The two assassins pause in the alley, eyeing her with mild interest. Kobaya's jaw clenches, sizing up the new rival, while the tattooed man squares his shoulders and ditches his rake in favor of a katana strapped to his back. The wayfinder doesn't smile. Blue eyes like a too-bright flame latch onto me.

"Meera, is it?" she says, her voice like water and ice. Two things which exist simultaneously like heaven and earth, flame and smoke, always touching, always sharing, but never at peace with each other.

"Yes," I say, my voice slick with fever. I resist the effect her voice has on me, the way my fingers want to loosen on the dagger.

"Did you poison an immortal being?" she asks, her eyes burning brighter. "A dragon?"

"We don't have time for this," growls the tattooed assassin, pointing the blade at her. "The police will be here shortly. And only one of us can get the prize. She's already dying from poison, so it will be me."

Poison. How long do I have?

Kobaya raises a brow, scanning the wayfinder's tattered elmwood cloak. "Stay out of this. Where did you come from anyway? Climb out of a tree?"

The wayfinder closes her eyes and takes a deep, calming breath. It seems impossible with the anger hanging thick like a curtain, a sword pointed at her, and Kobaya's stealthy movements closing the gap. When the wayfinder opens her eyes, Kobaya is almost in front of her. The tattooed assassin attacks. But the wayfinder dances out of the way without a nick in her cloak. She stops a few paces from me and turns to face her attackers who trip out into the alley entrance with puzzled expressions.

The tattooed assassin sways like a young pine in the breeze before he collapses against the wall and slides to the ground. Kobaya turns to stare at the wayfinder. Her eyes widen and a tear spills down her bloodied cheek.

"I'll avenge your mother," the wayfinder says gently, stepping forward to catch Kobaya as she crumples.

It's only then that I notice the single wound on their necks. *How had I not seen her attack?* It seemed like she had only danced away from their strikes, not returned with an offense.

I watch in mute shock as the wayfinder sweeps Kobaya's milk brown hair from her face and lays her body on the ground as if setting a flower into a pond. With a gentle movement, she closes the eyes of both assassins. Then she stands and walks toward me.

Only the face I stare into isn't one of pity. *Oh, hearts . . .*

I drop the dagger and let it clatter on the ground. The assassins were better equipped than I and fell before her in minutes. I take a fevered breath and meet the wayfinder's cold stare with my own. Only my legs don't get the notice to act strong. My left hip buckles and I stagger against the alley wall, bracing myself. There's no running with a mangled foot and poison throbbing in my veins.

"What did you do to him?" I ask, eyeing the bloodied cloak.

"The dragon . . . or the man?"

I gulp. *Is this a test?* "Soran," I say.

The wayfinder's eyes train on me, emotionless. How had the dragons managed to recruit an Ainur wayfinder to do their dirty work? The messengers of the Path who dwell in the northern lands of Ezo don't make deals. Papa had tried more than once to forge a treaty with them. They keep to themselves, to the forests, and to the Winterwilds.

"What did you do?" I ask again, wishing the blistering pain in my foot would stop. "Where is he?"

"I would never harm a dragon," she says stopping within arm's reach. "But men are another story. And he is neither without a heart." Her eyes narrow on me like an accusation.

"It was an accident. I was trying to save my sister. Soran understands that. And he's not without a heart. I plan to give it back."

"It's too late for that," she says. "The laws of this world are unforgiving. I can't let another dragon heart turn dark."

"Another? What do you mean?"

"They didn't tell you," she says, her mind visibly ticking beneath those icy blue eyes. "I volunteered to end your life to prevent this disaster from falling on the world again. But I wonder . . . be still, Princess, or you will end like them." She nods to the two bodies lying in the alley.

Obediently, I freeze.

The wayfinder scans me from head to foot with her sharp eyes. This close, I notice that she's about the same age as me, a girl of seventeen or eighteen winters. Her hair is a thick raven black falling to her waist with a voluminous wave. Sharp cheekbones and long cut eyes give her a fierce impression, but the smooth chestnut skin and gentle shape of her lips suggest a kindness hidden behind that imposing exterior.

Her eyes narrow as she presses two fingers against my forehead. "Don't move."

A tremor quivers up my spine, but I match her glare. "Tell me if Soran's okay."

She closes her eyes, an irritated tweak in her brow. "He will be," she says. "If you don't move. Don't try anything."

Reluctantly, I obey.

The wayfinder takes a deep breath, her fingers pressing firm against my brow. A shudder passes over her and she removes her hand. "I won't kill you," she says. "Our paths are too threaded. For better or worse, I cannot tell."

I step aside, biting back the stabbing pain in my foot. "What do you mean? What did you do?"

"You need to leave." Her eyes bore into mine, as if she'd just seen something horrible and wonderful all at once. Like the beauty of a sky ablaze with color and the fire behind it burning an entire forest.

"But what of the dragons and the trial? What did you see? I know what you are, the paths you foretell. I'm not unfamiliar with the Ainur."

"I am not a fortune teller," she says darkly. "I interpret the paths as the Saint shows them to me, but it's always for his will, not mine. To see life and protect it. But I can't make sense of this path. I can't see the end or the beginning. Only that it exists and so it must be honored. I've seen many paths, but this . . ."

A tear glistens in her eye. She doesn't bother to wipe it away. It's a gift to her people, the Ainur respect the water from ice to snow to the blood in their veins. Recognizing it as a gift, I bow at the shoulders. "Thank you for sparing me. What will the dragons do now?"

"I don't know. But take care, Meera. I wouldn't trade paths with you, not for all the gold in Taiga. Fate can be a cruel thing, but destiny is still yours to write."

The wayfinder turns to leave, but I call after her. "And Soran? Where is he?"

A wry smile touches her face as she sweeps the hem of her cloak to the side. A red gash carves across her thigh and seeps through the thick weave of elm bark. "He's one of the few who's marked me. I think he'll be all right."

I blink and the wayfinder is gone. Clatter from the main street fills my ears, along with a shrill whistle and the storming feet of Taigan militia. Men in black uniforms with white belts and studded batons sweep into the alley, shouting over the dead bodies. I'm barraged by questions and at least five city patrolmen. But I stare at where the wayfinder had disappeared, her words echoing in my head.

She'd seen my future, I'm sure of it. Spared me from inevitable death at her hands, but . . . I can't shake the fear that whatever future she'd seen had been worse than dying.

"It's the Ezo princess!" one of the patrolmen shouts.

An officer lifts me roughly in his arms and carries me through the street to a partially covered cart filled with straw. Chills rack my spine as the fever turns to ice and then hot again.

"Wait," I mumble. "I need to find my friend."

"Your friends are dead," the guard holding me says. "Worry about yourself. They say you tried to murder the duke. You might not have taken a fancy to him, but people around here look up to the duke since he won his title. You're coming with us until we get answers."

"I've done no such thing," I say, shoving my elbow into his chest. "I'm the Princess of Ezo. Put me down."

He does, dropping me into the back of the cart and slamming the half-door shut. A manacle snaps around my wrist, its chain bolted to a hitch at the rear of the cart. "The princess is going to be tried for the attempted murder of the Duke of Taiga," another guard sneers, pulling a cigarette from his pocket. "Enjoy prison, *Your Highness*."

"No! You've got it wrong," I say. "Ask him. Ask the duke."

The cart lunges forward in answer. I shove against the back gate to free myself. The chain rattles, but no matter how hard I pull on it, the metal refuses to budge.

Crowds eye me with curiosity, and not a few ring out jeers. One even pelts me with a cabbage. *How had I failed so spectacularly? How had Soran managed to wound the wayfinder and get away with it? Where is he?*

He wasn't by the rickshaw, and he hadn't followed the wayfinder. Had something else happened to him? It's not like a dragon to leave his heart unprotected.

My hearts beat in sync with each other for the first time. Both give a panicked thrum like a bird trapped in a cage, swirling in my chest and begging to be set free.

I've never been in prison before, at least not on this side of the bars. The cart took over an hour trundling across the city and into the outskirts. Green rice paddies stretch as far as I can see, reflecting the full moon and the mountains in the distance. By the time we reach the prison, I've worn myself hoarse demanding they release me and notify the Ezo ambassador of my condition.

My cries fall on deaf ears.

"Welcome to Fuchu prison," the warden says upon seeing me and motioning for the guards to take me to one of the radial wings surrounding the guard house. "Usually, we house murderers in that wing"—he points to a long row of cells at his right—"but considering your noble origins, we'll throw you in with the common riffraff instead while you wait for your trial. I hope you rot after what you tried to do to the duke."

"I didn't do anything," I protest. It's not exactly true—I did *kiss* Cass then leave him at the altar, but they won't care to know that.

"Walk." The guard shoves me in the back with a spiked staff.

Glowering, I do as he says and hobble into the prison wing. The stench hits me first, the putrid smell of urine and damp wood. It's like walking into a pig stable with slatted wood walls and short square doors, cages for animals. The officer grabs my hair and shoves my head down toward a cell. "Get in."

My good heel digs into the stone floor in protest. I won't be bowed like a beast in a crate. "Notify the Ezo authorities first. It's law," I say, knowing he won't listen. "I have a right to see the ambassador."

"Maybe you do. But no one will see you at this time of night. Get in."

"I need a healer." I lean against the nearest wall for support and hold out my injured foot.

"In the morning."

The guard squeezes the back of my neck and shoves me forward. Coughs and jeers sound from the nearby stalls, but I can't see inside any of them. Gritting my teeth, I bend and crawl inside the cell. The door slams behind me, bolted with not one but three iron locks.

My head brushes the ceiling which greets me with a shower of dust. I sit on the floor, tucking my shawl beneath me in a vain attempt to keep the fleas and filth away. The pain in my ankle is now a sweltering throb, the fever a steady heat that slicks my parched throat. *Poison. How long do I have?*

I will not cry. It won't do any good. My arms curl around my knees.

Dread pools in my stomach at the thought of dying here, locked away like a criminal. Flashes of memory assail me in the dark. The way I'd kissed Casmir only to betray his trust, the way I'd plunged the dagger into Soran's heart, even the way I'd cursed the saints.

And then there's the inherent disorder in my blood, leaving me weak and crooked—worthless. All my attempts to save my sister and the queendom have been in vain. I dig my nails into the palms of my hands, and then stare at the crescent shapes. I won't cry.

I peer between the wooden cracks, but all is dark outside. An idea strikes me. Taking off my brace, I angle the corners of the wooden shell at the outside wall where there's a small opening to pass night soil. If I can wedge the slats far enough apart, they might snap. As long as I work quietly, I could be out of here before morning. True, the ambassador might help me if I wait until tomorrow. But with the chaos in Ezo, he might not even be at his post. And poison has its own timeline.

It's too risky to wait.

I work until my hands ache and my fingertips blister. Hours pass. The fever worsens until I begin to see things. My eyes droop and the muscles in my arms have gone stiff. The opening has moved several centimeters, enough to almost slip my upper arm through. But I'll never break it open before dawn.

Who am I to save a kingdom? I can't even save myself. What will take me first—the fever or the guards the next morning? Dark thoughts rap against my mind like acorns pelting a window.

I dart upright. The sound isn't in my head.

An acorn flies through the widening crack and rolls to my feet. I pinch it between my aching fingers in wonderment.

Plink! Another pops against my skull.

I hiss, rubbing the spot and peer through the slat.

"I thought about leaving you in here," a familiar voice whispers from outside. "But my heart wouldn't like it."

I drop the brace and search the darkened farmland outside, hope beating a wicked dash against my ribs. "Soran? How did you find me?"

"I followed my heart."

"I'm serious," I say, throwing an acorn toward the sound of his voice.

"If I told you, then I couldn't track you anymore," he amends. "Now quiet, they'll hear."

I nod, though he can't possibly see me, and fumble to secure my brace with numb fingers. The backside of the wooden shell chafes my skin, but I'm beyond caring. There's no sign of anyone outside except the warm voice that had whispered and the acorns in my palm. I crane my head, listening for the guards or the stir of other prisoners—all is quiet.

"How are you going to get me out?"

Silence.

"Soran?" I press my face between the slats. *Where did he go?*

The rattle of keys in the lock answers me and the door grinds open. Soran's chest swells with a sharp inhale as our eyes meet, then he looks away. "Are you coming, or do I have to drag you out?"

I shake my head mutely and climb from the cell on hands and knees. I collapse onto the cold stone floor in the prison hall and force myself to straighten. Every bone in my body begs for me to stop moving.

Soran watches me with a sour expression, as if it's my fault that he has to be awake at this unholy hour and breathing in urine. He lifts me into his arms, his jaw tight with concern. "You're burning up with fever."

"Poison," I whisper, and his hands grip me tighter.

My bare feet dangle on one side, but he's careful to keep them from colliding with a wall. His movements are swift and silent. I curl into him, his body like cool water to my feverish skin.

I never thought I'd be so glad to see him.

I hold my breath as we pass the guards' insulated cabin in the center of the compound. One guard sits alert at a desk facing the window, a cigarette glowing between his lips. Another crosses the octagonal cabin, each side fitted with glass windows to keep a constant watch over the prisoners. Lanterns flicker across the five hallways filled with cells. But Soran clings to the shadows.

The guards' eyes pass over us, unseeing, and then Soran runs. Strong arms anchor me and my dirty rags to his chest. I listen for the familiar beat. *Dokun.* The reverberating drum is warm and fierce. The hearts in my chest answer with a harmonizing beat.

Dokun dokun.

I don't want to be carried. I don't want to share a heart with this . . . *man* feels like the wrong word. But with his strong arms shielding me, the warmth of his breath, the steady pace of his footsteps, it feels right too.

Soran stops at the edge of a large field and sets me down gently in the grass. I throw off my soiled shawl and shiver, welcoming the cold night air on my fevered skin. Soran approaches a large shadow lying on the ground. At the sound of his footsteps, the shadow lurches. A horse startles to its feet, tossing its head as if chiding Soran for being late. He rubs the horse's nose and then along the white blaze between its eyes.

I stare at my ankle, swollen and caked in blood. Lifting my chin, I rise and hobble toward the horse. Its ears flatten at my movement.

"You can't walk," Soran says. "You need rest." He reaches out to lift me onto the horse, but I push his hand away.

"Don't pretend you care," I whisper. He may have come to save me from the prison, but I can't forget his concern has a time limit. He needs me dead after the third trial.

Soran draws the horse closer with a gentle tug of the reins. It stops beside me with a snort. "The sun doesn't care about the earth, but it still warms it," Soran says. "I don't have to care to do what's good. Right now, you need a healer and to prepare for the next trial."

"I don't want to think about the trials," I say, fever slicking my brow.

"You have to." Without asking, he lifts me onto the horse bareback. I scramble to sit as I grip the horse's mane. Soran slides onto the horse behind me. He tucks me protectively against his chest and nudges the horse forward. We barrel across the fields, carefully avoiding the rice, taking the narrow paths the farmers use between the paddies.

"Where are we going?" I say after a long stretch of silence, my eyelids heavy. Vacant city roads appear, an unfamiliar part of Taiga in a hilled and spacious neighborhood.

"The duke's house," he says, voice tight. "They've prepared a room for you."

The house I would've traveled to after the wedding, the room Casmir and I would've . . .

I gulp, trying to force the questions from my mouth. *Why are you taking me there? Does Casmir know I'm alive? Who lives at his house now?*

The words don't leave my mouth. After several sleepless nights and a relentless fever, I succumb to the weight of being just another mortal slug—a human.

My head falls against my shoulder and Soran's broad arm. But in my dreams, I'm riding to the cathedral again for a wedding license and a dagger. Only it's not Casmir riding beside me, but a dragon the color of moonlight. The hoofbeats beneath me turn into the pounding drum of a heart. Then the dragon opens its mouth and fire devours the forest, my horse, and me.

CHAPTER 18
MEERA

A WOMAN WITH A SCARRED FACE and gentle hands greets us at the door. I'm half asleep, still held aloft in Soran's strong arms, but the pain throbbing in my foot keeps me from fully sleeping. Fever claws at my throat, slick and hot.

"Bring her inside," the woman says.

We pass through a wide door and into a warm living room with a blazing fire in the hearth. Soran holds me over it, and for a moment, I wonder if he'll throw me into the flames and watch me burn. But his fingers dig protectively into my skin, guarding me like a treasure chest holding his one and only fortune.

Dokun . . . the fever battles with my hearts . . . *dokun.*

"Where should I put her?" his voice is low, earnest.

"Set her down there," she says.

"The doctor is waiting upstairs," interrupts an older man with grayish-black hair tied in a ponytail. He stands beside the woman, the firelight lending his hair a silver sheen.

"She doesn't need a doctor," Soran says with authority. "They use healers in Ezo. Do you have monkshood and perilla leaf on hand?"

The conversation stills as if a cold breeze had blown in

through the window. "Pauper's medicine," the man scoffs. "A doctor is exactly what she needs. Look at her. The duke will be furious when he hears of it. How did this happen? The princess, here in Taiga, and in a brawl?"

"The story can wait," the woman says, touching my cheek with a tender hand. "She's burning up. Ambassador, fetch the doctor and tell him to tend to her in the great room."

"It's poison," Soran says, a protective ring to his words. He lays me down on a long sofa near the fire. "She was attacked by the bakuto in the market."

My fingers twitch, desperate to keep him near, but my body doesn't listen. I melt into the cushions with a groan and stretch my sore legs. I feel bad for dirtying the fine sofa's soft velvet and thick pillows. Apologetic words tumble from my lips. A warm blanket falls over me, hot and heavy on my stomach. The woman kneels and blots my face with a damp rag.

"You did the right thing," the silver-haired ambassador says to Soran. "Telling Madame Akane about her situation and bringing her to us. How much do we owe you?"

Soran bristles from where he stands next to me. "I don't take payment. I'm her guardian."

Guardian. I almost believe it to be true.

"A personal guard?" The man strokes his beard. "Where were you during the fight you told us about?"

Soran stares daggers. "Fighting another opponent. But I don't owe you an account."

The woman clears her throat. "That will be enough, gentlemen. Ambassador Richter, would you please fetch the doctor? Young man"—I imagine she nods toward Soran but my vision blurs from fever—"bring me lukewarm water and a fresh towel. I'll see about those herbs."

The woman's face bends over mine, her eyes kind pools of black honey beneath intelligent brows. I struggle to keep her in focus, blinking against the burning heat. Her smile is kindness and strength, making me feel safe. The last thing I notice are the burns, the way her skin crinkles into pale scars and puckers in brown lines like tree bark. The scars trail from her eyes, across the bridge of her nose, and along her left cheek.

The rag pauses on my forehead. "We all have scars," she says gently. "But most people carry them on the inside and suffer in silence." Her fingers press against my brace and I'm faintly aware of it sloughing from under my back. "Rest, my dear. I'll see to it that you don't bear any more scars than necessary. You've already borne a great deal."

Soran returns with the lukewarm water and stands stiffly over the sofa. "The doctor can't give her medicine," he says in a low voice intended for the woman alone. "It could harm her condition."

"The blue sickness?" Akane says, probably referring to my hereditary ailment. "I'm listening."

"Have the doctor clean and bind her wounds, but don't give her any Taigan medicine. She needs to get back to Ezo where she can be treated by her own healer."

"I'll agree with your assessment as her guardian," she says, her voice stressing the last word as if it hung by a thin thread. "But I must warn you, if anything happens to her, my son won't be forgiving."

"Casmir? It wouldn't be in his nature," Soran says dryly.

"Is your nature any different?" the woman says. "Or mine? No one is born a monster, but we all become one without love."

The fever crawls across my skin, burrowing deep inside until I can't hear, can't feel anything but the pain. Why doesn't Soran want me to have medicine? If this is about his heart, I'll murder him—again.

I writhe on the sofa, throwing off the blanket, but firm hands hold me down. Sleep takes me in fits of disorienting pain and nightmares and songs pure as gold.

Sunlight filters into my room and along with it, a hard shiver. My hearts hammer against my chest. The curtains are not mine. This bed is not mine. I claw out from under the covers and stare at my torso and legs covered in white silk pajamas—also not mine.

They smell of clean soap and cypress, of Cass.

"You're awake."

I startle at the familiar voice and pull the covers to my chest. My head throbs from the sudden movement, as if I haven't moved in days. "How long have I been asleep?"

Soran sits on a thick rug before a stone fireplace, one knee propped up and staring into the flames with a look entirely unhuman, as if he wants desperately to dip his fingers into the amber light.

"Three days." Soran doesn't offer a glance at me, but the flinch in his jaw and the . . . my eyes drop to his feet. A patch of crimson seeps from a bandage on his right ankle. A shimmering of white catches his hair in the firelight. "Infection set in and it took you a while to recover."

"Are you . . . all right?" Worry hitches my voice, but I clear my throat and amend to a more casual tone. Had he been here caring for me all this time? "You're injured."

I set the comforter aside and pull my feet from the bed. My own foot is puckered into a tight scar, three pink holes now healed over, the skin around them a prickly pink. The wound should be red and scabbed, more jagged from where the assassin's rake had dragged me. A worried breath skips through my chest.

I step out of bed, testing my ankle.

Soran jumps up, lips pinched in concern. "You shouldn't move yet."

I raise a brow. *Is that worry in his voice?* "You shouldn't be in the same room with me."

He glances down at his bare feet. "I come through the window every night. They won't let me in otherwise. I don't trust their doctor, and I don't like being away too long from—"

"Your heart," I finish for him softly. "I know."

He swallows hard and for a moment I wonder if he was going to say something else.

My feet thread the soft rug as I make my way to the fire and take a seat. He sits next to me, the warm glow of the flames softening his face and catching the gold specks in his eyes. He gestures for me to show him my foot. I do so, sticking out my left leg near the fireplace.

"One more song ought to do," he says, taking my foot into his hands.

"A song?" A flutter skips through my chest as his skin touches mine. The way his fingers trail the scars on my foot sends a warm sensation down my spine. I sit straighter, leaning in to observe as if I don't trust what he's about to do—and I don't—but the security I find in his hands is new, alarming.

"Can you be still?" He looks up between dark lashes, a tinge of white highlighting a strand of hair falling to his brow.

I reach out to touch it, and he swats my hand away. "I asked if you could be still."

"But when did you get that?" I ask, tugging at the pale hair drained of its rich, dark color.

He looks up again, his lips pursed in irritation. His fingers wrap around mine, twirling my hand away carefully as if it were a viper. My heart lurches. Or his . . . it's hard to tell anymore.

My thoughts spiral as I try to remain still. Soran cups my foot in his hands and begins to sing in a low voice. I turn my head to the door, worried that someone will hear and find us, like this, on a woven rug by the amber firelight.

Anxiety fades as his voice melts over my ears, ringing like

wind between the pines, the playful dash of waves, and a sound I can't place. It shifts through my mind, beneath the layers of my skin. I feel it from the inside out.

My second heart recognizes the beat. It soars to meet his words and a reverent awe comes over me. No human should be able to sing like that.

He sings of fire that refuses to be quiet, of love that words can't capture like a snowflake melting in your palm, and hearts that are broken to be made whole again. His voice doesn't taper off at the end of the song, it wrestles the air for space, it creates life where there had been none before. It takes breath from the air and gives it a soul.

I'd always known that dragons sing, and Runa wondered what they sang about, but now I know. It's too beautiful for human ears, too . . . *familiar.*

My feverish dreams hadn't been all nightmares. A gentle voice had soothed me when the fever dug in sharp claws, held me when I shook uncontrollably. I thought the song had only been a dream. Maybe it still is.

I lean forward, watching his lips form the sounds that shake my soul. The last syllable trembles to a stop and our eyes meet. The gold dust is like a flame, dancing with light, his skin pale from the song's toll. He releases my foot, shrinking away from me, and wraps his own foot in a fresh bandage. Blood seeps through the cloth.

My chest pinches in concern, but it's his pain too that I feel like an invisible thread connecting us.

"What have you done?" My fingers skim across my ankle. The scars are faint pink lines, and it moves freely without pain. I lean over and unravel the bandage from Soran's foot. My breath snags.

Blood oozes from three jagged wounds on his ankle. "It'll heal within the day," he says, voice clipped. "You couldn't walk otherwise, and we need to reach Ezo soon."

My mind reels. *How had he done it? Why is he in a rush to get to Ezo? What is he hiding from me?* "I-I thought you couldn't use your magic in this form? You said that you would die? I don't understand."

"Dragons are known to exaggerate," he says. "I can't use it, not like in my original form. I couldn't give it to you, for example—not that I would. But I can use it for a price. Barter against my own life so to speak. Though, the side effects are unpredictable." He curls the white hair along his finger, attempting to hide it in the dark mop. The highlighted strand is a bit thicker than before he sang.

I stand, the truth almost snapping me in two. "Your magic is healing? You could've saved my sister. You still could. I . . . why didn't you tell me?"

"You didn't ask." He rises, hobbling with his injured foot. "And my gift is fading in this mortal body. A few more days and I won't be able to help anyone." He tears his gaze away, frustration lining his brow. "For such a short lifespan, humans are quick to forget. You tried to kill me for my magic, to *force* me to give it to you. The only reason I help you now is to protect what is *mine*."

"And if I win the third trial? Would you give me your ancient art then?" I say. "In exchange for your heart."

He shakes his head. "Why must everything be deals and threats with you? A heart is meant to be a gift, not a prize. I wouldn't trust you even if you had both my hearts. The third trial is impossible. I'm counting on it. But you'll be lucky to make it past the second."

"Good thing I believe in choices, not luck," I say, voice going tight. "Thank you for healing me, but I think you should go now."

"We'll see what choices you make when stealing from your boyfriend, or should I say husband?" He cracks the windowpane open and peers out into the bright sunlight. "Everyone thinks you said yes at the wedding ceremony. Including the boy's mother. That was her who treated you when we first arrived, Madame Akane."

I pale, my knees going weak. "My . . . husband? Surely no one believes the gossip. They also said I tried to kill the duke. Casmir wouldn't have allowed the rumors—"

He laughs. "You should get to know someone better before saying you'll marry them. We leave soon for Ezo, the whole household. Sir Richter, the Taigan ambassador, is orchestrating the trip on the duke's orders."

"And your foot?"

"It'll be better," he says, jaw clenching. "But don't count on me to save you next time."

He sweeps out the windowsill, preparing to climb down with his injured foot. I don't want to push him away after what he's done for me, but what choice do I have? He's made his priorities clear. Still, I hate seeing him hobble. Is that how people feel when they watch me?

"What is the second trial?" I call after him. "What am I stealing?"

He looks up at me from his downward climb, using a nearby tree for support. "Casmir's signet ring; the dragons want it within the week."

"A ring?"

He nods. "I've heard he offered it to you before."

I gulp, recalling Casmir's pained face when I'd left him at the wedding, and the rumors he hadn't stifled. What would he think to find me alive? And a failure? My actions had done *nothing* to help the queendom and only pitched it further into chaos. And now I have to ask him for his ring—no, he won't give it freely again—I'll have to steal it.

I must gain his trust again to break it. There's no other way to get the dragon's magic and survive the trials. I just hope Cass will forgive me, again.

CHAPTER 19
CASMIR

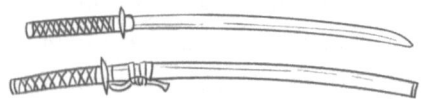

ALIVE. The word splintered Casmir's heart. A childish joy rose from some long-forgotten place, hope burst into ten, no, one hundred thoughts and plans. A single word had never impacted him so forcefully since his mother's admonition over a decade ago—*forgive*.

Casmir had received the letter from his mother about Princess Meera hours ago, but it stuck in the back of his mind like honey. She was alive and would be coming back to him within the week. One week to show her that he could manage the kingdom and save her sister.

Seated across from him, Jey spreads more paper on the cedar table, his thin hands pointing to one line of medicinal herbs and then to another. Poisons, cures, names of both high and low rank, and a flurry of marks linking them together.

One name jumps out from the stack of parchment. Casmir reaches across the table and snatches the paper detailing the trading routes approved by the ambassador of Taiga. His elbow clumsily knocks into a porcelain cup. Rich brown coffee pours across the desk, soaking into the white pages.

"You know," Jey says, "we'd probably solve this faster if you'd stop spilling coffee on our notes."

Casmir jerks his head up. He'd been lost in thought again. He rights his cup and takes the cloth Jey extends to clean up the mess. Thankfully, he'd saved the paper bearing his father's name from the deluge.

He never thought he'd see that name again. What was it doing on a list of trade approvals from Sir Richter? His father was nothing more than a bakuto now, a low-class criminal, disgraced.

He fists the coffee-stained towel.

"It's the girl, isn't it?" Jey asks with a wry smile.

"The princess?" Casmir says, taken aback. Jey was usually more adept at reading him, but then again, few knew the name Casmir's father had adopted after his disgraceful fall. He straightens, forcing himself to set the paper aside. "Princess Meera complicates things, in a good way." Casmir gives Jey a warning look. "Now, how close are we to the antidote?"

Jey nudges two glass vials across the table. "This," he says, pointing to a vial filled with a frothy substance reminiscent of jellyfish slime and bubbles, "is Dragon's Breath, a secretion made from their saliva and oxygen that lulls the victim into a drowsy state, sometimes inducing sleep or coma like—"

"I know what Dragon's Breath is," Casmir interrupts, leaning against the table. "What's in the second vial?"

Jey lifts the second vial between two fingers, turning it to catch the sunlight prying through the window. "Twilight Nocturne, a concentrate made from deadly nightshade, sweet-smelling and easily concealed in something innocent like a pudding. We found traces of both in the banquet hall."

"Good work," Casmir says, tilting his head back in thought to hide his suspicions. He didn't trust anyone, not lately.

The search for the antidote had left more questions than answers. Few people had access to the dragons, and even fewer had the gall to threaten one to summon the defensive response which would result in Dragon's Breath.

Jey had tackled the task with too much enthusiasm while Casmir busied himself with the politics of the kingdom: Rusa's stalled invasion and flagrant threats, the fleet of Seshu ships coming from the south, and unrest within the capital of Ezo. He couldn't hold it all while trying to find a cure for the killing sleep. But he would have to. If Meera's decision to face the dragon had taught him one thing, it was to trust no one.

That includes his personal guard and spy, Jey. He already knew he'd helped her get the dagger at the monastery. But why? Asking Jey directly would only arouse suspicion and set the man on edge. Casmir spins his signet ring, deep in thought. He would get answers from another source. It's not the elite who hold the most knowledge but pawns.

The next phase of the plan Casmir would need to undertake alone.

"They work you like a dog, don't they?" Casmir raps his fist against the open servants' door. He expected the small mouse of a girl to startle at his voice, but she doesn't.

Seira turns slowly, a wicker basket full of dirty laundry in her calloused hands and a practiced mask on her face. "They ask me to work like a servant, and I do. If you're looking for my brother, he's not here. He's out taking a count of the ships and their supplies like you ordered." Her voice drips with thinly veiled disdain.

"I'm not here for Kazuya," Casmir says, speaking of her twin brother who'd come to inspect the Rusan ships with him. He steps inside the room, shrugging off his outer jacket. He drops it into the girl's laundry basket and studies her for a reaction.

The slightest clench in her hands, but otherwise a wall of

guarded perfection. Casmir smiles. Servants are good at deflecting attention and concealing their true feelings, but not this good. His suspicions were onto something—they usually were.

He takes the basket from her hands and drops it on the floor, spilling its contents. He watches for another reaction. Most maids would be scared, uncomfortable.

"Your fiancée wouldn't approve of this behavior," Seira quips, holding her ground and raising her chin. He doesn't miss the slight tremor in her shoulders. She is unnerved, at least.

"My wife," he corrects, the lie knotting in his stomach, both a wish and a scar. He takes a respectful step back to give the maid breathing room. "What do you know about her? Hmm? I'm here because you have information I need."

Seira scoffs, bending over to pick up the basket and shoving the rumpled clothes back inside. "What information could I possibly give that you don't already know?"

"Surprise me," he says, blocking the exit when she attempts to scurry past him.

"I know she didn't want to marry you," Seira says. "Wouldn't have unless the kingdom depended on it. Meera wanted to join the saints even though her father forbade it. Her mother, may her path be eternally restful, admired the saints."

"You don't like me," Casmir says, bending down to help with the clothes. "I didn't force Meera. Besides what you may think, I care for her. And I'll find whoever poisoned her sister."

He grabs Seira's hand over a rumpled shirt on the floor and squeezes tight. "But I'm not here to talk about Meera. You were the only one who knew she'd be at the market that morning, besides Bastian. I've checked the records a dozen times. You mentioned the path just now. You and your brother are Ainur."

Seira gasps and tugs her hand. When he doesn't release it, she reels back to slap him with her free palm. Casmir catches it mid-air. "Runa and Meera never judged me because of my background. I wanted to keep it quiet, and they respected that. Please."

Casmir releases her hand, noticing how it trembles as she draws away. "The Ainur have a lot to gain if Ezo falls and loses its magic," he says. "They also have access to the dragons, the spume. Did you poison Runa?"

Seira shoves the basket aside and jumps to her feet. She swallows hard, her eyes swiveling to find an exit, but the only door is behind Casmir's back. "I didn't do it. I would never. She was my friend!"

"But you gave the spume to someone. Told them about it to keep your brother out of trouble? There's too much distrust in the military and among the queensguard for an Ainur to rise in the ranks that fast. The king found out and was going to send your brother back to the Winterwilds, wasn't he? Maybe even send him to work on the Prisoner's Road."

Seira pales, sweat beading at her temple. All signs of her careful facade melt. She nods tearfully. "Please, I-I . . . didn't know what they would do with it!"

"Who was it?"

She shakes her head, her hands prying into the laundry basket. "He'll kill me."

"And I won't?"

Seira takes a shuddering breath, her eyes flying to Casmir in horror. "Meera will never forgive you," she says between swallows. "She'll hate you forever."

"She's forgiving, unlike me," he says. "But if you cooperate —and refrain from mentioning this conversation to my wife when she arrives—then I'll keep you and your brother's secret. Does that give you some relief?"

"No, not really."

"I am unforgiving," he says, extending her a patient smile. "But I am also honest. I never break my word. Now, a name."

Seira gulps. "How do I protect myself from him? When he hears—"

Casmir cocks his head. "You should've thought about that before selling treasonous information. No more stalling. A name."

"They call themselves the Black Dragon Society," she whispers. "They have the ear of the emperor and the king. I . . ." She bites her lips. "I gave the spume to the ambassador."

"Which one?" Casmir steps closer, his impatience growing. This was it, the information he'd been waiting for.

Seira shakes her head, eyes wildly searching for an escape. "Please."

Casmir grabs her by the neck, his pressure firm but not suffocating. "A name."

"Sir Richter. The ambassador from Taiga," she squeaks.

He lets go and steps back, hardly believing her words. *His ambassador?* The one sent to look after his mother after Runa's coronation.

Seira's hand flies to her throat with a gasping breath. "Will you keep your promise?"

"Yes," he mumbles. "What organization did you say he's a part of?"

Seira wrings her hands on a towel, twisting it into a knot. "The Black Dragon Society," she whispers, still rubbing her throat. "Sir Richter left after Runa was cursed . . . you let him go. I-I assumed you were involved. The organization is so big, even some of the maids are members."

Casmir's hands flex at his sides, the ruby ring chafing against his skin. Sir Richter is delivering Meera back to Ezo. He'd heard of the Black Dragon Society. But he thought they died out with his father who'd tried to resurrect it. Apparently, they had crept beneath the soil, clinging to the shadows. And they hadn't just come for him, they'd come for everything he loved too.

Casmir strode from the room and hastily scrawled a letter for

Bastian to return home as soon as possible. Meera was returning with a monster.

But Casmir wasn't foolish enough to believe that Sir Richter had orchestrated the whole thing. Someone else was pulling the strings, but with Meera back and the net tightening, the game had changed significantly.

He couldn't stay the warm but calculating duke. He must become the Dragon Slayer again.

CHAPTER 20
MEERA

SAILING OVER THE RING OF FIRE with a dragon, a rival ambassador, and my fiancé's mother is about as smooth as netting a frightened pufferfish.

My room is sandwiched between the silver-haired ambassador, Sir Richter, and Casmir's mother, Akane. Soran sleeps in the underway cabin with the captain, keeping a near constant watch on the sea. With the dragons' oath to Ezo broken, the sentry is tasked with making sure the beasts stay afield of the ship. The ambassador had relegated Soran to outer guard duty for the duration of the ferry ride, no doubt trying to keep him far away from me.

I wonder if he'd heard anything the other night—ahem, the last *three* nights—when Soran had stolen into my room to heal my foot. Sir Richter watches us as if he thinks we are hiding something. He probably suspects a romantic tryst and not that I'm harboring a dragon's heart inside my chest. I'm not sure which idea frightens me more.

"Dragon, ho!" shouts a sentry from the crow's nest. A scurry of feet dash over the deck and up the railings, preparing scented bait to lure away the sea serpents and readying harpoons if that should fail.

Two dragons knife through the waves like porpoises, only much larger and more menacing. One is a nondescript gray, but the other is a shocking shade of emerald. My hearts catch in my throat and my skin burns at the memory of encountering the green monster in the cave. The scorching heat of flames intended to eat me alive.

Sharp curved horns, almost like deer antlers, cut through the waves at the side of the ship, a glint of green scales diving into the white froth. I hold my breath.

"They won't bother you," Soran says, standing at my side along the railing. "They want to see how you handle the second—"

Sir Richter strides by us, an arch in his silver brow and hair pulled taut against his pale skin, giving him a sepulchral look even in the sun. He shoots a pointed look at Soran. "Shouldn't you be sounding the foghorn to drive the beasts away?"

"The dragons out there aren't a threat," Soran says, meeting Sir Richter's eyes. "It's the ones you can't see that you need to worry about."

The irony of the comment isn't lost on me.

If Sir Richter knew he was staring down a dragon at that very moment, he would've wet his noble pants. In order to rendezvous and discuss the trial, and with what had happened while I was out with the fever, Soran had taken to imitating dragon cries at night to distract the guards and help me escape my room.

The first time Sir Richter heard Soran's dragon shriek imitation, he'd gone pale as the moon and retched over the side of the ship. Sometimes Soran did it during the day just for fun. I tried not to smile. I shouldn't encourage the monster, but we'd both taken a particular dislike to Sir Richter.

We spent the first night poring over records Soran had

procured regarding the assassins and their criminal histories. How he'd managed to steal them from the police barracks before breaking me out of prison, I'll never know. But he did. Each assassin belonged to a different region of the empire. We searched for links connecting them but came up empty-handed. We were to meet again tonight to discuss the second trial and Casmir's ring before docking in Ezo.

But that requires escaping my second personal guard, hand-picked by Sir Richter, a fit middle-aged man with absolutely no sense of humor. Slipping past him to meet with Soran at night had proven difficult to say the least. But the dragon cry came in handy there.

"I wish we could talk now," I whisper to Soran once Sir Richter leaves, barreling around the deck shouting orders about how to frighten off the two dragons tailing the ship.

Soran raises a brow. "We could."

I try to catch his meaning, but he has my hand before I can protest. We slip through the sentries and sailors, all occupied with the fierce dragons roughing the sea around the boat. One of the dragons slams its muscular body into the ship before dipping beneath the waves.

The wooden floor rocks beneath me and I stumble for balance. I've a distinct feeling they're doing it to unnerve me and warn Soran, but he's been silent regarding his telepathic communication with the dragons. I make a mental note to ask him about it later.

Soran leads me down a flight of stairs and into the boiler room. Steam puffs around us, slicking the walls with condensation. Soran nods toward one of the stokers working the coal and a grimy face nods back in recognition. I hope he's made friends with the workers down here or we'll be in more than trouble. My feet come to a stop, eyes adjusting to the dim, coal-dust laden air. Ezo had large transport vessels, but none had coal-fired steam engines like this one.

"Sir Richter is convinced you're my lover," I say, eyeing the steamy surroundings and dark corners. "You really think this will help alleviate his suspicion?"

"I don't care what he or anyone else thinks," he says, all business. "I might not be able to distract the guard again tonight, and it's our last chance to talk before the ship docks."

I glance around Soran at the stoker heaping another pile of coal into the furnace.

"The grimers don't like the guards and dignitaries. They won't rat on us," Soran says as though reading my mind.

Still not convinced, I tuck farther into the pipes, tugging Soran by the shirt until we're both out of sight behind a large engine. "All right," I say. "But we don't have much time. Let's start with the assassins. In spite of completely different regions and backgrounds, they all have one thing in common. Each one was hired by the dragons."

"And?" he says, as if expecting something more substantial. "Have you discovered how they're connected to the dragons? The emerald one mentioned something that gave me an idea."

I wet my lips and pull down my scarf. *It's hotter than the fires of Mortua in here.* "I wondered if they were speaking to you, telepathically, I mean."

He nods and then lowers his voice. "They're upset that I got involved during the last trial. There's not much I can do to help you with the next one or there will be . . . consequences."

"What kind of consequences?"

He shakes his head. "You'll think more clearly for the second trial if you don't know."

"Forget the second trial," I huff, wiping a bead of sweat from my brow. "I have a right to know."

"Meera." He takes me by the arms, locking eyes with me. "You need to think about the second trial. Let me deal with the consequences. It'll distract you, and you must be focused. Stealing the ring won't be as easy as you think."

I twist my lips, wishing there was a way to pry the truth from him. *How would the dragons punish him if he intervened again?* But the spark of gold in his eyes tells me he won't relent. "Fine," I say. "I won't need your help for the second trial anyway."

"I like your confidence," he says with a mocking grin.

"It doesn't come naturally," I say, rubbing my sore backbone. I loosen the collar of my robes, sweat beading down my neck. "Soran, I think I know what the assassins have in common. The wayfinder said something that made me think, and when I cross referenced the criminal records you found, it confirmed it."

He nods encouragingly, shrugging out of his outer robe.

"The wayfinder," I begin, "was the one thread that didn't make sense. It's what made me suspect something was amiss in the first place. Only Ainur can become wayfinders. The Ainur revere the dragons much like the rest of Ezo, even protecting them since the dragons gifted them with the art of wayfinding centuries ago. But when I pressed the wayfinder, she told me that she came to prevent another dragon heart from going dark.

"Which made me wonder, when had a dragon's heart gone dark and how did she know about it? There's nothing about it in the testaments of the saints. If she knew a secret like that, the dragons wouldn't want her to share it. And if she'd witnessed it, they'd want her silenced, wouldn't they?"

Soran's eyes narrow. "A dark dragon heart? Meaning . . ."

I shake my head and watch him closely, curious if he knows more than he's letting on. "I don't know. The dragons are supposed to be pure and just, warriors and guardians, impartial like angels in the Furan myths."

"Supposed to be?" He laughs softly. "They are. It's almost unheard of for a dragon to go against its nature."

Almost. I wonder if he's referring to himself. After all, he doesn't have a dragon nature anymore.

"What does it mean?"

"It means," he says, leaning forward, "that the wayfinder is under the impression that another dragon like the Beast exists."

Dokun dokun. My hearts thrum, one a warning to flee and the other drawing me closer to the barefoot man with a handsome face.

The Beast had killed the Bleeding Saint and was now locked into the deep below the watery world of the dragons—in Mortua, a world without return. He couldn't come back. Was the wayfinder saying that another dragon could turn dark like that?

I stare at Soran, a prickling feeling crawling up my spine. The dragon heartbeat rushes through my ears, warm and melodic. Without thinking, my hand goes to my chest and the pulse quickens beneath my collar.

"Is that why they want to destroy your heart?" Even as I say it, I don't want it to be true. There's something about the heart, like a beautiful song, that would leave the world dreadfully cold if it ceased to exist.

Soran's gold-flecked eyes meet mine. He steps closer. "No," he says with authority. "It won't go dark. That's not how it happened with the Beast. This is different. They don't want me to have it back for another reason."

I'm shaken by the force of his words, as if he's speaking a truth over his heart—willing himself to believe it.

A loud clank sounds behind me, and I turn. Two workers enter the boiler room, tucking their heads into the various crannies, searching.

Our eyes lock; we don't have much time.

"Quick," he whispers, tugging me farther back into the maze of pipes. "What links the assassins besides the dragons?"

"No, it *is* the dragons," I whisper, pressed against him in the narrow space. "The dragons hate each of them. The first two assassins were easy to figure out. The bakuto, the tattooed man, had killed a royal from Taiga. But the only Taigan royal whose been killed is Mitsuo Endo—he proposed a bill to stop the unlawful selling of dragon parts but was assassinated. I remember it in the news not too long ago.

"Then Kobaya, the girl . . ." My throat tightens. "She spent time in Fuchu prison for selling dragon scales on the shadow market. But she never used the money on anything they could trace. I bet she used it to fund her home, an orphanage the bakuto was trying to buy out to create brothels. I think she wanted to free them all."

"You think your would-be assassin was virtuous?" he asks, incredulous, and casts a glance toward the workers slowly making their way in our direction.

"I think she was doing the only thing she knew how," I whisper.

"So they all did something the dragons didn't like," he confirms. "People the dragons would prefer taken off the board so to speak."

I nod, my eyes searching his. "Soran, is the ring something they don't like as well? Something they want to destroy? Or is it just to spite Casmir?"

He takes a deep breath and I feel the rise of his chest brushing my arm in the tight space. My hearts leap, pulling me closer. He doesn't want to answer that question. Or perhaps he can't answer it. I don't know what the dragons have told him about the second trial except that I'm to steal Casmir's ring.

Knocks ring out on the metal pipes closest to us. The boiler room door bangs open. A new set of footsteps pound against the metal stairs. Soran steps in front of me protectively, but I grab his arm.

"Is it Sir Richter?"

"Worse," he says, lips flattening into a thin line. "No amount of lying is going to get you out of this mess."

"Then we don't lie," I say.

He turns to face me, brows lifting in surprise. "What will you tell them?"

"Yes," comes a smooth voice, pinched at the edges. "What are you going to tell me?"

My eyes shoot past Soran to the middle-aged woman with kind eyes and a scarred face, my future mother-in-law. But she doesn't know that. To her, I'm already married to Casmir.

Soran squeezes out of the narrow space to allow me room to meet her. Madame Akane waits on the metal ramp with two guards and the ship's captain. The guards struggle to hide the smile in their eyes, bemused to find us, well . . . I'd prefer not to think about what this looks like. The captain points at us with less manner.

"Told you I'd find them," he says. "No one can hide on my ship. Not a crevice I don't know about and haven't tried myself."

Akane gives him a look of pointed disapproval. "That'll be enough, Captain. I think I can handle this shipwreck if you'll keep us from any out there."

"Right, ma'am," he says, bowing toward her and taking off back up the stairs with a wink at Soran.

Heat flushes my neck, but I hold my head high anyway. "Madame Akane, I can explain—"

"I'm sure you can, my dear. But I'd rather hear it in private over a cup of tea to calm my nerves." She eyes Soran and gestures to the guards to take him away.

As he passes me, he squeezes my hand beneath my scarf, his fingers pressing against my ring finger. "Throw it in the sea," he whispers, his mouth brushing my ear. *The ring, throw it in the sea. Got it?* I stare wide-eyed at my future mother-in-law as she witnesses the intimacy. I'm doomed.

As soon as Soran's out of sight, Akane beckons me forward. "I know more than anyone how difficult an arranged marriage can be," she says, her lips drawn in disapproval. "But I thought better of you."

The words sting more than I'd anticipated. Protests lodge in my throat. I hadn't betrayed Cass, not like that. We aren't even married! But I couldn't explain that to her. Why would she believe me over the gossip and her own son?

I follow her out the door but stop at the threshold. I said I'd speak the truth, and I shall, even if no one believes me. "I'm not in love with Soran," I say. "I know what it looks like, but we weren't down here for some tryst. We've been trying to figure out who poisoned my sister, Princess Runa, and how to get the dragons' help."

Shrewd brown eyes scour my face for a long minute. Sweat trickles down my back. I'm keenly aware of the scarf knotted in my hands and the loosened collar of my kimono.

Akane's lips tuck into a sad smile. "Meera, dear, you may be telling the truth. But you're also blind to it. Now, come. The tea's getting cold."

I stare after her before scurrying up the stairs. What did she mean? Blind to what? I stow the thought for later and wonder what Soran is being treated to. Somehow, I doubt it will be tea.

Tomorrow we reach the Ezo mainland. One night left to plan my reintroduction to Ezo society, prove I'm not an adulteress, steal Casmir's ring, and deliver it to the dragons in the sea without anyone noticing. Piece of pudding.

CHAPTER 21
DRAGON

Ribs cracking under the weight of a fist is a new sensation. It doesn't help that the feeling comes first: searing pain, spotty vision, an amber flare of rage curling in his gut. *Why do men have to be cruel? But perhaps they aren't that different from dragons. Maybe this is what Meera felt like in the Celestial Court.*

"What did you do to the princess?" asks the ambassador, glaring from where he sits on the captain's sofa, twisting a cigarette between the fat of his fingers. "I'm supposed to find out just how deep your relationship goes."

Soran spits the acrid taste of blood from his mouth. *Would it matter if he answered him?* He doubted the beating would cease. The sailors holding him down seemed to enjoy it, all four of them. Perhaps it had something to do with the bloodied noses and swollen eyes they now flaunted. It was their fault for not making it a fair fight in the first place.

"Soran, is it?" the ambassador asks again. "I should throw you overboard, but the matron wouldn't like it. Besides, I think you have other reasons for being here. Are you a spy? Do you recognize this?"

A sailor jerks Soran's hair, forcing him to look at the ambassador. He flashes a card at him, a simple set of Blind Beggar, but with a black dragon instead of the traditional white crane.

He knits his brow, straining for a look of confusion, but he knows that symbol. It's been around for a century, slinking into taverns and the halls of palaces: The Black Dragon Society. A group dedicated to amassing the kingdoms under one banner alone, erasing the voices of anyone who objects.

The ambassador's keen eyes pass over Soran before he flips the card back into the velvet lining of his jacket. "You're easy to read with your heart on your sleeve," he scoffs, his lips curling. "Definitely not a spy. But you *do* know this."

Soran jerks against the men shoving his shoulders down and fisting his hands behind his back. The ambassador stands, eyes narrowing at Soran as the guards pull him to his feet. "You've done me a favor, ruining the princess' reputation," he sneers. "Taiga will rule all, it's our destiny. The duke used to be on board with that plan, at least in theory, until the princess' little stunt at the beach. I've spent years grooming him to take his father's place.

"No matter, the princess needn't face the same fate as her sister if she cooperates. But the sea is . . . turbulent. It'd be unfortunate if anything happened to her." He turns to the soldiers and motions to the door. "The dragons have followed this ship for too long. Let's give them a sacrifice."

Soran's eyes widen, his pulse pounding like a fierce drum. *If anything happened to Meera . . .*

His eyes harden on the ambassador, but he keeps tabs on the sailors restraining him with his other senses. A large man at his back, two at his side, and another man opening the exterior door to the quarterdeck where he would likely be thrown overboard.

In their dreams. Dragons don't go down without a fight.

The ambassador's lips curl as he flicks his cigarette in Soran's face. He exits the opposing doors, no doubt thinking

Soran's afraid for his own life. Nothing could be further from the truth. His life had been taken from him by a dagger and a girl with a heart that rivaled his own. Adrenaline rushes through him at the thought of Meera in danger, of her heart—and his— consumed by whatever vile thing the ambassador has planned.

The guards at his side snicker, one of them pulling a crooked knife as they shove him into the midnight air thick with sea spray. Soran follows, dragging his feet as though too weak to protest. The dagger glimmers in the moonlight as another guard grabs a spare halyard from the rigging.

At the last minute, Soran sweeps his right leg out, tripping the guard to his left, while simultaneously ramming his fist into the guard with the dagger. A sailor leaps on him from behind, another unsheathing a katana. Soran flips backward, slamming his opponent beneath him and freeing himself with a jab to the man's throat.

I am dragon, he thinks, a fire surging in his veins. All the warmth, beauty, and pure fury of a beast protecting its gold. He lashes out, blocking attacks with his arms, his shin, and returning jabs to major pressure points. The attacks feel almost natural, like water cutting into stone.

The sailor behind him buckles with a shriek as his arm snaps in two. Soran ducks beneath him, flipping him over the railing to stop the screaming. In minutes, the remaining men are lying on the wooden deck, groaning over their injuries or passed out. Snagging the rope, he ties them together and drags them back into the captain's cabin, locking the door from without.

We told you not to interfere, Soran. The dragon's voice is smooth as jade, a melody of wind and sea. *You remember the consequences. The second trial the girl must complete alone.*

I'm not interfering. He sends the thought telepathically, ignoring the splash of the sea as the emerald dragon keeps pace with the boat. *The trial hasn't started yet. Why are the elders asking for the ring?*

It's gold, the voice says, but it's not the whole truth. *Be warned, Soran, more is at stake than your heart. Don't interfere.*

He closes his mind to the voice and races down the deck, searching for Meera. What could the dragons want with the ring that would be more valuable than justice or his own heart? He shakes off the thought, focusing on finding the girl. He wouldn't let anything bad happen to her.

His blood warms as he nears the front of the ship, sensing the presence of the small gold pendant. She's close. He follows the scent and feel of gold until he's out of breath and staring at a slender woman leaning against the forecastle railing, peering into a black sea.

Why is she out here alone? Unguarded? His breath comes in and out in haggard puffs.

Meera leans against the red lacquered rail, her hands curled into a wool haori and scarf to keep away the cold nip of the midnight wind. Black waves the color of ink lap against the ship with a fierce howl as if urging her to turn back. But it has the opposite effect on the princess. She smiles into the breeze, steering her face homeward to the port of Silverwood somewhere on the dark horizon.

"Meera?"

She startles, but her eyes soften as he draws closer. "Soran," her voice hitches in worry. "What did they do to you?"

She reaches out to inspect a wound along his brow, but he snatches her hand on reflex and gently lowers it. "I'm fine."

"No, you're not," she corrects. "You're bleeding. Let me." She unwraps her white scarf and dabs the wool across his cheek and brow.

It stings and he flinches. His hand moves to stop her from tending to the cuts on his face. Scrapes and bruises he could deal with, but losing his heart?

With their hands overlapping, the pulse of his transplanted heart thrums against his palm followed by a subtler rhythm—

Meera's heart. It feels so much like his, almost indistinguishable but softer.

"What happened?" Meera asks.

His jaw clenches. He shouldn't think of her, shouldn't want to protect her other than to safeguard himself. But . . .

His eyes travel the length of her stubborn face, the eyes with sixteen shades of blue, the soft blush of her cheeks, and the courage that makes her stand tall when the world and her own body pull her down.

She slips her hand out from under his and presses the scarf back onto his brow.

"Oi, be gentle." He seethes as she touches another cut. He slides closer to her so she doesn't have to reach as far—or as forcibly—to clean the wound on his forehead. "We don't have much time. We'll arrive in Ezo by dawn."

"Did the ambassador do this?" She eyes him with a look that says 'don't you dare refuse to answer me.'

"Just some guards." He pauses to look at her. "You're in danger, Meera."

"Says the man bleeding with a busted lip and swollen eye." Her lips purse as Soran reaches to check his eye. She's right. It feels strange to him. The aches, the bruises, none of them hurt, not compared to the worry pinching his chest for this girl.

"We need to talk about the next trial," Soran says.

Meera turns her back on the sea and watches him with fiery blue eyes. "Why do the dragons want it?" she asks. "Casmir's ring?"

"It's gold," he says, repeating the emerald dragon's words.

Meera fishes the saint's pendant from the folds of her kimono and holds out the thin golden chain. "So is this, but you've not tried to snatch it from me."

"Stealing would be wrong," he says in a matter-of-fact tone. "And I'd rather you keep the gold where I can find it."

Her eyes widen with a flicker of understanding. "So that's how you've been finding me? This?"

"Mhm." He smiles, though it hurts with his cracked lip. Gently, he fingers the gold pendant, tracing the familiar mark of the saint. "I'm quite good at finding gold. Keep it on. I'll keep you safe."

"Safe." She tastes the word. "Until the third trial."

He nods, an uneasy pain squeezing his chest. *It's probably just the soreness from the fight.* "I'd rather you not think of the future. It would spoil the present, and it should be treated like a gift. It's a wonderful thing to live in the moment and know that you will never have another one like it. I understand now why humans can be so . . . impulsive."

Meera gives a soft laugh. "When was the last time you did something on impulse? The boiler room? Because that went well."

"Saving you," he says without hesitation. *No, he definitely wasn't imagining the tightening of his chest.* "I could've ended you in the sea. Put to death the heart you'd cursed and accepted my fate."

"Why didn't you? Because you wanted your heart returned?"

"Yes." He moves his hand next to hers, curiosity pulling him to feel that second, mortal heartbeat thrumming beneath her skin. "But that's not the only reason. Because of your courage. I wanted to know why you did it. Why you tried the impossible when you knew you would fail."

"Because I'm headstrong," she says, pulling her hand away and crossing her arms against the wind. "I thought there was a chance to save Runa and Ezo, however small. The saints say that hope is closer than the stars, brighter than the sun, and just as painful to hold." She shakes her head. "I tried to hold the sun, and I got burned."

"You held it," he says, meeting her eyes. "And you became the star."

"Which am I, a snail or a star?" she says with a smile. "Make up your mind."

"I think you already know the answer to that." He turns away to look at the dark sea, listening for any sign of the ambassador or the guards. It wouldn't be long before they found him, and he doubted they'd let him escape so easily a second time. He'd need to hide until the boat docked the following morning if he valued his freedom.

"I'll speak to Akane about what the ambassador did. He can't treat you like this," Meera says as if reading his thoughts. "We'll be on Ezo soil soon—my kingdom. I make the rules now. I'll keep *you* safe."

He laughs, but when he looks down at the blue-haired girl with eyes like iron in the flame, he believes her. "If I didn't know any better, I'd say you're worried about me."

"Why would I worry about an immortal being who can bend fire at will and heal with song?" She quirks a brow.

The answer falls on his tongue, but he bites it back. *Because you, dear Meera, have something I want. No, not just want . . . need.*

His heart calls to him, fueled by the empty ache in his chest. It twinges with a pain worse than all the beatings and insults the ambassador could throw at him. And it always hurts worse near Meera.

"I'm not immortal anymore, remember?" Soran says. "I'm still figuring out what it means to be human. Like . . . what does it mean when my chest aches around someone, or when my thoughts run off like mountain hares, or when my stomach pinches without reason?"

Meera raises a brow. "Did you not have feelings as a dragon?"

"I did, but thought came first. Now it's the other way around. Is that why you risked your life for your sister? You felt some-thing . . . like that."

"Something like that," Meera says, her voice soft.

"Can you tell me about her? About Runa?" he says. "I think I'm beginning to understand why you risked so much for her."

"What I did for Runa, it wasn't a feeling," she says. "It was a choice. Runa is my family, but she's so much more than that. I'd die for her. She's always been there for me, moved into the same room so I wouldn't be lonely since I had to live on the first floor with the blue sickness. She'd sneak out to visit the market with me against Papa's orders, even though she cherished the rules. She held me and kept me safe when Mama . . ."

Soran turns to look at her. She sniffles, her nose pink in the cold and her shoulders trembling. Tears run rivulets down her cheeks as she keeps a straight face, her eyes moving with unspoken memory.

Slowly, he places an arm around her, his throat going tight. She tucks her face toward him, wiping her tears with the silk sleeve of his haori.

"Thank you," she murmurs into his robe. "You know, I usually hate crying in front of people, but for some reason I don't mind crying in front of a dragon."

"Maybe that's because we came from tears," he says. "But we can't shed them."

She looks up, startled. "I hope you never have to."

Soran's fingers tighten and loosen as he pulls his arm away. He doesn't want to find out what tears feel like. He can't. Putting space between them, he clears his throat. "I hope your sister wakes up soon. Be careful in Ezo, Meera. Sir Richter has plans to stop you, he may have poisoned your sister, and Casmir won't give up the ring freely."

"Sir Richter?" she says, eyeing him thoughtfully. "I had another suspect in mind. What is it you're not telling me? Casmir gave me his ring once. The second trial seems almost too easy."

"I'm *not* telling you to steal the ring and throw it into the sea.

I'm *not* telling you to tear off your pendant and run away before the third trial."

"But what about your heart?"

He turns his back on her, on the dragons' voices clamoring to get inside his mind, on the heart beating for him to claim it again. Why does it feel like he's on the verge of losing everything? Meera might as well be the moon for how his heart tugs after her like the tide. These feelings will be the end of him.

He releases a pent-up breath. "I won't have the strength to tell you these things after you win the second trial. There's no way you can part from my heart and live. It's too connected to you now."

"I don't understand." She steps back, balling the bloodied scarf in her hands. "I told you I wanted to give it back after the third trial. Then you can give me an ancient art for my people. You've helped me make it this far—"

"Because I'm heartless," he says, a chill sinking into his words. "I warned you. I'll keep you safe until the end of the second trial. After that, everything changes."

CHAPTER 22
MEERA

WHEN I STEP off the ship, I'm no longer the same girl who dove into the ocean with a kiss and a dagger. The rocky shore shifts beneath my feet, white pebbles skittering as my boots crunch onto the southernmost dock. My world, too, has shifted.

I can't think about Soran.

The times he saved me, the way my pulse raced when he sang, how his protectiveness curled around me like an embrace. It'd all been a lie.

He'd told me as much, that he was a heartless monster bent on reclaiming what I'd stolen. But I'd grown accustomed to him. His absence was like an open hearth without a flame. I couldn't lace my own boots without thinking of him and his ridiculous bare feet.

What had he done after our meeting on the ship? Had Sir Richter found him again?

"Welcome home, my dear," Akane says, coming up behind me, the brightness of the morning sun temporarily obscuring her scars. The ambassador takes the position to her right, dressed in his finest suit and silver hair slicked back into a ponytail.

What did Soran mean about Sir Richter planning to stop me?

"Let's get the formalities over quickly," he says, dark smudges beneath his eyes. "I have unfinished business."

I force a tight smile. Maybe Soran had evaded him and the guards last night. *Don't care. Shouldn't care*, my thoughts race. I need to be thinking about the kingdom.

"Meera dear, they're waiting for you." Akane gives me a gentle nudge.

I stiffen, remembering where I am, skin prickling as the eyes of the kingdom turn toward me. Queensguard form a straight line up the beach, swords at their sides and vested in the traditional colors of Ezo, silver and blue. Beyond them, the beach turns into a wide cliff nestled with rows of low fences overlooking the bay and the white-walled castle above with its familiar tiered roof. Black shingles glisten like obsidian jewels in the morning sun.

Crowds press against the fence in the distance, shouldering the queensguard for a glimpse of the princess who leapt into the sea to face a dragon and lived. The faces that arrive to greet me warm my soul, but not as much as Runa's face would.

It feels wrong to step onto my homeland, to breathe in the fresh sea air and the scent of sweet cherries and spring with no sister to share it with. Bastian, too, is mysteriously absent. Had he received my letter? My eyes find their way back to the assortment of nobles on the beach, one face in particular.

Casmir's warm gaze meets mine.

Green eyes like a summer forest cover me in a welcome shade from the onslaught of curious glances in my direction. I fist my hands, nails digging into the fat of my palm. Questions swarm in the air between us.

Me: Why did you tell everyone we are married?

Him: Why did you betray me with a kiss?

Casmir swallows hard before stepping forward, dressed like a prince instead of a duke. A rich camellia-red jerkin beneath his silk jacket matches my dress perfectly. He waits a few paces from the gangway, his eyes riveted on me as if I were a pearl lost at sea that had miraculously drifted back to shore.

"Welcome home," he says.

I'd rehearsed this moment on the ship, but my thoughts escape me. I'd forgotten the warmth of his eyes, the care of a friend who also understands the trials of leadership, the curve of his lips. Heat bristles up my neck before I can stop it and I cast my eyes down to maintain composure.

Why had I kissed him before facing the dragon?

The red hem of my dress crests over my black boots. *Look up, Meera. This is your kingdom.* It's as if Runa is speaking to me. A chill brushes my bare neck and my gaze shoots up, remembering why I'm here—the queendom needs a queen.

And an alliance with Taiga might be the only way to save Ezo without the dragons' magic. Ezo needs another kind of fire to protect its shores—one with whiskey-colored hair and a will of iron.

"I thank the saints for my safe return," I say, smoothing my voice to a loud and polished tone for all to hear. It's imperative that the kingdom understands I'm safe and *whole*. That I faced the dragon and wasn't killed, even though I didn't accomplish what I set out to do. "I pray Ezo has fared well in my absence."

Casmir nods, sunlit hair falling from his carefully groomed facade. He extends his arm. "It has," he says and then lowers his voice for me alone. "And so have you."

I take his arm in mine, the warmth in my cheeks drowned out by the chill of the ocean breeze. I'm keenly aware of the message I'm stating with my current ensemble: I'm the wife of the Duke of Taiga. It grates against my hearts to go along with the deception, but what else am I to do? Casmir's eyes take on a clever sheen as I catch his gaze, a silent agreement that we are both pretending this marriage is real to save Ezo.

Cerulean hair twists around my head in a braided crown before trailing down my back, decked in tiny rubies and threads of gold. A crimson dress—one Casmir's mother had picked out as a gift when she heard of our wedding—fits against my slight curves and shows off the new black brace with the dual dragons of Taiga carved into its lacquered leather. Black boots studded in gold say I'm not just a princess for fancy balls; I'm ready to stop a war.

I stiffen against Casmir's touch as his arm links with mine, a gentle bend that seems like a perfect match. But is it?

What of the rumors he didn't stifle? The marriage is a ruse, but why has he let it take root?

Words unspoken swirl between us, hidden behind our faces schooled to please the crowd. A smile masks my emotions, demure and gentle—one that Runa would have approved and teased me relentlessly for too. Soran would've made some comment about how people hide what matters most while showing off falsehoods.

I cast a look over my shoulder, hating the disappointment when I don't see him standing on the rampart with his bare feet and unwavering candor.

The ambassador of Taiga and Casmir's mother disembark the ramp, and my father steps forward, acknowledging them first. "Welcome to Ezo," he says in his thundering voice. "Thank you for returning the princess to her home. We've made every accommodation for you."

Hello to you too, Papa.

Casmir's arm hugs mine as if in sympathy.

My father's gaze turns to me. He is ever the cold-hearted king: rigid, and concealing any sign of joy at my return. It's been a week—one whole week—which feels both short and like a lifetime.

"It's the least we could do," the ambassador replies. "We trust that Ezo is well and has contained the unfortunate sickness of the late Princess Runa?"

My feet grind to a stop. No . . . my sister isn't dead.

"The princess is just sleeping," the king corrects, his eyes hardening. "No cause for alarm. The house of Silverwood is a secure fortress, let me assure you. Now, come." He turns on his heel, the queensguard snapping to attention beside him, and strolls up the winding path from the castle's private beach to the southern gates.

My hand tightens on Casmir's arm. "My sister is alive, isn't she?" I whisper, thirsting for more confirmation.

"Yes," he says. "Though some are spreading the rumor that she's dead. Meera, it's only a matter of time until—"

"Runa will live," I say in a too-loud voice. A hush falls over the crowd. Let everyone think what they will of me.

"A cursed sleep can hardly be called living," the ambassador mutters loud enough for me to hear.

He wants to rile me.

Papa's hard brown eyes meet mine, lips pinched in disapproval. I've already caused a scene on day one of my return. I could keep quiet now, or act like a queen.

"Princess Runa is not dead," I say louder. "I will not permit such rumors to spread. As my father, the prince consort has said, she is asleep. I am queen regent until she wakes."

"Meera, let's talk first," Casmir whispers, leaning toward me. "A lot has happened since you left."

"No." I stiffen and cast him a wary glance. "Runa would want me to protect Ezo until she wakes."

The ambassador opens his mouth to speak, but Papa silences him with a bellowing voice. "I appreciate your concern for Princess Runa," he says, turning to me, the censure in his eyes searing. "But let's turn our attention to more pressing matters. Now that you're here, you'll be able to help the *regent* maintain Ezo's borders. Isn't that right, Duke?"

Casmir's arm tenses beneath mine. Whispers ripple along the nobles. The suggestion veiled behind the words is cutting, stealing the breath from my lungs.

"Regent?" My gaze shifts to Casmir's questioningly. *He* is ruling Ezo in Runa's stead? Not Bastian, or my father, but Cass?

Casmir averts his eyes toward the castle. "We've much to discuss, Princess."

The words aren't intended to silence me, but they do. *What have I walked into?* Questions stick to my throat. I've hardly spoken one word to the man at my side and now he is conspiring to take my crown? What is he to me? *My fiancé? My friend? Definitely not my husband.*

My eyes trail his hand for the ring—the one he'd offered me in the library with the ruby surrounded by diamonds. It feels like so many moons ago.

Casmir casts me a concerned glance, and I divert my eyes from the ring, smiling for the benefit of the crowd.

"Shall we?" Sir Richter says, a glimmer of victory in his eyes. He gestures for Casmir's mother to follow behind the king. Akane gives a respectful bow and strides ahead with a graceful step.

I cast another glance to the ship, wishing I could return to its swaying deck or even back to the hot spring inn nestled in the mountain. *How could I feel safer with a dragon than at home in my own house?*

The ambassador trails the welcoming committee, but his gaze wanders back to Casmir and me before disappearing around the snaking path. Only a few queensguard remain with us at the end of the procession.

"It'd be best to talk inside," Casmir says in a low voice.

"Yes . . ." I say, feeling strangely disoriented. *Regent. Why had no one told me? I should be queen regent. Or Bastian if something happened to me. Where is my brother?*

I glance back toward the ship, its impressive sails billowing taut in the wind. The red lacquered rails force my hearts to squeeze thinking of Soran and the beating he'd received because of me. I hadn't expected him to disembark the ship with the rest of us, but I find myself searching for him none-theless.

I turn to join the others, but Casmir doesn't budge. "What is it?" I ask.

His arm locks in mine. "Who's that?"

Dokun dokun. I know the answer before I whip around.

A man clothed in pink wide-leg pants and black haori with gold-dust eyes and a youthful jaw ringed with bruises stands at the top of the ramp. He makes his way down, humming as he takes each barefooted step. The morning sun seems to brighten from his song, but it's just my hearts rushing blood to my mind, making the world more saturated.

Soran.

He pauses at the last step where the rocks meet the wooden ramp, as if he'd rather not set foot on Ezo soil yet.

Casmir's eyes flick to the dragon's feet. He raises a brow, turning to me for answers.

"This is . . ." I wet my lips, searching for an acceptable explanation. "My guardian. He found me on the beach in Taiga where I washed up after the dragon attack."

Casmir's green eyes cut into me. He doesn't need to search for the truth, he knows I'm lying. I read it on his tight jaw and the pain behind the stare that softens as he realizes I'm reading him correctly. "How? No one survives a dragon attack like that, Meera."

The words are so simple, but they expose me completely.

Casmir faces Soran with a look that could spill blood. "Meet me at sundown," he orders. "You and I are going to have a talk."

Soran raises a brow and steps onto the rocky path. His lips curve into a derisive grin as if he'd like nothing more than to meet Cass in private and murder him. "I don't take orders," he says smoothly. "If you'd like to speak to me, next time ask nicely."

Casmir releases my arm and strides forward. *Great, just what*

I need, a brawl as soon as I land back home. "Cass," I whisper harshly. "People are watching."

The two men don't look at me but pause within striking range of each other. This isn't about me, I'm not foolish enough to think that, it's about who they are. Casmir feels it intuitively, Soran's otherness, the dragon in his blood, and it's driving him mad. "Who is he, Meera?"

"A bodyguard," I say.

"Not much of a bodyguard," Cass says, surveying Soran's bruises.

"Or a very good one," Soran quips, stepping closer. "My charge doesn't have a mark on her. And I didn't let her jump off a cliff."

An uneven breath hitches my lungs at the sudden emotion in his voice.

Casmir's knuckles turn white.

I step between them, wedging myself into the narrowing space and murderous stares. "I'd like to invite you both to a . . . banquet. Celebrating my return as queen regent."

Soran's eyes narrow at me, trying to decipher what I'm up to.

"Please." I smile at them both.

"You know what happened at the last celebration in Ezo?" Casmir stares at me in disbelief. "You could get killed," he says, lowering his voice. "The assassin is still out there."

"Then we do it to draw him out, and you two become friends in the process."

Soran laughs. "I'd rather become friends with a pirate than" —he gestures to Casmir in disgust—"that monster."

"I hate to agree with him, but the lout has a point," Casmir mumbles.

I pull Casmir aside with an apologetic smile. "He's not very polite, but he did save my life."

"Fine. He can stay," Casmir says, a tick in his jaw. "But in the stables. He smells like a dragon."

"He doesn't smell—"

Casmir's brow raises higher as if daring me to finish the sentence.

Like a dragon, I was going to say. Not that he smells like warm campfire doused by a spring rain or any such nonsense. But I get that it's beside the point. I *shouldn't* know how he smells, and now is not the time to defend myself.

Casmir turns and nods to the queensguard to lead Soran to his quarters—or stables—and then gives me his full attention. "We've a lot to talk about," he says, taking my hand. "Would you like a coffee?"

I'd like to see my sister, to rest in my own bed, to escape into the saints' library for answers—but I'm not here for me. I'm here to resuscitate a queendom and steal a ring. And both can be done over coffee. "I thought you'd never ask."

I risk a glance over my shoulder as Soran walks between four guards sent to keep him in line. He winks at me, and I've no idea if he knows how conspiratorial that looks or if he's trying to get me in trouble. Probably the latter. Nothing will keep him in that stable, not with his heart so close to the Dragon Slayer. But I'm not worried about him, not until the third trial.

Casmir is another story.

He takes me to my room and opens the door, motioning for me to go inside. I slip into the familiar chamber on the first floor, the least glamorous of rooms, but Runa had agreed to stay with me here so I wouldn't have to climb all the stairs with the blue sickness haunting my veins.

The so-called curse that made my hair blue and my spine crooked. I fear it made my heart sick too, but Runa never thought so. Fresh lilies lay across Runa's pillow, her clothes arranged for her in the wardrobe as if she'd awake the next day.

I turn back to look at Casmir, emotion making my voice stuffy. "Cass, I'm—"

"Don't say it." He shakes his head, raking a hand through his hair. The ruby ring gleams on his finger, right where the wedding band would be. He'd moved it from his index finger sometime after the wedding-that-wasn't. "We'll talk later, after you've rested. I'll send Seira up with your coffee."

"But Cass, I need answers and to explain—"

"Soon," he says, a weary kindness in his eye. He turns and strides down the long corridor toward the stairs.

How have I made a disaster of my first day back in Ezo?

Seira arrives shortly carrying a tray with a cup of frothy, decadent espresso smothered in fresh cream. She sets the tray down with a clatter and then throws her arms around my neck.

I rock back, nearly falling from her weight. Sobs rack her chest as she pulls back and squeezes my shoulders. "I thought you'd died, miss! Kazuya and I were so worried. We—oh, I'm just glad you're okay. The Saint really does answer prayers. And look at you, walking without a limp."

It's true, I haven't limped since Soran sang over me, but my back still aches from all the walking. "Slow down, Seira," I say with a smile. "Tell me, how are things at home? I've heard rumors. My father said that Casmir is regent. What does it mean? *How?*"

Seira pats a full-backed chair for me to sit down, brings me the cup of coffee on a saucer, and then drags a stool screeching across the floor. She flops on it, lips pursed in worry. "The rumors are a bit nasty," she concedes. "But not all are rumors. Are you sure you want to talk about that? You just got home."

I take a sip of coffee and my insides melt. "Yes, that's exactly what I want to discuss. Are they truly saying that Casmir and I are . . . married?"

Seira cocks her head, studying me with a dubious expression. "Aren't you? We all saw the ceremony. You kissed and—"

Coffee spews from my lips. "We kissed, yes," I say. "But I didn't say my vows or take his ring. I-I . . . jumped off a cliff, Seira. How can that be a yes?"

"You have a point." Seira's face pales as she twists her hands in her lap, as though debating something. "Everyone thought you'd cracked after losing Runa. The doctors called it *hysteria*, when a person gets confused, heart beats too fast, shortness of breath, that kind of thing. And Casmir didn't deny that you were married. Bastian himself announced it.

"The duke has been taking care of the border and foreign relations while you were gone. Your father named him regent since Bastian's been missing and everyone understood you were married. The kingdom couldn't rely on a figurehead like your father after the scheduled coronation, so he had to appoint someone." Her brows knit. "Why didn't the duke say anything?"

"I'd like to know that as well. What do you mean Bastian's missing? Where is he? I was surprised he wasn't at the docks to greet me. It's not like him."

Seira scoots her stool closer, eyeing the windows guardedly. "I'll tell you more, but not here. The castle has eyes. Just the other day, I was interrogated about your sister. The assassin is still on the loose, and Casmir holds tight reins on *everything*."

I flinch at the suggestion that Casmir is being too controlling. While I don't like that he became regent in place of Bastian, he can't possibly mean to keep the role. Regent implies a temporary position. "He's doing his job, Seira. I've an idea where no one will bother us and we can speak freely."

She lifts a brow. "Don't tell me the market, because they'll never let you go there alone again."

"The banquet hall," I say. "It's been too long since I last saw my sister."

Seira pales and shakes her head. "No, you can't."

"Runa never let anyone tell her what she couldn't do."

"Meera." Seira lays her hand on my arm and flinches when my eyes narrow at her. She bites her lip. "The killing sleep has spread. Going into the banquet hall is as good as saying you've got it too. It's spreading in Rusa now, but it's not just putting people asleep—they're dying." Her lips tremble. "You mustn't tell anyone I know, it'll get me in trouble and others besides. I beg you, don't go in there. The door is locked with solid silver. Not even the duke can enter now. It's off limits."

"Then find me a metallurgist," I say, finishing the coffee and setting it down on the dressing table. "There's work to be done. I'm going to finish the coronation where we left off, with my sister's blessing."

"But . . . the only metallurgist is still a child. The king has her locked in the dungeon. She's the one who sealed the doors on his orders and—"

"Seira." I turn to her, willing her to see my determination. "We've always been friends, and that won't change. But starting now, I'm also your queen. I have to do this."

Seira bows, her breath tightening. I hate how quickly she adapts from confidant to servant. I never wanted this, any of it. Runa was more fitted to the role of ruler. "What would you have me do first?"

"Send your brother to bring the metallurgist to me. I also want a report on all the delegates housed in the West Wing, if any of them have been in contact with Sir Richter. And Seira, thank you."

Seira blanches at the mention of Sir Richter. She nods and backs from the room before scurrying down the hall. I shouldn't worry about the feelings of house maids, but I do. There's something she's not telling me.

Steeling myself, I call for the guards outside my door. Only one thing left to do if I'm to make my coronation official and steal my betrothed's ring . . . and that's to set things right with my father. He was the one who made Casmir regent and my battle starts with him.

"I need to speak to my father," I say. "Take me to him."

CHAPTER 23
MEERA

THIS WAS THE WORST PLAN in the history of plans, which says a lot. Worse than leaping off a cliff on my wedding day, and definitely worse than putting a dragon in a kimono and daring him to tackle assassins. The dread of speaking with my father snakes around my spine like a cold fist, threatening to snap me in two.

Look more whole. Papa's words the day of my sister's coronation repeat in my mind like a spell, telling me who I am.

But it doesn't sit right with me. Soran hadn't deemed me worthy because of what I thought about myself. Who knew that thoughts could be curses too? But just like spells, they're meant to be broken.

I raise my head as the doors of the private grand hall slide open. Ignoring the queensguard and Taigan sentries on my left and right, I step inside. Enormous ink-washed murals of cherry blossoms and young pines against a warm golden palette greet me. It's a startling contrast to the stony king waiting for me at the front of the room. Father sits on a raised platform, his usually cold eyes weighted with worry. Though not for my safety, I'm sure.

I stride across the thick rush mats to the room's center and bow. The king returns the gesture, and I kneel with difficulty, waiting for him to speak first. It's not a coincidence my father chose this room, a formal space, for our audience.

"It's about time you returned to your senses," the king says. "Do you intend to move forward with the coronation? There are conditions to be discussed."

I swallow hard. "The kingdom needs hope for the future. I will take Runa's place until she wakes. Make me queen regent. It's the only way."

"You? Bring the people hope?" A laugh escapes the king's lips, choked out by a thick cough. "The people believe you abandoned them in a fit of madness. Thanks to you, the people believe that Casmir, a foreign duke, is their only hope. But"—Papa leans forward—"I will arrange for the coronation on the condition that you prove to the people of Ezo that you are . . . better."

"Better?" I scoff at his choice of words. As if better is an improvement from the word *whole*. He hasn't truly looked at me, seen me for who I am, not since mother died.

"How do I show them that I'm worthy? That I'm whole?" I ask, stressing the last word.

"You marry, properly this time." The king's eyes bore down on me as if I'm another soldier in his army and not his daughter. "You and Casmir will sign the marriage license and share the North Wing until the coronation. The alliance with Taiga is the only way to protect our borders. Ezo is not safe, even from within. When your brother arrives"—he coughs, hard, and presses a fist to his lips—"he will assist Casmir with the duties he maintains in Taiga. Your *husband* has done an excellent job of managing the kingdom in your absence. He's proven himself worthy for the both of you."

My breaths come in short. I know my papa's still there beneath the cold exterior, but it's hard to believe. If grief has become my catalyst to action, it's become his shield preventing any light or hope from cracking his icy heart. It's one thing for him to sell me off to an arranged marriage, quite another to sell our kingdom out of fear.

"I don't need marriage to become queen," I say, standing. "Mother believed each of us was worthy. Not Casmir or anyone else proves my worth. I carry it in here." I lay a hand upon my hearts.

"You are too similar to her," Papa says with a heavy exhale. His fist trembles upon his temple, brows knit together as if to block out any more kind words. "I don't say this because I doubt you, Meera, rash as you are. There is a threat within the castle walls. An alliance with Taiga is our only hope. You must understand that. Without Casmir, Ezo would have fallen already. It is a queen's role to do whatever is necessary to protect her people."

Papa uncurls his fist and waves a weary hand, avoiding my eyes. "Now leave. The duke will summon you. I've already let him know my intentions."

You are too similar to her. It's the best compliment my father has given me since Mama died. Too similar to the brave woman who fought off wolves to save her children. To the woman who carried Runa on her shoulders and sewed rabbits on our quilts with little button noses and smooth silver threads. Too similar to the mother who believed that the Saint threads all things together for good.

But this?

Marrying Casmir?

Accepting, once again, that I'm not enough?

I don't bow when I leave the great hall. My footfalls creak against the polished wood floor as I storm back to my room to await the summons. Even the queensguard has a hard time keeping up, and I manage to escape to my room and slam the door. *A summons!*

Hearts thunder in my chest at the indignity. Everything in me wants to rebel against my father, to prove that I'm worthy and can lead the kingdom like Runa would have.

But I'm not the queen my sister would be. The only reason Ezo is still standing is because of Cass.

I pace Runa's and my room for what feels like hours. My spine aches beneath the crimson dress as it rustles against my feet with a fire-patterned gossamer. I suck in air, feeling my chest expand beneath the black brace.

My fingers brush the stenciled images of dual dragons on the hand-lacquered leather. The texture is smooth as bone. The brace hugs my spine with a flexibility and support like no other brace has done before. I would have loved it in another version of my story; I suppose I still do, but the dragons feel off. Too savage. Too cold-blooded. Not as—my brows knit together—not as thoughtful as Soran.

Can't think about the dragon now. I won't.

A rap sounds at the door and my hearts leap.

I rush to open it. A Taigan guard stands outside and bows. "The duke requests your presence."

Within minutes, I'm standing outside Casmir's door and wondering what in the eight kingdoms we're going to talk about. We both know the marriage isn't official yet, not on paper or in our hearts, even if the whole kingdom thinks we sleep in the same bed. I haven't had time to even think about if I *want* to marry Casmir. But how else do I hold the kingdom together when it's falling apart? And what did father mean about not being safe within these walls?

Sir Richter. Jey. Had one of them poisoned Runa?

Two sentries stand watch in the hallway, but it does nothing to calm me. Threats grow around me like choking vines: Seshu and Rusa scheming to overtake Ezo, Runa fading with the killing sleep, the dragons preparing to rip out my heart.

Dokun dokun.

My knuckles rap on Casmir's door.

"I heard you'd be up here," comes a low baritone from behind me.

I turn around slowly, resisting the urge to spin in surprise. Casmir strides down the wide hall covered in old tapestries, his boots soft against the wooden floor but loud enough that I should have heard him coming. He holds an apple in one hand, chewing thoughtfully as he walks.

I raise a brow at the slight indecency.

"Your father told me he'd sent up a present," he says stopping a few paces from me. "But he needs to work on his manners. A gentleman never makes a present of a princess but offers her one instead."

I take a deep breath, my anxiety settling into a rippling pool. "I don't need a present. I've come to *talk*."

"I know," he says, taking another bite of apple. "You want to talk here"—he gestures to the bedroom with a roguish grin meant to unnerve me—"or elsewhere?"

I arch a brow and take a quick step away from the door. I was wondering how he'd taken the rejection at the wedding. Apparently not as a definite 'no.' "How does the library sound to you? The grand library in the monastery?"

"I could think of no place more celibate," he says, eyes sparkling with mischief.

We journey properly this time, notifying the appropriate officials and traveling by carriage instead of on horseback in the moonlight. It seems like ages ago we came here to procure a marriage license and sneak into the treasury in search of the fabled dagger. A dagger that had cursed Soran's heart.

My hand goes to my chest, feeling the familiar flutter of hearts working as one. *Would parting with the dragon heart really kill me?*

Casmir sits across from me in the carriage, giving me space to get used to him again. He still wears the official Taigan uniform he'd worn at the beach, a black suit with gold buttons, a wool jerkin the color of winter camellia, and the collar of his white shirt unbuttoned as if he were tired of the formality. Stress clouds his usually impeccable features, rough stubble shading his jaw.

How much has he been doing for Ezo while I was away?

"I should speak first," I say, leaning against the upholstered seat. "I'm sorry for leaving you at the wedding."

His smile is more of a grimace as he glances out the window into the dappled forest. "I should thank you," he says. "I've had few opportunities for humility. They say it improves character."

"Cass, please take the apology. I *am* sorry."

His jaw tightens, those green eyes studying me like I'd just asked the world of him. "Would you do it again? Face the dragon instead of marry me?"

Words clam in my throat. *Would I?* Knowing that my actions had done nothing to improve Runa's state, nothing to help Ezo? Instead, it had left our borders wide open and susceptible to attack. I'd wounded more than one person: Casmir, Bastian, Seira, and . . . Soran.

Cass smiles and shakes his head. "You'd do it all over again, wouldn't you? Loyalty runs deeper in your veins than your own blood."

"If I knew what I know now, that I would fail in saving Runa, then no. I wouldn't have done it. But I had to try. I'm sorry," I say again. "I'd do anything for my sister. No matter how small the chance. Magic is the only thing that can save her . . . or it was."

"Don't apologize," he says. "I'd give kingdoms for such loyalty. Your sister is lucky to have you. Now for my question."

"Wait," I interrupt. "Why did my father name you regent?

Was it to get Taiga's backing? I asked him about it, but the answer was less than satisfactory."

Casmir holds up a hand and begins counting on his fingers. My eyes don't miss the glint of his ruby ring. "One. The princess set to take the throne was cursed. Two. The younger princess leapt off a cliff instead of marrying me." He raises a brow at this one, smiling as though it amuses him. "Three. Rusa and Seshu declared war with armed fleets. Four. The prince decided to run off and search for his sister, who everyone thought was dead."

"I get it," I say, lowering his hand gently. An odd chill passes over me as I brush his ring. What do the dragons want with it?

"No, you don't get it," he presses. "Five. The killing curse spreads and the first case outside the castle was identified in Rusa."

"I've heard rumors," I say.

"Ezo needed hope, something new and exciting, someone with experience in war. The king as prince consort is merely a figurehead without power. The people need more. Your brother asked me to step in while he was away and your father agreed."

"Why didn't you quell the rumors about us being married?"

He gives me a sidelong look. "People need something to celebrate, and a strong leader. Both are very hard to find in times of war. But everyone loves weddings, and I'm something of a celebrity after your notorious runaway at the altar. By assuring everyone that we'd been married, it stabilized the kingdom."

Wheels crunch over gravel, and the carriage grates to a halt. We're greeted at the gates of the monastery by the nuns in their periwinkle-blue robes waiting on the steps. Mother Ema bows at the main doors, a kind smile on her weathered features.

"Welcome to the home of the Ladies of the Light," she says, opening the door for us. "We've reserved you a room in the library as discussed."

As discussed? I look to Casmir for answers, but he doesn't sate my curiosity.

Mother Ema's soft blue eyes light on my pendant as we step across the threshold. She doesn't mention the dagger, and I wonder if anyone had found out that it was missing. It certainly didn't seem like they regularly inspected the forbidden vault, but the knowing look in her eyes suggests otherwise.

I pause beneath her guarded stare, fingering Mama's pendant as my thoughts turn to the dagger at the bottom of the sea. "Thank you for supporting the kingdom while I was away," I say, willing her to see the apology in my eyes. "I'm trusting the Saint still has a plan for Ezo."

Mother Ema's weathered face softens. "He always has a plan. But it's your choice to follow it or not."

A small laugh escapes me. "I wouldn't begin to know the Saint's mind."

"You'll know when the time is right. May I?" She lifts my pendant between her fingers, admiring the flat gold circle imprinted with a star and crossed daggers. Her lips pinch in a curious smile. "Sometimes the difference between a queen and a thief is very small. Or between a saint and a monster."

"You speak in riddles."

"When you realize what makes them different, then you'll know the right path." Mother Ema drops my pendant.

"We thank you for the quick accommodation," Casmir says, nodding toward the saint. "Princess Meera wanted to peruse your books after her encounter with the dragon. We have some questions that need answers."

Mother Ema inclines her head. "We prepared all the books relating to dragons on the center table. Please let me know if you need anything else. May the light be with you."

The massive library doors close behind us. I spin toward Casmir. "Why did you lie to the mother? I didn't ask to—"

"And you haven't been lying? My next question." He closes the gap between us with a decisive movement. "How did you survive? And who is that man who found you? Why did you tell your father that you wanted to marry me for real this time?"

He takes my hand in his, the ruby signet ring smooth against my fingers and his palm warm in mine. "I-I didn't say . . . my father arranged . . ." I huff in exasperation. "That's three questions, Cass."

"That's because I'm afraid of the answer to the last one. And I'm never afraid, Meera." He draws my hands up toward his lips and places a gentle kiss across my knuckles, the look in his green eyes pleading. "I can handle the truth, but no more lies. No more secrets."

I nearly swear in the monastery but stop myself. To pull away now would be to say no most irrevocably to him, the man who had held my kingdom together while I was away. The last wall of defense sparing Ezo from war. There's a kindness in him I can't overlook, even if he wants my kingdom.

My fingers unwind from his, allowing myself a brief moment to imagine a future with him. I'd never allowed myself to go there when our arranged marriage was decided. It'd been a distant thing then, like a cloud that I could neither control nor wish away. Something my father had planned, and I shunned simply because he'd orchestrated it.

And then there's Soran . . . I shake my head, surprised my thoughts jumped there so quickly. But I find myself humming his songs unawares, noticing his favorite color with a new appreciation. Who knew I could find five shades of pink in a single cherry blossom? The way he'd protected me on the boat, laughed with me, it felt almost ordinary, in the best way.

Dokun dokun. A warm flush rises to my neck.

I pull my hand from Casmir and turn toward the books placed neatly on the center table, collecting my breath. "I've not had much time to think about us," I begin cautiously. "I survived because . . ."

Do I tell him about the dagger? Jey had warned me against it. To Mortua with Jey and his backstabbing schemes.

"Because I found the dagger of the Bleeding Saint. The one in the legends we'd talked about. I thought it would give me a chance to save Runa and the kingdom. And it did, sort of."

Cass' eyes narrow as he turns toward me, leaning against the table. "Jey lied to me about the dagger then. It's as I expected."

I nod, grateful he doesn't mention my own lies. *Chooses not to.* It almost makes me want to tell him everything. Almost. "That's how I survived the dragon, with the dagger. But the myths about the dagger aren't exactly true. It didn't work like I'd expected. I landed on a beach in Taiga and the man you saw on the docks, Soran, he saved me."

Casmir grabs a book from afar and plops it onto the table in front of me with an unholy smack. The letters, *Of Saints and Monsters,* stare back at me in embellished gold script.

"No one survives a dragon attack like that with a dagger, relic or not." His hand covers the page, a dark intensity in his voice I've not heard before. Powerful, almost threatening. "I'm not a fool, Meera. I saw the color of his eyes."

Dokun dokun dokun dokun. The dragon heart inside me begs to flee.

My hands clutch the table rim as I stare at the book. Casmir flips the pages and then hammers it with a ringed fist. Carefully sketched images of dragon eyes meet my own, each of them varying shades of black or brown—all flecked in gold.

"I'm not asking who he is," Casmir says, voice strained. "I'm asking, *what is he?*"

I wet my lips, hearts thundering so hard that I fear my ribs will bruise. The secret digs into my mind, hiding, begging for me to keep Soran's identity hidden. *Safe.*

But neither of us will be safe until I have Casmir's ring in my hand. So much for the second trial being simple. I'm treading shifting sand with the duke, with my kingdom, and with my hearts. Honesty is the only way to reclaim the duke's trust.

I flip the pages until I see drawings of the elongated beasts with their serrated spines and flowing whiskers, foxlike faces and razor-sharp talons. Handwritten letters scrawl in the margins, calculating sizes and measurements for each. Pointing to the picture on the parchment, I meet Cass' eyes.

"A dragon," I whisper. "The one I stabbed to be precise."

Casmir tilts his head slowly to look at me and then the picture, a furrow appearing on his brow. "It can't be . . ."

"That's what I said at first." I lay my hand over his on the page. The ruby ring presses against my palm. The one thing I need to complete the second trial. If I could make it through all the trials, I would live. The dragons would leave Ezo alone. I would have a chance at the heart magic to save Runa.

"But shapeshifting?" Casmir's face hardens. "It doesn't make sense. I've never heard of it before."

Dragon hunting is his profession, so the interest makes sense —too much sense for my liking. I flip to the end of the book, scouring for a small paragraph I'd seen years ago in my studies. "Here." I point to it and begin reading out loud.

"Although rare and no specific documentation is available for proof, it is theorized that a dragon may shift into human form under an enchantment. Many consider that this is what happened to the Beast responsible for the destruction of Taiga in the early Sangetsu period after he was destroyed, but scholars disagree. In order for a dragon to shapeshift it would have to lose one of its hearts."

"Impossible." Casmir tears the book away and combs the pages feverishly. "Even if it lost its heart, it would die, not change into a human form. Why would the monster save you?" He pauses, looking up from the book, a scowl etched on his handsome face. "And why would you bring it back to Ezo?"

My throat tightens. I want to tell him the truth, to ease the worried lines of his face and replace them with the carefree smile I'd seen not moments ago. I need him on my side to help Ezo. But he'd kill Soran and leave me with a dragon heart he could never love.

"Dragons are . . . complicated," I say, reaching out until our fingers touch and the ring is within my grasp. "Can I answer your other questions?"

He takes my hand, eyes peering at me with questions and pain and longing.

"I asked my father for a coronation, to make me queen in Runa's stead. But he told me that he'd already named you regent. He told me to seal the alliance with Taiga by marrying, for real this time, and he'd give me the crown."

"So it's for power?" he asks with a soft laugh and approving smile.

"No," I say, straightening my back. "It's for Ezo. I have a duty to my sister, to the kingdom, to keep it intact. Cass, I've never been one to dream of marriage. But . . . you've become a friend to me, to my family. You've stood by my kingdom when it began to crumble, but I—"

"How do you feel around me?" He runs a hand along my cheek questioningly.

I close my eyes, wishing away the warm feelings that spring on me. He must misread my reaction, because his other hand goes around my waist, drawing me closer. My eyes jump to his, scrambling for footing in that sunlit forest of green. "Cass," I mumble, searching for words.

"Do you still feel the same way about me?"

"I'm not sure what I feel," I confess. "And feelings aren't always the best indicator of what is right." One of my hearts pounds louder than the other, tugging me away.

"Your honesty is like an arrow," he says, his voice coarse and uneven. "It makes me want to fight harder to prove myself to you."

He leans in to kiss me, his breath stealing over me tasting of apples and fresh spring cedar. My stomach flips and my mind buzzes with warmth, but I step back and hold the space between us. My hearts aren't something I can trust to just anyone.

"Marry me, Meera." It's not a question. He slips the ruby ring off his finger and holds it out for me to take. His cheeks flush as if realizing his blunder. "Would you? For real this time? I've kept my promise to keep Ezo safe. To keep your sister safe. Let me keep you safe too."

But he can't. No one can.

I eye the ruby ring—my free ticket out of the second trial—and then meet Cass' warm gaze filled with possibility and promises. If I reject him now, there will be no going back. He won't forgive me a second time. He won't give me the ring.

"Can we make a deal?" I ask cautiously.

His brow flinches, but he recovers quickly. "You did this last time I proposed, and it didn't go so well. But bargains intrigue me, so go on."

I smile, grateful the duke has the patience to hear me out, but it's fading fast. My gaze flicks to the book spread open on the table, roaming over the curved dragons and gold-flecked eyes. My stomach pinches as though I'm about to lose something precious, a deep pang that I don't quite understand. I shut the book.

"Cass, would you promise not to hunt the dragons?"

His mouth quirks as if the request is amusing. To not hurt Soran. "Only if you say yes."

"And if I keep control of Ezo as part of the matriarchy, would you be content with that?" I raise a challenging brow.

He raises his to match mine, a smile playing on his lips. "You drive a hard bargain, but I've made worse deals as the Duke of Taiga." He turns the ring in his hand. "If you say yes."

I press my lips together, torn when a decision should be easy. Cass has been there for me, has forgiven me for leaving him at the altar, and has proven himself a friend of Ezo. He's handsome, maybe too much so, and our alliance would protect Ezo from invasion.

But he doesn't have your heart, my mind whispers. *He doesn't make you feel safe, whole, treasured. He can't save Runa.*

I shut out the thoughts—the impossible. Soran will return to being a dragon, and I have a role to lead my kingdom until Runa wakes. I will find a way to save her.

I slip the ring from Casmir's hand, my fingers curling around the gold band holding a magnificent ruby. If it means saving Ezo, keeping a dragon hunter from harming Soran, and securing my life with the second trial. I meet Casmir's deep green eyes and fist the ring in my palm.

"Yes, Casmir, Duke of Taiga. I say yes."

CHAPTER 24
DRAGON

HE WASN'T ALARMED when the guards slapped chains on him and locked him in the dungeon instead of the stables as Casmir had ordered. He'd expected nothing less from the legendary dragon slayer, the duke of murder, the irascible son of a disgraced noble who was part of the Black Dragon Society. What could Meera possibly see in him?

He noticed the way the duke watched her when she stepped off the ship, as if he'd woken up to his first sunrise and could almost touch the brightness and make it his own. Meera's reaction didn't help. Her lips had parted like the softest petals of a rose, her breath catching and hip shifting to compensate for the crook in her spine.

Would she ever look at him that way?

Soran knocks the back of his head against the prison wall. His eyes flick to the ceiling wishing for a glimpse of moonlight and sixteen shades of blue instead of cold, gray walls.

It's not his business what humans decide to do with their passions—however misguided. How could they feel so much with hearts smaller than a sparrow? Feelings that soared without wings and burned without fire.

Soran's jaw clenches. He wouldn't stay this way much longer; after the third trial he would reclaim his heart. There is no future for him in this world. Pain curls a tight fist around his ribs, filling the place his heart once occupied. He was becoming more and more human without it, and the feelings . . . hurt.

He fiddles with the lock on the prison cell door. If only his powers extended to metallurgy, the magical art of bending alloys. That was his sister, Kahnya's gift, not his. She'd bestowed it on some mining family seven years ago when they freed her from a devastating collapse at a silver mine.

The husband had sacrificed his life for the mine workers and Kahnya, leaving behind a widow with a baby. Back in the rural mountains where people still revered dragons as a gift from the Saint sent to protect them. Not as monsters for slaughter or hides worth a cart of gold.

Soran wiggles his bare toes against the damp stone. During his fight with the wayfinder, she'd mentioned a cell in his future, one that would tear his heart out. He laughs. If only she knew that it'd already been torn out—by a girl with hair as blue as the ocean and a will forged from the stars.

Keys rattle against the dungeon door followed by the creak of hinges. Soran tilts his head, listening. Footsteps. Too light to be the duke. The prison door swings open, and a boy bearing the crest of Ezo's sentry trots down the stone steps.

The youngest soldier who'd marshaled him off the beach, at least half native Ainur by the look of him.

"Water," Soran says, drawing the boy's attention.

The guard pauses at the bottom step. "My orders don't include—"

"Do you need permission to do what's right?" Soran raises his chin, beckoning the young guard to the bars. "Water, please."

The guard's brow flickers with indecision, but he scoops water from a nearby wooden barrel. He lifts the ladle to the bars, careful to keep his distance. "What did you do? The duke looked like he wanted to murder you on the beach. Probably would've had the princess not been there. I've seen him do worse."

Soran takes a long swig of water. It passes over his teeth with a greasy tang that tastes distinctly of rat. He grimaces. "The princess stole my heart."

"That's a joke, right?" A disbelieving smile pulls at the corner of his lip, fading slowly as he studies Soran's face. He leans closer, chestnut skin and hazel eyes barely discernible in the torchlight. "You mean it? Did you and the duke get into a fight?"

"No." Soran reaches through the bars and grabs the boy's shirt in his fist, jerking him into the metal grating. "But we will. The key."

"The duke will kill me," he protests, struggling against the hold.

Soran pulls until the youth's face is pressed against the slick metal. "Nonsense. Casmir has bigger things to worry about than you right now. The key."

"I'm supposed to use it for her," he says, attempting to nod in the opposite direction.

From the corner of his eye, Soran notices a wooden crate large enough for a horse. It's wedged between the other cells as if it belongs. A small, quiet shadow hunches inside the cage. The prisoner had been silent for the entire day, not even moving to relieve himself.

Soran squares the guard with a serious expression. It doesn't matter who he'd come down to release, this is his way out. Meera might have the ring at this very moment, making his heart vulnerable. She's completely unaware of the danger.

That ring is more than gold and rubies.

A dangerous theory plays at the back of his mind, one swirling with dragons and dukes and daggers glazed in poison.

Not long ago, another dragon had lost his heart. Soran remembered the trail of blood in the sea, the vacancy in the

Celestial Courts, and the songs laying his soul to rest before they'd even found trace of his red scales. Days later, they found the dragon's body decomposing in the sea he'd once called home. The elders struck the crimson dragon's name from record as though he'd never existed. There'd been no mention of his heart, but now that Soran *knew* the blade . . .

What if the crimson dragon's heart still beat? Only one mortal likely to possess it. Casmir had slain three dragons in the last several years. His grandfather had been a dragon slayer as well, which fit the timeframe of the crimson dragon's death. Had he known about the dagger or the poison? The heart would have clung to the purest vessel near it, desperate to preserve itself.

Soran faces the boy-guard with newfound urgency. "Let. Me. Out. I'd prefer not to break your teeth."

The guard clenches his teeth as if that would keep them intact. "It's not worth the punishment I'd endure for letting you out."

"Have it your way." Soran pops the boy's head against the bars with a loud clang.

The boy groans, sagging against the bars and holding his forehead. "No," he pleads weakly, trying to keep the door shut. "Don't—"

Soran pads the guard's pockets for the keys. Cool metal slides over his fingers as he locates them and unlocks the shackles on his wrists and ankles.

"My thanks." Soran swings the iron cell open. In one swift movement, he twists the guard's hand behind his back and borrows the short sword at his side before shoving him into the cell. He locks the door behind him with a satisfying click. "I know this might not seem like gratitude, but I am grateful."

"You'll be sentenced to the reefs for this!" The boy struggles to regain his footing.

"That doesn't sound pleasant," Soran says. "What's your name? You're going to help me out of here."

"Kazuya," he growls, rubbing his bruised forehead. "I won't help a criminal."

"Where's Princess Meera?"

He could find her by tracking the gold pendant, but it would take too long with all the gold in the castle obstructing his senses. This guard won't take too long to crack.

"He won't tell you now that you've locked him up," quips a small, hard voice.

Not two paces away, the scrawny prisoner in the wooden cell moves. Soran steps closer, his eyes adjusted to the darkness. A girl sits in a mound of damp straw, long black hair brushing her knees; she can't be more than eight years old. The wooden cell sits apart, each plank as thick as the width of his hand.

Soran shifts the keys, finding a crooked wooden one to match her cage. As soon as the door clicks open, the girl's eyes dart up, pinning him with an angry stare.

She bolts for the exit like a mountain hare.

"Whoa." Soran snatches the girl by the back of her soiled tunic. "What's your name?"

She spins, scarecrow arms tense and ready for a fight. Her brows knit in confusion as she looks from him to the imprisoned guard. "Sorachi," she growls, fierce gray eyes settling on Soran. "Who's asking?"

"I am." Soran releases her and bends to the girl's eye level, conveying that he wishes her no harm. Dragon magic flares within her sprightly heart, a cool, silver flame. "You're a metallurgist," he says, not concealing his surprise. "What are you doing behind bars?"

"They're made of wood, dummy." She spits on the ground, disturbingly close to his bare feet, and scowls. "Why'd they lock you up? Were those pink pants too offensive?"

Soran holds back a grin. "I don't need to ask why you're here. You probably insulted the wrong person."

The girl eyes him shrewdly. "You're not bad, mister. Not all bad, anyway."

"What did the guard want with you?" he asks, tossing the keys in hand.

"Good question." She snatches the water ladle as a weapon and spins on the guard behind bars. "What do ya want? I'm not gonna touch that door again!"

Soran grabs the ladle mid-air with a reproving look. The girl rolls her shoulders back, chafing that she can't hit something. He turns to the guard. "Answer her."

"The princess asked for her," the guard says, his tanned arms looped through the prison bars. "My sister is the princess' personal maid. She says they need a metallurgist for the wedding feast."

"The what?" Soran's jaw goes slack. He stills, a cold dread sinking into his chest.

"He said wedding feast." The girl elbows him in the hip before turning to march up the stairs. "That means food!"

"In the banquet hall," the guard says.

"*The* banquet hall?" the girl shrills. She stops on the bottom step. "Like the one the half-dead princess is locked inside with a curse and a bunch of bodies? Nope. Not touching that door again. Why on earth would they want to open it?"

"To send a message to the dignitaries, I think." The guard gives a morose laugh. He is almost resigned to the cell already, the fight drained from him. "I used to believe Princess Runa would wake," he says, tapping his fingers against the bars. "But she's probably dead. No one has opened that room in over a week. Any hope we had for Ezo is gone. The king was a fool to hand it over to the duke. I've spent the week helping him on patrols. The man's a monster."

"We agree on that point," Soran says dryly. "But I'm not so convinced Runa is beyond hope."

"What's it to you, Goldie?" The girl nods toward the stairs

and freedom. "Let's get out of here. I'm not sticking around for this."

Soran raises an affronted brow. "Who are you speaking to?"

"You, of course," she says. "You've got gold thingies in your eyes."

"My name is Soran," he corrects, the corner of his lip twisting into a reluctant smile. "Runa would be your queen right now if not for the curse. I think she deserves respect. Dignity."

The words surprise him, coming from a place of feeling rather than logic. Curiosity tugs at his chest. What would have happened if Runa hadn't succumbed to the killing sleep? If Meera hadn't taken matters into her own hands and changed everything? Part of him doesn't want to know, doesn't want to let go of all the . . . feelings he wouldn't have known otherwise.

Soran turns toward the guard. "You say the wedding feast will take place in the banquet hall where Runa sleeps? When does it start?"

"In two hours if the kid manages to open the door. They'll send guards to check if I don't bring her soon. Then we're all in trouble."

Soran eyes the guard thoughtfully. "Come with us. Your allegiance seems to be with the princess, not the duke. It will provide the best cover and you won't get tasked for our escape. Just misunderstanding orders."

"Why should I help a criminal?"

"Because we have the same goal," Soran says.

"What? Escaping the dungeon?" He shakes the bars. "You put me in here."

"No, seeing Princess Runa wake up."

The trek from the dungeon and into the main levels of the castle requires skill to remain undetected. The young guard,

Kazuya, begrudgingly doles out instructions with hand signals as they navigate a maze of wooden halls. A secret passage used by the queensguard trails the main corridor, walled off with thin planks that allow for easy listening between the walls.

"Watch your step and move where I do," Kazuya whispers, keeping his footsteps light. "One wrong move and the floor will whistle."

"What made you decide to cooperate?" Sorachi says, shouldering past him. "Embarrassed you got tasked by a little girl and Goldie here?" One of the floorboards gives a soft creak beneath her. She grins sheepishly and steps back.

"Because this country won't remain Ezo with the duke at the helm," he says. "If there's someone who still believes Princess Runa will wake, I'll take my chances. My people have a saying: hope is closer than the stars and stronger than ice. I guess I'd forgotten that as long as the stars shine, I shouldn't give up."

"I think you missed your life calling." Sorachi laughs. "You should've been a poet."

The guard pauses at the bottom of a twisted passage. A dark corridor opens from the square of flagstone, revealing a large oak double-door. The once ornate wooden transoms and oak planks are now a spiderweb of twisted silver. Metal stretches over the wood like vines clawing into bricks.

Soran casts a glance at the scarecrow of a girl at his side. She trembles at the sight of the door, her hands wringing together.

The child had done all that to seal it shut? Perhaps she couldn't control the magic yet; she'd been too young to receive it.

Four sconces frame the massive double doors, amber light guttering into the dark hallway and casting an eerie glow to the melted silver. Two men wait in the lamplight, one a queensguard in argent and blue livery, and the other a shorter man with nimble hands, restless dark eyes, and cropped black hair.

Soran slips back around the corner of the twisting stairwell to hide. He motions for Kazuya to commence the plan.

"Did you hear something?" the restless man asks the other guard.

"No, sir."

"I thought I felt someone watching . . ."

Kazuya shoulders past Soran and steps into the corridor, dragging the metallurgist by the scruff of her tunic. She claws at him and yells frightening obscenities. Her feet push against the stone in a vain attempt to stall their progression to the silver-encased door.

"Jey. Kimura." Kazuya greets the watchmen on guard. "Here's the prisoner."

"You're late," Jey, the restless one, growls. He scans the young guard with narrowed eyes as if trying to determine the best punishment for his tardiness.

Sorachi squirms and shakes off the guard's hold on her, turning to run. "No! I won't touch that door again!"

Jey laughs, blocking her path with a quick step. "You didn't have so much attitude when the king asked you to lock it in the first place."

She cuts him a look. "Well, I didn't think it would almost kill me and that he'd *thank me* by throwing me in the dungeon."

"That's nobility for you." A smile wrinkles Jey's thin lips. "Street rats live and die by their brains not brawn. Get smarter if you want a future. Now back to work."

Soran watches from the shadows as the little girl makes one last attempt to run. Jey snags her by the hair and drags her to the door, putting her hands against the metal. Sorachi cries out and it's no longer an act.

Soran's stomach knots, the cruelty burning an angry fire inside him. It takes all his focus to remain hidden.

"The door," Jey demands.

Sorachi's arms tremble as she touches the massive oak doors

strangled by metal vines. The silver convulses at her touch, rising to meet her tiny, calloused hands. Feet shoulder-width apart, Sorachi strains for balance as she channels her heart magic into the unwieldy metal.

Vines curl and flick silver tongues at her in protest before pulling inward, converging in the center of the door until a large handle appears in the shape of a metal rose.

Sorachi's knees buckle and she staggers. With an exhausted huff, she collapses onto the cold floor. One hand still touches the door, her fingertips drawn to a curling metal vine.

Soran's jaw tightens. Forcing a child to use so much magic is cruel. It's beyond her endurance. But he can't step forward yet.

"Move her," Jey commands.

The queensguard grab Sorachi by her twig-like arms and haul her limp body to the side of the corridor. She doesn't protest, her energy drained like the last dregs of soup spilled through a crack in the floor.

"Open it." Jey nods toward the door.

The wood heaves a sigh as if the air pent up behind it had been pushing against the doors for months and begging for release. The two queensguard exchange a look, neither wanting to open the magic-laced door into a chamber possessing a killing sleep and an unknown number of bodies—living or dead.

Soran glances down at his livery borrowed from the guards' room, a lapis lazuli blue uniform with silver buttons and trim along the shoulders and sleeves. His bare feet grip the flagstone beneath him, the stone's coolness reminding him to be strong and unbending like it.

The banquet would bring him one step closer to finding Princess Meera. One step closer to his heart. The longer she has the ring, the more opportunities for disaster. Meera undoubtedly has it in her possession if they are organizing a wedding feast.

"Do it!" Jey barks, waving an impatient hand. "Open the

door. Don't make me wait or I'll have you both strapped to the reefs."

Soran seizes the opportunity. He breaks from the stairwell and strides forward. Grabbing the silver handle, he pries the door open with uncanny ease. A cold, rank smell sweeps from the opening and coils into the hallway.

Soran steps back, holding his breath. He extends a subtle bow to the commanding soldier, imagining the short ruthless man screaming in a pit of dragonfire to keep composure.

Jey raises a brow, unflinching, as the stale, putrid air saturates the hall.

Soran clears his throat. He'd need to explain his presence. "The princess sent me to make sure her sister looks presentable."

"I see," Jey says, dark eyes scrutinizing. "You"—he points to Kazuya standing dumbstruck in the hall—"fetch the maids. It'll take an hour to clean this mess. And you, what's your name, guard?"

The words jam in his throat. It feels wrong to share his name with this man. "Goldie," he says, cringing on the inside.

"You're in charge here, Goldie." A humorless smile cracks Jey's lips. "Clean this room and prepare for the feast. The duke and princess will be here within the hour. And . . ." Jey swivels his sharp gaze on him as if trying to find a reason to doubt Soran's story.

Soran doesn't miss a beat, he strides into the newly opened banquet hall and begins ordering the arriving maids. If he keeps active, the commander might leave him alone. Before any of them begin clearing the rotten food and moving the still-sleeping bodies strewn across the floor, Jey throws a bag full of gloves onto the flagstone.

"Use those if you touch anything," he orders.

One of the maids lifts a glove from the bag and her jaw goes slack. "It's silk."

"Yes, we found that cotton and leather don't prevent the killing sleep from spreading."

"And silk?" the maid asks, a slight inflection in her voice.

"We haven't tested it yet." Jey shrugs. "And I'd recommend wearing shoes too." He gives Soran a pointed look and then turns down the hall to command someone else.

The now-open banquet hall chokes on its own silence. Kazuya stands beside the other queensguard, while a half dozen maids pluck gloves from the bag and linger at the foot of the door, waiting for his lead. The scrawny metallurgist lies propped against the exterior wall, eyelids heavy from exhaustion. Soran fingers the white strand of hair over his left brow. He, too, knows what it's like to use so much magic without leverage.

He'd not had his other heart to balance the magic so it had borrowed from his own life. Soran faces the assembled staff.

"We have an hour to clean this room," he says. "Everyone wears the gloves and *no one* touches another person. Remove the food, wipe the tables, polish the floor, but touch no one. Understand?"

One of the maids chokes on a relieved sob.

"What are you going to do?" Kazuya asks, coming up alongside him. The boy casts an assuring glance to one of the maids, presumably the sister he mentioned.

Soran stares at the half dozen men strewn across the floor; no one had paid any regard for the life still beating in their veins— or for the now-rancid bodies that had once housed something sacred.

His gaze shifts to the princess reclining in an opulent chair, her head tilted back unnaturally. The girl's face is moonlight pale and streaked in greenish veins, food stains her crimson dress, and long chestnut hair rumples over her shoulders like blanched seaweed. Most would think her dead save for the shallow breath in her lungs. He swallows hard.

"I'll move the bodies."

"Aren't you worried? The killing sleep is contagious."

Soran smooths back his unruly hair, his fingers pausing over the white streak that'd cost him at least a year of his life. He'd felt it, the time ticking away from him, the unknown of when he would die but the certainty winding a hole through his already empty chest.

If he stayed human, he would never reach an old age, never live to see the next generation, never count his thirty-thousandth and three-hundredth sunrise like most mortals. Things he'd never imagined losing that now seem of more worth than gold.

But if it salvaged his conscience, gave Meera what she was willing to die for—the life of her sister, it's the least he could do before she died in the third trial. He wouldn't steal his heart like the girl had.

He would pay for it.

Curiosity tugs him toward the poisoned princess. Ratsbane, foxglove, deadly nightshade, even green tea brewed underground. He'd seen enough in his years as a dragon to know that no poison is powerful enough to become contagious without the aid of magic. Ashfallen magic. Dragon made.

The servants whisper behind his back, their expressions almost reverent. He'd not seen that in the eyes of men in a long time.

"Don't worry about me," Soran says, giving Kazuya a firm pat on the shoulder. "I have the antidote for fear."

Kazuya raises a brow. "Oh, really?"

"It's simple," Soran says, swallowing the knot in his throat as he lays a hand on the sleeping princess. "I sing."

CHAPTER 25
MEERA

I HADN'T PLANNED on taking a detour to the duke's bedroom before the wedding banquet that would announce my coronation as queen.

Casmir removes his jacket and hooks it with a finger over his shoulder. "Promise this won't make us late," he says, sweeping the bedroom door open. "I have a few things I need to square away before the banquet."

His foot props the door wide as he gestures for me to enter with a simple flourish. Protests flood my mouth. Everyone thinks we're already married, there's nothing improper about it—except that we aren't. Until we actually say our vows before a saint and sign the papers, it's just an act to frighten the other kingdoms with our alliance.

"I can wait outside if it won't take long," I offer.

He throws his coat haphazardly on the bed, green eyes glittering with amusement. "What makes you think my business doesn't involve you?"

I stiffen in the entryway, heat blooming up my neck. "I-I . . . think we need to talk before—"

"Before filing an embargo on Seshu?" He grins, waving a stack of papers at me with a devilish wink. "I completely agree."

My breath escapes in a much too loud huff, and I smile. "You know, I'm completely against an embargo on Seshu. This could've been deal breaking. I'm glad we discussed it."

He laughs and reaches past me to close the door, his arm brushing mine. There's a methodic slowness to his movement, as if he'd much rather linger here next to me. But he draws away suddenly, like he feels the wall I'm holding between us.

"I'm sorting out proposals for the ambassadors and diplomats we've been keeping in quarantine," he says, slipping back into his composed self. "We can appease a few of them with reduced tariffs and silver production, while others need a firm hand to remember where Ezo stands among the kingdoms"—he offers me a smile, one that I would call shy on any other man—"as much as I'd love to discuss other things."

My hand flies to my brace as if to hold me together, but my eyes get lost in the green forest gently asking if I'd like another kiss. I twist the signet ring that hangs heavy around my neck, strung alongside my pendant of the saint. My eyes snap to the floor, breaking his spell over me.

"We don't want to be late," I say.

"You don't need an excuse," he says, stepping back. "I'm in no hurry."

I'm thankful he doesn't look at me as he says it. I'm sure my cheeks are as pink as those ridiculous pants Soran wears. My hands clench. I shouldn't think about the dragon, he only wants my heart—*his heart*, actually—but it's beginning to feel oddly familiar. The twin beats thrum within my veins and a slight ache pulls at my chest.

I take in the large room while Casmir occupies himself with the papers. The North Wing used to be my favorite place in the castle, overlooking the ocean and the narrow straight that connects Ezo to the rest of the eight kingdoms. The sun rises from this window, the first light in all the world.

Mama used to sit with me on the balcony, pale blue curtains blowing in and out, tickling our faces. I finger the embroidered silver threads in the drapery. The stitched shapes are imprinted on my memory: stars and moons and rabbits.

It still smells of Mama, of mountain wintersweet and miso from her time helping in the kitchen. *A queen is always with her people*, she would say. My siblings say that Mama was a wild, stubborn spirit like me. But when she faced the wolves, I'd done nothing. I'd frozen. I'd no courage in my heart then. Now it's me braving the wolves—men from the neighboring kingdoms waiting to claim our land. Having a celebration dinner with Runa would show them that I don't take treason or scheming lightly. Sir Richter and Jey in particular.

I slide the full-length window open, letting the breeze hit my face and erase all these feelings. This time I *am* doing something to save my family, my kingdom. Even if it's marrying for power to hold everything together. The world must see Ezo standing on its own feet, even if it sees the shadow of Taiga behind it.

I bite my lip, tasting the salt-laced air. Would Runa approve of my marriage to Casmir? While I don't love him, he's respectable, hardworking, and patient.

Dokun dokun. My stomach pinches. Perhaps staring at the sea so long is making me sick.

I finger the gold necklace weighed down by the saint's pendant and Casmir's ruby ring. If only the sea were closer and I could throw the ring from this window and be done with the second trial. Maybe then this decision wouldn't feel so . . . wrong.

What do the dragons want with the ring anyway? Does it hold some magic? Had it belonged to a dragon's treasure cache and Casmir had stolen it?

"Are you ready to show the kingdom your worth?" Casmir's

voice slips in from behind me. His hand slides from my shoulder to the soft curve of my neck where my gold necklace rests. "Are you going to put on the ring or just hoard it like a dragon?"

"Soon," I say, fingering the gold chain. "But I want the dignitaries to see my worth without it first."

"They'd be blind not to."

I turn to face him and grip the ring tightly, dual hearts pounding.

Casmir's forest-green eyes meet mine. No gold flecks dance in their gaze, no depth like the sea or wonder like a man wishing on a star. I tear my gaze away and look at the ring instead.

What's wrong with me? I need a clear head to meet the nobles and introduce myself as queen. Gold flecks, who needs those?

An unwelcome flutter skips through my ribs at the thought.

Casmir's hand trails to the ring, covering my own. I marvel at the brilliance of the fiery ruby. Even in the shadow of our hands it burns with an unnatural radiance—like a living flame. "I'll wear it after the banquet," I say. "Maybe we can go somewhere quiet . . . like by the sea to put it on."

I'm almost relieved Soran isn't around to help. I don't need whatever consequences the dragons had promised if he intervenes. It's better for everyone if he stays out of this. A sharp pain pulls at my chest and I draw a tight breath.

This heart is more opinionated than I'd bargained for. If it doesn't stop acting up, I'm going to start jogging to make it suffer.

"Are you all right?" Casmir asks.

"I just need some sea air. Something refreshing after we deal with the dignitaries."

"The last time I let you near the sea you almost died," he says, voice wary.

Who's to say I won't this time? Whatever the dragons want

with the ring, it's not to stash it in a cave. It could be a trick, like the first trial, one I wouldn't have survived without Soran.

I offer Cass a practiced smile. "Magic has its pull. But I've made my choice. This is my kingdom and you promised—"

A loud knock hammers at the door.

Casmir stiffens and turns. He whisks the door open and the Taigan guard on the other side nearly tumbles into the room. "Apologies my lord, but it's most urgent."

"It better be."

"The king has been poisoned." The guard's eyes shift from Casmir to me. "You are both needed immediately."

"What kind of poison?" Casmir's warm demeanor shifts to a detached calculation. "Details, quickly and to the point."

"Is my father all right?"

"He's . . . holding on. The healers are tending to him now. It wasn't the killing sleep," the guard says, his face paling. "Deadly nightshade, likely dosed in his tea over the course of the week. The princess was the last one besides the guards to see him."

"You will not relay this information to anyone else," Casmir says. "Was Jey one of those guards?"

"Y-yes, my lord."

Casmir's voice drops to a whisper, but I'm almost certain he threatens to silence the man. The guard bows and hurries from the room, leaving the door open.

A thoughtful shadow descends on Casmir's face. "I'm sorry about your father. Do you need time alone?"

No, Papa couldn't be poisoned. How does Casmir take it so calmly? When did he become suspicious of Jey? Soran said it was Sir Richter conspiring against me.

My legs shake mutinously, threatening to buckle. I just saw my father. How could he have fallen in so little time? I remember his cough, the weariness in his face. Is the assassin sending me a warning? I force myself to match Casmir's gaze. His green eyes bore into me with a fierce confidence.

"I can meet the advisers if you prefer," he says delicately.

"No . . ." I'm only barely conscious that my hand trembles against the windowsill, holding me upright. Without Papa the kingdom has no ruler, not even a figurehead at the helm. There's no time to mourn a vacancy on the throne—only to fill it. "The coronation banquet will continue as planned," I say. "The people of Ezo need a queen."

I don't have time to process my father's close encounter with death when the dignitaries staring at me clearly wish for mine.

The six remaining nobles and ambassadors from the surrounding kingdoms round the banquet table at a distance. All wolves assessing a kill. No one makes a move. The only kingdom strong enough to unite the lesser kingdoms is Taiga and its lord is standing at my side.

None of them know about my father yet, the poison waging war in his veins. Except, perhaps, the one responsible. I've a suspicion he lurks in this very room.

Sir Richter and the ambassador of Seshu stand farthest in the back, avoiding the centerpiece at all costs—my sister. Instead their eyes fix on the glass wall that looks into the ocean from beneath the waves or at the chandelier imported from Furan.

Not at what matters most.

Runa fills my eyes the moment I step into the banquet hall.

I'd feared to see her near death, a living nightmare asleep upon the forsaken table. Fear conjured images of her chestnut tresses grown into long vines and poison running green rivers down her veins. The memory of my sister choking on poison is stamped upon my soul.

But Runa's hair is brushed and free from the sticky strands of pudding. A soft blanket covers her spoiled dress, and someone has dabbed away the dried blood once caked on her forehead.

My hearts lodge in my throat, warmth flooding my face and threatening tears.

Had Casmir ordered one of the servants to tend to her? Which of them had the courage to actually touch her, to risk their life to give my sister the decency of a clean face?

I approach the chair where Runa sleeps, ignoring the dignitaries as I pay tribute to the one soul braver than them all. My sister's head tilts to the side against a small cushion. Her skin is a smooth chestnut cream, no trace of poison leeching her veins. It's as if she merely sleeps. Like she'd eaten too much dinner and couldn't stay awake for another of Bastian's seafaring yarns.

My eyes cut to Casmir and the few others I trust to some degree. Seira bows her head with the other maids, all dressed in white pinafores with matching gloves. Madame Akane's shrewd brown eyes observe my every interaction with her son, her thoughts secreted behind a kind smile. And in the entryway . . . Bastian. I scarcely contain the gasp of shock as my brother's tawny-brown eyes catch mine.

"Meera," Bastian's warm voice envelops me before his bear hug. I'm pressed into his thick jacket, smelling of salt and herring as though he'd just stepped off a boat. "It's good to see you, little sis."

"You too." I return the fierce hug before pulling away to soak in his face. "We've a lot to catch up on."

Bastian grins. "That we do. Here." He holds out a black scarf embroidered in half-moons and rabbits. "A present for your coronation. You might need it."

"A scarf?" My palm shifts beneath the silk and meets a glimmer of silver. A dagger, about the length of my hand, nestles in the black folds. "I might need it, huh?"

Bastian cocks his head, a sad smile dimpling his face. "After what happened to Father." His voice drops to a whisper. "I imagine the nobles aren't too pleased at being cooped up like chickens. It's a good idea to keep it on you."

I hold the dagger up to the warm chandelier light, unsheathing it to inspect the blade, and then tuck it beneath my brace. "Have you been at sea all this time?"

"Looking for you," he says, rubbing a hand across his stubbled jaw and then along the back of his neck. "Casmir took over as regent while I was away. You, uh, sorted things out?"

"We resolved things, mostly," I say, pursing my lips.

Sir Richter clears his throat. He'd snuck through the other delegates and hovered over our conversation without my noticing. Anger prickles my skin as I make a concentrated effort to smooth my face into an emotionless mask.

"We've been waiting for a long time," Sir Richter says, his gaze skipping over me dismissively before settling on Casmir as the final authority in the room. "Shall we begin?"

"My sister is the one who's been waiting," I say, resisting the urge to glare at the man. "A few more minutes won't hurt."

"I forget that time is figurative in some of the lesser kingdoms." Sir Richter laughs at the veiled insult. "The nobles have waited anxiously to meet you since your marriage to the duke. I see no reason to delay the banquet more unless there's something the princess doesn't wish to disclose."

"Sir Richter, you and I both know that the nobility are full of two things—bones and secrets. Break one and the other shatters. Or you can feed them both, which is the intention of a banquet." I smile, feeling Casmir's approving eyes on me.

These men are wolves. I won't survive by treating them like lambs. My pulse quickens altogether too fast, telling me I can't keep this up for long.

The alliance to Taiga is a thin thread. The dragons aren't protecting our shores. My father is ill. Is there anything I'm not hiding?

My hands slide to the brace supporting my back and my eyes flick to Akane wearing her scars boldly. I'm not hiding my weakness.

Casmir holds out his hand to me, offering to lead me to the queen's chair as my equal.

Instill confidence in the leadership of Ezo. Make a show of solidarity in the face of the nobles. I know this game. My sister played it well. Acting the part shouldn't be so hard, but pride lodges in my throat like an unwelcome fishbone.

It's evident that I'm taking too long to react. All the nobles watch the exchange like wolves sniffing for blood, for weakness. Waiting for me to tell them why it had taken so long for Ezo to find a queen. Sir Richter's mouth curls in a crooked smile, knowing he's bested me.

I look at Casmir's hand again and then grip it with my own.

Casmir closes the gap between us, lifting our hands in unity. "Taiga will support the queen," he says to the room at large. "And it's worth your time to listen to the future queen's announcement too."

Where is he going with this? My shoulders tighten into knots, keenly aware of every eye in the room staring at us.

"Queen Meera spent the last week making a deal with the dragons," he says in a loud voice. "To fulfill the wishes of her sister that Ezo would once again have a land steeped in magic and an alliance with the great kingdom of Taiga."

I gape at him, struggling to contain my shock. Soran's last words to me on the ship bolt through my mind: *There's no way you can part from my heart and live.*

Casmir's words imply the dragons will freely give us their magic, but nothing could be further from the truth. I'd told him the dagger hadn't worked. Is he out of his mind?

A chill dances up my spine followed by the frenzied thrum of hearts.

Questions erupt from the pack of dignitaries, but Casmir silences them with a wave. "Gentlemen, please take your seats. We will discuss all during the coronation banquet."

Dokun dokun. Hearts slam against my ribs as though sensing something approaching. *Could Soran have followed me here by tracking the gold pendant? Where had he gone?*

A low, eerie howl fills the room.

Candle lights flicker, nearly extinguishing, as the Furan chandelier sways gently from the ceiling. I pivot, my eyes homing on the floor-length ocean window. A dark shape rushes past the glass in a torrent of green scales, flowing whiskers, and claws. Thousands of bubbles erupt in a flurry of dark swirls and glittering currents. A hollow, piercing howl rattles the chamber. Dagger-like talons furrow into the once immaculate glass, leaving three unmistakable needlepoint lines before the beast disappears.

"A sea dragon," Akane breathes, clutching her chest. "Casmir, I thought the dragons weren't active in the waters near the castle. What is the meaning of this?"

"No need to worry," he says, stepping toward the glass as a crease forms on his brow. He traces the claw marks with a gloved hand and stares into the water as if hoping the dragon would reappear. "They've been farther out at sea, keeping pace with ships from Seshu, protecting Ezo. A statement of their support."

"They're following me," I say, not daring to look at the others. "But they won't attack Ezo . . . as promised. It's a warning, that's all."

A warning that I need to hurry up and complete the second trial.

Casmir's eyes narrow on me. I know what he's thinking, *a warning of what?*

"Do you think they'll come back?" Bastian cuts in. "Because I don't know how many warnings that window can take."

"The warning is intended for anyone who crosses Ezo," Casmir lies smoothly, finishing his inspection of the underwater glass. We both know that's not the situation.

"The beasts could break the glass," Sir Richter says. "We

should move the banquet. This location was highly inappropriate with the curse still in the room."

"I will not abandon my sister on the day I take the throne!" My pulse spikes and I struggle to control my voice. "Or any day hereafter. Gentlemen, please take a seat. We don't need to be afraid of what's out there. It's the assassin within these walls that concerns me. My father was poisoned a few hours ago." I let the pronouncement sink in. Now is the time to surprise them. To watch them squirm as I figure out who's responsible. Before continuing, I harden my features. "And I will find the one responsible before this dinner is over."

Sir Richter blusters red in the face. "It's highly irregular to begin a coronation by blaming—"

"I've blamed no one," I say. "I've only asked you to take a seat."

The men exchange apprehensive looks, but the ambassador of Seshu is the first to speak. "Is this an insult that you bring us to the same table that stole our prince? We've been prisoners in Ezo for over a week. We come only to discuss our immediate release."

"Reconsider your tone," Casmir says. "No one speaks to the queen in that manner." Power reverberates from his voice, daring anyone to counter him. "We will discuss the release of our *guests* after we've celebrated the marriage between our nations and the queen's coronation. Those who do not wish to celebrate may meet with the dragons on their way out. I believe they're more than happy to oblige."

I shoot Casmir a look. *We hadn't discussed that. Surely he's only saying it to keep the dignitaries behaving properly.* But the sharp lines of his jaw and the subtle rings beneath his eyes from stress say otherwise. He means every word.

I lay a hand on his muscled arm and smile for show. "Please, take a seat, gentlemen."

Bastian promptly takes his seat, followed by Akane and the

stern-faced ambassador of Seshu. I stare down each man until the sound of scraping chairs fills the hall. Sir Richter sits in the last available chair, on the right-hand side of Runa, his fists clenched.

I'd anticipated feeling pleased, a spark of vengefulness surfacing, wanting these men to suffer for the way they had treated my sister like a plague. Not only my sister, but the nation, as a thing to be bought and won and discarded. But Casmir's threat sits heavy in my stomach. A warning ticking in the back of my mind. *I'm playing with fire.*

Queasy faces eye the food as if it were poison. It could very well be. A plate appears before me, and I try not to shift in my seat. The back brace digs into my shoulder blades too tight, chafing. "We've had every plate tested by royal tasters," I say loudly, addressing the room.

"Are they alive?" snorts the green-robed ambassador of Thesia.

Casmir shoots a warning look and the man sobers immediately. Despite being half their age, Casmir commands unquestioned loyalty. Why then does he value my loyalty so much? I shake off the questions, trying to keep my thoughts on the present.

These men had been under careful surveillance for a week, and only a handful remain suspects in my sister's near-murder. By bringing them all into the same room and making them uncomfortable with Runa's presence, I hope to identify the poisoner. Or at the least, to send a message that Ezo won't be subdued.

"A toast," Bastian stands from his chair, raising a glass. "To my dear sister, Meera the Queen of Ezo, and my friend, Casmir the Duke of Taiga. May their rule prosper and bring peace to the eight kingdoms."

Goblets raise toward the ceiling.

Casmir lifts his chalice toward my sister and then to me. "To the future queen of Ezo," he says, swirling the glass before draining it.

I draw the cup to my lips hesitantly.

Dokun dokun.

The fear of poison clings to the air. I must take the next sip, to demonstrate bravery and extend trust. My eyes meet those I most suspect at the table, Sir Richter and the shadow guard, Jey, standing at the back of the room. I hate how my muscles tighten and ache, how sweat beads along the rim of my brace at just seeing Jey again. Remembering his threats. With the goblet fisted tight, I tilt my head back and take a long sip.

Smooth, warm wine trickles down my throat and leaves a tingling sensation on my lips. A hum rolls over the smooth taste, filling the air with music and strings like summer wind chimes. A familiar voice fills the hall, not with words but a slow and enchanting sound as though music could be taken from the air itself.

My fingers tremble as I set the goblet on the table. Gold-dust eyes meet mine and an uneven breath squeezes from my lungs. A man stands at the far side of the room near the ocean window, the water's reflection dancing across his skin.

All eyes turn toward him as he plays on a simple, stringed instrument and sings like an angel fashioned from the stars. No, from the Saint's tears.

Soran.

CHAPTER 26
MEERA

I'VE NEVER WANTED to touch a sound before. Not unlike the childish desire to catch a firefly, to hold a rainbow, or even to safeguard a snowflake.

Dokun dokun. My lips part at the sound that had once healed me. Gooseflesh covers my arms, and I realize too late that I'm not the only one staring.

Casmir stiffens beside me, his hand fisting the emptied goblet.

Sir Richter visibly twitches and attempts to summon Akane's attention, but she ignores him. From her peaceful expression, I take it that I'm not the only one affected by Soran's song. Other nobles lean back in their chairs, listening to the song that could mend a broken bone. No one else seems aware that the man dressed as a common servant was once the same as the dragon that had ravaged the window moments ago.

Raven-black hair hangs in disarray over his eyes. He stares at me like I'm part of him, like he's the fire and I'm the gold shining in it. Like he hadn't just told me days ago that he's heartless and I'd die the moment he became whole again. The thought breaks me from my trance but not the swooping sensation in my stomach.

Applause rings out as Soran finishes his song—a normal song without the heaviness of magic—if anything that man sings could be considered *normal*. I flush, realizing I've been gawking far too long.

Sir Richter eyes Casmir from across the table, clearly trying to communicate that Soran is a criminal. I don't applaud. I can't. The ruby signet ring hangs heavy around my neck on the same golden chain that holds Mama's pendant. This is why Soran's here, not for me. But the dragon trials can wait one more day— my kingdom can't.

"My best wishes to the Queen of Ezo," Soran says, offering a dignified bow before his eyes narrow on the ring. I don't miss that he didn't give Casmir any well wishes. The shock of white hair over his brow pinches my chest. It's thicker than before.

Had he healed someone else? My eyes rove to Runa's clean face and the warm hue on her once bruised skin. I draw in a sharp breath.

He wouldn't have . . . couldn't have . . .

The gold-dust eyes refuse to meet mine as he passes the stringed instrument to another servant. Questions bubble to my lips, desperate for answers. My gaze lingers as he takes up the position of a waiter at the back of the room. Soran collects a pitcher to refill the drinks as if his presence hadn't upended all my plans.

The thought of Soran attempting to heal Runa punches the air from my lungs. *Had he actually sung over her? Why?*

Conversation picks up around the table as music lilts softly in the background. Casmir leans over to whisper in my ear. "Are you sure about keeping dragons around? I'm happy to get rid of them for you."

"No," I say too quickly. "You promised."

Cass gives an unsettling smile. One that means something

else entirely. "Loosely agreed would be a better term for it," he whispers, following my eyes toward Soran. "I never promised."

My jaw tightens. "The dragons won't harm Ezo."

"It's not Ezo I'm worried about," he says pointedly.

I try not to make eye contact with Soran. The ring weighs heavy against my chest and my hearts thrum with more energy than is necessary for a dinner party. Casmir's threats are full-bodied and sharp; he's not bluffing. My father is sick and Runa sleeps at the end of the table, present but as distant as the moon. The only true ally I have is my brother, but even he's won over by Casmir's smooth tongue.

Is there any way to survive the trials and save my kingdom? I'd already tried winning it back with dragons and daggers and dukes. Now, all I have left is . . . just me.

Talk deepens around the table as the diplomats slowly overcome their fear and eat the food. Runa and her curse seem forgotten. Both Sir Richter and Jey make continued glances in her direction, though I have solid proof against neither of them. A hand slides past my shoulder, bending over me with a pitcher of water.

"I told you to throw away the ring," Soran whispers. "There's no time for decorum if you're to survive. Throw it in the sea."

"You shouldn't be—"

"Here? This is exactly where I need to be. Get rid of the ring, Meera."

I turn, staring at the fiery gold in his eyes. He hardly passes for a servant with his lean, muscular build, the soft lines of his face, the unassuming confidence in his eyes.

I hate that I notice the little things too, like the way his brow forms a slight V when he's frustrated, or how he has two freckles at the corner of his eye that remind me of a teardrop.

"Why are you looking at me that way?" he says, refilling my cup.

"I'm not." I shoot him a warning look. "I'll get rid of it later—"

Water sloshes over my dress, cold seeping between my legs and down my thighs. I jump up as Soran takes me by the elbow and propels me away from the table. All eyes in the room swivel toward me, the queen, with a wet dress that looks like I've peed myself.

Perfect. Exactly the thing to inspire confidence in a new ruler.

"You're causing a scene," I hiss, spinning on him.

Soran offers me a hand towel as if that solves the problem. "I told you, it's not the time for decorum."

Casmir sweeps to his feet. "Please excuse the queen for a moment," he says, nodding toward the diplomats before cutting between us.

Soran straightens, ditching the servant's meek posture. "I believe Meera invited us both to the banquet. Though, I hadn't realized it would be a wedding feast."

"Your memory's infallible." Casmir eyes Soran as though seeing him for the first time. "A mark of your heritage, no doubt." He snaps his fingers, beckoning three guards from the perimeter.

Jey and two queensguard step forward at his command.

"Escort the queen back to her room so she can change. Jey, watch over the diplomats while I'm gone. This won't take more than a few minutes."

"It's customary for the queen to make the orders," I correct, silencing the guards and Casmir with a look. *So much for displaying a united front before the wolves.*

"Casmir." My eyes entreat him to humor me, counting on his desire to make our alliance more than just a political one. "You're the only one I trust to protect our guests. Don't let the delegates get bored while I'm gone."

Casmir rakes back his dark blond hair, coldness steeling over his eyes. "My queen," he says, much too compliant.

A chill scurries up my spine. He's playing along for the sake of the kingdom, or for his own pride, but it's not a slight he'll forgive easily.

I step out into the hallway followed by the two queensguard and Soran, head bowed as though he were a reprimanded servant. The guards close the large doors behind us and marshal Soran forward, waiting for my command.

The red silk dress sticks to my legs, but I lift my chin. "A cloak," I instruct one of the guards. "I won't punish the staff for mishaps. Though we all know he's not one of us."

The queensguard exchange glances. They've both served my family for over a decade and have no doubt noticed by now that Soran doesn't belong among the servants. A soft gray cape drapes over my shoulders, embroidered with silver stars. It would be too warm come summer but for the tumultuous seaside spring, it's perfect.

"Stand guard at the door and alert me if anyone interferes," I say, my eyes pinning both guards with a severe look. "You served my father and my mother. Now I ask for your loyalty too."

"You have it," they say in unison.

"Good." I pull out Bastian's dagger. "Because I'm taking care of the intruder alone."

Without casting them another glance, I point the dagger at Soran and gesture for him to move down a narrow hall to a back door.

He raises a brow but complies, a silent smirk tugging at his lips. I can practically hear his thoughts: *Going to stab me with another dagger, Princess?*

I nudge him in the back, telling him to hurry as we make for the exit to the southern docks and the sea. I'll throw the ring into the ocean and be done with it. Soran need not interfere again.

The dragon was going to get himself killed if he stayed near Casmir.

Soran strides ahead with a gentle gait, his bare feet soundless. My chest pinches at his nearness. The fact that we are alone, again. But it's not like before. I am the queen holding Ezo together by a fraying thread, and he, a heartless dragon with claws to sever it.

Our worlds don't belong together. They never should've crossed paths.

I throw open the back door, the evening breeze curling through me like a hard fist. I cast one glance down the hall to make sure the guards didn't follow, and then step into the garden. An orchard of cherry trees sprawls before the steep cliffside that dips into the sea.

Soran follows me onto the sandy path wending through the garden, ducking beneath low-lying limbs held aloft with bamboo ramparts. His silence is telling.

The cliffside pavilion for the queen's coronation isn't far. Where he'd lost his immortality to my dagger. *What does he feel coming back here?*

I traverse the dark crags beyond the fenced-in walkway and tumultuous sea winking in the fading sunlight. When we're far enough from the castle's wall, I tuck into the pavilion partially veiled with large wisteria vines.

Soran swoops beneath the archway, turning to lean against the closest balustrade, arms crossed and fixing me with a searing stare.

"What were you thinking?" I spin on him, our faces a breath apart. Heat rages in my gut, mostly at myself, but it's so easy to hurl it on someone else. *Where had he been since the boat docked? Why only come to help me now?*

"Do you have any idea how fragile this kingdom is?" I say. "You've ruined my first act as queen. I don't need your help, or whatever you call this." I gesture to the wet dress beneath my cape. "I can finish the trials on my own."

Soran's eyes train on me. *You can't win*, they seem to say. *You're going to fail.*

Of course, he's betting on it. His life *depends* on my failure.

The wind steals my breath, salty and a touch of chill. Cherry blossom petals dot the rocks and sand like pink tears, forgotten and swept into corners. Their scent has faded in the week since I've been gone.

"Why are you here?" I take a deep breath, already knowing the answer. "You don't need to follow me. I'll keep your heart safe until the end, then you can have it back."

The look he gives is pained, torn. "Meera, you don't know what you're saying—"

"I mean it." I draw the cloak around me and step back, shutting out the tenderness in his voice. "Promise me that you'll use it to protect Ezo, return magic to my kingdom and bring my sister back." The petition is raw in my throat. "I know you can. You tried to heal her, didn't you?"

An awkward silence follows, and I'm forced to meet his eyes.

"Consider it a parting gift," he says. "A thank you for taking care of my heart."

"And the kingdom? Will you heal that too when you have your heart back?"

"No." His lips pinch at the corners as if he wanted to answer differently. "The battles of kingdoms may seem important to you, but nations come and go. No kingdom was made to last forever. It's not my fight."

"But if I win the third trial," I press. "And return your heart of my own accord. What then? Would you make a deal?"

"The kingdom isn't worth the cost," he says, stepping forward and brushing a wayward strand of hair from my cheek. His fingers carve a warm path across my skin, one that leaves a tingling whisper filled with the words he didn't say: *it's not worth losing you.*

I catch his hand and lower it, quickly wishing I hadn't. My stomach flips at the touch, defiant to all my well-laid plans. "It's worth it to me."

Soran takes my hands and the warmth pooling in my palms spreads. His voice is low, earnest. "Just finish the second trial, Meera."

"Not until you make a deal with me."

"The Grand Elder may be merciful, but the process of losing your heart won't be." Soran squeezes my hands as if to convey the message. "Magic is impartial to pain, much like love and other poisons."

"Would you really compare it to poison?" I say, raising a brow. "What do you know of it, dragon?"

His brow furrows like it does when he's angry, but I've a suspicion that there's something else behind it entirely. "More than I should."

Heat races between my ribs.

"If I win the third trial, save my kingdom." I say, struggling to focus on why I came out here. I'd failed to win the dragon's magic with a dagger, failed to save my sister, failed to unite the kingdom with the duke at my side. My life must be worth this at least.

"You won't win," he says, pushing me away and striding through the garden to the crags.

"Promise me!" I shout, following him as the sound of breaking waves grows.

"You wouldn't trade your sister's life for this kingdom," he says over his shoulder, not stopping. "Why is yours any different?"

I don't have answers, and he knows it.

My feet hurry, stumbling over a stray root. Soran pauses at the discordant sound of my footsteps, and I collide with him. He catches me by the arms and steps back, his eyes dropping to the ruby ring hanging from my necklace. "Finish the second trial and leave. I meant what I said on the ship."

"What, that you're heartless? I don't believe it." I counter his step, closing the space between us. "Why did you try to help Runa? You care about the kingdom, admit it."

"You want me to prove that I'm heartless?" Soran gives a disbelieving laugh. He takes me by the waist and pulls me close, his other hand cupping the back of my neck where it burns like fire. His eyes steal over my face as if devouring every detail before sliding to the ring between my beating hearts. "Throw it in the sea and by the third trial you'll not only know what heartless looks like—you'll feel it too."

An uneven breath tugs at my lungs. His words are sharp claws meant to frighten me. But I see through them. His eyes pinch at the corners, trying to remain distant, trying to push me away. His shoulders knot tight, a vein ticking in his neck.

But more importantly, the heart in my chest rises to meet his with a steady tempo, calling his bluff. There's something he wants to show me, but it's not heartlessness.

I slip my hands from his easily and place them around his neck. I'm not sure what makes me do it. Maybe it's the heart that tugs at me whenever he's nearby. Maybe it's the way he tries to act tough but always ends up helping me and making me feel safe. Or maybe it's those blasted gold flecks in his eyes that fill my world with stars.

Whatever the reason, I rise on my toes and kiss him.

CHAPTER 27
DRAGON

So this is what a kiss feels like.

Soran had seen them from afar, heard tales of them in poems and ballads, but the physical ritual had never interested him before. No one had said the mere brush of lips could reverse the flow of time or banish the most well-laid plans. His gut knots as his remaining heart makes a wicked dash against his ribs.

She wasn't supposed to taste like music, like the rise and fall of the sea with every breath. The girl presses her lips to his again, gently this time like a question whispered between close friends.

But they were not friends. Could not be.

Tell me I'm not the only one who feels this way, her kiss seems to say.

You're not. His hand traces the soft curve of her jaw, a familiar beat calling out to him beneath her skin. *Dokun, dokun.*

But just because it feels right doesn't mean it is.

He pulls back, wishing he hadn't seen a flicker of pain cross Meera's brow. Her cheeks flush a deep pink as her hands slip to his chest and then down to her sides.

"You're not heartless," Meera says before stepping back.

Then what is he?

Is it not heartless to harbor feelings for her when *a future* could never be part of their vocabulary? Heartless to protect her, shield her, crave another day and all the tomorrows when he knows they can't have them. Come the third trial, the girl will die.

End of story.

Pretending otherwise is the definition of heartless.

Meera turns away. Without thinking, he catches her hand, asking her to stay. Her eyes narrow at him in question, chin raising to cover her wounded pride. "Can you still tell me it's only your heart you care about?"

Words lodge in his throat, things he wants to say but can't. He shouldn't even be letting the feelings take root. The girl is fierce, loyal, stubborn, reckless, caring, . . . *beautiful.*

"I . . . care," Soran says. "But it's against my better judgment." He shakes his head and tilts it back to collect himself. "There is no future between us, Meera."

Her eyes drop to his hand. "Then why don't you let go?"

Because I don't want to.

Soran's jaw tightens. In all of space and time, this is the only moment he will ever have like this one. The thought hurts. But not as much as the space between them. Soran pulls her closer. *Maybe the ring could wait a little longer.*

"Hope I'm not interrupting." Casmir stands a stone's throw from them, arms crossed, and anger radiating from his shoulders like heat on a summer day.

Meera jumps back, a hand flying to the ring hanging from her necklace. "Casmir."

"The guards wouldn't speak, so it took me a while to find you. But I must admit, I wasn't expecting *this*." His eyes cut to Soran with a murderous stare. "I know what you are."

Soran steps toward him. He'd always wanted to face the duke in combat; now seems like the perfect opportunity. He assesses the duke, taking in the sword at his side and the wide, square shoulders ready for a fight. "I'm assuming Meera told you. Doesn't seem like something you could divine yourself. Unless . . . you've met another like me?"

"I've met plenty of your kind," Casmir says. "Though, none quite like you. But don't worry, you'll get the same treatment."

"Cass, this isn't what you think." Meera steps between them.

"I'd love to hear your explanation of the events," he says, raising a brow. "Because from where I'm standing, the queen has fallen a lot further than when she jumped off the cliff."

"I'm the one who dragged her out here," Soran says. "Your fight is with me."

"Listen." Meera draws up straight. "If you two are going to fight, then I'm going to stand between you and make sure neither of you gets killed."

"Dear, that's the purpose of a fight—for one of us to die," Casmir says, side-stepping her.

"Cass, no!" Meera blocks him. "I made a promise. You said that you'd let the dragons be." She unclasps the necklace and slides the ruby ring from its chain.

"You call that keeping your promise?" Casmir raises his voice, pointing at Soran.

Soran straightens, realization drawing his chest tight. "You made a deal with him?"

Meera nods and slips the ring onto her finger. She raises it for Casmir to see. "You promised," she says. "No more harming the dragons."

"Darling, he's not a dragon anymore." Casmir pushes her aside and draws his sword as Soran steps forward. Steel glints in the sunlight's western descent. The same blade that had slain numerous dragons. Unbeatable steel forged in the silver mines and doused with the healing waters of Fever House.

Meera clutches her fingers and gasps in pain.

Soran's gaze jolts in her direction, checking if the sword had accidentally grazed her, but a swordsman like Casmir wouldn't be so reckless. A bone-deep fear slinks to the front of his mind. The ring . . .

Meera's lips part, her teeth clenching as she pinches her left hand as though trying to halt poison from a viper's bite. The ring glows with an unearthly fire.

"Get it off!" she cries, tugging at the ring. Sweat beads against her brow.

Casmir lowers his sword. "Meera? What's wrong?"

The girl shudders, skin blanching. Greenish veins bulge from her finger, spidering up her hand and then arm. Meera grabs at her chest, back arching in pain.

"Meera?" Casmir lowers her to the ground, kneeling in the dirt and holding her head up. His eyes cut to Soran. "What did you do to her, dragon? Has she been poisoned?"

"There's a dragon heart in your ring," Soran says. "A dark heart."

Deep creases knit Casmir's brow. He doesn't deny it, but perhaps he's not entirely sure of it either. A vein throbs at his temple as his eyes panic over Meera's face. "It doesn't make sense. The ring has never—"

"She has my heart," Soran says, hating the way Casmir's eyes round in horror at the revelation. "The two cannot exist together. It's waging war against it."

"Can your heart defeat it?"

"I don't think so," Soran says. "But maybe hers can. You must throw her in the sea."

"Are you mad?" Casmir stands and lifts the girl in his arms.

Soran doesn't waste time. "If you won't, then I will."

CHAPTER 28
MEERA

Is this what dying feels like? Fire rips through my senses, burning me from the inside out. Voices break in and out of my conscious, but I can't make out the exact words. Only the general feeling that I'm being held, teetering on the edge of a precipice.

"Let go," a voice says. "Open your hand."

But I can't. The fire is so bright. So warm. It's the most beautiful thing I've ever seen burning inside the ring like a star made of molten tears. *The dark heart.* The moment it slid across my finger, I knew.

Pain and fury entered my blood, crawling through my skin like poison. Maybe it *is* poison. It slithers through my veins, predatory, searching for another heart to consume and take its place. Fever racks my body, pain bursting along my spine. I never knew I could feel so much suffering at once.

"Stay with me, Meera," a voice washes over me. Close. So close. "Don't give in. Tell it you won't."

I won't give in . . . I won't.

The pain doubles in response. My spine curves upward, drawing my body into violent contortions.

The heart, a dark voice creeps into my mind. *Give me the heart. Where is it?*

"No," I gasp. "No. Please, make it stop."

"She's mad with fever," a second voice calls out over me, muddled as though I'm hearing through a fog.

Wind slices against my fevered skin. The sun is too bright. Too hot. I claw at whoever holds me, begging them to make the pain stop. To make the monster inside go away.

I won't give it Soran's heart. Never. Let it eat me alive from the inside out, but I won't sell his heart to this . . . thing. I feel it inside, dark and twisted, scouring my body. It hurts most above my chest, where my own heart thunders.

Throw the ring in the sea. The thought floats to the surface of my mind. That's what the dragons wanted. They knew the ring contained the dark heart of a dragon and they meant to destroy it so it wouldn't do this. So it wouldn't try to overpower anyone, to consume and destroy.

"You're mad!" the second voice shouts. *Casmir.* "She needs a doctor."

"No. If she doesn't take this ring into the sea, she will die."

"I'm not letting her back in that ocean," Casmir snaps. "The dragons are waiting down there to devour her. Get a healer. Now!"

I'm vaguely aware of Soran reeling back and punching Casmir. My body tumbling to the hard earth and gentle, strong hands lifting me. Curses ring out, but I'm running. Or rather, Soran is running while holding me.

Give up the heart, the beast within me cries.

My throat burns and my spine feels as though it will split in two. "Make it stop . . ."

"I'm sorry, Meera." Soran anchors me to his chest, his voice frightened. I'm propped onto my feet, Soran bracing me as I wobble with a violent shudder. I'm faintly aware of the rocks beneath me and the crash of the waves. Soran's arms hold me upright. "You have to jump."

Jump? I can't even walk.

Sharp pain stabs at my abdomen and my knees beg to touch the ground. *There will be consequences if I interfere again.* Soran's words from the ship ghost through my mind. I have to do this by myself. I struggle to stand and take in my surroundings, the rock face ends only a few steps from me, the ocean stretching beyond it.

"We do it together," Soran says, supporting me with one hand around my brace and the other hoisting up my arm. "One, two . . ."

Pain splinters across my chest. My body curls in on itself. I take two staggering steps but the effort is pointless. Soran curses and then lifts me into his arms.

Together we fall into the sea.

The water's surface is harder than I expected. It breaks across my skin with a hard slap and folds over my head. I'm pushed down in a stream of bubbles and swirling currents.

Dragons weave through the sea with armored scales, threads of silver and gold, green and blue. Their coiled bodies slam into me, spinning me into a violent whirlpool of their making. But Soran finds me, his arms a protective shield as he tries to propel us toward the surface. He holds out my ringed hand for the dragons to see.

Soran must be communicating with them telepathically because the dragons slow their frenzied churning. The green dragon faces us, its foxlike face curved into an unnatural grin, teeth bared. I push through the pain, willing my mind to listen, my eyes to observe.

A new kind of pain nestles in my chest—one that longs for air.

The emerald dragon lunges with an open mouth, its spine cutting through the water.

Don't die. Not yet. Fear gives me enough clarity to reach within my brace. I fist the short dagger I had been keeping there —Bastian's welcome home gift.

The green dragon is almost upon us. Curved fangs angle for Soran and me, each one larger than my dagger. There's no way to stop the beast. I'd learned that the first time I jumped into the sea.

Soran holds me tight, his arms unrelenting. He would face death with me. But I won't go down without a fight. I'm no longer a little girl trapped by fear. My suffering and circumstances don't define me, it's my choices.

I take one look at the dagger and the ring glued to my hand. *This ring, this is what the dragons want. This is what's causing pain.* Biting the inside of my cheek, I place the dagger over my ring finger, isolating it, and then slice. Intense fire burns through my hand at the cut. My lips press tight to hold back the scream.

Soran knocks the dagger from my hand, bubbles escaping his lips in surprise. My eyes flick from the charging green dragon to the ring and part of my finger sinking to the bottom of the sea. The ruby glints in the swirling water as it falls deeper and deeper.

The green dragon twists at the last second and chases after the ring. A guttural snarl rips past us as it nosedives in pursuit.

Soran doesn't waste a second. There's no telling how much time we have before it returns. He kicks toward the surface, gripping me tight. But I can't hold my breath any longer. Water pours into my lungs. An acrid taste climbs up my throat. I look down for the green serpent, afraid it will return.

The emerald dragon is a dark ribbon in the deep. Blood trails behind it—my blood—seeping into the ocean like a spool of crimson ink. Spots cloud my vision. Gold-dust eyes bore into mine.

Hold on, Meera, he seems to say. *Don't give up.*

For a moment, I wonder if I really hear him in my head like

he speaks to the dragons. If I've been hearing his thoughts all along. I reach for the gold in his eyes as if it's the sun calling me to the surface. Pain swallows me and the sea turns black.

CHAPTER 29
DRAGON

SHE CUT off her own finger to save them.

The blood leaking into the ocean feels like his own. Soran holds the girl afloat above the waves. Her dead weight pulls against his arms as he struggles to stay above the water. Brave, beautiful, stubborn girl. He would get her out of the sea if it cost him everything. He calculates the distance between them and the rocky shoreline. A quarter mile perhaps; the dragons had pushed them farther out with the currents.

His stomach tightens. It's not that he doubted his ability, even with the girl in tow, but she was losing blood. He could go any distance as long as his thoughts remained focused.

Silver scales break through the waves as another dragon approaches. Soran treads the water, holding Meera in front of him to help her stay afloat. The silver dragon crests the water's surface before swirling around them. Its armored body forms a cage of scales and teeth, preventing escape.

You've broken the agreement, the silver dragon says, speaking into his mind. *We told you not to intervene in the trials. You brought the ring into the sea, not the girl. She failed and so have you.*

She jumped, Soran sends the thought, cradling the girl to his chest. *It was her will. Her decision.*

Yes, but you helped. There will be consequences. Ash and bone, my old friend.

No! The innocent . . .

The green dragon returns from the deep, weaving in a circle around them. Soran attempts to dive beneath them toward the shore. But the emerald dragon slashes at him with its spiked tail. Amber light whirls within its chest, too bright for a normal flame. Soran retreats to the surface, breathing hard.

Humans are not innocent, the green dragon hisses in his mind. *You should know that, especially now that you're one of them.*

Soran recognizes the tight fishing noose formed by the two dragons, a common hunting technique. The green dragon would come from below and swallow them whole while the silver one kept them in place. There would be no escape. *Is this part of the consequence the elder had spoken of? Or is it the emerald one dishing out her own medicine, apart from them?*

The dragons' will is usually tethered to the elders and their deep knowledge of the Saint. Whatever free will they have is buried deep down, forgotten. But at times, it had been known to surface.

Soran grits his teeth as he struggles to hold the girl afloat. It wouldn't end like this. Not if he could help it.

But he didn't have a dagger, and the idea of harming one of his own is a punch to the lungs. They are no longer his brothers and sisters. He understands something they don't, the will to choose. The feeling that comes alongside the mind to shape our choices, the heart to be afraid and to still fight—to have someone worth fighting for.

The silver dragon cranes its long neck out of the water, the rest of its body forming a tight noose around them. A few minutes and they'd be gone. Soran's mind hammers against his skull for a plan.

He reaches for Meera's gold pendant to tug it from her neck and distract the monster's aim. The chain holds tight, tangled in her hair.

Wait until the last trial! he shouts in his mind.

No more waiting, I have what I came for. The green dragon says.

Sploosh! A sudden shriek erupts from the silver dragon above. Soran squints as the dragon flails and flops its head beneath the waves. Casmir pries his sword from its finned back, cursing at the dragon while pushing off its body with the heel of his boot.

"Blasted worm!" Casmir yells, struggling to stay afloat. "I'll skin your hide and stretch it out in front of my fireplace!"

"Nice of you to join us," Soran says.

Casmir growls. "You're next, so don't go thanking me yet."

A cold current surges beneath them. Soran pushes back. "Below you!"

The emerald dragon rushes Casmir, slamming into him at a dangerous speed. The duke pivots, deflecting the worst of the attack and retaining the grip on his sword. He cranes the blade at an expert angle and shears the scales from the dragon's back as it whirls past. The beast howls in fury as the silver dragon returns to its aid. Green scales glitter the sea along with an inky cloud of blood.

"Can you keep them occupied while I take her to shore?" Soran yells over the waves.

"Can I?" Casmir laughs darkly. "I'll hack them into bits so small the minnows can feast."

Soran nods. "Hold them off for at least ten minutes, until I get to shore."

"Go already!"

Soran seizes the moment and swims toward the rocky

surface. He fights to hold Meera above the waves, her head tilted back, lips nearly as blue as her tangled hair. Determination fuels his limbs, aware the dragons will come after him shortly. The duke can't hold them off for long, not two dragons and the emerald one among them.

Why had Casmir jumped in to save them?

Did the emerald beast swallow the ring?

A new horror tightens his gut. The dark heart would consume the green dragon's own heart. The beast had known that. It wasn't destroying the ring she'd been interested in, it was taking it for herself. Had she used the trials to her advantage? Twisting the elder's ear to get what she'd wanted all along?

The consequences and the trials begin to make sense. *It had been rigged from the start.* The assassins, the ring . . . It wasn't only about justice; some of the dragons had turned against the Saint. And now, they could take back the land like the Beast had done.

Soran grabs hold of the shore, clinging to the dark rocks that make up the rough coastline. He pulls Meera upward, hoisting her safely upon the rocks. His arm trembles from exertion as he climbs up after her. The clothes on his back hang heavy with water, his breath more so. Soran carries Meera farther up the shore where sand meets the crags in long golden stretches. Her head rolls to the side, sand plastered against her ashen face.

His knees sink into the sand as he presses two fingers below her jawline, checking for a pulse.

Shrieks and howls sound near the coast, but he doesn't look back. No time to distinguish between the cries of men and dragons. Hopefully the duke can hold them off a little longer.

He can't feel a heartbeat.

"Meera." He leans over her, laying his ear upon her chest. A faint thrum meets his ear, but it's not the one he's listening for. It's not the heart that beats like the wings of a dove. Not the heart that fuels this mortal soul with life and warmth. He ignores the steady *dokun dokun.*

Where is her heart? Her wild, beautiful, unstoppable heart.

Soran supports her neck, wishing all the life into her thin body. He rubs her shoulders and arms, trying to warm her and return life. "Wake up, Meera. Wake up."

Blue hair spreads across the sand, the same color as her lips and the waning tint of her skin beneath the sunlight. He unstraps the brace from her back, hoping it will allow the air to come more freely into her lungs.

She lies motionless, growing paler like the moon.

"Meera." He rakes a hand through his hair, his gaze sweeping the beach for help where there is none. He breathes into her lungs, attempting to impart life to her. *"Come back!"*

The girl doesn't move.

He cups her face, her back, and then draws her into his lap and cradles her to his chest. Could warmth bring someone back? He'd seen the fishermen mourn a drowned friend, seen a few— so very few—return to life after warming their bodies and shedding tears.

If only dragons had tears.

The girl coughs, her ribs contracting in a painful lurch. She gags and hurls the contents of her stomach across his knees.

A hard cough rattles her shoulders. Slowly, her pale face resumes its natural color. She wipes her mouth with the back of her hand and then her eyes round in shock.

"Shh, don't look at it," Soran says, pulling off his collar to provide a fresh bandage around her mauled finger. He'd been so concerned about her breathing, he'd forgotten to check on it again. "You're okay. You're whole."

He wills her to believe it. The truth.

"My hand . . ."

"It'll be fine," he says, studying her to make sure she doesn't go into shock. "I need to get you somewhere safe. I'm sorry, Meera."

Confusion and pain nestle into her brow as she looks up at him. "What for? You saved me."

He gulps, wishing he hadn't complicated things. But he couldn't just let her die. He had to intervene. There was no other choice. She wouldn't like the consequences.

Meera glances toward the sea and pulls herself to her feet, cradling her maimed hand. He steadies her, following her gaze. Casmir stands on one of the rocky crags partially submerged in water, wielding his sword at lightning speed. The silver dragon lashes its tail at him while hurling flames to force him back into the sea.

"He won't make it," Meera says.

Soran would gladly cheer to that, but he holds his tongue. Meera leans against him for support, her gaze fixed on the dragon slayer as she squeezes her injured hand.

"Soran, you have to help him."

"No, I don't."

Meera gives him a beseeching look, the lines of her face tight with pain. "Casmir is holding this kingdom together. I need him to live."

"The kingdom's not my concern."

"But it is mine. I'll go out there if you won't." Meera struggles to untie her boots with one hand. "I don't stand much chance in this condition, and neither does your heart, but—"

"That's low," he says, frowning. "I'll need a weapon."

"Fetch the queensguard," Meera says. "They should be stationed nearby. Quickly."

Soran hesitates, unwilling to leave her side when she could easily lose consciousness again. If the dragons finished Casmir, she would be their next target, in the sea or not. But the quavering strength in her voice and plea in her eyes compels him to run. He finds two sentries at the north gate, not far from the beach, and leads them to the sea.

Meera turns at their approach. The soldiers' eyes widen at the sight of her drenched robes and the bloodied rag on her hand. She lifts her chin, ordering one to retrieve Bastian and a healer. To the other, she demands his weapons. She passes Soran a simple dagger from the guard's belt.

"I'm tired of daggers." Soran drops it in the sand. "A real weapon."

Meera grabs a katana from the guard and smacks in it his palm. "Be safe."

"I don't pick my battles based on what is safe," he says. "Some things are worth fighting for no matter the cost."

"Like Casmir's life?"

Soran smiles, wishing the wind didn't toss her blue hair like ribbons and her lips didn't look like they needed warming. "No," he says, biting back the words at the tip of his tongue. "Like my heart."

He wades into the sea before the girl can say something that makes him reckless. It doesn't take long for him to reach the dragon and the barely-standing duke. The silver dragon sees him coming but ignores him in favor of trapped prey on a lonely rock. Amber glows hot in the dragon's belly as the duke prepares his stance for the next attack.

Soran climbs up the rock beside Casmir, pulling out his sword as the duke's blade comes down at him before halting mid-air.

"What are you doing?" Casmir snarls, jerking back the blade. Blood seeps from a wound on his brow and another deep slash across his arm. His clothes are scorched and torn.

"Saving you."

"I don't need saving." The duke parries, sliding down the rock and cutting at the silver dragon as it throws its serrated tail against the rock. A crack splits the stone, water dashing up the middle. "But you could be useful as a distraction. Then I'll kill it."

Soran fists the sword tight and nods. *Distract it. Easy enough, but kill . . .*

The silver dragon lashes at them again with its spiked tail and a howl of flame. They duck, stomachs hitting the hard rock, before jumping back up. The dragon plunges into the water where they cannot see, no doubt circling them for a vulnerable opening.

"Where is the green one?" Soran asks, his back to Casmir's as they survey both directions should the dragon resurface.

"West," Casmir snaps. "Unless it changed directions underwater. How should I know?"

He wished the silver dragon would just leave now that the emerald monster had gotten what it wanted. But it remained on the green dragon's orders, meting out a punishment without thought. Not so unlike humans who take orders without asking the right questions.

The silver dragon resurfaces like a flash of lightning. "What are you waiting for?" Casmir shouts. "Distract it!"

Soran leaps from the rock, landing behind the beast's scaled head. He grabs its horn and drives the sword's blunt handle into the soft scales there. Casmir attacks at the same moment, his blade slicing through the dragon's neck from below, plunging all the way to the hilt.

The silver dragon shudders, its body going limp against the rock where it had landed. The part still in the sea lilts to the side like a sunken ship. Soran releases the sword with a trembling hand. His fingers trail over the rows of perfect scales until he reaches the empty black eyes flecked in gold.

Like his.

Grief lances a bitter arrow through his ribs. Dragons aren't supposed to die, not like this. He had spilled ancient blood. Even if he got his heart back, things would never be the same.

"A bit too close to home?" Casmir spits blood from his mouth, staring down at the dead dragon. He attempts to pull his blade free, but it refuses to give. Casmir shoves his boot against the dragon's head and rolls it into the sea, swiping his blade free as it falls.

"Don't forget you're next," Casmir says, swinging the sword dangerously close to Soran's neck.

Soran doesn't flinch.

"After I beat the green one." Casmir lowers the blade. "Where did it go?"

"To fight another day." Soran stands and peers back at the beach where Meera now sits accompanied by several guards swarming the sand.

"Then I suggest we do the same," Casmir says, diving into the sea and swimming to shore. Soran follows, hating the way it feels like part of him has died. The dragon had left them little choice. Fight or be killed.

Soran hauls himself to the beach and sinks exhausted onto the sand, throwing a hand behind his head. Casmir stands with the queensguard and Meera closer to the castle walls. A warm robe blankets her shoulders and one of the healers tends to her injured finger. Bastian, too, stands on the shore, his banquet robes forgotten and looking every bit the pirate. He stomps down the beach, boots crunching to a stop just feet from Soran's head.

"A dragon's been sighted in the city," Bastian says, staring out at sea. "The diplomats are in a panic. One of them struck down a guard and attempted to commandeer a ship. It's chaos."

Soran pushes up on his elbows, eyeing Meera's brother warily. He has the same round eyes and thick, dark lashes, a familiar stubbornness in his chin. "Why are you telling me?"

Bastian gives him a sidelong look. "Casmir isn't the type to get jealous unless there's a real threat. I just hope not everyone saw the way she looked at you in the banquet hall. Do you care for her?"

Soran flinches in surprise. Had it been so obvious? But *care* seems too soft a word, like a sentiment for the weather. Whatever the feeling is, it's more of a tempest, not that he'd tell Bastian. "You've not answered my question," Soran says.

Bastian rolls his neck with an audible crack. "You single-handedly managed to throw this kingdom into more chaos. A trait I admire in a pirate, but not in a brother-in-law. I want you to fix it."

Soran laughs and his ribs squeeze in mutinous pain. "Don't worry, I'm not after her heart." *Only the return of the one that rightfully belongs to me.* "And it's not my job to salvage your kingdom." Soran trains his eyes straight ahead, on his tenth sunrise as a mortal. Persimmon and honey drip from the sky as the sun makes its westward descent.

"I'm not asking. The dragon sighted near town started a fire. We need every man available to put it out." Bastian throws a pile of clean clothes onto the sand, the uniform of a shadow guard and a pair of pink pants. "But I am asking you to keep my sister out of trouble. She won't listen to Casmir or me, but for some reason, she might listen to you."

Soran rises to his feet and dusts the sand from his wet clothes. He scoops up the clothing, accepting the offer. He might not care if Ezo falls, but he still has a heart to protect. "I promise you, she listens to no one. Present company included."

"What is this about the city in flames?" Meera runs up to them, spinning on Bastian. "The guards told me."

Bastian shakes his head. "It's a dragon. It blasted the wharf and then flew off."

"It what?" Casmir thunders, joining them, one hand cupping the open slash on his arm as if to hold it together.

"It has . . . wings," Bastian stresses the last word, searching for an answer on the shocked faces before him. "It will probably return. The scouts say it retreated to the mountains surrounding Silverwood, near the cathedral, but it continues to circle. We already dispatched a regiment of soldiers to the market and set a perimeter around the castle, that's how we found you. Not that any of you will tell me what's going on out here. It looks like you all left for a swim, and it turned into a bloodbath."

"That's a fairly accurate assessment," Soran says.

"Did you say a dragon with wings?" Casmir's hand clamps too tight on his arm, blood squelching to the sand.

"The ring . . ." Meera pales and her blue eyes snap to Soran's before taking in the others assembled. "Do you think the green dragon took it?"

"Most certainly," he says.

"What does a dragon want with a ring?" Bastian's eyes land on Meera's necklace now bare of the signet ring.

"I'll fill you in later," Meera says. "First, we deal with the threat to Silverwood. If a dragon is attacking then we need to evacuate the town, bring the people into the castle walls. Use every man and woman prepared to help. Send one squadron to the harbor to secure our ships."

The queensguard bow, dividing the order and hurrying to the castle to do as the queen commands. Meera turns to Soran, her voice a broken whisper. "Is this the consequence you spoke of?"

"Consequence of what?" Casmir grimaces as a healer pokes at his arm.

Soran's shoulders sag, too tired to fight another battle. He looks at Meera, willing her to see reason. There's no stopping the destruction, not with the dark heart alive within the emerald beast. "They warned there would be consequences if I intervened. The dragons promised to burn Silverwood to ash and bone if I stepped in. I'm . . . sorry."

"You could've said this sooner," Casmir growls.

"We can't erase the past," Meera says. "But we can change the future. My city will not be destroyed. Cass, you're the strategist. What do we need to do?"

Casmir swears and shoves the healer away. He snatches the

bandages, his face paling from the loss of blood. By the size of the gash, it needs stitches. "First, we recover. We'll be useless against the monster like this. Give me one hour. Change clothes, mend wounds, prepare weapons. Send your soldiers to evacuate the town but don't put everyone in the same place. You want to diversify the targets so the beast will have to choose."

"Right." Meera turns to Soran, her eyes bore into him in a way that makes his stomach tilt.

"I'm sorry," he says. And he means more than interfering in the second trial.

"Don't say sorry with your words." Meera swallows hard. "Show it with your actions. We're going to stop a dragon —together."

CHAPTER 30
MEERA

BATTLES AREN'T WON by charging into the fray without a plan. Casmir is a born leader. Or perhaps he wasn't born that way, but a lifetime of suffering and impossible choices have carved his soul into the warrior who sits with his back toward me. The guardhouse is empty save for an armory of crossbows, spears, and swords, a guttering oil lamp, and the duke and me.

Our personal guards stand watch outside, waiting for us to finish preparing for the battle ahead. The only way to salvage the damage I'd done at the banquet is to stand by the duke's side with unflinching focus. I want nothing more than to jump on my horse and lead the charge to the market where the dragon had last been sighted encircling the city like a bird of prey. But beyond this, I have no plan.

How do we take down a dragon that can fly?

Casmir slumps over his arm on a wooden stool, his wide, muscular back slick with sweat and scars. The silver needle glints in the lamplight as Casmir sews the long stretch of muscle from his elbow to the back of his shoulder, mouth twisted in a tight grimace. He focuses on the bloodied thread with remarkable precision. Biting off the cord with his teeth, he douses rice wine over the stitched wound. He seethes as the alcohol burns into his flesh and then ties off the bandage with an experienced hand.

"The healer could have helped you," I say, throat tight.

Truth be told, he wouldn't even let me offer aid. I had to force my way into the guardhouse, shouldering Jey aside. Why does he keep that shadow around after suspecting him? He must have a reason. The only word Casmir had spoken since our brief encounter on the beach was a low growl I interpreted as *get out.*

Which of course, I politely ignored.

"I don't trust anyone," Cass says, breaking the silence.

Those words wouldn't have included me before, but they do now. I let the sting settle over my skin, knowing I deserve it.

"I haven't stayed alive this long by trusting people," Casmir continues, anger rolling off him in the tightness of his shoulders and the hard turn of his lips.

I'm no fool. Anger's one of the few emotions that can quickly cauterize a wound like heartbreak. And I'm not cruel enough to rob him of that one comfort. Not when my kiss had left a scar and I wanted Casmir to suffer no more of them. His back is full of scars already, some long and straight, others crooked and notched.

"How long have you known about the dark heart?" I ask, sliding onto a wooden stool opposite him.

"I suspected it," he says, examining his bandage and the range of motion in his arm. "The ring had belonged to my grandfather. He'd told me stories of its connection to the dragons, of its power. My left hand was always stronger with it, and I came to prefer it to my right. But I didn't know for sure about the dark heart until you told me about . . . him."

"You mean Soran?"

He grunts, washing his hands in a wooden bowl and splashing his face. Casmir tugs his shirt on over his bandaged arm and chest before laying his sword out on the table near the oil lamp. He scans the blade, inspecting it for damage.

"I've killed four dragons now. Each time I've come away with a scar. But I think I'll carry this scar the longest." He pauses, dark green eyes boring into mine. "Is he what you want, Meera?"

I take a deep breath, ribs expanding. The question is sincere and without malice. Words stick in my throat, unsure, afraid of the answer. "I want my kingdom to be safe."

His brow rises, lips slanting in a disbelieving smile. "I think you might be as blind as the emperor. Listen," he says, sheathing the katana. "I didn't spend the last few weeks in Ezo because I like this cold, mountainous island. I didn't bleed to protect your homeland. Yes, I'm invested in claiming Ezo for Taiga, but there was only one reason I held back." His eyes flick to mine. "Whether or not you feel the same, I'm still going to take down this dragon. Just give me your answer when it's over. A final answer, Meera." He drags out the last words, letting me know that this is my last chance.

"Cass, I—"

"Save it for after the battle. You going to fight?"

I nod and stand, welcoming the change of subject. My hand still throbs beneath its bandage, but the pain-relieving herbs the healer gave me take off the sharp edge. "If I don't protect my kingdom, I can't expect anyone else to."

He slaps a leather belt fitted with two daggers onto the table. "Here, a present since you lost the last one."

I didn't just lose the last one; I used it to cut off part of my finger.

The belt fits perfectly around my waist. I've changed into my training clothes from when Bastian and I used to spar with the shadow guard. The dagger glides smoothly into my palm. The blades are black as night but glimmer like mirrors, and the handles are engraved with dragons and a singular ruby in each. "Beautiful," I say, losing my breath.

"And deadly, if you wield them right. But I don't think I need to teach you."

"I'll use them well."

He sheathes his sword and gives a curt nod before pushing the door open. Jey waits outside and snaps to attention the minute we step into the night. I narrow my gaze at him, letting him know I haven't forgotten his part in all this. He'd tricked me and I'd never fulfill my bargain with him.

"Where is Kazuya?" I ask, glancing in both directions for my chosen guard, and noting our horses already tacked and ready for the excursion into Silverwood. Occasionally the guards would take better positions to cover us from attack, but they never went far.

"I replaced him." Cass nods to the far gate where someone leans against the wall, mingled with the shadows except for a pair of conspicuous pink pants.

"Soran." A breath skips through my chest at the sight of him.

Casmir takes my horse by the reins and checks the cinch before passing the reins to me. "He's a decent bodyguard. And they say to keep your enemies close."

"See, you did become friends after the banquet," I say with a sweet smile.

Casmir rolls his eyes and helps me onto my horse before turning to take his own steed. "If this is what you call friendship, I'd hate to be on your bad side, Meera."

"The fires have started," Jey says, carrying a case full of weaponry to the wagon loaded with supplies for our mission. "The scouts report that they can't hold the dragon off much longer."

Casmir swings into the saddle and pushes his horse forward with a nudge of the knees. "They won't have to."

We taste the smoke before we see it. Our party of six storms out of the castle gates with nothing but four horses, a wagon, and angry hearts at the sight before us. Casmir and Bastian take the lead, followed by Soran and me, each on horseback, and the wagon trailing behind us with the guards.

Ahead, the city bleeds the color of sunset, a flame against the rose-pink sky. Smoke churns toward the castle walls. The air is a thick flurry of ash like snow. Our horses rock their heads, ears pricked at the slightest sound. A frightened rumble comes from my mare, its footing unsure as it clops into the market square.

"The scouts said it only started an hour ago," Bastian says, his voice raw. "We're . . . too late."

I follow his gaze to the destruction choking the city. Overturned carts and rickshaws abandoned in the street, bones glistening white and scorched lay scattered among the rubble of tumbled buildings and blackened bricks.

How many had the soldiers rescued before the fires started? This wasn't their battle, the innocent men, women, and children.

Injustice bites a savage hole in my stomach. The dragon would pay.

"Fire doesn't need time to burn," Soran says darkly, pulling his horse to a stop at the beginning of the street. The boulevard of zelkova trees Runa and I had often slipped down in secret now stands like a skeletal candelabra, leaves falling like melted wax to a deserted strand.

Soran positions himself on my left side and Casmir on my right. Soran has no weapon, and I wonder how he plans to help defend me as a guard or stop the dragon. But I don't ask. Perhaps killing one of his own kind had been too painful.

Bastian reaches for the axe strapped against his back. "I don't see the beast now. Could it be hiding in the ruins or has it moved on?"

"It's possible." Casmir leans back in the saddle as he scours the remaining rooftops. "Depending on how clever it is and what it wants." His gaze flicks to Soran. "How do we defeat it? This dark heart or whatever you call it?"

"It can't live on its own," Soran says. "It's like a parasite living off whatever host it can find. While contained in your ring, it couldn't harm anyone. It probably drew energy from you in small amounts so you wouldn't notice. Would have revealed itself in trivial signs like the shadows under your eyes or your overdependence on coffee."

Casmir glowers, shooting me a look as if I had somehow betrayed his coffee indulgence.

"It might have lent you strength at times," Soran continues, ignoring the glare. "To help you to stay alive, but it couldn't merge with a mere mortal. Not to keep the immortality it craves."

"To what end?" Bastian asks, his eyes scanning the buildings as we pass.

Soran stares ahead. "To destroy everything the Saint created. Every last thing."

Dokun dokun. Hearts thunder in my chest. Soran casts me a brief glance as if he hears them too. *Is this why the dragon elders were so bent on killing me? On destroying Soran's heart? So it doesn't turn into a monster?*

We enter the round courtyard which fans out like the spokes on a rickshaw's wheel. The bakery where Runa and Bastian had stopped to buy pudding last week sits on the left. Shattered glass litters the pavement.

Soran motions for us to stop. "Release the horses. We go on foot."

"We don't even know if the dragon is still here." Bastian

squirms in his saddle, pulling his horse to a halt. "Shouldn't we find out where it went before dismounting?"

"The glass will lame the horses," Casmir says, untacking his black horse.

"He has a point." I slide out of the saddle and pat down the mare's neck before reaching behind its ears and slipping off the bridle. She would find her way back home to the stables without me.

The others follow our example, and we watch as our horses toss their heads, a few giving a frightened kick before bolting back the way we had come.

"The dragon's here," Cass says, eyeing the courtyard like a hunter and pointing to a scorched path leading toward the docks. "We need to get out of the open, now."

A low roar comes from the far side of the square, down one of the alleys. Casmir motions for us to take cover along the wall as we approach. We form a small army with our personal guards, Jey, Soran, and Jade—Bastian's new guard—and the three of us in the front. I should've asked Bastian to stay back and watch over the castle and father in his sickbed, but Kazuya would do a good job of that. The boy had a strong moral compass and plenty of training.

"That road leads to the warehouse and trading post, doesn't it?" Cass asks, his back pressed against the wall.

"It's the Silverwood harbor," I affirm. "It ends at the red-brick warehouse where the trading ships come in. It's large enough to hide a dragon, if that's what you're thinking, and close to the sea so it could slip away. Most of the merchant shops and healers line this street."

"Let's go." Soran steps forward, but Casmir pulls him back.

"We need more intel first. Why does Meera have your heart?" Casmir demands. "Is it the same as the dark heart?"

Was this part of his anger? Fear that I would somehow be corrupted by the dragon's heart?

"We aren't here to discuss your love life," Bastian says. "We need intel on the dragon."

Casmir points at Soran with a disgusted scowl. "He *is* a dragon. We don't have time to explain. Shut it and listen."

Bastian gapes, clearly thinking Casmir has lost his mind.

"The blue sickness," Soran continues, swallowing hard.

My ears perk at the mention of the illness that had painted my world in shades of pain and loneliness. What did Soran know about it?

"Meera was born with a piece of dragon magic, too small for any to notice with an untrained eye. As you know, the Ezo queens are connected to the dragons after their coronation ceremony. In rare circumstances, that magic is passed along to their progeny, but it has side effects and usually isn't potent enough for them to use. That's why the blue sickness as you call it only runs in the queen's bloodline." His gaze turns to me. "Your sickness isn't a curse; it's your strength."

"Then why does it hurt?" I ask, one hand fisting near my brace. "Why would dragon magic do this to me?"

"I don't know," he says, meeting my gaze. "But if I've learned anything this last week, it's that beauty is most vibrant in what is passing, even broken. Maybe the same is true for magic and curses. It shines brightest in the weakest vessel."

"She's not weak," Bastian says, defending me.

"It's not an insult," Soran says. "Cherry blossoms are fragile, but no one ridicules them. Your queensguard bear the symbol on their swords and helmets. It is very strong indeed to be fragile and beautiful and not afraid."

The dual hearts squeeze my chest. *Did he just call me beautiful and strong? What would have happened were I not a cerulean princess? Would Soran's heart have gone somewhere else like the dark heart had, and the dragon simply let me drown in the sea?*

I close my eyes, shutting out the thoughts. Smoke scrapes my lungs, a potent reminder of the danger we face along with the people of Silverwood.

"That's an interesting theory," Bastian says, eyes shifting between the three of us. "But how do we stop this thing?"

"The dragon must die," Soran says. "The dark heart is like a parasite. It's bound to the emerald dragon and now it lives or dies with her. But it can change host quickly, so you need to be on your guard."

"I'll not play host to some monster," Casmir growls. "What else do we need to know?"

"Knowing the dragon's ancient art might help," I say. "If we know what kind of magic it can wield against us."

Soran laughs, the look in his eyes dark. "Nightmares."

"What?" Casmir's eyes round in horror.

"Nightmares. Bad dreams. Hallucinations. Not the kind of dragon you want to face."

"You call that magic a gift?" Bastian casts a nervous glance down the narrow street, surprisingly untouched by the flames that had devoured the rest of the city. "You'd think the beast would grant dreams, not twist them."

"She can do that too, but if you're talking about weaponizing a gift, that's how she would do it."

"And your gift?" Casmir narrows his gaze.

"Doesn't matter. I lost it."

I lead the way down the street to the red-brick warehouse, feeling like I'm walking into a trap with every step. This wasn't a dragon. It was a monster.

CHAPTER 31

MEERA

BATTLING DEMONS isn't for the faint of heart, so it's a good thing I have two of them—hearts that is. The monster must sense our energy as we near the red-brick warehouse that processes trade in and out of the port city. Skeletal green wings stretch into the sky from the building's once beautiful skylight.

I recognize the emerald glint of the dragon's scales and the long, spiked tail, but the similarities to the sacred sea dragons end there. Hooked claws sprout from its wings and dig into the bricks as the dragon rights itself, drawing its fat belly through a hole in the roof. A horrid shriek rends the air as it claims a new stronghold. Dark eyes gleam whenever the early moonlight hits them at the right angle, but no gold dusts the hollow orbs replaced by serpentine slits.

The dark heart has seized complete control.

Soran grabs my hand and squeezes tight, whether to comfort me or himself, I'm not sure. We brought swords, arrows, and shields to fight. But who could win against such a monster? I fist the black dagger at my side. Despair refuses to hope, but that's not my destiny. My kingdom won't be stolen. I won't make excuses for powerlessness. This fight is mine, whether I'm enough for it or not.

Queensguard race along the wharf, guiding merchants and families away from the smoldering harbor. Wails sound in every direction as people flee, tears etched on their ash-strewn faces: A mother carrying a young boy, an elderly woman who sold rice balls for those working late, a dockhand scavenging tools from a burning yard.

A few men attempt to stage a defense, angling pitchforks and bamboo spears at the dragon. Soldiers armed with matchlock pistols take aim, but the bullets ricochet off its impenetrable hide.

The dragon rears its head, chest heating with an amber glow.

"Run!" I rush down the hill to warn them. My legs pound the dirt road and pain slices a wicked dash to my hips, but I don't care. "Get out!"

My legs give out as the dragon arches its neck and blasts the marina with flame. Even from this distance, heat scorches my face. When I glance up, Soran shelters me with his own body, taking the brunt of the flames with a shield.

"What were you thinking?" His winded voice rakes through me, fearful, as though he scarcely got to me in time. "Are you okay?"

I nod, stunned by the narrow escape. Soran offers me a hand, the gold dust in his eyes sparks of fire. My left hip catches when I straighten, so I ease into a lopsided stance. Words form tangled knots in my throat. "I-I'm fine, but . . . they aren't."

Soran turns to follow my gaze. Within the red-brick warehouse, the dragon paws through the remains, snapping at any movement.

"We need a plan," Casmir says, coming alongside us. "Its blast is considerably larger than the sea serpents. We use our shields to get closer. Bastian and Jade, if you can pin the dragon's tail, then I can get to its neck. Trap it, and I can kill it."

"Confident as ever." Bastian gives Casmir a sharp nod before shouldering his axe.

My breath pinches tight in my chest, begging him not to go. But my brother saunters down the hill, shield strapped to his back and axe in hand, as if he's fighting another warrior and not a fire-wielding demon sitting atop a fortress of brick and bone.

His shadow, Jade, follows close behind, sporting a throwing chain draped over his thick neck. At least Jey is no longer his shadow. Casmir had ordered him to remain behind with the supply wagon.

While the dragon is busy digging through the wreckage, Soran, Casmir, and I make our way toward the compound, everyone within range of a shield in case the creature spies us. There will be no time to run for cover if it attacks at close range.

I limp to the towering brick wall and slouch against the hot stones. My bones haven't bothered me since Soran's song. *Of course* they act up now.

The dragon's tail dips into the main chamber from the broken skylight, swaying like an irritated cat. It stretches its wings as though preparing to take flight again.

"As soon as they pin the tail, the dragon will turn on us," I say. "Cass, you have to be on the roof before we make our move. We have one shot at this."

"I'll need something for my hands," he says. "The ladder is metal. If I climb it like this, I'll burn."

Soran shrugs off his outer robe and hurls it at Casmir. "It's Amami silk."

"How unfortunate." Casmir offers the worst sympathetic smile I've ever seen and then promptly rips the precious black silk. He wraps the torn strips around his hands, before throwing the scraps back at Soran. "I don't want any more dragons in Ezo once we're done with this. And I mean none."

"I could say the same for dukes," Soran says, eyes narrowing as Casmir swings onto the ladder.

My eyes rove a tad too long over Soran's loose white shirt and broad shoulders. I grip the handle of my dagger with my good hand and eye Soran's belt for a weapon. "How are you, um . . . planning to help exactly?"

"There's more than one way to fight a dragon." Soran reaches into his pockets, fisting a glass jar with a cork stopper filled with powdery pills. "I'm here to help everyone survive. The healer gave me these." He reaches into his other pocket and pulls out bandages and ointment.

I raise a brow, looking around for someone we can help while waiting for Cass to get in position. It doesn't take long. A few dockhands remain in the wreckage, injured and trapped beneath debris. "You can start with them, over there."

Soran nods, his eyes calculating the distance between those needing help and me. "Come with me. A guard never leaves his charge."

I nod. "Okay, but we have to be quick."

We start outside the warehouse, freeing a man trapped beneath an overturned crate, then a boy with a broken leg encamped beneath a splintered boat. The child refuses to budge until Soran sings him a fisherman's song. While the boy is distracted, Soran sets his leg, muffling the startled cry with a warm hand and kind smile. We work until the bandages are completely used up and the pill bottle near empty.

"The dragon's getting restless." Bastian calls our attention from the shadows of a nearby wall. "We need to move."

Soran scans the warehouse, his jaw tight.

I follow his gaze to the hollowed-out building, a shell of red brick and iron, one side entirely exposed as though struck by cannon fire.

Casmir whistles from the roof, imitating a white-tailed warbler—it's time to kill the beast. Swallowing hard, I follow Bastian. Together, we crouch next to the smoldering bricks and peer inside the opening.

"Are you sure this will work?" I grip my brother's arm.

"Of course it will." He flashes an impressive grin. "Don't forget, I'm leading this mission."

The tight breath I'd been holding unwinds a little at his playful words, but I don't miss the way his brow furrows when he thinks I'm not looking. He's never killed a dragon, especially not one with wings.

No one has.

"Where is Casmir?" Soran peers around the wall to the broken skylight and dragon. "It's going to fly again."

"How do you know?" Bastian asks.

"He knows," I say, not wanting to explain again how my bodyguard is . . . *was*, a dragon.

Bastian shakes his head and then points at Soran. "Keep her safe."

Without waiting for another signal, he and Jade race into the warehouse and seize the dragon's tail which hangs down from its perch on the third story. Sharp dorsal fins ridge along the top of the tail, threatening to slice into their hands, but together, they pin it to the ground.

Jade ties a chain around the tail, between the spikes, and secures it tight. With Bastian's help, they loop the opposite end around a shipyard anchor. The more the dragon pulls, the tighter the chain becomes. The tail slashes madly, upsetting boxes and crates, blasting an entire ship within the warehouse from its hanging.

"You could've tied it a bit higher!" Bastian calls out, ducking the massive spear-like tail.

"It won't hold," Jade yells, eyes widening as the dragon pinpoints his voice.

The beast begins to climb down from the roof, a monstrous head with glowing green eyes scouring for the source of irritation. I spy Casmir from the broken skylight, not a stone's throw from the monster. He grips his sword in both hands. The emerald dragon can't see him sneaking up from behind while it peers down at us.

It's a clean shot. Take it!

Casmir lunges for the back of the monster's head. The dragon whips around, blocking the attack with its fangs. The sword scarcely makes a dent. Wings bat down on Casmir, attempting to push him down and crush him. His sword whirls, throwing impressive strikes from all angles when least expected. The blade shreds a hole in one wing, hopefully rendering it flightless. But the sword catches in the narrow wing bones, and for one brief moment, Casmir is defenseless.

Sharp talons grab him and pin him to the hard shingles.

I can't watch anymore. A dam of desperation breaks inside me. Fisting my dagger, I rush forward to distract the beast.

A wall of muscle stops me.

"Don't." Soran's lyrical voice holds a hard edge to it. "It'll kill you."

My chest squeezes at the plea in his eyes.

"Casmir needs me. A dragon slayer is the only one who can end this." I duck under his arm and run into the smoldering warehouse. He doesn't try to stop me again. Iron beams hang from the ceiling where the dragon had broken through to the roof, and rubble groans under my weight.

This monster will not kill my friends. Without a second thought, I drive my dagger into its tail.

The emerald dragon roars.

It knocks Casmir aside, nearly crushing the air from his lungs, and then it grabs the broken edges of the roof with its talons and cranes its neck into the desolated warehouse. Slitted eyes meet mine, a flicker of recognition in the dark pools.

A voice sinks sharp teeth into my mind. *No one escapes me. You are mine.*

I freeze, my legs may as well be pillars of stone. It's not the green dragon speaking but the dark heart racing through my mind with the dragon's telepathy. I'd felt the same insidious force inside the ring.

Laughter shrills within my skull. *You worthless fool! To think you could stop me.*

I close my eyes to shut it out, but it's no use. Vaguely, I make out Soran's voice calling to me, but it's so faint.

The dragon's wolf-like face with twisted horns descends into the warehouse, circling to my left as it eyes me unflinchingly. The elongated body follows, its coils filling the gutted room as wings bend and fold along the snakelike frame.

Images assail my mind. My worst fears turned into dark nightmares. Runa choking on the pudding. Father coughing on his bed. Casmir being torn apart by the monster. Soran dying without a heart. Me, healthy and whole, but too afraid to help any of them. Worthless even with a perfect body. I grasp my head, curling in on myself.

Why does the darkness feel so real? So true?

A roar breaks me from the nightmares.

Bastian rushes the dragon with his axe, swinging for the soft flesh between its talons. He makes one cut before it bats him aside. His back smashes hard into a brick wall. There's a loud crack as the chain tethering its tail breaks.

My hearts slam against my ribcage. I-I . . . can't move.

You thought you could beat me? Save your friends? The voice laughs. *You can't even walk. Worthless. I'd wanted to play with your dreams more, like I did with your sister. But I grow bored.*

Runa.

Had this monster infected my sister's dreams with darkness? Was it responsible for the killing sleep? But how? I fist my remaining dagger and hobble forward. "I won't let your darkness infect anyone else!" I shout. "Light sets the boundaries, not the darkness."

A gleam enters the dragon's eye. *Give it your best shot.*

"Meera, run!" Soran grabs me by the arm and pulls me toward an opening in the wall. *Whoosh.* The dragon's tail lashes free from its chain and slams into my abdomen. Air punches through my lungs. My hand slips out of Soran's and something hard cracks against my back.

The ceiling opens to the sky, pipes and metal beams jutting from the broken edges, but the stars smile down at me as if my world isn't ending.

Soran. Bastian. I must get up.

I push myself upright, wincing at the pain throbbing against my ribs. The dagger is gone. Soran is already on his feet, racing toward me. But the dragon shoves him aside, serpentine coils blocking him from view. Quickly, I scan the room for the rest of the crew, assessing injuries and hoping that at least one of them has a clear shot at the monster.

Bastian lies unconscious beneath the dragon's talons. I can only imagine what nightmares he faces. Casmir staggers to his feet and attempts to climb down from the roof but his arm seems broken. Soran and Jade are nowhere in sight, lost behind the enormous ribbons of dragon scale.

The wolf-like head lowers toward me, so close I make note of where the scales shift to soft fur around its horns and at the side of its jaw.

Still think you stand a chance? No one can stop me. The dragons will no longer be locked in the sea. We should've been held in higher esteem than man. History will be rectified. With the dark heart, I am all. Can take all. The dragon bares its teeth, lifting Bastian in its talons and slamming him back against the ground. My brother moans, his head rolling to the side.

"BASTIAN!"

The scream steals more than my breath. It steals all sense of self-preservation. I run to my brother, empty fists pumping at my sides. *Reckless.* Casmir would've said. *Foolish.* My father would've said. *Worthless.* The kingdom would've said.

And they would be right.

My run is a limping snail's pace compared to the dragon's speed. Its tail barrels me over and pins me to the ground. Sharp scales lift me, coiling me into a tight fist from which there is no escape.

I push against the dark green scales with my free hand, but it's no use. In a flash, I remember the white dragon holding me in the sea, a similar burning in his eyes, the amber glow of his chest. But this time I have no dagger; no one is coming to my rescue.

The queens will no longer demand our magic, the voice hisses. *I'll show the world how worthless human life is. How small and weak. Imperfect. Dragons were always superior. It is we who should rule the world, not men.*

The dragon opens its mouth, jaw adjusting to swallow me whole. My hearts lurch, the panic flooding my chest taking a new rhythm.

The queen. The oath.

A gift of the gods for a human queen, if worthy she is found.

"I may be imperfect, but I'm also worthy!" I shout, my voice trembling against the dragon's hot breath. "I am Queen of Ezo, and I demand your magic, dragon!"

The beast's fangs crash down, stopping a breath from my face.

"I . . . am . . . worthy." I force out the words I'd struggled against my whole life. Believing them with every part of me. Doubts surface, all the reasons I can't be worthy because of my brokenness, my weakness, my deformity and lack of confidence, my foolish mistakes, my chronic not-enoughness. I let it wash over me—part of me—and I am not ashamed.

Feelings can't tell me who I am, that power rests with a deeper magic. With the light and truth that sets the boundaries of this world. I must face my darkness, my weakness, and write on it with light.

"I. Am. Worthy," I say again, my chest expanding. "I claim the oath."

You can't! the dragon hisses, shrinking back a fraction. *You're not pure, not whole. You're married and not eligible for the oath's prize.*

"I may be broken, but that doesn't make me any less whole. It makes me more so. As for my wedding, it was a farce. I'm every bit eligible for the oath and I demand payment. Now!"

Soran manages to climb over the dragon's scales at the far side of the room. His eyes go wide with concern as they latch onto mine and he fights the monster to reach me. But I know what I must do.

I stretch out my hand and the dragon quivers. Its terrible muscles convulse beneath the scales. Then, as if forced by an invisible hand, it presses its muzzle to my palm.

The oath demands it obey a worthy queen.

A spark bolts through me, piercing my chest.

I inhale sharply, power spreading through my chest until it reaches the tips of my fingers. Dreams and nightmares pour into my mind from the beast's heart magic. Hand pressed firm against the dragon's muzzle, I meet its slitted gaze, remembering the once gold-flecked eyes of the emerald dragon. The dark heart had stolen from this creature, and as much as it had destroyed in its selfish quest, pity finds a small place in my heart.

"Sleep," I say, willing all the magic back into the dragon.

NO, the dark heart hisses. *You can't!* But the hideous voice fades as the dragon closes its eyes and its head falls, smacking into its own scales.

Casmir seizes the opportunity. He leaps from the second-story overhang onto the beast, strides over to its neck, and with one hand, thrusts the blade into the one vulnerable spot behind its horns. Soran clamors over the rows of lifeless scales and pulls me from the heap of coils.

I sink against him, the power drained from me. Whatever

spark of magic the dragon had given to its queen is now gone. My body doesn't listen when I tell it to stand. Soran catches me by the arms and allows me to lean against him, my ear to his chest wondering what it would be like to hear the steady *dokun dokun* warm against my skin.

His heart skips a wild beat against my ribs, echoing the sentiment.

"Help Bastian," I say weakly.

Soran nods and passes me off to Casmir. I wish I had enough strength to watch the interaction between those two. Cass holds me at a distance from himself, his body rigid and warmth radiating from his arms slick with sweat. Blood splotches his wool jerkin and white sleeves.

"It'll stain," I say, plucking at his sleeve. His fingers flinch in surprise. "I'll ask Seira to clean it for you."

He scoffs. "I should start charging you for every shirt you destroy. I'd be quite rich."

I smile even though my head throbs. "Thank you."

"For what? You're the one who beat the monster. It seems you've broken off our engagement officially. Did the dragon really have to be the first to hear it?"

I offer a sad smile, wishing I had the words to heal his pain. Friendship isn't what he wants, but I can't offer him anything more. "I owe you so much, Cass," I say, leaning against him. "You will always have a friend in me."

"I don't need your friendship, just your kingdom." He smiles as if it's a joke, but we both know it's not. Then he helps me hobble over to where my brother and Soran wait. Jade joins them with a maimed leg and burn marks across his jaw. Cass sets me down on a low wall and barks orders for Jade to fetch horses and send word to the castle.

Cass vanishes behind the role of duke. I'm impressed by the long list of commands, details on how to dispose of the dragon's body and preserve parts for trade in Taiga, medicinal supplies needed, where to construct temporary housing for the displaced persons. Jey takes over the task of removing the dragon and Soran gives me the last of the pills in his medical kit even though I protest that others could use it more.

"Nonsense," he says. "Knowing your worth means knowing when to accept that you need help too."

"If you're helping me, does that mean the third trial has been called off?"

"I doubt it." He swallows hard, avoiding my gaze. "Though I'm fairly certain the green dragon acted alone. The Grand Elder will explain the third trial soon enough. Until then, let me help you."

I gulp down the bitter pill, closing my eyes as we wait for help to arrive. Soran pulls me into his arms and hums over me. Nothing magical or dazzlingly beautiful. But the sound of his voice, the hum of his chest against my back, is all I need to quiet the nightmares.

Don't leave. I hold the wish in, not daring to voice it.

I won't, he seems to whisper back, holding me tighter.

And for a moment I don't care if the third trial will be the end where I lose his heart . . . and mine. I'm only glad that I'm not alone.

CHAPTER 32
DRAGON

THE NIGHTMARES DON'T END the next day or the day after. But even bad dreams can't dampen the castle's spirits.

"A monster slain by our own princess! A curse broken!" the townsfolk cry in the streets.

When Soran arrives at the castle, carrying Meera in his arms, someone is waiting to greet them at the drawbridge. A girl with chestnut tresses and ruby lips. She leans forward in a rickshaw, sweat slicking her brow, and tawny eyes glued to the horizon with a worried fever as though anticipating a falling star.

Runa.

No one had explained what Soran feared to be true. That a dragon had partnered with someone to make the killing sleep, a dragon harboring an ancient heart magic that could spread dreams and nightmares. The one piece of the contagion they'd all been missing had slithered before them the whole time. And now that the monster was dead, the princess had awakened.

So too had the others poisoned by the killing sleep. The maids, healers, the prince of Seshu, all still suffered from the effects of poison, but without the unrelenting nightmares and cursed sleep, were making a smooth recovery under the care of the saints. Casmir had sent his personal guard, Jey, and the Taigan ambassador packing—no doubt to curtail the investigation Bastian had ordered to look into the poisonings.

Soran doubted the duke had played a hand in it, not with how invested he seemed in Meera's happiness. But he hadn't cooperated. Someone had worked with the green dragon—certainly not Sir Richter who was terrified of the serpents—which left the shadow, Jey. Soran shoves the thoughts aside, focusing on the sleeping girl in his arms.

Ahead, an assortment of guards and healers stand by Runa's rickshaw, admonishing her to return to the castle for her health. Soran's arm tightens over Meera as she slumps against his chest, their horse keeping a slow and steady pace across the drawbridge. He pulls the horse to a stop before the newly awakened princess, their eyes meeting for the first time.

"Is she well?" Runa's voice frays at the edges.

"Sleeping and healing," Soran says, the rise of his chest meeting the bent curve of Meera's back. "Welcome back, Princess Runa. Your sister was worried sick about you."

Runa's eyes jump to his. "You're the dragon Kazuya spoke of, aren't you?" Her lips pinch into a grin as though remembering a particularly humorous conversation. "The one who took away some of the poison in the banquet hall when I was asleep? Who helped defend Ezo from the green monster."

His breath winds a tight fist against his ribs. She made him sound like a saint, but he isn't. Meera leans heavily in his arms, the dual hearts beating steadily against his chest. He would become a dragon again—when he reclaimed his heart.

One week, and the third trial would commence.

He would have his heart returned.

And she would die.

Soran nudges his horse forward. "I'm not a dragon anymore,

but no less a monster as you call them. I'll be gone within the week, Your Highness."

"You're not either of those things," Runa says, her eyes trailing after him and falling on her sister in his arms. "From where I'm standing you have the heart of a saint, not a monster. But maybe you don't know that yet."

CHAPTER 33
MEERA

I DREAM OF SONGS that thread my city together, of heat that doesn't burn but soothes the wounded hearts and souls who had lost homes and loved ones. I dream Runa walks into my nightmares and leads me out of the maze. She brushes the hair from my fevered brow. She laughs with Soran, their voices two wind chimes clinking in the breeze and making me thirst for sunshine and blue seas.

I feel her hand on me now, cooling my cheek. My eyes open and wince at the bright light coming through the bamboo blinds.

"What . . . how did I get here?" I focus on the blurry face.

"She's awake." Soran's voice jumps out at me, but farther away from the corner of the room.

"Your guard carried you back from the warehouse," a tender voice says. "He hasn't left your side for more than a moment. Meera, can you hear me?"

"Runa?" I push up in the bed, my eyes centering on the soft chestnut hair, nearly blonde in the dappled sunlight. Ruby lips part in a welcoming smile, tawny eyes misting with tears as my sister covers her mouth with one hand, hiding a quiet sob.

"I'm here," she whispers, holding me. "I'm here."

"Runa!" I throw my arms around what must surely be a ghost. But her shoulders melt into mine, her strong arms squeeze me back with the ferocity of a tiger. "When? How? I knew you'd wake up," I cry, afraid to let go.

Runa pulls back, her warm eyes searching my face. "You're something else, little sis. I'm lucky to have you. Your guard filled me in on your adventures this last week. Though I'm positive he's not telling me *everything*." She arches a brow, lips puckering in a mischievous grin.

I straighten in bed, taking a better look around the room. I'm in our old chamber with the two beds on the lowest floor of the castle. Soran sits in a round chair in the corner of the room, looking at the door like he'd prefer to escape and avoid whatever Runa was insinuating with *everything*.

"How did you wake up?" I ask. "What happened?"

"He can explain it better than I." Runa nods toward Soran. "I woke when you defeated the dragon. The killing sleep was partly the dragon's doing. It was using its heart magic to keep multiple people asleep while the poison was administered to each of them individually. Someone was working with the dragon to get the dark heart. An organization called the Black Dragon Society."

A hardness enters her eyes. "We'll find out who is involved. All of this for the corrupted heart of a monster. The idea that Casmir was carrying it around in his ring gives me the creeps. But he didn't know it was there, so he's not to blame. Though, I'm sorry to hear about your engagement getting called off."

I sober, throwing back the covers and rushing to stand. "But we already know who did it. It was Sir Richter and Jey—"

"No." Soran breaks his silence for the first time. "There isn't enough proof—at least, not for your courts. And they have political immunity in Taiga."

"They can't get away with it!"

Runa gives a sad smile. "Don't worry. We'll catch them. I

have a plan or two once I become queen. But for now, you need to focus on recovering."

"Queen . . ." I can hardly keep up with the changing world around me. "Is Casmir still here? Did he announce that our wedding wasn't real to the whole kingdom?" Sooner or later the ruse would come to light, but having it leaked while I was unconscious stings.

"Shh." Runa pats my hand. "He's still here. It's only been two days. I think everyone was so grateful the dragon was defeated that they didn't make too much fuss about the marriage ruse. Most of the diplomats have already left. Some might try to stir up trouble later, but I think we can forge new alliances. Thanks to the duke, we have a tonic for the poison left behind by the killing sleep."

"That's because his guard made it to go along with the poison," Soran says. "Casmir let those criminals get away and I want to know why."

"It's dangerous to jump to conclusions," Runa chastens.

"Where does Taiga's alliance stand?" My throat goes dry. *Would Casmir turn Taiga against us?*

"I think the duke is waiting to talk with you before he leaves, though he's too proud to say it. Are you really sure about breaking it off with him?" Her eyes sparkle with questions. "Because he is rather handsome . . ."

I smile. "Now I know it's my sister and not a ghost. Don't tell me you've found your true love in the two days I've been out."

Runa laughs and the sound fills my heart. "He won't even look at me. But we've had to meet a few times now that I'm to be queen."

My eyes shift to Soran in the corner. Something about his face tells me that he's heard from the elders about the third trial. That I might not quite be done with dragons yet.

"You're going to make a magnificent queen," I tell Runa.

"And you are going to have to explain your new guard," Runa whispers, a mischievous twinkle in her eye. "Whatever is between you, it feels like magic."

Runa's choice of words is too close to home.

Dokun dokun. My hearts grow restless, as if sensing the third trial is near. Assassins. Evil rings. I don't want to guess what the third test will be.

I'd tried to ask Soran, but he remains uncharacteristically silent. Not even caving with pithy comebacks. To make it worse, whenever I'm near him my hearts skip through my ribs, making a fool of me. I swear he can hear it.

"Meera, we need to talk."

Soran catches me outside the evening bath, on a pebbled walkway leaving the bathhouse that springs from beneath the mountains. It's a small building surrounded by bamboo fences and seasonal gardens with bathing pools for the royal family and staff. Seira trails behind me carrying our dirty clothes in a basket, both our faces a pink sheen from the delicious heat.

"Seira, I need a moment," I say.

She nods and hurries ahead on the path, leaving Soran and me alone.

When she's gone, he reaches out and brushes my fingers. "How is your hand?"

I pull away, stinging at the week of distance between us. My pulse pounds at the first touch since we faced the dragon together. "Healing," I say, tucking my disfigured hand behind my back. "Sometimes I still think that finger is there. But tell me about the trial. I know you've spoken with the dragons."

His eyes stray toward the horizon. "This isn't easy for me," he says, as if I should understand that stealing his heart back won't be easy for him. That watching someone die isn't easy.

"What did they say?" I pull my robe tight about my shoulders, willing my voice to be calm. "Do these pools connect to the Celestial Courts? Is that how you've been communicating with them? No one has seen dragons in the ocean since—"

I can't bring myself to mention the attack. The damage stares at me every time I trek into Silverwood, but it's still hard to talk about it. Soran had joined in those daily excursions too, sharing in the building projects, serving food to the homeless, sweating along with us in the inglorious labor. My stomach tightens. I can't think about that side of him, not now.

"Yes, they've scheduled a time for the third trial." He stares at his bare feet, shoulders rigid, before meeting my eyes. "It's now."

"Now?" Shock spirals through me. "I thought I'd have more time. I haven't said goodbyes or—"

"I didn't want to tell you sooner. To ruin the days you had. I wanted you to enjoy them without worry. If I was wrong to withhold it, forgive me."

I notice he doesn't correct me about the goodbyes. He doesn't think I'll win this trial. But he thought the same thing about the last two. I take a calming breath and shake my head. "No, I prefer it this way. But I was hoping the elders would decide that a trial wasn't necessary anymore."

"They are grateful for your help in putting an end to the dark heart," he says. "I raised the point with them myself. But they stressed that now you must understand why they cannot allow a dragon heart to live outside its true home."

"Your heart is different."

"Yes and no," he says. "I'm fortunate my heart latched onto someone like you, but the heart can't remain transient forever. It must have a real home."

"It's certainly made itself at home," I say.

"But it's loyal to me. It's not home yet. The dark heart in Casmir's ring was transient for years and turned on itself, darkened by hatred and loneliness and pain." He runs a hand through his hair. "The third trial stands. Either you die with the heart or" —his jaw catches—"I get my heart back and you still . . ."

I take his hand, squeezing it and willing his eyes to meet mine. "Or I beat this trial like I did the last two and live. We find a way to get your heart back without me dying. There's always a way. We just need courage to find it."

He sighs. "You make me want to believe you."

"Then believe me," I say. "But if I do lose, would you give Ezo some of your magic, help Runa to keep the kingdom safe?"

"You know I would." He shakes his head as if he can't believe his own answer.

I offer a small smile at this consolation. "So, where is this trial?"

"I'll show you." He takes me by the hand and leads me outside the bathhouse courtyard. A carriage waits on the dirt-packed walkway, the same one Casmir and I had taken to the cathedral for the wedding license. I approach the two horses, rubbing the forelock of the gray mare which nods its head in appreciation.

"Do you want to tell anyone before we depart?" he asks. "To say goodbye?"

"I won't be needing any goodbyes," I say. "Besides, I think it's better if we don't tell anyone. Runa and Bastian have been through enough without worrying about me."

"Then after you." He whisks open the carriage doors, and my hearts leap toward them.

Toward him.

And the death the dragons had promised should I fail.

CHAPTER 34
MEERA

I NEVER THOUGHT I'd come back here. My feet step onto the carefully manicured path that winds into a grove of wisteria near the top of the mountain. The smell of sulfur and cypress tangles with the rich highland air surrounding Silverwood. The cathedral of the Ladies of the Light rises before us with its huge stones and stained-glass windows.

If I turn to the left, I'll see it . . . the hot spring where I'd hidden while mother died by the teeth of wolves. I'd forgotten it was so close to this sacred spot, blocked it from memory. But for some reason, now it feels safe to look at, to remember.

The wound is still there, but I no longer fear it.

Soran helps me from the carriage, his pink pants and black robe getting caught in the breeze as he stares ahead at the immense cathedral.

Has he ever been inside one or met the saints?

"Let's go," he says, taking my hand gently. "They're waiting."

My hearts lurch at his touch, but the coldness of his words gives me pause. *Just how strong is the heart's hold over him? What will the third trial hold?*

I follow, turning back once to look at the hot spring outside the cathedral gates. *Is it one of the sacred pools connecting the dragons to the Celestial Court? Had the dragons seen what had happened to my mother all those years ago?*

Soran pushes open the garden gate, stepping onto an overgrown path surrounded by roses, hydrangeas, and azaleas. Lizards scurry between the rockery, and yellow butterflies float on gentle wings. In the center of the lawn, outside the cathedral's shadow, stands an arbor knotted thick with wisteria. Beyond that is a rock coppice fitted with a statue of the Bleeding Saint, his arms outstretched.

Welcome. A dragon speaks into my mind with piercing clarity.

I jolt, searching for the voice in the shrubbery and the cathedral wall beyond, but its source is nowhere to be seen.

A princess should face her last judgment with pride. The words grate against my skull.

"Do you hear it?" I squeeze Soran's hand.

He nods and quickens his pace to the rock coppice. On closer inspection, it's a round hovel made from white stone with a single entrance. I duck inside, keen to escape the voice prying into my mind. I scour the room for any sign of dragons.

"Please, come in." Three saints bow in greeting from where they stand before a long table set with flickering candles and incense. One holds a sizable bowl filled with steaming water. Her hands tremble beneath the weight as she sets it upon the table.

My pulse quickens. "Is this the third trial?"

Soran's hand tightens around mine and he takes a step back as if we'd made a mistake coming here. I tilt my head to question him, but he doesn't look at me.

"Yes, my dear." A saint waves me forward with thin fingers. "A trial you must endure *alone*. Take the bowl."

I try to slip my hand from Soran's, but his fingers curl against mine.

"Whatever the third trial is, I can beat it like the others," I say. "Have a little faith. We're almost at the end."

"That's what I'm afraid of"—he grips my hand in one last squeeze before letting go with a haggard breath—"the end."

I fist my hands and step forward to peer inside the bowl. A dark, hazy reflection stares back at me from the hot spring water: a foxlike shadow of horns and smoke and gilded eyes.

That black dragon. The same one who defended me in the undersea tribunal, the Grand Elder. The image ripples as if in affirmation, and I half fear it will leap from the bowl and devour me. But the dragons have only come for what is rightfully theirs —or should I say, Soran's.

"I'm here for the third trial." I grip the edge of the bowl, hearts beating fast. "What must I do?"

The saints will explain. The voice needles into my mind like a searing thread. I sense the black dragon's magic saturating the room, filling it with a strange scent. *No one leaves until the trial is complete. If anyone does, they will leave without a heart.*

"What do you mean?" My hands snap away from the bowl. I spin toward the door we'd entered and meet Soran's gaze. His eyes widen, confirming that he, too, hears the dragon's voice. How far is he willing to go for his heart?

If anyone leaves this room, their heart will stop.

I step toward the open door, disbelieving, but Soran places a hand on my arm and shakes his head. "He speaks the truth. You have to finish what we started."

My throat goes tight as I stare at the open door. What magic does the black dragon possess that he can stop the blood flowing in my veins?

"It's all right, my dear," one of the saints says, her voice a soft blanket to my nerves. She reaches beneath the table and procures three chalices. The saint sets each one on the table with a hollow clink, refusing to meet my eyes.

"The door," I say. "Did you know about this? That if you leave, your heart will stop?"

The saint sighs. "The Grand Elder is the most powerful of serpents. There is no changing his will."

"Your dragon," the middle saint begins, her already rosy complexion deepening, "asked us to participate in the trial. He thought you would be more comfortable if the Ladies of the Light conducted the last ordeal here, instead of with the dragon tribunal. We volunteered to help."

Recognition hits as I stare at the short saint in the middle, the one who had congratulated Casmir and me on our first venture to procure the marriage license. I flush, shame curling in my gut at the very tangled path that had led me here. But it's her words that arrest my full attention.

Soran had thought of me. He'd put me first in the timing of the trial, the location. It couldn't have been easy to negotiate with dragons, especially not after one of them devoured a dark heart. Is it possible that he cares more for me than . . . ? No, I can't hope.

I turn to look at Soran, trying to divine the answer from his eyes.

He's moved to the entrance of the stone room as though blocking the door. He stands tall, his jaw set in a firm line. Soran looks like he was cut from these mountains, unbending in the wind and untouched by the harsh realities around him. There's a coldness to him I've not seen since we first met.

"Soran." I say his name like a wish. That ours was a different story. That a heart and a dagger and a curse didn't stand between us.

His eyes meet mine, acknowledging our bargain. Whether I win or lose this last trial, I will try to return his heart, and he will safeguard my kingdom.

I just hope to be alive to see it.

To make sure the dragon keeps his promise.

"Mother Ema will be here soon," the third saint says, stealing me from my thoughts. "She's bringing the other guests before we begin."

"The others?"

I spin toward the saints and the bowl, all trace of the black dragon gone except for the steam rising from it. The three saints bow from behind the table, an apology for not answering my question. A metallic glint catches my eye. The chalices.

One gold. One silver. One that looks like bone.

"What exactly *is* the trial?"

"You must pick the right chalice and drink," the rosy saint says, her words anything but cheerful.

What are they not telling me?

The saint lifts the nearest chalice and dips it into the bowl. She dips the second goblet into the steaming basin and then the third. Hot spring water laps at the chalice rims.

The door opens and Mother Ema strides into the candlelit room with two guests behind her. Seira breaks into a run when she sees me.

"What is this about?" Seira says, surveying the saints, the table, and the barefooted dragon eyeing the full chalices with a stony expression. Her eyes narrow on Soran for a long moment. "Why is he here? It better not be another running-away-to-get-married stunt because I've had enough of that. Meera, are you in trouble?"

I pull her into a hug, and she stiffens at the informality. "No. It's only a . . . test," I say to dispel her fears. "The queens always have a confirmation trial in the cathedral."

"But you're not queen anymore. Runa is." A deep baritone echoes off the rounded walls.

The last time I heard that voice, we'd slayed a monster together. I peer around Mother Ema and take in Casmir's familiar face. His forest-green eyes glower at Soran and the saints as though he'd like nothing more than to level the place.

"Cass, what are you doing here? I thought you'd gone back to Taiga."

"I came to take you home." He strides across the room and halts abruptly at the table. His nostrils flare and his eyes cut to Soran. "This room is full of dragon magic. He lied about his power."

"It wasn't Soran," I say.

"Is there another dragon in the cathedral then?"

I gape, unsure how to explain it to him.

Cass takes my hand and pulls me toward the door. "The saint told me there was a trial going on. They have nothing to try you for. I'll kill any serpent who says otherwise. Let's go."

My heels dig into the hardened earth. "No, Cass!"

He tugs harder, frustration lining his brow. And then he steps across the threshold. Casmir's face pales and he drops my hand, staggering forward as though the air has been knocked from his lungs. I wrap my arms around him and pull him back, nearly falling from his weight. But Soran is at my side, helping hold Casmir upright.

Casmir gasps for air until his breath normalizes, one hand squeezing his left arm. He turns to me, a look ghosting across his face before his eyes focus. "What devilry is this?"

"Your heart stopped," Soran says.

"I noticed," Casmir mutters. "Was it your magic, dragon?"

"No," I say. "Another dragon has placed an enchantment on this room. If anyone leaves, their heart will stop. Until I finish the trial set before me."

"Unfortunately, you were lucky," Soran says. "If you had stepped both feet outside the door, nothing would bring you back."

"We're trapped here?" Seira says, hands cupped to her chest.

"Meera doesn't need to face a trial. She's done nothing wrong! She saved Ezo. I don't understand."

"I stole something, and I have to make it right. It's their law."

"Nonsense." Casmir dusts himself off. "You didn't steal anything of value."

"Says the man with a stolen heart in his ring that nearly killed us all," Soran says.

"You just want your heart back—your magic." Casmir reaches for his katana.

Mother Ema clears her throat from where she now stands at the front of the table. "Thank you for coming. I am honored to stand beside Meera as she finishes what she started."

The last trial.

The last chance to live.

To give my kingdom the magic it needs.

A hush falls over the room. Mother Ema reaches out, beckoning me to approach. "You are so much like your mother," she says. "That pendant I gave to her when she was your age, as a gift for her courage. When your grandaunt, the last cerulean princess, died during her coronation ceremony, your mother swam out to the rocks in an attempt to save her. I tried to calm your mother, to explain to her that the dragons hadn't deemed your grandaunt worthy. Do you know what she said?"

"No." I hold my breath, thirsty to hear my mother's words about the last cerulean princess—and me.

Mother Ema's eyes crinkle at the corners. "She said, 'We are all worthy. It's part of what makes us real—human. Some people just haven't found it yet or they've buried it so deep they don't believe that innate worth is there anymore.' As the dragons would say, the earth is full of gold; you need only to find it. The same is true of the human heart. I'm proud of you for finding it. Your mother would be too."

The air that fills my next breath feels richer, fuller.

"She would've said something like that."

"This trial will test your worth," Mother Ema explains. "Everyone makes mistakes on a journey, but not everyone keeps going. That's what makes you extraordinary, Meera. You don't quit. I hope the dragons will see the gold in your heart too."

In my hearts.

I glance at Soran. I hadn't found my worth alone. It took connection, trust, and friendship with an unlikely monster. No, a saint.

"The trial begins." Soran steps up to the table and raises his voice. His demeanor shifts entirely, taking on a strong, impartial tone. "The Elder has asked for me to speak for him and lay out the terms. It's a sign of honor for you, Meera, that he's allowing me to conduct the trial. But if you, or the guests, disregard the terms, the offenders will be punished most severely."

"By that he means death," Casmir grumbles, still holding his left arm.

Soran scowls—a don't-make-this-harder-than-it-is look on his face. He spreads his hands over the three chalices and drops a different liquid into each one.

"The trial is simple." His eyes bore into mine. "There are three goblets, and two are poisoned. Pick right, and you live."

"That simple?" I swallow hard. For once, the gold dust in his eyes doesn't calm me. Everything about Soran is as hard and unbending as the mountains surrounding us. The fears and worries he'd expressed earlier are buried somewhere deep inside.

"Three chalices," he repeats, a cold determination in his eye as though the trial couldn't end soon enough. "One is deadly nightshade, one is foxglove, and one is healing water from Fever House. Choose wisely, and you will live. But whatever cups you do not drink will be given to your guests."

Soran motions to my friends.

"Given to the guests?" Seira murmurs, eyes rounding into dark moons as she presses her back to the wall.

"You've got to be kidding!" Casmir fists his sword, his

empty hand slashing the air in an emphatic 'no.' "Nightshade is a painful way to die," he says. "First her eyes will dilate and then delirium will set in before the final stage where it severs the breath from her lungs. Are you okay with her going through with this, dragon?"

"It's not my choice," Soran says, a muscle clenching in his jaw. "I tried to find another way."

"Can I inspect the chalices?" I ask.

"You cannot smell or taste them," Soran says. "Nightshade is sweet-smelling and the waters of Fever House thick with iron, either would give them away. Once a goblet is chosen, it's over."

"Meera, you don't have to do it," Seira calls out. "Mother Ema, please make it stop!"

"There is nothing to be done," the saint says.

"Pick a chalice," Soran says, but the words seem a thousand yards away. "If you refuse to drink, then the dragons will devour you and all witnesses to protect this world from the possibility of another dark heart. They thought this punishment would be . . . kinder."

"Kinder? To have her heart stopped or the breath ripped from her lungs?" Casmir hisses.

"Meera, what is he talking about? What dark heart?" Seira reaches out to me, her eyes wide with fear. "You don't have to do this."

"If I don't, we all die."

I step up to the table, a knot tightening in my gut. Seira cries into her hands. And Soran's gold-dust eyes meet mine, an intensity beneath his gaze meant for either my heart or his. I can't tell which.

"The choice is yours," Mother Ema says.

The choice is always mine. It's the one thing no one can ever take away from me—choosing how to respond. No person, no trauma, not even a crooked spine can steal it.

Death has followed me every step of the way. First with the

dagger, then the assassins, the innocent lives lost in Silverwood, and now this. I can't look at Seira and Casmir. It was unfair to drag them into this. The dragons were supposed to be pure and protective spirits watching over the earth. There could be nothing good about this.

Why test me in this way? Does Soran know which cup is poison and which is safe?

I search his eyes for answers, but his thoughts are a veiled wall. How can I possibly know which cup is life?

I can't.

I offer my friends a comforting smile and take in their warm faces and the threads that have connected us over the years. *The future is yours*, Cass had told me weeks ago. I must face the darkness, write on it with light. I know my worth. The worth of everyone here in this room. Yet two people will die no matter what I choose. It's too high a price to pay.

My finger trails the base of the first goblet. Or I could just take the first cup for myself and hope it's the poisoned one to save one of my friends.

Seira stifles a cry, her hands cupped over her mouth. But then she would have to drink the remaining chalice. One of my friends would die.

No. I won't let anyone else suffer. A wild plan darts into my mind.

I fist the first goblet, cold metal slicking beneath my sweating palm.

Soran's brow furrows, the only signal that he is worried, or possibly that it's the wrong chalice. His voice is a distant rumble. "Meera, choose carefully who will drink which."

"I choose," I say, lifting the first chalice.

My eyes bore into Soran, taking in one last long breath of gold flecks. I tilt the cup back and drink, liquid pitching into my abdomen like fire.

Quickly, I take the second goblet. "No one else dies."

That too swirls down my throat, sweet and cold. I force back a shiver and reach for the third chalice. Mother Ema grabs my arm and attempts to pull the third goblet from my grasp.

"Stop!" Casmir rushes toward me.

My head swims and my vision blurs. Mother Ema's fingers dig into my arm. No one else will taste this cup.

"Soran, you're not heartless," I say as he too runs toward me, and then I swill back the last chalice.

Fire explodes in my throat, burning all the way down. Sharp pain doubles me over. I reach blindly for the table to balance myself, but I topple, my arm hitting the wood. A hard shudder passes from my head to my toes. I search for Soran, finding his face drained of color like an empty porcelain cup and his chest rising and falling impossibly hard for a heartless dragon.

Drink the chalice, he'd said. *Three goblets, pick one.*

I drank them all. So no one else would have to.

Soran is at my side with Mother Ema and Cass, their faces hovering over me. I hear their words, but their lips move out of sync like a badly orchestrated play.

"You weren't supposed to drink them all!"

"Dear, dear, girl, stay with us. You—go get help!"

"Is she going to be okay?"

I try to focus on the sounds and faces, to put together which is which. Chills rack my body. My vision blurs. My hearts, they're so . . . slow, erratic. I reach out, but I don't know why. Maybe it's so I won't be alone. I've never liked being alone.

It's cold.

Familiar arms lift me from the ground and rush me outside. Sunlight filters through the wisteria arbor painting a haze of purple light across my face.

"It wasn't supposed to happen like this." Soran grinds his teeth, arms gripping me with tender strength. "I brought tonics for two of them, but it will do no good now. Casmir's gone to fetch a healer. Hold on, Meera."

"It's yours . . . the heart," I whisper. "Keep your promise."

"No!" He fists my hands tighter, pressing them to his lips.

"Stop yelling. She needs to remain calm or the poison will spread," Mother Ema scolds. "With two hearts, it's spreading faster as it is."

"You're not going to die." Soran sweeps back my hair, a fever to his eyes that set the gold flecks ablaze. "The healer is coming. I made sure one was close by."

"Your heart deserves a home." I choke out the words.

A violent chill overtakes me. My skin turns clammy. *Why is it so hard to breathe?* I can't hold his hand anymore. Where is it? I'm so tired. The sky is purple with flowers and gold dust.

I made the right choice.

I know I did.

Breath rattles from my lungs and it doesn't come back.

CHAPTER 35
DRAGON

THE GIRL BLEEDS STARLIGHT AND CRIMSON onto the dirt floor. Soran cradles her in his arms. One hand wraps beneath her neck and the other cages around her like a protective shield. Where is that healer? Casmir had better hurry in fetching them.

"Soran, she's gone." Mother Ema's words carry a sharp finality.

A deep ache burns in his chest, pain shattering him from the inside out into a million sharp shards. The sun glimmers above through tangled branches of wisteria, casting a hazy mauve glow on the girl's last moments.

Meera does not breathe.

He should have done something sooner. *Why hadn't he stepped in? The dragons would've killed them all to stop the next dark heart, but . . . she can't be . . .*

"No." He breathes the feverish word as if it has the power to bring her back. "No, no, no. Don't go." *You stubborn, beautiful girl.* "Why'd you have to give your heart?"

"Soran?" The maid, Seira, places a hand on his shoulder, her voice soft. "It's too late. She's dead."

He shrugs her off with a growl. "It can't be too late. It's not."

"Let him be," another voice says.

He doesn't care who speaks. The healer must help.

"We need to alert the queen," says another. "And the dragons. Tell them what has happened."

Soran blocks out the sounds and words and hearts beating around him. He blocks out the world as he looks down at the small, peaceful face and blue eyes he'd memorized like the night sky. He doesn't need the world; he's already holding it in his arms.

A tremble passes through him, starting at his core and spreading to his fingertips as he runs a hand through the girl's silken hair, trying to hold onto her, the essence of her—whatever is left.

Wake up, wake up.

He leans over Meera, listening for a heartbeat, checking her pulse.

Silence.

Oh, how he misses the sound of that mortal heart.

A song rolls from his lips, jumbled with something hot and wet in the back of his throat. Were he a dragon, he could heal her. He pushes through the song, desperate to bring her back. Power flickers weakly in his veins, unresponsive, tapped out, useless.

Soran tilts his head back, biting his lip as something fills his eye. Tears brim to the surface and spill down his cheeks.

Dragons can't shed tears.

Blast it all, he would embrace being mortal. It doesn't matter anymore. Immortality is not nearly as powerful as love.

A cry strangles his throat, and he worries it will shatter him until there aren't enough pieces of him left to hold. He'd heard that mortals could die of heartbreak. Perhaps this is it.

"You could've kept my heart," he whispers over her. "It's yours. I give it to you. It's where it belongs."

Do . . . kun . . . do . . . kun . . .

Soran jolts back. He cups Meera's face, studying it for any hint of life. *Was that his heart? Where?*

"Quiet," he snaps to those nearby. Meera had drunk to save them. Broke the rules to do what was right when no one else had thought of a way forward.

He leans over Meera again, listening. The beat is faint, a whisper of what it once was.

Could it be like the dark heart? Had his heart fled once the poison threatened it? Had it survived?

He sinks to the floor, checking her pulse again.

Nothing.

Wherever the heart had gone, it wasn't within her body. Soran strains his ear to follow the heart's gentle, uneven pulse. It's struggling, but where? Dragon hearts are unruly things, loyal to a fault, but . . .

Soran lifts Meera's pendant from where it lay across her collarbone. The round golden pendant is warm to the touch, energy pulsing through it like a flame. He traces the image of the saint on one side, the four-pointed star with crossed blades on the other. Quickly he sets it down against her skin again, hope rushing through him.

Dokun dokun. The heart is in the necklace.

It had stayed close to Meera, loyal to her, and protecting them both. Maybe even keeping her alive. Dash it all, he didn't care how much of a chance there was. Any chance is better than none. But how long could it sustain her within a golden charm?

"The healer is here." Casmir kneels across from him. He shrugs out of his wool jacket and drapes it over Meera's body, his hands stiffening as they meet her cold skin. "I'm . . . too late. We should get her back to the castle. I'll carry her to the carriage."

"She's not dead." Soran presses the pendant against Meera's cold skin. "I just don't know how to bring her back."

Casmir's voice is slow, pained. "It's okay."

No, it's not okay.

Somewhere in his brain, it registers that he could take back his heart. Pluck it from the necklace and place it back in his chest. It would be eager to return home and restore his ability to heal, restore his mind and heart to that of a dragon again. But there would be no bringing Meera back to life without a heart tethering her to this earth. No dragon magic could raise a soul from the dead—no matter how powerful. That belongs to the realm of miracles.

His fingers grip Meera tightly, holding on to the distant hope that his stolen heart keeps her alive. He lays Meera upon the ground, on a carpet of dirt and wisteria, and adjusts the wool cloak over her to keep her warm. Then he lifts the pendant in his palm, careful not to remove it too far from her body. A small, warm glow emanates from the gold. If he looked hard enough, he could see the wisps of blue flame beneath the metal, the subtle glow of a dragon heart struggling to find its place.

"You belong with her," he says. "I release you."

Bright blue light sparks from the necklace, specks float in the air above it like fireflies, drawing together until it forms a blaze of cerulean light the size of a flesh and blood heart. Soran reaches out to touch it, the familiar warmth caressing his fingers.

Dokun dokun. The flame hovers over his hand without burning him.

"I don't need you anymore," he says firmly. "But she does." Then he turns the heart in his hand and places it over her chest.

Blue flames fan over the girl, spreading across her chest, her arms, until the entire body is encased in a warm, blue fire. Flames sink into her skin like ink disappearing on a blank page. Meera bolts upright with a gasp, hand flying to her chest as though an arrow had struck her through the heart.

A flutter of excitement murmurs through the onlookers, but no one moves. All eyes fix on the cerulean princess with a dragon's heart.

"Meera," Soran voices her name like a wish, afraid to touch her as if she might vanish. "How do you feel?"

She stares down at her chest, at the breath coming in quick, rapid gulps. Her lips part, eyes widening as she takes in the beating of her heart. "Seira and Casmir, are they . . . ?"

"Safe," he says, taking her outstretched hand.

She heaves a deep breath before looking at her hands. "How am I . . ."

"Alive?"

Meera nods and her hands cover the soft skin below her collarbone. "I know this heart. I *know* it. Soran, it belongs to you."

"Not anymore," he says. "It's right where it belongs."

EPILOGUE

I WISH I COULD SAY THAT OURS IS A HAPPY ENDING. But no end is perfect. No life is without the scars and dirt that build up along the way. I'm not trying to hide anything. My leather brace fits snug against my chest, outside the gold kimono that skirts my ankles, long sleeves fluttering in the summer breeze. Runa says wearing the black brace to her coronation will be a bad omen.

But I don't believe in luck. I believe in choices.

After five months, Silverwood is mostly rebuilt, the warehouse improved, and foreign relations with Rusa and Thesia off to a smooth start. I can't say the same for Seshu or Taiga. But whatever comes, we'll be ready for it, because a kingdom united can stand any tempest.

I smooth the black brace with dual dragons, the dagger Casmir had given me for a present carefully concealed inside. Whenever I marry and if I have children, I'll be sure to tell them not to go anywhere without a dagger and a big heart. Those two things had saved my life.

Bastian swoops in from behind me and leans over the seaside rail jingling a silk bag full of zeni before me like a carrot. "Runa wants me to buy some puddings to celebrate, but I'm thinking you can decide on the dessert this time."

I laugh. "How about chocolate? I hear it's even better than egg custard."

"I'll look into that possibility," he says. "But it's highly doubtful. Whose idea was it to orchestrate a town festival for the coronation anyway?"

I look out from my perch at the merchants of Silverwood, the drums and zithers playing in the street, children running about with carp streamers and water balloons tied on strings, banners with sea serpents inked on their faded colors, and it fills my heart.

My beautiful dragon heart.

"Who do you think? I'm rather fond of parties, anywhere there's food in general." I elbow my brother in the ribs. "And I scheduled a parade for you to lead. There's an archery event and a ribbon cutting ceremony for the new School for Ancient Arts. I would've asked Father to cut the ribbon, but he's still too sick. The metallurgist girl will be the first student and some wayfinder friend of Seira's."

"You did what?" Bastian rakes his hair back, a disgruntled half smile dancing across his face. "You're just trying to make me work for my keep, aren't you? Or was it Runa?"

"No, I'm just trying to get you out of the way so I can spend time with someone else."

"Right," Bastian says, suddenly turning red and taking a few backward steps down the hill toward town. "I warned him that I have high expectations for anyone courting my sister."

Soran steps out from one of the vendor booths lining the narrow path. His dark hair catches in the wind, face focused on the two sticky rice balls skewers he carries, both dripping sweetsap onto his favorite pink pants. "I'll have to wash them myself," he grumbles, passing one of the sticks to me.

"Seira will wash it for you," I say, nibbling the sweet gelatinous rice.

"She threatened to throw them away next time I put them in the wash," he says, clearly affronted. *"Future princes don't wear pink,"* he imitates her censuring tone. "I told her that dragons do, and she went off on a long rant. I couldn't listen to all of it. Something about turning my pants into kitchen rags or handkerchiefs."

"Did you walk off in the middle of her speech?" I clear the first rice ball from my stick and lick my fingers to savor the last drop of amber sauce. I'm so glad Runa's queen and not me. Manners and rules were never my style.

"Something like that," he says. "I've more important things to do than listen to scathing opinions on my favorite color."

"Like what?" I say, leaning closer to him and drowning out the crash of the ocean and the chatter of the festival below.

"I've a song scheduled for the sailors. They want an authentic rendition of my namesake, the traditional fishing song."

"*And?* Isn't there something else?" I pluck the rice balls from his hand and hold them out of reach.

"The castle does need a new guard," he says. "Every castle needs a dragon to protect it, after all."

"And a princess to rescue?"

"No, not to rescue." A smile dances in Soran's eyes as he pulls me close. "To believe in."

THE END

THANK YOU FOR READING

CASMIR

IT WASN'T SUPPOSED TO END THIS WAY. The princess should ride into the sunset with the handsome dragon slayer, not pity the monster and run off with it instead. A blight on every fairytale and love story known to humanity. It made for a beastly bedtime tale.

And to make matters worse, *it was true*.

Casmir leaned across the desk and pinched his brow, wishing sheer willpower could silence the blistering headache plaguing him all morning. It was no use. Every time he closed his eyes, he saw the princess. The girl with blue hair like the sea, a fiery heart, and a loyalty worth a dungeon's ransom of treasure. She was supposed to be easy, a willing bride second in line to the throne with no other suitors due to her crooked spine. But she'd rejected him at the altar.

The Duke of Taiga.

The champion of the dragon invitational tournament.

The first in command of His Majesty's armed forces and calvary.

All worthless things to her, and now insignificant to him. Not that he was nursing a wound. He was above that. No time for personal feelings when war brewed beneath the surface and diplomacy caused delays in the most recent shipment of coffee beans from Furan.

That's what this headache was about—coffee.

A man cleared his throat, and Casmir glanced up from his desk where he'd been reading reports from the western unit stationed in Kagano. A request for reinforcements and provisions in the fight against the rebelling countryside protectorate. The emperor had tasked him with keeping the country united, winning the affections of the newly acquired provinces. A difficult feat when he couldn't even win the heart of one girl.

Two emissaries from Candor stood before him, shuffling in their boots like impatient school children. Buttery sunlight cut through the lattice windows to crash against their sharp jaws, catching on the fibers of their crisp uniforms. They dressed as if they belonged to the room. Green from their tailed coats matched the dragon hide adorned behind his desk, ivory from their stiff collars harmonized with the embroidered chairs, and an impatience just like the ticking of the clock on the wall. A servant bowed out of the room and shut the door.

"State your business," Casmir drawled, paying them no mind.

"My lord . . . we sent a request a week ago. Candor needs a dragon slayer. It's most urgent. The beast has laid waste to crops and reduced the governor's villa to ashes. They will pay handsomely—"

"I don't need money." Casmir waved them off without a second glance.

"But you're the best dragon slayer in the land," the younger emissary cut in, his words desperate. "The best in the world. You can't say no."

Casmir lifted his gaze. "I just did." He located the request form on his desk and held it over a burning candle. "Tell Candor to find another dragon slayer," he said. "I'm retired."

The paper crumpled like so many other things when exposed to flame—homes, dreams, love . . . Mother once told him that his heart was a flame, and all hearts are raging fires that need tender care.

"Be careful what you feed it," she had said. *"Hearts can burn brightest blue or flicker like embers, but it's the purpose of the flame that matters, not the size."*

A slight smile tugged at the memory and then he dropped the blackened paper into a metal pail.

TO BE CONTINUED IN . . .
DUKES & DRAGONS

HISTORICAL & CULTURAL NOTES

While strictly a fantasy novel, *Saints and Monsters* pulls inspiration from historical and cultural elements of Japan during the Meiji Restoration (1868-1912).

I've always loved this time period as it's imprinted deeply on my city from the street names to the historic buildings repurposed as shopping malls and museums. That Japan is more than green tea and samurai goes without saying, but this rich time period helps illustrate the beautiful fusion of culture and creativity that Japan is famous for today.

When I first started this story, I found myself fascinated by the architectural beauty of the Red Brick Warehouse, one of the central inspection houses that processed goods from the West. Nestled on the bay, I imagined a cinematic scene with the brick and iron beams torn down by sea dragons instead of the Great Kanto Earthquake.

Other scenes came to mind as I considered Tokyo coffee culture, the historical biographies of foreigners living in the Yamate Bluff, the confusing clash of cultures at the turn of the century when pistols, gaslamps, and western clothes began to coexist with the old ways. And I found ample inspiration in the accounts of dragons scattered through the countryside.

I wove small details into *Saints and Monsters* like Casmir's obsession with coffee (made popular by the emperor taking a daily dose for health), the hot spring inn with western dining inspired by a famous 1870s hotel, tattoos to indicate crimes were often seen on *bakuto* (precursors to the *yakuza*), and even the modern rendition of rock paper scissors or "jan-ken" which is still popular today. Even the saints' cathedral is inspired by some of the early monasteries in Japan where you can still buy their famous butter.

Of course, I took liberties and made a truly fantasy world. Meera's "blue sickness" is largely a fantasy portrayal of my own struggle with chronic illness and autoimmune disease. It often comes in unpredictable flare ups and can make everyday tasks feel like trials. In this time period, no one understood such conditions and its easy to believe it would have felt like a curse. Braces for scoliosis did come on the scene, but were quite clunky and impractical.

And because I love the 72 microseasons, I wanted to emphasize seasons throughout my books. So, for this one, I needed a spring flower. The cherry blossom, or *sakura,* uplifts the spirit throughout Japan. In fact, there is a yearly forecast to see when it arrives at each prefecture!

Samurai often used this flower pattern on the lacquered deer leather of their helmets and armor, a pattern known as *kozakura.* It's a symbol of hope. A reminder that while life is short and fragile, it's also beautiful and worth fighting for.

Remember reader, *WORTHY DOESN'T MEAN PERFECT.*

ACKNOWLEDGMENTS

Writing a book is a lot like facing a dragon. It's daunting to create worlds and characters from a blank page. A task that would be impossible without courage, hope, and a party of good friends.

I can't tell you how many times that blank page snarled at me, whispered that I couldn't do it, that no one would read it, that I wasn't good enough. But here you are, Reader. Thank you for taking a chance on this debut fantasy.

The world of Saints and Monsters has swirled in my mind ever since I read historical accounts of the Meiji Restoration and found one off-hand comment about actual sea dragons pulling a boat. I'll never know what the observer saw in real life, but it fascinated me and planted the idea for this book.

Thank you to my friends and critique partners extraordinaire, Nova McBee, Candace Mieding, Laura Frances, Melissa Poett— your friendship is worth more than gold. This book wouldn't exist without your encouragement and faith. The four of you are wayfinders through and through. Readers, if you are looking for more great books, you can't go wrong with theirs!

Thank you to all my beta readers for finding the plot holes, spelling mistakes, and cheering for these characters: Catilin Miller, Megan Gerig, Moriah Chavis, Constance Lopez. To all the advanced readers and those on the street team, thank you so much! Many of you encouraged me to write the next book for Casmir and Runa, and I haven't forgotten it!

Huge thanks to my biggest supporters, my husband and my three boys. And I give thanks to the most creative Author of all, Jesus Christ, for giving me a passion to write.

About the Author

Ellen McGinty is an author and editor of Young Adult fantasy and historical fiction. She lives in the Tokyo metropolis with her husband, three boys, and a hypoallergenic cat. When not writing or editing, you can find her exploring the wilds of Japan with an abundance of espresso and the occasional kimono.

For more books, updates, & giveaways join the newsletter:
https://ellenmcginty.substack.com/

Leave a review on Amazon or Goodreads

www.ingramcontent.com/pod-product-compliance
Lightning Source LLC
Chambersburg PA
CBHW030243120726
47903CB00005B/1598